MADISON MICHAEL

Bedeviled

A BEGUILING BACHELORS ROMANCE

BOOK THREE

Contents

This book is dedicated to Sandy with my humble thanks for her insight into mysteries and suspense, and for her friendship.

"Secrets are made to be found out with time."

Charles Sanford

PROLOGUE – SOME YEARS EARLIER

It all came about so quickly. He barely knew what happened before the horrible deed was done. Adrenaline was pumping through his veins; he felt his young heart would explode from it.

Breathe. Just breathe slowly... and think.

But he couldn't think. He stood in shock, noticing only the blood seeping from the body splayed out on the floor in front of him. It was thicker and darker than he expected blood to be. Not at all like in the movies.

He needed to move swiftly, before anyone passed by the front window or before his wife came through the back door from their tiny apartment above. He stood paralyzed, though, knowing he needed to move, but was not sure whether to hide the body, the weapon, or just run.

No one would believe it was self-defense. There were no witnesses to corroborate his story. His family engaged in questionable activities, and he was young and poor. He could never afford the legal help he would require. It would cost him everything he had in the world just to try defending himself. He was certain it would not be a good outcome.

Run! Run now!

It was his only choice. Once he concluded that, his clumsy feet moved quickly. He locked the front door and bolted out the back. The young man grabbed all the money he had stashed in the apartment. He grabbed a few small items that he and his wife received as wedding gifts, items that might sell for a few extra dollars quickly and without questions.

"Pack a suitcase. A small suitcase. We are leaving," he barked as he ran about the apartment.

"What are you doing? What is the matter?"

"We are leaving. Now. I will explain everything after we leave this place.

"Explain now."

"Do you love me?" he asked urgently, staring deep into her beautiful brown eyes, willing her to understand and trust him.

"With all my heart. You know that. Why do you ask me like this?"

"Then please, pack a bag now and come. Ask questions later."

So, she moved as quickly as she could in her current state, feeling his alarm and absorbing it as her own. She mumbled some discontent under her breath as she gathered what would fit in her small suitcase. She understood she would not be back.

"What about my parents?" He could hear the fear in her voice.

"We will contact them later," he said with a weak smile meant to reassure.

"When later?"

Without an answer, he remained silent. He looked around the old apartment where they had enjoyed wonderful times. His eyes passed over their belongings, but all he took was their wedding picture. Lifting it from atop a small table, he tucked it safely inside the front of his jacket. Taking her hand gently, he pulled her into the unknown and never looked back.

CHAPTER ONE

*C*harlotte was hiding something.

Alex could feel it in his bones. Since they had met in June, she had been elusive and mysterious - even cryptic sometimes. If she wasn't so damn alluring, he would have walked away by now. He had never waited around for a woman in his life. They had flocked around him like pigeons. Not Charlotte.

He had vacillated between wanting her and wanting to get away from her, but wanting her always won. He had wondered if she was keeping some deep dark secret or if it was a suddenly overactive imagination, but today, once she had 'the accident', he was sure. She was definitely hiding something.

Their morning had started much like any other. Their run had been companionable, ending near the beach where they watched the last tinge of pink leave the sky over Lake Michigan.

"Good time today," Alex praised, shaking off his constant, simmering desire for her long enough to stop staring at her. He checked his stopwatch as they toweled off and gulped from their water bottles. Sitting on a low stone wall, the beach behind them, Lincoln Park, and the Chicago skyline before them, they shared the sunrise of a crystal-clear morning and the healthy exhaustion that followed their workouts. "We have to go longer tomorrow."

"I know," Charlotte had responded, annoyed. "I hate early mornings. Yeah, yeah," she headed him off before he gave her a lecture, "I know we have to do it, and once I am running, I'll be fine, but until then just let me complain. Not all of us can just talk ourselves into ignoring pain and exhaustion."

Alex listened to her non-stop loathing of that early morning alarm. It was a routine by now, repeated out of habit.

"I'm tired," she would complain. "It's those stupid nightmares I have. They wake me up and then I can't get back to sleep."

"Talk to me about them. Maybe that would help," he offered as he had countless times before.

"It's nothing, really."

But he knew it was something. Another piece of the puzzle that was Charlotte. "You have them all the time, Charlotte. It's not nothing."

"Just drop it," she sighed and so he did, reminding her instead that if she wanted to train with him, she would have to get up early. She complained, but she always showed up and she always ran hard.

Their training was shorter runs interspersed with long runs requiring the 5:30 a.m. start that she so vociferously complained about. She hated those long run days, but with only six weeks to go until the Chicago Marathon, they were pushing each other hard.

Pushing each other's buttons, too.

"How long will you be around this time?" she queried, breaking into his thoughts of her, of her funny habits and quirks that he had come to know, of her body so temptingly close to his. He could smell the light floral scent of her soap or shampoo mingled with the smell of perspiration. The combination aroused him, as always.

What had she just asked him? Concentrate, you dolt.

"I head to California week after next. You?"

"I need to be in Boston next week, so it looks like our schedules won't overlap – for a change. What keeps taking you to L.A. anyway? This must be your second or third trip this month. You were gone all that time over the summer, too."

So, the verbal dance began.

"Just business. The usual," Alex gave her his standard answer.

"Whatever that means," came Charlotte's sarcastic response.

"Well, what's with all your trips to Boston?" he turned the tables on her.

"Harvard stuff." Her response was too quick and equally vague.

"Whatever that means," Alex mimicked in a sing-song voice. He dropped the subject, though.

I can't push her if I don't want her hounding me, damn it all.

Alex clammed up. He could share little of his life with this woman unless he was prepared for her to notice discrepancies, pick up on his little mistakes. Even after decades of cover up, he worried about letting something slip. He didn't have to stay on his toes as much with the vapid L.A. models he usually dated.

Alex tamped down his curiosity, resisted pursuing further questions on the subject and allowed her to do the same. Instead, he let their conversation returned to the mundane while they caught their breath.

"I wanted to ask you for more advice on structuring the financing for my deal in St. Louis. I could really use your logical approach on this one."

"I'm happy to help, Charlotte, but you know you can do it on your own. You always can."

So, we will stick with finance. I shouldn't get in to trouble with this topic, but of course, neither will she.

"But this is my biggest deal yet. I think I covered everything, but I would feel better with a second set of eyes on it, especially yours. Maybe I could come by after work today or tomorrow?"

"Sure, I am happy to help. Not today though, I have too much going on. Tomorrow?"

"We could do lunch. I'll buy," she offered, persistent.

"Okay, that works," Alex readily agreed.

Lunch keeps things casual so that maybe we can talk about you for a change, Charlotte.

Alex knew Charlotte didn't need the help she was requesting. She might lack the confidence in her new job, but she was brilliant. Too brilliant. She was certainly smart enough to fool most of the world with very little effort if she wanted to. Alex recognized that if she had secrets, she was far too clever to be found out easily. They had been running together every day for almost four months, at least when they were both in town. Add the fact that they usually followed their runs with coffee and all that togetherness meant a lot of talk time.

They had covered a lot of territory in their conversations, speaking easily on a variety of subjects. She was extremely well educated, from a blueblood Boston background. Surprisingly, she was not well traveled. She had never even been to California, so she was always asking him about L.A. or his school years in Palo Alto. She was well read and quick-witted. They discussed books, theater, and politics.

Of course, they conversed on financial topics too, from what it was like for him to run an entire bank to dissecting her new position as Director of Finance at Lyons Howe Real Estate. Her ability to crunch numbers in her head and see the long-term impact of them staggered him, but of course it was that ability that had earned her the new job and brought her to Chicago.

She was easy to talk to, warm and interesting. And interested in him. Too interested. She asked way too many piercing questions. He had learned to deflect the conversation back to her by asking her about settling in Chicago. Charlotte talked about the challenges of living in a new city, finding her way around, using public transportation – which had surprised him too. He expected her to have a driver, or at least take taxis. But she was more down to earth than that. She was openly excited about exploring her new home. They talked about how they spent their time and their careers.

They didn't share anything intimate. They certainly didn't share the truth.

Both were focused and ambitious, and that emerged in their debates. Clear about their futures, they could describe their career goals and what steps they would take to achieve them. But any discussion of either's personal life was always a bit sketchy, with the details murky. The conversation always returned to safe topics.

"So, how are the wedding plans coming?" Charlotte asked, as by tacit agreement, they headed in the direction of the nearest Starbucks.

"I am so glad to be leaving town. There are too many parties. I am sick of them. It thrilled Aubrey to see everyone, and I think she is enjoying the attention. My parents' house is overflowing with gifts," Alex laughed. "God only knows where Aubrey will put everything, and there are still two months until the wedding."

"How about your brother?" Alex asked, keeping the conversation in safe and innocuous territory. "He should be graduating soon, shouldn't he? Those gifts must be coming in by now, too. Kitchen stuff, I would imagine. Has he shared any new recipes with you this week?"

Charlotte's brother was graduating from the Culinary Institute of America in the winter. It was one of the few things he knew about her family. He also knew there was another, older brother that had graduated from Harvard. He had no idea what he did. Besides 'business'.

"And how is the rest of your family?"

"No new recipes this week, sadly. But did I tell you? Don is starting to receive job offers already. I am so excited for him. The Culinary Institute is the Harvard of cooking schools, so I shouldn't be surprised."

"Speaking of Harvard, didn't your parents have a problem with your brother choosing to be a chef? I would imagine they wanted him to follow in your footsteps. How do they feel about a chef in the family after you and Jake both got Harvard MBAs?" Alex presented the question innocently enough, but he noticed the instant Charlotte stiffened up, and that she tried to hide it.

"Of course they don't mind. They love us and just want us to be happy. It's like you feel about Aubrey, protective and full of brotherly love. It's how I am sure your parents feel about you, although you have certainly exceeded everyone's expectations, haven't you?" Charlotte changed the subject, as she always did when he asked about her family.

Oh yes, she is hiding something, and I am tired of waiting for her to come clean. Either she trusts me, or she doesn't.

Today's chat had been open and easy when discussing ways to improve the economy, but when they switched to her family, she shut him down. When they discussed plans for the Chicago Marathon next month, she was fully engaged, but when they attempted to schedule their next several training runs, Alex watched Charlotte become vague – again.

He was amazed that he noticed since it was difficult concentrating with her so near. He was caught up in the feel of a lightly grazed arm, the sight of her fit body in her running clothes, the way she periodically pushed her hair behind her ear.

Despite their relaxed banter, Alex was acutely aware of her every move, her every breath, so he recognized the moment she 'went fuzzy' on him, as he liked to call it. That was when Charlotte, decisive and articulate, suddenly forgot things, confused things, or failed to mention things. It was a complete shift in her speaking style, full of the lengthy pauses she needed to create a good story or remember the previous lies, so she didn't contradict them. An unintelligent woman would have made more mistakes. Not Charlotte: she was anything but stupid.

Keeping his mind on the topic always took all of Alex's effort, anyway. When Charlotte sat hip-to-hip with him as she had today, he felt the heat of her skin, saw the long length of thigh exposed in front of him, heard her heavy post-run breathing until he was in sensory overload. She smelled so good, not stinky and sweaty like he must. Charlotte smelled classy and expensive, with all those clean, floral scents. She smelled like a woman he could trust.

More like a woman I want to trust.

Thinking back, Alex recognized that she had been hiding something all along. When he wasn't lost in a sensual fog, he was able to zero in on where the conversations lagged when she got testy with his probing or tried to change the subject. It had something to do with her life in Boston before she moved to Chicago, and it was something that had been going on for a while. She was practiced at her excuses by the time she used them on him. She was making too many trips back East for 'Harvard stuff.' She had met Regan Howe through this same 'Harvard stuff', yet Regan went back to her alma mater only once or twice a year, if that.

Oh yeah, Charlotte is definitely up to something, and I intend to find out what. I have been patient long enough.

Sitting waiting now for Charlotte to arrive at Starbucks, Alex promised himself that he would get to the bottom of this or walk away.

Since she had declined his offer of a ride, Alex currently sat at a shady outside table enjoying the last of summer, waiting for her to walk over and speculating on her possible secrets. He was planning his subtle interrogation during the few minutes Charlotte would need to make her way across the park,

Stubborn. She should have just accepted the ride.

"You driving over or walking?" she had asked him once they caught their breath.

"I have the car if you want a ride?" When she hesitated, he tried tempting her. "I have the new car."

Alex was the proud owner of a brand new Mercedes AMG. The sleek, luxury sports car suited him despite most people's image of him as logical, conservative, and staid. The need for speed was actually deep in his blood. "You will love it, tight on the curves, fast and quiet. She purrs," he had bragged.

Charlotte hesitated on his last remark, and Alex had been sure she would accept. "The new car, huh?" she sounded intrigued. "I am excited to see it at last, Alex. You have certainly been talking about it long enough."

"I need to walk off this tight hamstring, so I'll have to pass this time," she had replied reluctantly. "Meet you there in ten." Of course, Charlotte had been Charlotte, and that included being unpredictable.

Charlotte, leaving Alex standing there, had taken off across the park without a backward glance. Alex stood dumbfounded a moment, watching her slow jog-walk toward the trail across the grassy lawns of Lincoln Park. She was heading directly toward their usual post-run Starbucks and if he didn't get moving, she would be there first.

Still, he stood, willing her to look back and flash him that smile that changed her whole face. She didn't, of course, and Alex was left standing there, admiring her lithe figure and the smooth bunch and release of her muscles in those tiny running shorts as she moved into the distance. Reminding himself to close his gaping mouth, Alex jogged to the parking lot, trading an extra moment of admiring a beautiful woman for a few short moments admiring his beautiful new car.

Arriving at the coffee shop several minutes before Charlotte, Alex was forced to cool his heels. He spent the time piecing together anything he could think of to uncover Charlotte's deep, dark secret. Admittedly, he needed the ten-minute head start away from her to give his overheated blood a little cooling time, too. He kept envisioning the two of them in that sweet ride, sitting close with their sweat-slicked bodies. The image had intensified the jolts of electricity already coursing through his veins from running beside her scantily clothed body.

Too bad she turned me down. One of these days we will be in tight quarters, all alone, and I will make my move. I have resisted too long already.

Since the mention of her tight hamstring, all Alex could think about was massaging her leg and moving up from there. Did the woman not understand what she was doing to him? After all, he was a healthy red-blooded man. How long was he supposed to watch her round little ass wiggle in front of him, or the glide of muscles in those incredible legs - or OMG - her breasts bob up and down in those little running tops? The woman was killing him. He wanted her so badly he could taste it.

He chided himself to stop thinking of her that way, as he always did when he lusted after her. He would catch himself wanting her and repress the overwhelming sexual response that had plagued him since the beginning. She was so much more than just beautiful and sexy. She was a brilliant woman, funny, witty, complex, and delightful. She considered him a running partner, and a friend...

...but that body, oh, that body. Stop it!

Alex determined to stay focused on what she might be trying to cover up and got his desire under control. He reviewed the signs - when she changed topics or failed to make eye contact. e carefully dissected her words while he waited for her to arrive. He knew she was being intentionally elusive. Alex resolved again that today would be the day he found out what she was concealing, beginning as soon as she arrived.

Speaking of arriving, Charlotte should have shown up long before now. She would have unless something had happened. How long had he been sitting, pondering? How much time had passed?

Heart racing like a freight train, Alex ran into the park. Unsure why, he was terrified of what he might find.

CHAPTER TWO

The ambulance arrived within minutes. To Alex, it felt like hours. He paced like a caged animal and cursed like a sailor until the EMTs jumped from the vehicle, did a quick check of Charlotte's bloodied body, and pronounced that she would be fine. She had told him the same thing while they waited for the professionals, trying to convince him that she could lean on him to get home rather than go to a hospital.

"What were you doing so far off the path?" he barked at her once he was sure she was not seriously injured. His frustration and fear were getting the better of him.

"Was I? I hadn't realized," she responded vaguely, her voice quiet, as if she had to work hard to find the breath. She must have really hit her head. She seemed shook up and distracted, asking more than once, "Are you sure we are alone? Is anyone around?"

Alex was not sure she understood what she was saying, but when she repeated the questions again, he became concerned. "Like whom, Charlotte? Was someone here? Was someone bothering you? Is that why you are way over here? Did someone drag you here?"

"Of course not," she had retorted quickly, suddenly more alert. "I just was embarrassed at the idea of someone seeing me fall on my face." Was she trying to laugh it off? Was she lying?

Running through the park, it took Alex a few minutes to spot Charlotte, flat on her face in the grass, well off the path she should have taken. She was lying near a copse of trees that were not in a direct line to the Starbucks - not even close. She was face down in a more isolated area, almost completely hidden by bushes and trees. If the grass had been longer, if her running clothes had not been a vibrant magenta, he would have missed her. She wasn't moving, not making a sound. His first thought was that she had been accosted, dragged to this spot, and left for dead. Alex's heart had stopped cold.

"Oh God, please, please, please let her be alive," he prayed repeatedly, rapidly approaching her still form despite his trepidation. As soon as she sensed him beside her, she mumbled his name and he leaned close to hear her soft voice, relief flooding him. When he helped her roll over, he saw her battered face.

Alex wanted to kill someone with his bare hands.

"I was afraid to move too much without help in case I broke something. My ankle is killing me," she had told him calmly in a raspy voice. She looked shaken up, trembling slightly, but it was only moments before they switched roles and she was reassuring him. He feared internal injuries, a concussion, the worst. He insisted that that they call for aid and transport her to the nearest hospital.

"Just help me up so I can go home and clean up. I don't want to make a scene, Alex. I will be fine." Ignoring her, he called 9-1-1. One look at her and he knew she needed professional assistance while he needed an outlet for his anger and adrenaline.

As they waited for the first responders, Alex went through the motions of checking Charlotte for obvious broken bones, although he had no formal training and little idea of what he was actually doing. Wrapping his hands around her small ankles and wrists, lightly moving them over her cool skin, reminded him that Charlotte was not physically the larger-than-life persona she projected.

Her personality always filled any room. Since the moment they had met at a party, he had noticed no other woman but her, despite his continued dates on the West Coast. He would have described Charlotte as taller than most women, but now he recognized that she was only of average height with a slim, small-boned build and the long, lean muscles of a runner.

Charlotte had aristocratic, fine features and a pixie-like heart-shaped face where two large bruises were forming on her cheek and forehead. She had a long scrape, as if she had been dragged across the concrete sidewalks and there was pain and fear reflected in her enormous golden-brown eyes. The tears she was trying to hold back were clinging to the fringe of exceptionally long, straight lashes.

Her hair was swept away from her high forehead in a sleek, short bob. Even now, with grass stuck to the strands, it was styled perfectly. It always was, despite her habit of sweeping one side behind her delicate shell ear when she was animated or nervous, only to have it fall forward again, thick, dark, and lustrous.

Charlotte's mouth was a grim line of pain, but usually the small bow was widened by her bright smile, showing her small white teeth and that one 'snaggletooth' on the bottom that she hated so much. It was a lovely, patrician face, appropriate for a descendent of the original New England settlers. Right now, disturbingly, it was the scraped and bruised face of someone who had been savagely attacked.

Where are those damn EMTs?

While they waited, Charlotte answered questions reluctantly and in a reedy voice. "Tell me again what happened," he asked her gently. He was determined to keep asking until he was able to piece together a coherent story.

"I was just jogging over to meet you when I caught my foot and took that stupid klutzy spill."

"Charlotte, that is not like you at all. Are you sure it wasn't something else?" Alex asked gently. The lines did not ring true to him. "I have never seen you be anything but graceful, even when you are exhausted."

A fall was inconsistent with her known behavior and the bruises developing on her face didn't look like they came from a fall either, at least not to him. She was in an odd location in the park, too. The whole thing made absolutely no sense. It had to be a fabrication, but he could not imagine she would cover anything up, especially not if there was an attacker in the park who might hurt someone else. Charlotte would be cognizant of doing anything she could to protect others.

Yet, that was her story. She just fell. She lost her footing and went down hard. Alex knew better. Although he had no understanding of her motives, he sensed she was lying. After all, he had run with Charlotte several days a week for many months now and he knew her to be graceful and surefooted. Something else was going on, something that made no sense.

She was behaving strangely, too. Even under these unusual circumstances, she was being uncharacteristically fretful. It could have been the injuries, but it felt like something menacing to Alex. It seemed to him that she was frightened and specifically fearful of something, of someone being nearby. Add the questions earlier about being alone and Alex became convinced that someone had done this to her.

"Are you sure, Charlotte? You can tell me if there was someone here. In fact, you should tell the police if you were attacked," he encouraged her.

He sensed that she wanted to engage the police, but she refused. "The police are completely unnecessary, Alex."

"Someone might hurt another woman," he pointed out.

"That would be true if I had been attacked," she told him, tired of talking but repeating her assertions. "No one else was here, though. I just fell, so no one else is at risk." Despite her repeated assertions to the contrary, she was definitely hiding something. The more Alex reviewed the situation, the more he feared it was something sinister.

She looked like hell, battered, and bruised. She had two skinned knees trailing blood down her shins and into her shoes, the cuts and bruises on her face and a scraped elbow and wrist that seemed to be causing her a lot of pain. He wondered it she had broken something. Her hand was a mess where she had put it out in front of her, trying to break her fall.

She had that ugly bright red gash bleeding on her right cheek like someone had cut her and he could also see bruises forming near her shoulders and on her neck.

While these marks were inconsistent for a fall, they made perfect sense if someone had grabbed her and tried to choke her. Her thin voice supported that theory too. She was definitely struggling to speak and eventually she stopped answering any questions from him.

Once he had reassured her that they were alone, she grew quiet, although she repeatedly complained about a pain in her ankle. It didn't look broken to him, and although he was no expert, he wouldn't allow her to stand up without help. He was frightened by the scope of her injuries, but in order to keep her calm, he strove hard to calm himself.

"How bad does it look?" she asked when he finally heard sirens growing louder.

"Not so bad, really. Just a few minor cuts and scrapes."

"You're a bad liar, Alex."

If you only knew, Charlotte. If you only knew.

Laying there, she looked heart-stoppingly beautiful, vulnerable, and fragile. She stood toe to toe with him when they were running together, matching wits and physical endurance and while he never forgot for a moment that she was a woman, Alex had never seen her as he did now – defenseless. Alex felt an overwhelming need sweep over him. He wanted to be this injured woman's defender, her knight in shining armor. It was a completely chivalrous emotion, one that he had never experienced before.

Rein this in, Alex. You cannot fit a woman into your life right now. Especially not a brilliant and deductive woman who is harboring potentially dangerous secrets of her own.

Alex moved back as the EMTs carefully lifted Charlotte onto a stretcher and skillfully assessed her. He stepped away slowly and allowed them to take complete control. They wheeled her into the ambulance. She was already hooked to an IV, the needle protruding from the fragile hand he had held only moments earlier. Reminding himself that she was in capable hands, he released her to the experts with reluctance, standing alone as the doors closed behind them.

This is a sign, Alex. Just let her go. Now is not the time to take on Charlotte. Not a chance. No matter what.

CHAPTER THREE

Charlotte was aware of the muted sirens as the ambulance inched through morning rush hour traffic toward Northwestern University Hospital, just blocks away. The EMTs were giving her something through that tube in her arm, but still she lay in a haze of pain. She assured herself that she was being well cared for by the professionals, but she was unable to stop the trembling that had begun as soon as she left Alex and she allowed herself to let the paralyzing fear overcome her.

How had everything gone so wrong, so fast? How could she have been stupid enough to let her guard down, even after so much time?

You know better.

It had been such a glorious morning, and she had been so happy. She had started the day too early, true, but she had watched the sun rise over Lake Michigan briefly, turning the grey-blue water to fire and it was almost as dazzling as the smile of the man beside her.

Alexander Gaines. She met him at a rooftop celebration back in June and still she remained in awe of him. She had been saying her goodbyes, leaving the party where she had known only a colleague or two, when he made his entrance. Popular with everyone, Alex was sinfully handsome and so confident. He was a cross between California surfer-boy - tanned and blonde with white, white teeth - and a rugged pitch man for an expensive foreign beer, tall, built, with deeply chiseled features and the hint of a bump in his aristocratic nose. His dishwater blonde hair was even lighter now, bleached by a summer in the sunshine, setting off his eyes of deep, piercing blue. He had the body of a Greek god, tight butt, long legs, broad shoulders. Alex was a devastating combination of lean runner and muscular swimmer. He had all that and a brain.

A phenomenal brain. A dangerously astute brain.

They had hit it off immediately, finding finance in common and quickly discovering their shared passion for running. "Marathons? You do marathons?" she had asked him, incredulous. "But I am a marathon runner too."

"Well, isn't that a lovely coincidence?" He was flirting shamelessly. "Perhaps we can egg each other on a bit?"

Were they still discussing running?

"Where do you train? What is your training routine?" she asked, and they were heads together comparing workouts for a solid ten minutes until the conversation moved from training through a competitive debate comparing their financial knowledge, all the way to favorite movies.

"Is there anything you don't know? You're incredible," she had finally conceded.

"You should only know," he laughed, flashing a sexy grin that took her breath away.

"Wait until you discover all the great things there are to do in this city," he had told her when the conversation turned more general, but no less flirtatious. "If you like museums, we have some of the finest in the world. Sports? We have the best fans you will find anywhere. I dare you to pit Red Sox fans against our Cub fans," he had laughed. "We have beautiful beaches, unbelievable parkland, clubs, fantastic restaurants. Seriously, Boston cannot hold a candle to Chicago."

Alex had bragged like a true native, describing all the places to see, all the things to do in Chicago, and she believed he was hinting that he would show her those places - that he had been working up to asking her for a date. Disappointed when he kept it strictly platonic, she never let it show. They had been meeting almost every morning they were both in town since to train for the Chicago Marathon and she still had hopes that their relationship might shift into something more romantic.

During these last months, Charlotte had come to know and admire Alex. He had opened up to her, and she had come to know a man who worked hard his whole life, first in school, where he won both an academic and a track scholarship to Stanford, then in college. He now headed the private bank he had joined almost a decade ago, after completing his MBA at Northwestern's Kellogg school. She admired his work ethic, his logical approach to setting and achieving his goals. She saw her own determination mirrored in his.

She also saw a man who loved his family unconditionally and who was unfailingly loyal to his friends. He was serious and logical in his approach to everything, never letting his emotions get the best of him. Alex was passionate about national and local politics about which he could debate her to death, and an aficionado of Chicago restaurants and cuisine. He loved running, swimming, and hockey, and excelled at all three. He was warm and funny and sexy as hell.

It didn't hurt that Alex was one of the richest men in Chicago, as well as a renowned philanthropist. Hell, she was sitting in the emergency room in the Alexander Gaines wing of the hospital right now. He was a whiz at financial matters and had amassed a fortune quickly, then given much of it away. He'd helped her work through complex decisions several times since she had taken the position of Director of

Finance for Lyons Howe Real Estate earlier this year. It was no surprise that he was running a huge bank at such a young age.

She enjoyed verbally sparring with Alex. She respected his opinions on almost everything and she enjoyed his company immensely. Charlotte queried her new boss about him, but all she got from Regan was 'he's elusive as hell, but if you can catch him, he's definitely worth it." It wasn't encouraging, but at least it told Charlotte she had no direct competition from her one true friend in her new hometown.

Regan knew Alex's complete history, but she was close mouthed on the subject. If she wanted, she could share so much about him. Alex was best friends with her older brother, Wyatt, and had been since childhood. She had grown up around him, but she offered little.

"You should form your own opinions," Regan told her on the few occasions when Charlotte tried to pry information from her. "I refuse to interfere or get in the middle," Regan had announced before stepping away, allowing the pair to discover each other on their own, and in their own time. "But you should know he has a string of models he is dating on the West Coast. They constantly show up on Instagram."

"A string is okay," Charlotte countered. "That means he isn't settled on anyone special."

Alex hung out with Charlotte almost every day as long as he wasn't travelling. He was extremely busy with many demands on his time, but he started his day with her at least briefly, usually for a grueling run, then they would linger for 30 minutes over coffee. That routine had provided them the opportunity to grow comfortable with each other. It might not be the fast and furious method of dating today, but it suited them. Despite their hectic work and travel schedules and their cautious natures, Charlotte had grown to know and like Alex and knew he liked her too. They had progressed to her joining in when Regan and others went out for drinks with Alex and his friends and there had even been a business event or two where she had attended as his 'plus one'. It was progress.

Charlotte liked him so much, in fact, that he fueled her fantasies and revved her engines. Alex was the epitome of Charlotte's dream man—tall, hard-bodied, brilliant and all man. He was beyond sexy, kind, and generous, clever, and witty. They shared interests, conversed easily and from the moment they said farewell, she was counting the minutes until they were together again. He made her heart race. She knew that he found her easy to be with, and she believed he found her attractive. It was enough to build on. She'd been willing to take it slow—for a while. Recently, her patience had been wearing thinner, and Alex had appeared ready for more too.

In Charlotte's estimation, things were moving forward - they had been promising, in fact. That was, at least, until Alex showed up with a gorgeous and famous model at a business event late last month. Not just showed up. He actually flew the stunner in from Los Angeles just for the night. Then, to add insult to injury, the pair pawed each other incessantly before leaving the event early, with obvious plans for a night of hot sex. That episode definitely dampened Charlotte's spirits and until last week, she had been intentionally aloof, almost cold. Charlotte knew she had lost any ground she had gained previously. She strongly considered just giving up. After all, bringing the model to Chicago was a strong message to just walk away. But Charlotte Roche was no quitter.

Despite the small voice of reason in her head, Charlotte stopped being angry, unavailable, and amped up her game. Instead of packing it in, Charlotte had doubled her efforts by investing in new workout clothes, lower in the front and higher on the leg. As the clothes became smaller, Alex's eyes grew wider. She saw the new way he looked at her, riveted, as if he was seeing her for the first time. His hand strayed to her hair, her hand or her arm, a bit more frequently than before. She had a tight, fit body and beautiful tawny skin, tanned from the summer sun. She had been determined to show off both until the dense man noticed that she was a woman.

Alex had definitely taken notice. When Charlotte saw the new light in Alex's eye, she had been ecstatic. She felt easy with Alex, yet she struggled to get a reading on how he felt about her, to figure out whether to keep trying. It looked like she had finally read him right. Then she second-guessed herself yet again.

Maybe it's time to do something even more overt and find out if we can make this work. Or is he just looking for a quick lay? Maybe you should just give up. Char, you know perfectly well you should give up. The man is brilliant, and you are just begging for trouble.

She thought that she was getting to him, that her small efforts, and small togs, were encouraging Alex. Trying to push things even further, Charlotte had poured the last of her water bottle over the top of her head this morning, letting it run down her face and chest, cooling her off only slightly. She didn't care about the temperature, since her purpose was to draw Alex's eyes to her body, not to air-condition. She was gratified to see the ploy work as his gaze strayed to her pert breasts and lingered there.

She calculated that the small effort, plus the deep V-neck sports bra, might finally get the man to see her as more than a running buddy. She enjoyed training with him, truly, but so far, he had thwarted all her subtle and not so subtle attempts to move things from the track to something far steamier. She needed him to see her the way he saw that model from L.A.

I should have taken the ride.

Coming back to the present, and the pain, Charlotte berated herself. She debated sharing the short ride with him to get coffee but had decided not to feed his already impressive ego. She did not want to give Alex the satisfaction of accepting the short lift. He had just purchased a Mercedes AMG GT in a brilliant blue that matched his eyes, and he was like a little boy with his new toy. His need to show it off was telling, but she saw the ride as a way for him to regain the upper hand.

Charlotte had negotiated with herself for a moment before turning him down. Being enclosed in the sleek two-seater, damp, close, barely dressed, would have been heavenly, but keeping him guessing and unsure was important too. She had battled with herself before refusing. The man asked too many questions and he was especially inquisitive today. She recognized the light that he got in his eyes when he was trying to ferret out an answer. Charlotte finally opted to forego the sweet ride. Besides, she needed the time apart to get past the potent attraction before she lost her concentration and made any big mistakes.

She would ponder her next move and buy herself a few extra minutes to let her desire-fogged brain clear before meeting Alex for a skim latte. The five-minute jog would be her strategizing break.

Walking her foggy brain back through the morning, she prayed she had not said or done anything to give herself away to Alex before the EMTs arrived. He had been panicked so perhaps he wouldn't remember, even if she had mumbled too much or slipped. In an odd role-reversal, she had been the one calming him. She could only hope that worked to her advantage.

This is why being around a super smart man is a very, very bad idea. Take your own advice here, Charlotte. It's time to cut and run.

She had been weighing whether to run away or stay, further pursuing that possible mutual attraction, when she started the short jog toward Starbucks. Alex was everything she wanted. She could not have conjured up someone more perfect. She loved that he was incredibly smart and even sexier. The polished executive was a perfect match for her serious, career orientation but she also adored the fun-loving, easy-going guy. He made her heart beat faster, made her smile wider, made her run fast to keep up, physically and mentally. He kept her on her toes. She had never been more attracted to a man, never had a better time being with a man. She had decided then and there that she wanted to push things forward. She wanted to be with him and damn the consequences.

Now that she had made up her mind, now that she had clarity, Charlotte decided she would ask him on a date this very morning, or at least discuss changing the nature of the relationship. Suddenly anxious to see him, Charlotte picked up speed, jogging past a small, wooded area.

No more waiting. She would take her chances and look for a way to knock Alex right off his feet.

"Oh, please God, no!" she cried out when she spotted someone moving in the trees ahead. Before she could scream for help, she was knocked off her feet instead.

CHAPTER FOUR

Having arrived in an ambulance, Charlotte bypassed the administrative and waiting areas and was behind a curtain in the ER with medical personnel all around her. They were treating her as a priority patient, although Alex heard her say at least a dozen times she could walk, that others might need more attention, that she was 'fine'.

"Just let them help you," Alex commanded, pushing back the curtains to let her know he had arrived. "Stop fighting and let them do their job."

"I am fine. I am sure it looks much worse than it is."

"Are you a doctor?"

"No." Her voice was soft and her expression sheepish as she acknowledged his point.

"OK, well then, that's settled. I have called my physician to come assist these lovely emergency room doctors and he should be here shortly." Alex was charming but with an authoritative air. People around him automatically became deferential. He lowered his voice to that sexy timber she couldn't resist and added, "Please, Charlotte. Please let them help you."

"Sir, are you family?" a bustling, rotund nurse challenged, jumping between Alex and Charlotte. Jennie, according to her nametag, was of indeterminate age and was clearly unimpressed by Alexander Gaines. She had a headful of tight curls against her scalp, dark smooth skin, a deep bosom, and a serious scowl on her face. When Alex shook his head, she indicated the waiting room, gleefully running her world like a Drill Sargent. When he hesitated, she ushered him unceremoniously from the curtained area, then pivoted on her heel, leaving him watching her large backside roll with each indignant step she took back toward her command post.

Alex huffed in frustration, but he remained in the colorless waiting room. Circling once, ignoring both the oversized clock and the silent TV playing 24-hour news, Alex fidgeted with the dog-eared magazines on a nearby table and then with his phone, removing and replacing it in his pocket nervously.

Realizing he could do something productive, Alex focused on his iPhone, making a list of the things Charlotte would need - nursing care, healthy food, medicines, DVDs, books, clothes. He poured himself a cup of warmed-over, weak coffee and longed for the Starbucks he'd missed out on earlier. Dropping into an uncomfortable, faux-leather chair, he focused on completing his list, guessing what Charlotte would need while he awaited a status update. A light bulb had gone on for Alex the moment he realized Charlotte would need a lot of help today, and perhaps for the next several days. He knew that she had colleagues at Lyons Howe Real Estate, but she had known them only a few months, since the beginning of the summer when she had started her job. She had only been working there a week when Alex met her. He had spent more time with her than any of her coworkers.

Except for her boss, Regan Howe, there was no one she was close to that he knew of. If Regan and she had not met at some Harvard events before Charlotte accepted the job, he wasn't sure she would be close to her either. He could not remember Charlotte mentioning socializing with Regan or anyone else from her office, unless they went out together for drinks or lunch in a group. Regan had never mentioned her to Alex before she showed up to begin at LHRE. Reflecting on it now, he was not sure that the women were close, either.

She had no family in the area either. That meant that he was her closest friend in Chicago, and he had no problem accepting the responsibility for her well-being. Alex felt completely comfortable, even welcoming the opportunity to care for this smart, funny, brash woman. He would assure that she recovered fully and was well again. He stopped obsessing about her contretemps and started thinking about her care.

I need to look after her. I want to look after her.

The idea repeated in his brain and took a firm hold. He started pacing, aware of the obligation and its significance. The chivalrous emotion he had felt earlier returned. He would move her into his place and provide the finest medical care money could buy, along with all the creature comforts of luxury surroundings. He would work from home and be available around the clock if she needed anything. After ensuring that his personal physician checked her out from head to toe, he would play nursemaid - if that was acceptable - or hire a professional, if it came to that. He was surprisingly comfortable with the idea of Charlotte staying with him indefinitely.

True, this was not how Alex had envisioned getting Charlotte into his bed. He smiled to himself, but she would be there just the same. Once she was a little better, she would be captive under his roof, at least temporarily. He intended to make the most of it. His earlier chivalry morphed to a much more recognizable sensation.

Hell, I'm no saint.

He would have to cancel his trip to L.A. It couldn't be helped. That would require some work on his part. Charlotte was supposed to go to Boston for a 'Harvard thing' that would need to be cancelled as well. When she was feeling better, he could have Regan bring her some work. But he would not allow her to overdo things. She must take things slowly. Alex intended to make certain she remained in his care as long as necessary.

Necessary for what?

All the logistics handled, and a mental list made of the phone calls and emails to attend to later, Alex strode to the nurses' station to get an update. No one would tell him anything, although he moved about the floor like he owned the place. Not even close, of course. There were only two wings with his name on them.

Or was it three now?

Once he understood he would still have to wait awhile before they discharged Charlotte, Alex got another cup of the dreadful coffee and started making phone calls.

"Jo," he barked at his assistant the moment she picked up the phone, "I won't be in today and I need you to cancel my trip to L.A. for next week. Make a note for Brian to let the board know we will do everything via conference call until I make it out there. Have them send him any necessary documents. Call Regan Howe over at LHRE and let her know that Charlotte Roche will not be in today. Hmm? Oh, just say she had a minor mishap while running and will be in touch later. Call my mother to let her know I will be in town in two weeks for that dinner party, please. Oh, and have some groceries delivered to my place. Enough for several days. Healthy stuff—lots of fruits and veggies, yogurt, tea and juices. Plenty of fresh juices. Yes, Jo, I said groceries."

Alex waited while his newest personal assistant, Joanne Reese, laughed in his ear. She knew, as did anyone acquainted with Alex, that he never set foot in his gourmet kitchen. The man was a legend at every restaurant in town. Despite frequenting dozens of places, he ate out so often that he was a regular everywhere.

"Another thing, Jo, if you can stop laughing, find a pharmacy that delivers and text me their number. Get the name of a place that can deliver a hospital bed, and home nursing care too. No, I am fine, but a friend of mine was in an accident. Oh, she will need clothes too. Ask Regan if she has a key to Charlotte's apartment. If not, you get to go shopping. Use the corporate card."

Alex listened and chuckled. "No, you can't just shop without checking, much as I know you would like to. Ask Regan first. Okay, that's it for now. I will be in touch later, from home."

Although it was still early in the day, Alex listened as Joanne prevented him from hanging up, rattled off a list of to-dos and messages that had already piled up at his office. He gave her answers to several of the questions she asked, then had her transfer him to his administrative assistant, with whom she would coordinate. Alex knew he could count on the two of them to handle things seamlessly and waited for the admin to come on the line.

Alex silently counted his blessings that he had found Joanne. His life ran so much more efficiently with her helping him manage his personal and philanthropic tasks. She was the best PA he had ever hired, efficient, intelligent and often one step ahead of him. She was also discreet. His last PA had learned the hard way that he would not tolerate gossip. That had opened the door for Joanne, who had continued to impress him these last six months.

His admin, Brian, a man in his early thirties with an impressive resume, had been with the bank for five years. He was crisp and efficient in his conversation with Alex and clearly had everything under control.

"Sounds to me like you have it all covered, Brian. Just coordinate with Jo, so I don't have to call you both. Perfect, thanks."

Alex checked his phone once more, saw the pharmacy info was already there, as well as an excited text message from his sister about his attendance at the dinner party. Joanne was certainly efficient. It was barely 9 a.m. He jiggled his long legs nervously in the uncomfortable seat, then moved them out of the way as a distraught-looking family came in and took seats across from him. They acknowledged each other's misery silently and retreated back to their own problems. Alex checked the time repeatedly until finally he saw Marty Levin wander out from the emergency room almost two hours after Charlotte's accident.

Everything took so damn long.

"So?" Alex asked, bounding from the seat to meet Marty before he could cross the room. "What's the verdict? How is she? You were in there a long time."

"I was only there a few minutes Alex. Hospitals take time, paperwork and tests take time. Relax."

"So, she's okay?"

"Ever heard of HIPAA, Alex? I can't tell you much unless you married that pretty girl when I wasn't looking, because I know she isn't your sister. Could be a smart move, my friend."

"Nope. 'Fraid not," Alex told the older man, annoyed. After a frustrated hesitation, Alex blurted, "But I called you, not her."

"True, and I am glad you did. But Charlotte is my patient, not you. However, you are in luck. She is asking to see you, so why don't you come on back and I suspect she will be more than willing to tell you how she is."

The two men matched long-legged strides, turning a few heads with their good looks as they moved past admissions and the nurses' station. Alex considered resisting an arrogant look toward Jenny, but the imp in him won and he flashed her a 'yeah, just try to keep me out' look. She just ignored him, denying him pleasure from the moment.

Charlotte was sitting up in a hospital gown with a large bandage around one arm, a smaller one on the other, and a third on her face. Alex was relieved to see her eyes were bright and alert.

"Thanks, Dr. Levin, I appreciate the care," Charlotte responded sincerely after she okayed Alex's presence while the physician reviewed her discharge instructions.

"I will see you in my office in three days, young lady." His broad smile belied his stern order.

"Yes, sir. And remember what we discussed."

"Of course, Charlotte. You, and only you, are my patient here." He gave Alex a warning look, and Alex knew they were talking about her privacy again. The brief exchange just confirmed Alex's suspicion that she was hiding something. It just solidified his decision not to leave her alone in her apartment. She was coming home with him.

Alex watched the exchange, waiting anxiously for Marty to leave so he could ask Charlotte about her condition and about that last brief comment from the doctor.

"How are you feeling? What did the doctor say? Is anything broken? Will you be okay?"

Why the need for all this secrecy?

"Alex, relax, sit over here near me and I will tell you everything, but one question at a time, please. And whisper. I have a pounding headache."

Alex took the seat near the head of the bed, reaching for her hand, careful of the intravenous line still hooked there. Quickly realizing her hand was bandaged, he wrapped his large fingers around the tips of her fingers. He noticed her nails, a sensible length and unpolished. So different from most of the women he knew.

So Charlotte.

"You look like the mummy," he said, making her laugh.

"Don't make me laugh. It hurts."

"Sorry, I am so sorry. I should have been there to prevent this."

"This was not your fault, Alexander Gaines, and don't you think for a second that it was."

"Okay," he took a deep, calming breath, "tell me everything."

"Everything?" Charlotte teased before finally settling in to tell Alex what the doctor had said. She had to remind him repeatedly not to interrupt.

"No concussion, no broken bones. Those are the two most important things. I sprained my ankle, so no running for me for a while and the marathon is definitely out."

"I am so sorry, Charlotte. That is so unfair after you trained so hard."

"I have a couple of badly bruised ribs that make breathing—and laughing and frankly everything—painful, but they should be good with just a week or two of bed rest. My face will heal and should not scar. Your Dr. Levin is great. He brought down a plastic surgeon to look, just in case."

"He is good. That was why I wanted him here."

"My arm and hand are a mess. Everything will be a little difficult there for about a week, maybe more if my wrist doesn't get better. But they should come by to discharge me soon, so you need to get out and let me get dressed."

At that moment, almost as if Charlotte had conjured her, the efficient nurse returned, giving Alex a glare, and pushing him unceremoniously from the room. A large, no-nonsense woman, Alex knew not to mess with her. He stepped just outside the curtain and waited while Charlotte got dressed.

She completely ignored my question about secrecy.

When the curtain slid back with a metallic swoosh, Charlotte was standing uncertainly in a rumpled pair of drab green scrubs with a big black boot enclosing her left lower leg.

"This thing will be a bear," she said, trying to cover her concern with a pitiful laugh before wrapping her ribs to protect them. "I was trying to remember how many stairs there are to my front door. I think it is twelve or maybe fifteen, but either way, I am going to have to learn to balance better. I should have rented the first-floor apartment, I guess."

Jennie held Charlotte gently while she took a few tentative steps, exhibiting nothing but kindness and patience. Charlotte found a few places to use her fingertips for balance.

"I've got you, Charlotte," the big nurse told her reassuringly. "You are doing just fine." It turned out that Jennie was a tiger to Alex, but she was a pussycat with Charlotte.

"That a girl," she encouraged her now and with only a few steps, Charlotte had the hang of the boot. Although she was moving slowly because of the sore ribs, she was walking.

It took another twenty minutes for the hospital to process paperwork. During the wait, Alex sprang his plan on Charlotte.

"I've taken care of everything I could think of, so I don't want you to worry about a thing," he stated, very matter of fact and efficient. Pulling his phone from his pocket, he reviewed his list. "I let Regan know you would not be in today but would call later, I arranged for a pharmacy to deliver medications once we have the prescriptions, I have a guest room that will be perfect—no stairs—and I am having clothes and food delivered there now so you will have everything you need."

"I am not going to your place," Charlotte countered without missing a beat. "I am going home. People navigate stairs on these stupid things," she pointed at the heavy black boot on her leg, "and if they can do it, I certainly can."

"Of course you could, Charlotte," Alex responded. "I am confident you could do anything you set your mind to, but you have the bruised ribs and hand, and you need a little help which I can provide. I am happy to provide that."

"I don't know you well enough, Alex, and I absolutely cannot take advantage of you like that. Besides, you will be out-of-town all week, so I would still have to care for myself, just in a strange apartment."

"It's not strange, Charlotte. It's flat and comfortable. You would have everything you need there. Oh, and I cancelled my trip. I want to be here for you."

Charlotte blushed at the last few words, silenced for a moment. "Alex, you didn't need to do that. All this attention is embarrassing. I can't let you do this. I have only known you a few short months, and it's not like we have that kind of relationship." She was blushing furiously, unable to make eye contact.

Lifting her chin and looking deep into her tawny eyes, Alex made sure she would hear and understand what he said next. "I can and want to do this for you. I am your closest friend in Chicago, and I have the space, the ability," Alex paused for effect and chose his words carefully, "and the desire to care for you." He stressed the word 'desire.'

Alex held his breath. Did she understand what he was telling her?. He couldn't have been more obvious, even if she was in a medicated fog.

"But, Alex," she stammered.

"Don't but Alex me, just agree."

"You are being so generous, and I am so appreciative..."

"Great, I will just go get the car."

"... but I really can take care of myself, Alex. I still have to say no thank you."

"I have an elevator, grocery delivery, assistants to run your errands, enough space. Hell, we don't even have to see each other, as long as I know you are safe and cared for." He knew she was wavering.

"It's too much, Alex," she explained. "You are so thoughtful, and I appreciate it, really I do, but I simply cannot impose on you. Go to California. I will be fine."

"It's a secure building," Alex reminded her, hitting her where he suspected she was most vulnerable. "You can trust me, Charlotte. I will keep you safe."

Charlotte's head shot up and he knew he had struck a nerve. Sometime in the past, she had been frightened. It made so much sense now—her need to be strong and independent, her skittish behavior if a man got too close.

"Why did you say that?" She looked more frightened than he had ever seen her. "What would make you think you have to keep me safe?"

"I just meant that even if I am unavailable, you will still have a security person downstairs that you can call for help. Don't you want that assurance, Charlotte? Don't you want to know that you control who comes and goes while you recover, and that, even when I am not there, help is just an elevator away?"

He watched her expression as she hesitated, weighing some factor she would not discuss with him. He knew now that she was more afraid than she admitted and hoped this security argument would tip things in his favor.

He could tell she was about to refuse again, and Alex poised to go in for the kill, ready to tell her he was certain she was lying about being attacked in the park. It was unnecessary. Surprisingly, Jennie sealed the deal for Alex.

"Honey, with that headache, the sprain, your bandaged hands, and those ribs, you are going to need a bit of care for a week or two. Just let this handsome devil take care of you. It will be a role reversal for him, I can just tell." She winked at Alex just before she disappeared down the corridor, but Alex could hear her laughing at her own cleverness.

She was right, though. It would be a change for him. First, he would have to let Charlotte deeper into his life, then he would have to let her leave. Both would challenge him greatly. Alex hoped he was strong enough to let Charlotte go at the end of a few weeks—and that she didn't see too much in the meantime.

CHAPTER FIVE

C harlotte was still laughing about the botched attempt to get into the AMG. Alex had been determined, but the car was just too small and low to the ground for Charlotte to maneuver into with bruised ribs. She could not lower herself without excruciating pain. Giving in finally, Alex signaled a taxi, handed the guy a twenty, gave him the address and followed the bright yellow Prius through traffic to his condominium only blocks away.

"Stop making me laugh," Charlotte scolded again while Alex helped her to disembark from the taxi in front of his building. He was handling her like a delicate flower as she hobbled to the doorway, leaning on him heavily with one arm and carrying a small plastic bag containing her dirty and destroyed exercise clothes and one bloodied shoe in the other.

"I promise I'll try," Alex said while crossing his heart with his index finger like a small boy. It only made Charlotte laugh again before she gave him her most ferocious—and fake—scowl.

"You live here?" she asked as she looked up toward the top of the modern building. She had passed this prestigious address, just one block west of Michigan Avenue, many times, always longing to see inside. The lobby was elegant and subdued through the tinted windows, with large sofas and gorgeous oversized displays of exotic blooms on traditional wooden tables. There was even a fireplace. The décor, while not consistent with the clean, soaring lines of the glass and concrete structure, set the tone of opulence and prestige.

"Yeah, is it a problem?"

"Oh no, not at all. I am only a temporary guest and besides, I have heard it is a nice building."

Nice. That should bring him down a peg or two. What an understatement that was. It was only one of the most sought-after addresses in the most desirable neighborhood of the city.

"It is nice. Come see for yourself." He took her gently by the elbow and helped her through the revolving door, crowding with her into the space designed for one.

Immediately, a doorman—well, door woman in this case—jumped to assist, holding open the inner door and greeting Alex deferentially.

Alex helped Charlotte cross the large lobby, holding her like spun sugar. He introduced Charlotte to a young, petite Hispanic woman who looked like anything but a security person. It gratified Charlotte that Alex didn't give the very attractive woman a second glance as he explained Charlotte was staying "for a while" to recuperate. "Has my assistant arrived yet, Elizabeth?" Alex asked as he maneuvered Charlotte through the inner door.

"Ms. Reese is already upstairs, Sir, and Ms. Roche. You call me if you need anything, Ma'am - anything at all." Elizabeth was polite and efficient and flashed a warm smile that made Charlotte believe she really could call if she needed help.

Charlotte returned her smile, thanked her for the offer and hobbled with her help and Alex's the short distance to the elevator. She watched as Alex entered a key card into the bottom of the numbers panel and then pushed the button for the 70th floor—the top floor.

"The top floor? Really?" she challenged him as if he were a spoiled brat, and not the sharp, well-educated, and experienced banker who had earned this space through hard work—and perhaps some family money. "How predictable."

"It's comfortable," he shrugged nonchalantly, "and Wyatt helped me get a fantastic deal during the housing slump."

"Ah, of course. Good old Wyatt. You guys certainly take care of each other," Charlotte observed without rancor.

"We try. We have been watching each other's backs since we were in kindergarten. It's a habit now, as well as a pleasure."

The elevator had moved swiftly and silently, covering the distance to the top uninterrupted. The doors slid open directly into the penthouse unit, explaining the need for an elevator key. Charlotte ignored the apartment and furnishings. The view immediately grabbed her attention.

The expanse of windows looking toward downtown afforded a view of the entire city laid out to the south, east, and west. The elevator and walls blocked her view north. Trump Tower was in the foreground, Willis Tower off to her right and beyond that, the museums and parks, Soldier Field, and the South Loop. She had to limp closer to the glass to look below her. Far below was the Wrigley Building, with its gleaming white terra cotta façade, the sandcastle top of the Tribune tower and an enormous expanse of Lake Michigan. All of this lay at Charlotte's feet. The lawns of Lincoln Park, where she had fallen hours ago, were out of sight, but Grant Park was a green carpet in the distance.

"This is some view," Charlotte told Alex, turning to find him watching her as she took in the space. Finally, she allowed her eye to rest on the soothing neutral tones, muted rugs, and open floor plan of Alex's enormous apartment. "Nice digs."

"Thanks. When you feel better, I will show you around the place. For right now, though, let's get you settled where you can rest."

Limping through the massive living room, Charlotte got a quick impression of low modern furniture, variations of wood tones and beige and massive spaces. She glimpsed a long black dining table and the kitchen beyond, a large masculine office, and then they entered a long hallway that was obviously a wing of bedrooms. Alex led her to the second door on her right, a bright airy room with walls painted blue and large windows offering a more limited version of the earlier southern view.

Gently helping her to sit on the king-size bed, he offered to get Joanne to help her get undressed and in bed and left the room quickly. She sat less than 30 seconds before a young African American woman of about twenty-five entered the room. She was small in stature, but she had a glorious head of hair that added several inches to her height. Her dark eyes were sparkling, but her mouth was set in a stern line and there was a furrow between her brows.

"I'm Joanne Reese," she said, extending a hand before realizing that Charlotte's was bandaged. Embarrassed, she fussed about the room, explaining that she was unable to get into Charlotte's apartment to get clothes.

"I talked to Regan Howe though, and she was very helpful. Between us, we guessed you are a size 4 or 6, so I got two of everything, just to be safe. I got you a couple of nightgowns, but mostly I bought jeans, tops and dresses, even some business attire. Mr. Gaines never explained your injuries, or I would have selected differently and bought more for comfort. I will buy more for you later today, or if you prefer, I can get things from your apartment." Charlotte could see that she took every aspect of her work seriously and that it disappointed her not to get everything right.

"I am positive your selections will be perfect," she reassured the young woman, "but sweats and tees are all I can wear for a few days, if that." She was trying to see everything in the closet. Even with her limited view, Charlotte quickly comprehended that little in the closet was appropriate for her injuries.

"Sorry, he just said buy clothes," she repeated awkwardly. Joanne was holding a diaphanous, white nightgown in her dark hands, clearly designed for seduction, not recuperation. Behind her, the closet was jammed with designer dresses and business suits, classic trousers, stunning blouses, and a few skirts. The floor showed heels and strappy sandals beside four pairs of running shoes, all in a neat row.

"It's fine for now, but a robe might be the first order of business," Charlotte offered. She nodded at the running shoes with frustration. She couldn't even wear those now, at least not both. Some changes would have to be made. It explained the consternation Joanne was showing and Charlotte set out to make the young woman feel comfortable. "Regan would normally be right about the shoes you got, so I can tell that a lot of thought went into your work. I appreciate it. You should shop for me all the time. I have zero fashion sense, but I can see you picked beautiful things."

Appeased by Charlotte's kind words, Joanne went to work helping her remove the borrowed scrubs. Charlotte was self-castigating as she regaled Jo with her story of insisting that she should wear her running clothes home from the hospital. When she had barely made a hand into the dirty, ripped clothes, the hospital staff had offered the scrubs. The pain of getting anything on, Charlotte admitted, was exceeded only by the pain of removing it. It took several minutes, but eventually the two women had Charlotte in the wispy nightgown and tucked into the queen-sized bed, a pile of down pillows supporting her back and smelling faintly of lavender.

Joanne fussed for another moment before Alex entered the room with a tray, and she excused herself. Charlotte was propped against the pillows, her dark hair framing her pale, scraped face and pained eyes. Alex took in the sight of her long neck, creamy shoulders and the hint of breast showing through the nightgown, despite her best efforts at modesty. Charlotte watched, gratified to see Alex's eyes take on a smoldering gaze before he turned away.

Even through her fog of pain and painkillers, Charlotte had a moment of triumph at that look. Although she had resisted Alex's offer to host her for quite a while before giving in, she was glad he had won the argument. She would get excellent care in a luxurious and secure location and a chance at the elusive Alexander Gaines, too.

Except for these damn ribs, this might be perfect.

Smiling at the ridiculousness of seducing Alex in her present condition, Charlotte gave herself a mental shake and turned her expressive eyes up to meet Alex's as he gingerly sat on the edge of the bed, careful not to jostle her.

"Marty prescribed some pain meds. You are to take them no matter how you feel for the next two days, then as needed. I had them delivered, so you will start them in a couple of hours. I brought water, tea, and orange juice since I wasn't sure what you might want. Food too. You never got breakfast, so I brought cereal and yogurt. You pick."

"Tea, please, and the yogurt, and then rest. I just want to let these meds do their trick and sleep through some of this discomfort."

"Of course, of course." Alex placed a starched linen napkin across her chest and handed her the yogurt, along with a fine silver spoon. He apologized for the flavor, although she did not complain, and added a Splenda to her tea before handing it to her. He quickly realized she couldn't hold the cup with her bandaged hand, so he tipped the cup carefully to her lips as she took a sip. His eyes stayed there until she nudged him to indicate she was done. He fed her yogurt and tea in silence, their eyes speaking volumes.

"Can I get you anything else? Anything at all?"

"I'm fine, Alex." Charlotte nibbled at the yogurt until the carton was empty, surprised by her hunger until she remembered she had been running earlier. "Go take a shower. Go to work. I just need to sleep. I don't want to be an imposition. Go about your day. I will be fine."

"Char, you are anything but an imposition. But you need to rest." He placed a light kiss on her forehead, as if she were a child, and used a small remote control on the bedside table to close the blinds over the multi-million-dollar view.

"Holler, if you need anything at all. Joanne and I will be here all day." He looked at her, clearly torn between staying with her and letting her get the sleep she needed.

"I will, Alex. Go."

Charlotte was left in the quiet darkness. Using both hands awkwardly, she sipped the last of the tea slowly and revisited her morning.

Oh, God.

That had been no ghost she saw in the stand of trees, Charlotte remembered with a shudder. All she had left behind when she escaped to Chicago appeared to find her early this morning. The hospital had brought back bad memories, not that she needed any reminders. He haunted her sleep almost every night, caused her to look over her shoulder every day. But she was less vigilant lately, believing the miles between them were enough.

I am so stupid. Jail, the police and restraining order after restraining order had not stopped him. Why should a plane ride?

She knew that if he could find her running in the park, he had been watching her. What else did he know? Did he know where she lived? Where she worked? All her running had clearly not been enough. She needed a new game plan before he cost her everything she worked so hard to achieve, or worse, everyone she loved.

Putting the cup back onto its saucer with a rattle, she rested her sore and shaking hands, trying to get their tremors to subside. Charlotte allowed her eyes to droop shut. Her problems would just have to wait. She would need a much clearer mind to make all this go away because, she realized with startling clarity, she didn't want to flee again.

CHAPTER SIX

There was moonlight filtering through the blinds when Charlotte awoke. Disoriented until her mind cleared, she remembered this was Alex's guest room. Wiggling her fingers and toes, Charlotte gently moved around, checking her pain levels and found she didn't hurt as much as earlier. When she tried to sit up to get out of bed, her body told her another story entirely. Her ribs really hurt like hell.

Sliding her way out of bed awkwardly, protecting herself from the stabbing pain, she hobbled to the bathroom on one foot and a tiptoe. Where had Joanne put that stupid boot? Charlotte limped her way back to the closet, found the boot on the floor under some of Alex's shirts and suits that had been pushed off to the side to make room for the new things Joanne had hung up. Grabbing a faded blue work shirt, Charlotte held it to her nose, hoping for a sniff of Alex—expensive aftershave and rugged man. Nope, nothing. It had been laundered too well. She put the shirt on, made sure it covered her private parts, then bent painfully and wrapped the boot tightly around her leg with the Velcro closures and wandered out of the room to find her host.

Once she opened the door and entered the hallway, Charlotte heard the sounds muffled by the thick door. Moving unsteadily toward Alex's murmuring voice, Charlotte passed priceless art pieces along the wide hallway.

He had excellent taste.

The work was mostly modern, large canvases, huge sculptural pieces and, oddly, an African wood carving as tall as she was that worked in the space somehow. There were artists she recognized, museum quality pieces that she assumed were the real thing.

The man had way too much money.

Following his voice, walking carefully to avoid reaching a hand against the walls or tripping on the edges of priceless Turkish rugs, Charlotte discovered Alex in his office, back to the door, talking business on his speakerphone and running a pen through his fingers like a card sharp might a playing card.

She stood quietly, taking in the surroundings, a large wood paneled room with floor to ceiling windows on one wall and a large telescope poised to look out of them. The two remaining walls were built-in bookshelves covered in hardback and leather-bound books interspersed with small paintings, pottery, wooden objects, and a beautiful stone orb. The desk was wood, with clean lines and an efficient lamp with a moveable arm. Currently, the files and papers covered the desktop, and a laptop computer sat on one corner. There were several straight-backed leather and wood chairs scattered about the room, with small tables set beside them in intimate conversation groupings. She selected one and dropped into it carefully.

Charlotte studied the space while she waited for Alex to notice her. The ceilings were very high for a modern apartment building. The priceless rug rested over the carpeting, absorbing sound and contributing to the overall feeling of calm in the functional room. She allowed her mind to wander, thinking about the last few months while she waited for Alex, who was winding up his call.

How strange she thought it to find herself here.

Charlotte remembered meeting Alex at Sloane's party. She was saying her goodnights when the sexy man had struck up a conversation.
Uncomfortable before that, Charlotte felt out of place with all these
strangers. But Alex had her laughing quickly and enjoying her evening.
He helped her make new friendships, almost as though he understood she needed them, drawing other into their conversation. She'd
believed she was monopolizing the time of someone else's husband
or boyfriend, since this brilliant hunk of man couldn't possibly be
available.

Then she worried that her boss, Regan, was with or interested in the
gorgeous blonde, but her new colleagues quickly set her straight. Regan was circling another friend of her brother, Tyler Winthrop. The
two had been dancing around each other for years and both had eyes
only for each other. ,Once she understood she would not offend her,
Charlotte had outright asked Regan about Alex, getting that cryptic
response about him being elusive. But she didn't discourage Charlotte
from pursuing him, and that was all the sanction she needed. Regan
had clarified that the field for Alex was wide open.

"But very competitive, Charlotte. If you are interested in him, it is
only fair to warn you. He plays the field aggressively. He dates both
here and in L.A. and never with the same woman twice."

Despite the warning, Charlotte had been relieved. Although new
to the job and the city, she had met an interesting and attractive man.
It was a promising start. Had Regan been interested, Charlotte would
have stepped aside reluctantly, but her boss would pose no interfer-
ence.

She wanted to heed Regan's warnings, but her attraction to Alex
had been instantaneous, a new sensation for her. Sure, she had met
many men in her thirty-one years, but she'd dedicated herself to her
studies, then her work, and dated infrequently. Charlotte had been

involved with only one serious boyfriend, and that relationship had ended disastrously.

Since then, she guarded her heart, preventing herself from feeling too much. Never had she experienced such an immediate, visceral reaction to another human being. Instead of being her overly cautious self, she had thrown her hat in the ring for Alex—Charlotte style—slowly but steadily.

"With my studies behind me and the landing of my dream job, I feel like I finally have some time to breathe and enjoy life," she had told Alex with exuberance. "I am in a new city, making a fresh start." What she didn't say was that Alex offered a chance to achieve all her dreams for an exciting personal life with a special someone.

The charming man had remained a mystery. He spent time with her on the track, escorted her to an occasional business event, took her for coffee and smoothies after a run, even called just to talk once in a while. The friendship had formed naturally and comfortably, at a relaxed pace for her. Until recently, she had been content with that. Now she wanted him to make a serious move.

Charlotte believed she was making headway finally, that the man was just as cautious as she was about jumping into something with a virtual stranger. He was right to be careful. After all, Alex was a major catch—handsome, smart, funny, successful, and extremely wealthy. Women actively pursued him, some who wanted him for his charm, and many who just wanted the material things he could provide. She could understand why he might be hesitant.

At first, she had actually tried to talk herself out of being interested, reminding herself that she was new to town and needed some time to get the lay of the land. Charlotte reminded herself that she had just landed a plum job and should do nothing to risk it. But logic gave way to desire, and as the attraction grew, she subtly pursued Alex, waiting for him to reciprocate. She was an old-fashioned girl, so even in a modern world, she preferred he make the first move.

She was patient with him and frankly concerned that he was so secretive. But he was so damn attractive. She felt so good around him. She countered her fears about his mysterious demeanor by telling herself that she knew his friends, where he worked, where he lived. Alex might keep to himself, but with his childhood friends surrounding him, she at least knew he was no threat. Except to her heart. She never felt the need to run a background check. He remained suave and sophisticated, even if he didn't share his secrets. Charlotte could pick up bits and pieces about who he was and how he lived from the things said around him, from being with him. She wanted him to trust her. She wanted to trust him.

When he had flown in that gorgeous bimbo from L.A. last month, she was crushed. The woman was stunning, hanging all over Alex in a barely there dress. Charlotte got a dose of reality as if she'd been doused in ice water, and with cooler blood, she stepped back from Alex. Jealousy was a new and miserable experience for her. She longed for a friend to talk to about her emotions, about Alex, but Regan was still her boss, so she remained miserable and alone.

Charlotte had fought for everything in her life, but she'd never fought for a man. Except was no quitter. She didn't get a scholarship to Harvard, then remain at Harvard for an MBA by being easily dissuaded. She earned top grades, did everything necessary to join the right clubs, and deserved all she achieved. Tapping that fighting spirit, she redoubled her efforts with Alex. All leading up to today when she had decided she was done with slow and steady, with waiting to be pursued.

She'd intended to make a move at coffee just that morning and now, here she was, with a golden opportunity to get close to the man at long last. Charlotte intended to take every advantage of the situation.

"Well, once I feel like I can breathe comfortably again."

"Did you say something?" Alex turned to punch off the speaker button on the business phone buried under his haphazard papers, seeing Charlotte at last. "You startled me. I didn't realize you could move so quietly on that," he pointed to the boot. He was openly pleased to see her.

"Clever," he mumbled under his breath on seeing her attire. She had to admit it worked well as a robe. She could see his disappointment, reassuring Charlotte she was discreetly concealed. "How are you feeling?"

"Better," she told him with relief. "Except the sore ribs, nothing seems to hurt too much." She lightly fingered the bandage on her face with a scowl. "The tape is bothering me more than anything."

"Well, it has to stay on another day or two, doctor's orders."

"Yes, sir," she smiled. "I have one issue. I'm starving."

"I bet you are. It's after 6:00."

"You're kidding? I slept the whole day away."

"Not the whole day," he corrected, "but half of it. Can you walk? Want to follow me to the kitchen and we'll get you some food?"

She nodded and slowly moved to stand. Alex was instantly at her side, helping lift her out of the chair, then hanging on while they walked through the living room and into the enormous kitchen.

"This place is huge," she remarked, looking around her. "How much space does one man need, Alex?"

"Yeah, it's a lot, but I like the open feel. Really, I just bought it for the pool."

"The building has a pool?"

"It does, but I meant my pool—out there." Alex gestured vaguely toward the wide outdoor decks and manicured gardens surrounding his condo, where she spied a large pool surrounded by deck chairs hidden behind a hedgerow.

"A pool of your very own?" Charlotte asked in wonder.

"Yep, with a cover to use in the winter, so I can take advantage of it almost year-round. I like to swim."

"But you have an expensive gym membership?"

"That's for lifting. For swimming, I like this better." With that matter-of-fact statement, Alex changed the subject. "What would you like to eat?"

"What have you got?"

Alex opened the double doors of a wide stainless refrigerator and stood in front of them. "Let's see what we have. Joanne stocked it for us today."

He stood there so long, letting out all that cold air, that Charlotte finally limped over to see inside the fridge herself. There were all the fixings to feed a family of ten or more. She saw rotisserie chickens, containers of pre-made meat loaf and turkey breast. There was a large bowl filled with every fruit imaginable, an entire selection of fruit juices, another bowl with a salad already made and covered with a French-linen towel.

"Are you expecting company?" Charlotte laughed gently before grabbing her ribs again. "There is enough food here for twenty people. Joanne must come from a large family if this is her idea of getting us food."

"I told her to get plenty," Alex admitted with a sheepish grin. "So, what can I get you?" he questioned, turning to see what she liked. When he made eye contact, she saw the deer-in-the-headlights look in his eyes.

"Alex, can you cook?"

Alex dropped his chin to his chest to break eye contact and shook his head. "Could you tell?"

"Only from that fear on your face. You have this fabulous gourmet kitchen, and you can't cook?" Charlotte was incredulous.

"I entertain a lot of clients," he defended. "We eat in restaurants."

"Not tonight. Tonight, we eat here," she commanded, pointing to the salad bowl, which he lifted from the shelf. She had him carry two cheeses, the turkey breast, a lemon, and the jar of already minced garlic to the countertop. She carried a small bottle of Dijon mustard and a bottle of Rombauer Chardonnay.

"A bowl, a whisk, a plate, a cutting board, a decent knife," she looked at the contents before her, "olive oil, crackers and whatever herbs you can find." Charlotte took command of the space like a ship's captain, barking orders. She looked completely at home, wrapping a towel around her waist as a makeshift apron, grabbing the plate, placing the cheese and crackers out for them to nibble while she halved the lemon, squeezing the juice from it and pouring it, the oil, and the herbs over the lovely salad. She never measured, confident in her amounts and choices, and Alex watched from the sidelines in fascination until she pointed to the microwave and held up five fingers to tell Alex to heat the turkey while she went back to the fridge in search of more items.

"Dinner plates," she demanded. He handed her two expensive china plates that she piled high with salad, slicing a small bit of the cheese to lie across the top of each. She sprinkled both with pepper, without asking, added slices of apple and pear, then motioned to Alex to add the turkey slices to the plates and carry them to the other side of the counter where there were stools to perch on.

Alex carried them from the kitchen to the dining area instead. There was a large glossy black table in the center with a matching buffet under a large square painting, an abstract of the skyline in a riot of color. The room had windows on two sides that appeared to slide open to the wide deck outside and beyond that were views galore.

After putting out woven placemats and matching napkins, Alex poured wine into their glasses. Placing the plates carefully, he went back to help Charlotte maneuver into a chair. She had sliced a fresh loaf of bread with some pain and was carrying it until Alex took it from her and gave her his arm to help steady her as they moved across the room. He went back for a crock of creamy butter before joining her at the table. After Charlotte completed the painful task of adjusting in her seat, they dug into the food with gusto.

"This is great," Alex said in a surprise voice.

"I just threw this together with what you already had. With a bit of planning, home-cooked meals can be significantly better than this," Charlotte responded, a hint of a scold behind her words. "You really should eat at home. It's a beautiful space to sit in, a fabulous kitchen to work in, and the food will be so much healthier."

"Yes, dear," he responded obediently.

"Okay, I am done nagging. So," she said, changing the subject, "I knew you were comfortable, but I had no clue you were this comfortable." Her arm swept up to point out all the space and the view before she remembered how much the gesture hurt. She lowered it again quickly.

"I live well. I work hard and I'm not ashamed of it, if that is what you are implying." There was steel in his voice. Charlotte quickly backtracked.

"I am not implying that at all, Alex. After all, I know how generous you can be, too. I was in the Alexander Gaines wing of the hospital today, for starters. I am just saying this is way more than I had envisioned. It is a new, unexpected side to you."

"Sorry, I didn't mean to get defensive." He reached to remove her wine glass, pushing the water toward her instead. "No more wine with those pain meds," he explained when she pouted. She nodded her agreement and sipped the cool water. "I try to give away a good chunk of what I earn, but there is always someone who thinks I should donate more. I worked hard for my success, but sometimes even I have to admit it is excessive. Why should I have so much when others have so little? Then I try to do more."

"No problem. You don't owe anyone an apology. So, what is your story, anyway?"

"My story? You know my story." He seemed surprised by the question, and Charlotte watched as his walls dropped firmly into place. He dug into his food, avoiding eye contact.

"Tell me anyway. Now that I see you in these surroundings, I have a new image of you and a lot more questions."

"You shouldn't. I am still just me." He kept his eyes on his plate.

"Well then, tell me about 'just me'. Start at the beginning. I know you grew up in the suburbs with Regan."

"Yep, Lake Forest." Alex began, finally looking up at Charlotte. "We all lived near each other, went to the same private schools—Wyatt, Randall, Tyler, and me. We hung out together, played sports, chased girls. We just clicked; you know? Regan was always tagging behind us, the annoying little sister. Look at her now, CEO of Lyons Howe. Who would have thought it?"

"I would," Charlotte responded. "The woman is killer on the job. She is going to take that corporation far. She is intelligent, innovative and fearless. I am so lucky she hired me."

"I am confident that you deserved it. Anyway, a less-fearless Regan always tagged along when she could. So did Ethan and my sister, Aubrey, who's even younger. I know we have talked about her upcoming wedding. She's too young to marry, in my opinion, not that anyone asked me."

"We have discussed it, but from what you've shared, she seems very mature. She's what, twenty-five?"

"Twenty-six, actually. She still seems like such a little girl to me, but she isn't anymore. I really should admit it."

"Probably. No kids between you two? That's ten years' difference."

"Nope, I think my folks tried, but... So anyway, we all hung out together until college when we split up. I went to Stanford on a track scholarship and studied business. Wyatt and Tyler went to Cornell. They are inseparable. Eventually, we all believe they will be family, but Tyler will have to get off his ass first. Randall headed south. I loved California but my life was here, and my work was too, so I came back, got my MBA, and joined the bank."

"And now, at 36, you run it. That is mighty impressive."

"Just wait, Charlotte, I predict that in five years you will be running some big company, too. I would put money on it. And that, my dear, is my story."

"Excuse me, but I think you left out quite a few details."

"Old girlfriends? I have dated a lot, nothing serious. I travel a lot," he offered in explanation.

"No, not old girlfriends, silly. What about your family? Your interests? Your life? I don't want a resume; I want to know you better. What is your favorite color? What is your favorite food?"

"Seriously, there is not a lot to know. My mom is from California, born and raised near L.A. Charles is from Lake Forest. They met at a dinner party when she was here visiting in the area and staying with relatives, fell madly in love and got married. My grandparents are no longer alive. I have a smattering of cousins here that I am moderately close to and some in L.A. that I am not close to at all."

"My sister, Aubrey, is the light of my life. I would rather they waited longer to marry, but Adam is undeniably a catch. He is the son of a US Senator and a genuinely nice guy. He loves her. It's obvious to anyone who sees him. I am avoiding talking politics with him until I marry her off in a couple of months. Like I said, in my head she is still my annoying kid sister, but somehow, she has grown into a confident woman."

Charlotte had to agree that it was not every day that a girl became engaged to a US Senator's son, and it suitably impressed her. They were planning a huge society wedding, Alex explained, for right after election day.

"They are killing me with all these showers and events," he complained. "I have attended about six in the last two months alone. Too much small talk for me and they all seem the same. She needs a lot of parties, although I don't know why. I go to some restaurant or some hotel and eat too much food and stand around listening to the same toasts over and over. I am happy for Aubrey, really I am, but enough already."

"I think they sound heavenly. You know you do well at these things. You can talk to anyone about anything."

"Now that you are here recovering, I have canceled my next trip west. That means I will be here to go to the next insipid dinner being given in their honor. If you feel up to it, you can come along and meet everyone," he said.

"I'd like that. I am sure it will be lovely."

"It will be better than most. This one is at a house at least, so it will be slightly less formal. But it will still be a bore." Of course, he described the dinners as a waste of his time. That was what made Alex, Alex.

"Sounds great to me. I better be well enough by then. Otherwise, I think I will tear my hair out. Tell me more. Your parents? Do you get along with them?"

"Oh sure. We are not as close as your family, but we get along."

"No one is as close as my family," Charlotte agreed. Alex knew she was constantly calling home, reassuring her mother, father and older brother that she was safe living in Chicago, that her job was secure. If she missed a call to them, they all called her in a panic, uncomfortable with her out of their sight. He didn't know how she tolerated it. Alex had rightly observed that they wished she lived much closer to home.

Not a chance.

"This is not about my family," Charlotte insisted. "We are talking about you tonight."

"Ok, let's see. You know I swim. I love the water, always have. There is a pool in the backyard at my folks' house and I spent every summer swimming in it like a fish. The hockey came because the guys all played, and frankly, I am a pretty good goalie."

"And track?"

"Oh, interestingly, I just started running to burn off steam one day and kept on going. I got pissed off at something—can't even remember what," he said too quickly. Charlotte suspected there was something Alex wasn't sharing. "Turned out I was a good long-distance runner, and I liked it. I liked the routine, the time to think, even competing against the clock. So, I joined the track team and here I am, still running. But I have a prettier running partner now."

Charlotte blushed bright red at the simple compliment.

"Enough about me. What happened to you out there today? The truth."

"I fell. Really, that was it. Besides, we have not finished with you. Tell me about this place."

"You really want to know, or are you avoiding my question? I'm not boring you? You aren't too tired?" When she nodded no, he continued. "The guys all live nearby, so when a place with a pool came available, Wyatt thought of me. It's big, no doubt about it. Who needs four bedrooms, a media room, a library, and an office? There is that huge kitchen you saw plus a butler's pantry and a laundry room and a full two-bedroom apartment for live in staff, which I use for storage. There are four and half baths. One has a steam shower that might be great for you in a few days, or the soaking tub might be even better. You'll enjoy all the patios too. I am told the kitchen is a big deal, but, while you are obviously completely at home there, I grew up with housekeepers and a chef and never learned a thing about cooking."

"It's all really beautiful. I can't wait to explore."

"Feel free. I worked with a good decorator so they could photograph it for "Architectural Digest" right before I moved in, but it still feels homey to me. A lot of the art comes from my travels, giving it something of a personal touch for me. The rest I bought with Wyatt or his sister, Missy. They are on the board of the Howe Art Museum and Wyatt is on the board at the Art Institute. When he says buy something, I usually do. Then he has me loan it back to his museums, the bastard," he concluded with a laugh.

"Now, that's enough," Alex said, clearly sick of talking about himself. "It's late and you need to rest. Time to put you back in bed."

Charlotte didn't argue. Realizing she was exhausted, she allowed Alex to help her from the seat and back to bed. Despite her offer to assist, Alex insisted he would handle cleanup. He escorted her down the hall and to the bedroom, but she refused to remove the work shirt and get under the covers until he left the room. Alex used the time to head into the adjoining bathroom and fuss for a minute or two, before hollering "are you decent?" and returning without waiting for her answer. He helped her take her pain medication, refilled the water glass beside the bed 'just in case' and asked twice if there was anything else she might want. Was he stalling?

Charlotte thought he might be reluctant to leave, then assumed she was imagining it.

"Well, goodnight," Charlotte finally said shyly.

"Good night, Charlotte," Alex bent to turn out the bedside lamp, but instead he leaned over her prone body, carefully bracing his hands on either side of her head, and hesitated, his face only inches from hers. She could feel his breath on her skin, warm with the lingering scent of chardonnay.

She locked her gaze onto his eyes, marine blue, and questioning. He must have seen the answer he was seeking, because his head lowered, and she felt the faintest whisper of his lips against hers. It was the softest, swiftest kiss and yet she felt her body respond. He pulled back, again wanting answers, or acquiescence. Her eyes were wide as saucers. He had surprised her with the kiss and her body had surprised her with its swift response. Mesmerized, craving more, she lowered her sooty lashes slowly, then opened them again in an age-old sign of invitation. Alex's eyes blazed.

Lowering his mouth to Charlotte's, Alex kissed her, claiming her mouth and body in a manner nothing like the previous soft foray. She felt the firm pressure of his lips on hers, the rasp of his tongue demanding her response, probing her to open to him. Heat oozed into her sore muscles, turning her body to warm liquid as her heart pounded in her chest. His tongue explored her mouth, capturing hers in a dance suggestive of so much more. She tasted Alex, all dark and mysterious, moist, and inviting and gave him what he sought.

"You taste like heaven," he whispered, moist and intimate in her ear. "I should have done that, ages ago. Now, I want to do so much more, Charlotte. So much more."

"Mm," she responded, "me too, Alex."

He dipped his mouth to hers once more, and she felt the velvety touch of his lips before he took hers hungrily. Shockwaves of lust rocketed straight to her core. She kissed him back, passionately, and completely, as his strong lips moved against her softer ones. Charlotte felt her body rising to meet his, felt her mouth insistent for more. She reveled in the taste of him, the feel of his tongue tangling with hers. The more he gave, the more she took and gave in return. Their bodies touched only at their lips, but the heat from him was as powerful as if they were naked and glued to each other from head to toe. The man could definitely kiss.

The kiss lasted only a minute, but it changed everything. She could never be the same. Now she knew how he felt, how he tasted. She needed more, and he seemed to as well. They had taken the next step and couldn't take it back. He finally saw her as a woman, and Charlotte was heady with power and weak with desire.

A hint of a soft breath moved through her hair. "Sleep now, Charlotte. Get well soon." He reached and turned off the light, pushed a stray hair away from her face in the dim light from the covered windows, and left the room. She watched the shadow of his lean frame back-lit from the hall and she wanted him with an overpowering hunger. Then he was gone.

Charlotte willed him to come back, lay with her and hold her through the night. She longed for the feel of him beside her, his strength keeping her ghosts at bay. She wanted to wrap herself around him and pull him into her body.

All that from a kiss. She'd have injured herself sooner if she'd known what a good kisser he would be...

Charlotte forgot all about her injuries and focused on the power of that drugging kiss. Snuggling deeper into the soft Egyptian cotton, she drifted into a deep and dreamless

CHAPTER SEVEN

en days later, Charlotte was recovering well and moving as freely about Alex's opulent home as if she lived there. She kept telling him she was doing well enough to return home, but he insisted she stay through the end of the week. He played on her guilt by reminding her he had cancelled his business trip to be there caring for her, and his ploy worked.

She didn't fight him much.

She had to admit that life was far easier for her staying in his condo. She had Joanne to handle everything outside the apartment, from refilling medication prescriptions to arranging a car to get her to and from her doctor's visits.

Although she never asked him to, Brian started carrying files to and from the LHRE offices for her, helping with various tasks and even creating a PowerPoint presentation. The two assistants worked long hours, clearly devoted to their boss. By extension, these days, they were equally devoted to her.

She could get used to this.

They stocked the refrigerator with healthy foods—and a few unhealthy snacks at her specific request—and the kitchen was far superior to her own. She was living in the lap of luxury, and she knew it. She basked in an incredibly decadent soak in the extra deep tub in her bathroom, piping in the music of her choice while sipping a glass of

Alex's fine wine as soon as she was able, then she interspersed that with the moist heat of the steam shower. It was heavenly.

She was quickly back to work, but now she reviewed financial documents from Alex's landscaped outside decks, moving from chaise to couch to table as the sun shifted, and the day progressed. The outdoor space was as elegant as the indoors, with comfortably upholstered rattan or teak furniture, weather-safe rugs, and professionally groomed gardens still colorful with golden delphiniums and mums.

Charlotte regularly mixed sitting in the sunshine with work, spreading her files on the table safely weighted by a cup or garden rock. She would sit there lost in the unobstructed views of Chicago, appreciating the background music and an outstanding Wi-Fi connection. She spent more time doing research on the sites below than on the real estate business.

After following the sun throughout the day, Charlotte would marvel at the fiery sunsets each evening. They felt close enough to touch, painting the sky in shades of reds, pinks, and oranges. She tried photographing them with the camera in her phone, then complained when she failed to capture the majesty. On the nights he was home, she encouraged Alex to share in the moment's beauty, pouring them each a glass of wine and standing beside him quietly as they bid the day farewell.

Oh yeah, she could definitely get used to this.

Of course, there were the security aspects that she never took for granted. No one phoned her directly except on her cellphone. No one came through the door that Alex and the team hadn't preapproved. Everyone was keyed into the elevator by a doorperson. She felt the stress leave her body when she remembered that, and she slept better for having the added protection. How would she give that up and go back to looking over her shoulder every minute of the day?

Charlotte and Alex were almost like an old married couple by now, sexless, comfortable together, able to finish each other's sentences. There had been no repeat or escalation of that first night's kiss, although she tried to give him small hints she would welcome more. Sometimes Charlotte would find him looking at her like he could devour her, but he kept his hands—and those magical lips - to himself. Alex seemed to have rethought things, and he kept a disappointing distance.

She knew his routine by heart. He rose no later than 5:30 and went for a run. With the marathon closing in, he would be gone until 8:00, then he showered and went to the office, but never before he made her coffee, carrying it to her in bed. Alex looked elegant and aloof in his Brioni suits, while she lay rumpled—and she had hoped inviting — in his guest bed. He would crisply announce his schedule for the remainder of the day, promising to come home in mid-afternoon, or reluctantly telling her he had dinner meetings. Alex wasn't joking when he told her he dined with clients a lot. He was gone at least twice a week, more often three or four nights, and Charlotte knew he was declining invitations when he could in order to be home with her.

Although he rarely ate at home, he had Joanne stocking the refrigerator constantly. She would arrive at the condo promptly at 8:30 so that she crossed paths with Alex before he left for his office. Most days, she would work from the condo, sitting behind his desk like she owned it and efficiently managing their lives. Charlotte enjoyed having her there. Alex never said it, but Charlotte knew he didn't want her left alone.

Joanne would join her for a breakfast of eggs, cereal, yogurt, and every imaginable juice in the fridge. "Alex believes in the power of fruit juice. He believes it cures everything," she told Charlotte with a laugh.

"No wonder he drinks so much of it."

When she felt better, Charlotte started baking scones and muffins to add to the breakfast menu. She was a natural in the kitchen and the baked goods disappeared quickly.

The two women became close friends quickly, sitting over those breakfasts. "You are so down to earth," Jo told Charlotte one morning. "When I heard you had double Harvard degrees, and the Roche name, I just assumed you would be a snob."

"Thank you, I think," Charlotte laughed. "I am just a normal person. My family loves to sit around a table laden with great food and laugh. I miss them. All that eating was why I started running. I needed to burn off a ton of calories."

"I'll have to be careful too, if we keep eating like this," Jo laughed and patted her flat stomach. "Do you miss them terribly? I can't imagine living without everyone close by."

"My family? Oh yes, very much. I am very close with my brothers and my parents are very protective. I talk to them every day. They would be happier knowing how I spend every single second of the day, but I have not told them about the accident. They would be too worried. I am overdue for a visit, though, so I have to get out of this boot. How about you? What is your family like?"

"Big. I have seven siblings, all still here in Chicago. In fact, my older sister, Clarice, is good friends with Keeli Larsen. That is how I found out about this job."

"Clarice Washington? I have seen her sculptures. In fact, I think that is one of her pieces in the hallway, right? She's amazing. Wow, you two couldn't be more different."

"Oh no, except for our jobs, we are really alike. Clarice is focused and organized, like me. I grew up following her and my brother, Ronnie around like a puppy. I wanted to be just like them."

"I don't know your brother, but your sister is an outstanding role model. I wish I had sisters, but my brothers are so dear to me."

Over the days of breakfasts, Charlotte learned about Jo's education and her ambition, her fashion sense, and her friends, and more about her boisterous family. Joanne learned about Charlotte's work and her studies at Harvard.

"You don't share much, do you?" Jo finally asked one morning while she savored a warm apple cinnamon scone. "You and Alex have that in common."

"I don't know what you mean," Charlotte tossed off before she announced she was late for therapy and limped away from the table.

Charlotte had started physical therapy for her ankle and her wrist, three mornings a week, although she was still dragging the heavy boot everywhere and lingering bruises were still an ugly shade of yellow across her ribcage. Her face had returned to normal, and her hand and wrist had healed nicely. In Charlotte's opinion, Dr. Levin was being overly cautious, but she went to therapy without complaint. She loved her therapist, Becky, and it was as close as she got to a workout, sweating through what appeared simple exercises until she tried to do them.

Regan and Ethan both came to visit, and after the first few days, they started conducting work from the patio or dining room table to accommodate Charlotte. Charlotte had assured everyone that she was well enough to return to work, but Regan had insisted on meeting at the condo.

"Alex has made it clear, Charlotte. He will kill me if I take you out of here without his express permission, and he is nowhere close to giving it." Regan's no-nonsense face told Charlotte that Alex was being adamant about her safety. Regan thought nothing of it, but

Charlotte was grateful she had shared the information. It told her that Alex suspected something.

Charlotte didn't press the point. Soon she would return home and until then, she would have to do a better job convincing him that there was no one else in the park. And she would have to deal with the problems that she had avoided these last 10 days. Regan's words were a jolting reminder. Just thinking about returning to her apartment alone set her shaking.

"Don't think about him," she repeated to herself. *"Enjoy Alex and a few more days of blissful serenity."*

Charlotte knew well that reality awaited, so she savored this time even more. He was still out there, growing more frustrated, more enraged, and more dangerous since she dropped out of sight. He didn't like to be thwarted.

CHAPTER EIGHT

Charlotte's social life was better than ever. Besides her growing friendship with Jo, Regan had taken to coming over, Tyler Winthrop in tow, with carry-in Chinese or pizza. Charlotte observed the two carefully, and it was obvious to Charlotte that there was something happening between the childhood friends. Exactly what was anyone's guess. The glances Regan and Tyler exchanged were either steamy or longing, but the conversation never strayed from the ordinary, even banal, chit-chat.

Charlotte tried broaching the topic with Regan one afternoon, when she and Regan were taking a break from work. Sitting at a patio table under a large umbrella, Charlotte thanked Regan again for bringing dinner earlier in the week.

"I had such a good time. It feels great to laugh again without being in pain," Charlotte began. "Tyler seems so straight laced, but he is so funny. I would never have guessed."

"Oh yes. Tyler has many hidden depths," Regan responded cryptically. "You woul be surprised by how different Tyler is away from his work persona."

"Really? I am intrigued. Tell me a few of Tyler's secrets," Charlotte all but begged. Regan smiled serenely, but she shut the conversation down completely.

"You like him, don't you, Regan? Is there something between you two?" Charlotte tried to push it, but she reminded herself that she really didn't know Regan that well. Ultimately, Regan was her boss, not her friend, and she would do well to remember it. When Regan remained tightlipped, Charlotte dropped the subject. She also learned from the exchange. Charlotte, too, became reticent, declining to discuss her relationship with Alex, although she longed for some girl talk.

She would not have known how to explain her relationship, anyway. Alex was attentive and engaging, warm and friendly, but he kept his distance unless he was helping her move about. Then he held her like a porcelain doll, gently and carefully. If she leaned into him, he let her. If she took his hand, he didn't drop it. But he still made no overtures.

Charlotte felt frustrated by their return to relationship uncertainty, but in every other way they were doing so well together, their ideas and plans so in synch, their personalities so well matched. After deciding to pursue him, then moving in and after that scorching kiss, Charlotte was reluctant to just let things take their own course, but she did - adding a bit of prayer when she was alone.

Each day, Charlotte would wander the gourmet kitchen in awe, preparing a nice dinner whenever Alex was home. She loved working in the space, obviously designed for a serious chef. She baked more than she cooked, trying new recipes for bread, muffins, and the occasional serious pastries. But she cooked often, too, making healthy salads full of fruits and nuts and cheeses, and dinners of comfort foods like pastas, meatloaf and grilled chicken or beef. She introduced Alex to his huge gas grill, almost a second kitchen filling a corner of the patio, showing him how to grill steaks and spicy Chorizo sausages.

One night Charlotte pulled Alex into the kitchen and together they roasted a whole turkey. They invited Wyatt, Keeli, Regan, Tyler,

Sloane, and Randall to sit down for the meal as big as a Thanksgiving feast. They kept teasing, but she loved watching all the friends together enjoying a meal she had prepared. She baked fresh bread and a squash casserole, and the group marveled at her cooking skills. They fawned over dessert, suggesting she start a bakery. She turned scarlet at the comment, embarrassed by their praise.

"If you had told me I would be eating a home cooked meal at your house, I would have said you were lying," Randall teased Alex before turning to Charlotte. "Did you know he has his own table at every restaurant in town?"

"Not every," Wyatt corrected. "Only the superb ones." "And a hot dog stand or two," Tyler added.

They all laughed easily, moving the conversation to new restaurants that were good and which ones were great. "I am fine with the status quo, Charlotte. Don't get him too used to home cooking," Tyler told them. "This way, I always get a table when I need one. I just use his name."

"He picks up the tab, too," Randall added, getting a laugh as the group readily agreed.

"Do you always pay for this motley crew?" Charlotte challenged. "Why would you do that?"

"It's the only way he gets our company," Randall quipped with comedic timing, getting the laugh he sought.

"He is the best restaurant critic around," Keeli praised, "and Tyler is right about getting a table anywhere. Even the busiest place on a Saturday night will find a table if you drop Alex's name."

"Actually, we had Alex to thank the night we met you, Charlotte," Sloane announced. "It was his connections that got us the rooftop at Soho House on such short notice. He really is useful."

"For more than just reservations. He's a damn fine goalie," Tyler offered, causing everyone but Alex to laugh.

"C'mon guys," Alex stepped in. "Don't let Charlotte think no one would want me without some pull at the right joint. I am trying to impress her." He gave his friends a pleading look. They met it with silence.

"Nope," Randall finally teased, "Can't think of any other reason."

The group laughed when Alex's face fell, and they rushed in to heap praise on him after they regained their breath. "Smart", "brilliant", "logical" and "an incredible friend" were just a few of the compliments they paid him. Alex sat taller and beamed under the praise. Charlotte watched it all indulgently, learning more about each of the people sharing her meal and liking them enormously.

They piled the dishes up for later and the group moved to the spacious living room, settling into the sofas with digestifs and coffee. Conversation and laughter swirled about the room. Keeli caught everyone up on her upcoming collection, a piece of which was twinkling on her finger. Sloane filled in the business gaps associated with the designer's launch. That led to conversations about the current financial climate in Chicago, which segued to city politics and heated debates that had to be cooled repeatedly.

It was after two in the morning when the group finally broke up. The time had flown by for Charlotte, standing arm in arm with Alex as the elevator door closed behind their friends. Standing in the quiet, Charlotte rested her head on Alex's shoulder in contentment.

"That was perfect."

"If someone else was cleaning up, it would be. But you were perfect." He dropped a kiss on the top of her head. "They all like you so much. You fit right in."

"Is that good or bad?" Charlotte teased, throwing a dishtowel at him and pointing at the cluttered countertops. Alex hated washing the dishes, but he did it while she stood by and dried. He had suggested leaving everything for his cleaning staff, but Charlotte had insisted they clean up each night rather than leave the mess for the morning. They worked well together in the kitchen, comfortably trading tasks, rehashing the highlights of the night until Charlotte was yawning repeatedly.

"Let's leave the last of these for morning," Alex suggested bravely, turning down the lights and taking her by the arm. "You've certainly earned your sleep."

"I like your friends so much," she mumbled as they moved down the hallway, shutting off lights.

"Our friends, Charlotte. They are your friends now, too."

"Remember that first night we met? I didn't even know Sloane yet there I was helping celebrate the sale of her business. Regan had to drag me there. She blackmailed me by reminding me I was new to town and needed to make some friends."

"I am so glad you listened to her," Alex said. "So very glad."

"Me too. Now I really feel like they are my friends. I wish we could do this all the time," she let slip. Charlotte had finally vocalized the wish she had often felt since arriving to stay with Alex. She was happy in the space that had at first overwhelmed her. She lounged in the media room with him in the evenings watching indie films on the enormous screen, nestled into the generous cream sofa while he sat beside her, her feet in his lap.

They enjoyed similar films, but she introduced him to some foreign films, and he introduced her to action films with spies and exotic forms of torture that sometimes forced her to avert her eyes. It would make him laugh when she did that, and he would call her 'a wimp.

Sometimes they would sit together, reviewing emails or doing nothing at all. Then they would slide open the floor-to-ceiling doors and let the night in, sitting quietly or talking softly about their plans and aspirations.

Charlotte had just voiced a dream of hers, to be by Alex's side, doing normal everyday activities, entertaining friends, cleaning the kitchen, going to bed. She hoped that the bed was where they were heading, but Alex announced he was heading for a swim instead.

"Now?" she asked incredulously. "It's really late."

"Actually," he said dryly, "it's really early. I need to work out some kinks. I'll be quiet as a mouse, Charlotte. Go to bed."

Charlotte often heard Alex splashing in the pool late at night or in the wee hours of the morning. He would pad through the house, a towel slung low around his hips, making her mouth water. Less than an hour later, he would come in, unconcerned with the puddles he would leave in his wake. She admired his dedication to the sport. She admired his hard body more.

Charlotte loved being near Alex, watching him concentrate on work or try his hand in the kitchen or just moving about the expansive apartment. His earnest expression fascinated her when he was dealing with client issues, as did his determined scowl when he took charge on a business call. His masculine cool aroused her, whether he was prone on the large sofas or slung low in a chair with his long legs stretched in front of him. She couldn't take her eyes off him as he prowled about the house, his long muscles stretching into graceful lines of male perfection.

Charlotte recognized the sound of his walk, knew his laugh, anticipated that he would play with a pen when he was strategizing or jiggle his leg when he was upset. She knew the strength of his jaw, the power, and the gentleness of his hands, appreciated his tiny butt and wide shoulders. Selfishly, she loved having him all to herself and took pleasure out of seeing him with his friends.

Charlotte was falling hard for Alex. These days of proximity were doing the trick for her. As always, she couldn't tell what Alex was feeling, but at least she knew him better. He shared more with her, although she still knew little about his past or his family, or those constant trips to California.

But tomorrow, all of that would change.

CHAPTER NINE

Tonight would be different. Tonight, for the first time since her accident, Charlotte was stepping out into Alex's world.

Alex was taking Charlotte to the party for his sister, as promised. It was not the first time she had been out since the accident, although she had kept her forays to a minimum. She had been to follow up with doctors a few times, to physical therapy and they had done quick trips in the neighborhood, for coffee twice and once for a glass of wine. When she told him the views were better from his rooftop than the famous Nomi rooftop bar, he vowed not to disappoint her in the future. They had stayed in since then.

He was very protective of her out in the world, watching to be sure no one bumped or jostled her. He made her feel safe, and she appreciated it. It allowed her to let her guard down a bit and just have fun. Charlotte was excited about tonight, about the glamour of the event, and seeing Alex in this setting, but nervous about being in a room full of strangers and meeting Alex's family. How he would introduce her? A friend, a colleague, his roommate, or his girlfriend?

Charlotte checked her appearance one last time, still uncomfortable about the dress choice. The Carmen Marc Valvo dress Joanne had selected was undeniably beautiful, but the orange and purple floral silk was vivid. Accustomed to muted colors and business suits, Charlotte felt feminine and lovely, but didn't want to draw too much attention to herself. Admittedly, the high round neck, cut-in shoulder, and pleated skirt were becoming, and the obi-styled belt at the waist made her figure look curvier than it was. She felt pretty, beautiful, in fact, with no bandages or scrapes showing. She wore one low strappy sandal and the clunky boot. It couldn't be avoided.

Charlotte took a deep breath, trying to calm her nerves. Not only was she meeting Alex's sainted sister, she was being introduced to a US Senator and his family. It thrilled Charlotte that Alex had invited her to this event. It would be the biggest party of Aubry's events. Charlotte tried not to read too much into it, but this was a date, an actual date. She had high hopes of using it to rekindle the change in their relationship she had experienced her first evening under his roof. A lot was riding on tonight.

Fingering off a bit of lipstick that had gone astray, Charlotte decided she was happy with her overall look. She had a pair of Keeli Larsen Design earrings shimmering against her dark hair. She was overdue for a trim, but that meant the thick strands were staying behind her ears. The bob was sleek, her makeup was light but effective, and her eyes looked enormous in her small face. Her lipstick was pale and looked good with the dress. She gave a nod to her reflection, opened the door, and stepped into the fray.

"Wow, you look fantastic," Alex greeted her, taking her arm to help her maneuver. "My family will fall in love with you in an instant."

Charlotte beamed at the compliment. "Great, that will save me from having to impress them with my wit and wisdom."

"You will wow them with those, too," he assured her.

Alex looked good enough to eat. The man knew how to rock a suit. The dark jacket and trousers fit to perfection, accentuating his broad shoulders and narrow hips. Alex looked taller than his already tall 6'1", lean and fit, and still sporting his late summer tan. His deep blue eyes looked even bluer and his white teeth even whiter. He wasn't model-handsome, being a bit too rugged with his deep cut dimples and cleft chin. He made Charlotte's mouth water all the same.

The lake smells were strong on the unseasonably warm evening air as they drove past families lounging in the parks and even some teens braving the chilly water. People were taking advantage of the very last of summer, knowing that a Chicago winter would descend in just a few short months. Once they cleared the rush hour traffic of a Friday night, the Mercedes was sleek and fast, great on the twists and turns of the ride north. Eventually, the high rise building obstructed the lake views and then they passed increasingly opulent homes along Sheridan Road, moving from one suburb to the next into Glencoe.

The driveway alone told Charlotte they were not hanging in her usual spots. The stone façade was invisible from the road, hidden down the long driveway and behind high, well-tended bushes. They'd cut a wide concrete swath between the thick stand of elm, green ash, and red oak trees, creating a canopy overhead. It was totally exclusive until the drive expanded into parking enough for a dozen or more cars.

As she stepped from the car, Charlotte inhaled the strong fragrance from manicured flowerbeds that were a mass of color and beauty. A lanky, teen-aged valet jumped forward, eager to drive the showy sports car. He was efficient, but his speed prevented her from studying the house's exterior without being obvious.

Alex ushered her through the double glass doors into an entry hall that ran straight to the back of the house, a wide formal stairway rising to one side and a massive window with an expansive lake view straight ahead. Charlotte had only a moment to admire the oriental rugs and elegant furnishings before her hosts, Ethan Howe, Melissa Howe Wilder, and Missy's husband, Stephen Wilder, were greeting them.

"Gently, Ethan, Charlotte's still recovering," Alex chided Ethan as he stepped forward to give Charlotte a welcoming hug. Charlotte had met Missy once through Regan, but she knew her brother Ethan from the office. He was clearly excited to see her out and about at last. Alex stepped forward quickly to curb his exuberance. "Be careful, you clod." Ethan took the direction in the good-natured manner Alex offered it, shaking her hand gently with a sheepish grin.

"It is so great to see you," he gave Charlotte a peck on the cheek after looking over at Alex to see if he was overstepping. "We have missed you at the office, more than I can say."

"I have been phoning in daily, Ethan, and we held two meetings at the condo. Are things falling through the cracks?"

"Oh no. You are great, Charlotte. But it's not the same not having you around, you know?" Ethan was the youngest of the Howe family, still apprenticing with Regan to learn the ropes at the huge real estate conglomerate. He had the wholesome blonde good looks of his brother, Wyatt, in a younger, toned-down fashion.

"No shop." Missy stepped in to greet Alex and Charlotte. "This is a party, remember? I am so glad you could join us, Charlotte. It is lovely to see you again."

"Thank you for having me," she said. "Your home is lovely. I can't wait to see more of it."

"When the crowds thin later, I will give you the ten-cent tour and we can catch up a bit. Right now, since it is such a beautiful evening, everyone is on the back patio." Missy pointed in a general direction and, after promising Ethan that they could catch up later, she broke up a tête-à-tête between Stephen and Alex to make room for more guests streaming in behind them. Alex took the cue to keep moving and led Charlotte through room after room to get to the patio.

Charlotte found it difficult not to gawk. They walked through two enormous living rooms separated by a stone fireplace. The rugs absorbed the sound of their footsteps in the high-ceiling rooms as Charlotte turned around, staring at everything. First, there were floor to ceiling arched windows with an unimpeded view across a large, sloping garden to the gray-blue waters of Lake Michigan. Then there was artwork covering every wall, each piece more arresting than the next. The formal rooms looked like something from "Architectural Digest" but livable and comfortable too. Much of the furniture looked antique. Charlotte was afraid to touch anything, although the uphol-stered pieces looked inviting,

"Pick up your chin, silly. It's not the first impressive house you have ever seen, Charlotte. Not even close."

"But this artwork is remarkable, and these photographs are muse-um quality."

Alex drew Charlotte away from the artwork, including the fabu-lous photography, after explaining that Stephen was himself a famous photographer with pieces in museums around the world.

"Ah, that explains it. This is as good as any museum," Charlotte responded, moving away reluctantly.

"Well, of course, the Howes built a museum, too. In fact, that is how Missy and Stephen met. More on that later. Let's go find my sister. I promise you can peruse more after dinner."

With that, they moved through a large family room toward the patio. Charlotte quickly peeked into two large offices and the dining room. It appeared set for a state dinner. She wanted to see the enor-mous and bustling kitchen, but a busy server shoved her back, coming toward her with a full tray of hors d'œuvres. After being jostled, she latched on to Alex's arm and let him lead her without complaint.

"This place is unbelievable. It goes on and on," she said in awe.

"Yep. It's huge, but they have three rambunctious toddlers who will grow up and fill all this space, or at least that's their plan."

Moving toward a wall of windows, Charlotte allowed Alex to lead her out to a multi-tiered patio crowded with elegant women and handsome men. There were small lights surrounding the space, illuminating the growing twilight. Tuxedoed servers passed enticing tidbits, their aromas mingling with the aromatic scent of flowers. There were blooms in the English gardens on both sides of the lush lawn, and in abundant arrangements carefully placed edging the patio. The setting was flawless, but the sixty guests seemed oblivious to it all. Charlotte found it breathtaking.

"Come on, I'll introduce you to the guests of honor," Alex said, taking her hand and weaving carefully through groups of people, taking two glasses of wine off a tray as it went by and handing one to her in a fluid motion.

"Aubrey. Sorry to interrupt," Alex said, leaning into a group of six people chatting, and planting a kiss on the cheek of a petite woman with dark hair. "Come meet my date."

A lovely, delicate woman in her mid-twenties turned to look at Charlotte, extending her hand automatically. Her eyes grew wide, and she broke into a luminous smile very similar to her brother's.

"I am so delighted to meet you, Charlotte," she said formally. "Please allow me to introduce my fiancé, Representative Adam Jensen. Adam, this is Charlotte, the first woman Alex has brought to an event that is not a vapid model."

Alex smacked his sister's arm playfully.

"Lay off it, Aubrey."

"Well, it's true."

Charlotte, feeling more uncomfortable by the moment, took control, interrupting the banter between the siblings. "So, Adam, your father is in the Senate, and you are in the House? I don't think Alex shared that with me."

"Yes, but I am a state representative. I have a long way to go to catch up with my dad." Aubrey's fiancé was a good-looking man. Although only a few inches taller than her, he had a powerful bearing, and from his posture, Charlotte suspected he had a military background. A bit of probing proved her correct, and the conversation flowed easily around his overseas tours, his transition only last year to the state legislature and then to how the two lovebirds had met.

"I was really lucky, actually," he began, looking at Aubrey with open admiration. "I was doing a town hall meeting at the same hotel where Aubrey was leading a training session. We met in the elevator."

"It got stuck." Aubrey picked up the story. "Such a cliché, but that extra ten minutes was all Adam needed to ask me out."

"The rest, as they say, is history," he concluded, giving her a lingering kiss on the cheek. "In less than two months, she will make me the luckiest man alive."

"Well," Charlotte offered, "I wish you both only the very best."

At that moment, Alex's parents walked up, and he made introductions. While Charlotte could see a bit of a resemblance between Aubrey and Alex, he looked nothing like either of his parents. His mother, Laurel, was a bird-like woman, petite and with dark coloring. His father, Charles, was of average height, and while he might have been trim once, his belly reflected a man who enjoyed his food. They made an unlikely couple until Charlotte conversed with them. Both were fun loving, intelligent and engaging, all aspects that Alex seemed to have inherited.

Circulating with Alex around the patio, Charlotte was relieved to discover she knew quite a few people through her connections at Lyons Howe. Regan came over to say hello and give her a gentle hug.

Alex jumped forward as if to protect her, then self-consciously stepped out of the way when he realized Regan was being careful.

"I cannot wait to get you back in the office," she admitted. "It just isn't the same without you down the hall."

"Ethan said the same thing. It's so nice to be missed," Charlotte laughed, sincerely flattered by the compliment.

The evening went by in a whirl of superb wines, great food, and interesting conversations. Charlotte met the senator, who was down to earth and jovial and not above asking for her vote in November. It surprised her to learn that he was running a campaign and marrying off his son within a matter of weeks, until his statuesque wife explained he was doing nothing for the wedding but showing up when and where she told him to. They all laughed, but Charlotte could tell that Mrs. Jensen needed no help to rule the roost.

"Don't forget, I am also paying the bills," he corrected, with perfect comic timing. He got the laugh he sought, and the conversation flowed easily between them all with no mention of politics. They discussed Charlotte's recent move, and the group fell over each other, trying to tell her the best sights to see, and restaurants and museums to visit.

"The Howe Art Museum is rather spectacular," Wyatt chipped in, to chuckling. "Seriously."

Someone rang an actual gong, filling the space with its low reverberation. In response, the group passed into the massive dining room and found their places at the long table. Charlotte, seated between Wyatt and Alex, admired the gorgeous flowers and table setting. Everything was the height of elegance, like stepping back into "Downton Abbey."

Course after delicious course was served until Charlotte thought she would explode. She had tried to just take a taste of each dish, but the intricate flavors exploding in her mouth were irresistible. The corn chowder with lobster was creamy and flavorful, so she ate most of it. Picking at a salad of beets and goat cheese allowed her to eat more of the incredible wood-roasted arctic char that followed. When the rack of lamb was served, Charlotte thought she wouldn't be able to eat it, but she managed most of it, along with a taste of three cheeses and all of her chocolate truffle cake.

She definitely needed to get rid of her boot and get back to running. How could people eat all this?

After dessert and a flurry of toasts, Missy drew her aside, offering to take Charlotte on the promised tour of the house. Charlotte was delighted at the chance to see the house and walk off her dinner.

"It's ridiculous, really, almost 12,000 square feet, but Stephen fell in love with it. The schools are fantastic, and it is halfway between his work and my family," Missy explained as they moved from room to room, admiring the artwork and the architecture. Missy poked her nose in the kitchen, bustling with caterers, only to step back out to the doorway before being knocked over by a fast-moving server. "I guess I can't really show you the kitchen tonight."

"No problem," Charlotte laughed. "I almost got run down earlier. They are working so hard; we should leave them to it."

"You guys did fantastic, as usual," she hollered into the kitchen from the safety of the entryway. Pointing to the man in the chef's hat, she asked Charlotte, "Do you know Theo? No? He and Keeli are fast friends, and he is the best caterer for miles and miles."

"Well, dinner was fantastic, so I would have to agree. Too much food, but so delicious. I ate it all."

Moving back through the family room, Missy suggested they start on the lower level "where all the fun stuff is." Using a sturdy bannister to make her way down a wide stairway, Charlotte followed Missy into a huge hallway with doors and entryways in every direction. Missy guided her through the temperature-controlled wine cellar, the media room with large recliners and the biggest screen Charlotte had ever seen.

"It's a 90-inch screen. Ridiculous, isn't it?" Charlotte loved how easy-going Missy was and pictured them becoming good friends.

"We all have our weaknesses."

"Exactly!" Missy agreed with a laugh. "Speaking of..." Missy opened the door to a moderate sized room, flicking on the light to reveal a golf practice room.

Charlotte was speechless.

"OK," Missy admitted, "even I think this is over the top. But it makes Stephen happy, and he is showing our oldest how to hold a club."

"Maybe I should use it too. I stink at golf," Charlotte confessed. "I see what you mean about all the fun stuff. This floor is like a mini-amusement park."

Wandering up to the top floor, Missy stopped to tell Charlotte about all the artists, as well as how they had gained the art pieces on their walls. Charlotte was on sensory overload until they stepped into a serene, pale blue master bedroom and stepped to the window to admire the gardens below. The waning light muted the views, but Charlotte could imagine what it would look like with the sun rising outside the large picture windows.

"This is a magical place," she told Missy in a whispered breath.

"Let me show you my favorite room." Missy led Charlotte into the master closet, a huge square space with an island of drawers in the middle.Charlotte's mouth formed a perfect 'o'. It was the size of her living room. A wall of shoes, a built in, lockable jewelry safe and clothes hanging neatly in a row, sorted by type and color, were the icing on the cake of a lifestyle she could barely understand.

"This is my dream room. I want a closet like this, and I want to have the fashions to fill it." Charlotte whirled, grabbing a wall to save herself from falling. "I have no fashion sense," Charlotte confessed without shame. "Ooh, I want to make love on the floor, like Carrie and Mr. Big did in that 'Sex and the City' movie." Charlotte whipped her hand over her mouth in embarrassment. "I didn't mean to say that out loud."

Missy laughed and suggested she be sure to get all the designer shoes made famous by the show, too. "I knew I would like you the moment we met," Missy said. "You don't seem at all stuffy like most of the Boston-Brahmin people I have met. I really want you to stick around. Do you think you and Alex will keep things going when you move home?"

"Well, you don't pull any punches, do you?" Charlotte felt pink rising into her cheeks.

"It's just that I want to be sure we will get to see more of you in the future. I see a strong friendship forming between the two of us. I would hate to see Alex ruin it."

"We will have the Regan connection either way," Charlotte responded, evading the original question.

"Cagey, but I will accept it unless you want to share more?"

"No. I think you know what I hope for with Alex, but frankly, I am as clueless as you are."

"Did you all grow up in houses like this?" Charlotte asked Missy, changing the subject as her curiosity was getting the better of her.

"Pretty much. This is a bit much, but it's not that different from how we lived. Lake Forest has neighborhoods of winding wide streets and big houses. Tyler lived around the corner from Randall, who lived about a block away. A long block, because the yards were huge, but close enough. Alex lived another five minutes past that. The guys were friends, and Aubrey and Ethan were in school together, so I got to know her along the way. She's a lovely girl, smart and quiet. Alex completely dotes on her."

"I can tell that they are great together, despite the age difference."

"Yes, I guess his mother miscarried before she had Aubrey. She and Charles were desperate to have children together, or so my mother always said."

"But they had Alex," Charlotte corrected.

"Oh, Alex is Laurel's son, but he is not Charles' child. His father was from California, but he died when Alex was still an infant. I am not actually sure how he died since no one ever talks about him, but I remember Alex going to spend a summer break or two with his father's family in California when he was a teenager. Nothing ever came of it, though, and when Laurel married Charles, they arranged for Alex to be adopted."

"Well, that explains the lack of resemblance," Charlotte remarked. "He's so reticent. I have known him for four months and he never once has referred to any dad but Charles."

"I guess he doesn't even remember his own father," Missy theorized. "Charles would be the only father he ever knew."

They completed the house tour by peeking in on the children, tucked safely in their beds, with an obviously competent Au Pere watching over them. Charlotte looked at the cherub faces surrounded by toys and stuffed animals and smiled at the thought of them wielding golf clubs.

Backing quietly from the room, the women made their way back to the patio, where coffee and pastries were still being served. Only a few guests besides the families remained. Regan had left while they were touring, but Wyatt and Keeli were sitting holding hands on two lounge chairs, their heads close together in conversation. Ethan had turned ESPN on in the family room to get 'the scores' and he and Stephen were discussing the upcoming Bears season. Senator Jensen and his wife were saying goodnight to Missy's parents and once they were gone, it was just another Friday night of hanging out at home.

The caterers had cleaned until the only things remaining of the party were the aromatic flowers, a few bottles of wine that were being emptied rapidly, and Theo, emerging from the kitchen to say goodnight.

Keeli jumped up to give him a big hug, and they talked for a few minutes while Alex explained they used to share an apartment "in their poorer days." It was obvious, the caterer and the jeweler had come up in the world and they missed one another. Animated, they were laughing and punching each other like siblings might.

"This was great, Alex. I really enjoyed meeting everyone. Thank you so much for including me."

"It was my pleasure," he said, looking her full in the face for the first time in hours. Charlotte saw the heat flare in his eyes as they locked with hers. Could he read the same in her eyes? Their attraction was instantaneous. "Let's get the hell out of here," he suggested in a low, seductive voice.

They said a quick goodnight. Charlotte thought they were rude, but Alex was almost dragging her out the door. He helped her into the car and sped down the driveway, tires screeching as he pulled onto the winding lakefront road heading back to the city.

They drove in silence for about a mile before Alex spun the wheel left, into a small, deserted public park. He stopped the car, spanning two parking spaces. Then, as if he hadn't just driven like a maniac, he calmly suggested a short stroll before the drive back.

Helping Charlotte from the car, Alex kept hold of her hand as he moved, surefooted, along the beachfront path while she limped alongside in her boot. He stopped at the base of an old, gnarled elm tree and pulled Charlotte toward him, holding her around the base of her spine so that she could feel the hard length of him against her.

"You look so beautiful," he told her in a husky voice. "I have been wanting to do this all night."

Alex lowered this face to hers, pulling her close against him as he leaned back until all her weight was leaning on his and she had no choice but to twine her arms behind his head or the tree trunk. His lips captured her slowly, softly pressing against hers. One hand rested low on the curve between her back and her behind. The other came up to tangle in her short hair, holding her head still as he deepened the kiss. His lips demanded a response, plundering her mouth with his tongue. He tasted of expensive wine and Alex as his tongue explored the recesses of her mouth, hot and insistent. Her breasts were flattened against his rock-hard chest, her hips tight against his as he held her to him.

When he lifted his head, it was shadowed by the moonlight behind him, preventing Charlotte from reading his expression. Unsure and unsteady, she waited, catching her breath. Blood was coursing through her veins, hot and urgent. Her heart was pounding from just one kiss.

"God, I want you," he rasped, the words torn from him, raw and insistent, before he dipped his head to kiss her again. She returned the kiss, opening her lips to his insistent ones, entwining her tongue with his, increasing the pressure against his mouth as she ran her hands up into his hair. She held fast to him, feeling his hand move from her hair to her neck, down along her bare arms, tracing a pattern there with his fingers. The feel of his hands on her skin was warm, strong, and sure. She had longed for his touch and now desired it everywhere.

Alex lifted his head reluctantly. "If we don't get back in that car now," he told her, his voice hoarse with longing, "I will not be responsible for my actions."

He lifted her away from his body, steadied her and then hefted himself away from the tree and wrapped his arm around her shoulders to lead her back to the car.

She felt bereft without the solid warmth of him hard against her. Neither of them said a word until he opened her car door and closed it again, without allowing her inside. Instead, he pushed her gently against it.

"Sorry, I can't make it home without one more." Alex took Charlotte's mouth in a searing kiss that took her breath away, sucking her lower lip into his mouth, then sliding his tongue over it and into the moistness of her mouth. He kissed her senseless until she would have happily made love there in the sand, and the world be damned. She wanted this man as she had never wanted anything before.

Charlotte kissed him passionately, running her hands up and down his muscular back as she tightened her hold on him, wanting to get closer, to feel his bare skin, until finally they mutually agreed to some restraint and dragged apart from one another. He kept his fingers touching her lightly until she got in the car, and he closed the door behind her.

"Jeez," he stated with a rough chuckle as he folded himself into the bucket seat, "I hope there are no cops out, cause I am planning to break speed records getting you home."

CHAPTER TEN

Alex was careful to keep the speed reasonable by his standards, no more than ten to fifteen miles over the posted limit. The car handled the twists and turns like a dream, first on the almost deserted back roads and then as he weaved between slower cars in his quest to get Charlotte home. Soon they were back on straight open roads with bright lights overhead and light traffic.

When they emerged from the darkness of the residential areas, Charlotte finally broke the silence.

"You only date models? I thought that was a joke when I heard everyone say it. I mean, I did see you with that woman from L.A., but only models?"

"Not only, sometimes actresses, too."

"Was that sarcastic?"

"No, honest."

"Is there a reason? Why only models and actresses?" Charlotte strived hard to keep the jealousy and insecurity from her voice.

"I try to avoid entanglements. I mean..." he trailed off uncomfortably, considering the kisses they had just shared. "It's only that I travel so much, and I am busy."

"But don't you want to settle down at some point and have a family? Do you plan to do that with a casual fling from Hollywood?" She didn't mean her voice to sound so accusing. "I mean, I am sure many of them are really sweet. That didn't come out the way I meant it to."

"No, the ones I date are pretty dumb, if I am being honest," Alex admitted, getting a relieved laugh from her in response. "I have just resisted letting anyone get close. It's a habit now."

"And me? What about me?"

"Yeah, what about you? I have to admit," he shook his head, "you sure as hell don't fit the mold."

"Is that good or bad?" She held her breath, waiting for his response.

"At the moment, it is very good." Alex reached over to run his fingers lightly up the skin of Charlotte's thigh, and, after several strokes, rested his hand there heavily. "You are an enigma, Charlotte Roche. You seem to have wiggled under my skin when I wasn't looking."

"Well, I don't want you to feel uncomfortable, Alex." When he said nothing, she added in a disappointed voice, "How about we just see what happens after tonight? No strings, okay?"

"No strings," he agreed slowly, working over the words. "For now, no strings."

Alex moved his hand from her thigh to her arm, running his fingers up and down, up, and down in a mesmerizing pattern, inching closer to her neck, her breast, her face, then returning to the back of her hand before repeating the movement. He stroked the soft silkiness of her skin, the long lean muscles underneath, felt the shiver of her response. Alex kept his other hand on the wheel and his eyes on the road, but his right hand fingers seemed to have a will of their own, feeling every available inch of Charlotte they could reach.

"So, you never mentioned that you were born in California. I just assumed you were born here. I thought Charles was your father."

Alex's head whipped around, trying to decipher Charlotte's expression. "Who said he wasn't?" Charlotte saw a brief panic cross Alex's face in the strobing streetlights. Then it was gone.

"Missy told me."

"Why were you discussing me with Missy?" Alex barked. Taking a calming breath, he continued, "Charles has raised me since I was a baby. I think of him like a dad."

"But what about your real dad?"

"What about him?" Alex took another deep breath. "There isn't anything to say about him. We moved here when I was just a baby and my mother left all that behind. I was still an infant when she remarried."

"But Missy said..."

"Damn Missy and her big mouth!" Alex cursed in the small space, causing Charlotte to cower back into the leather seatback. "I'm sorry. I shouldn't have snapped at you."

"It's okay. Obviously, I have hit a nerve and I apologize. I didn't mean to snoop." Charlotte had never expected such a vehement reaction, even from the highly private Alex. "It's none of my business, Alex. Just forget I asked."

"No, it's not you. It's just a touchy subject for me right now. I still have family out west. I tried to have a relationship with them, spending a few school vacations and stuff. But you know how boys are at that age. I wanted to be with my friends here and my California cousins felt like strangers.

"Besides," he continued, "my mom really felt strongly that she wanted me here with her. She believed the California side of the family was a bad influence on me, so she made sure I stopped hanging out in L.A. Once Aubrey was born, that was it, regardless of what my

California family might have wanted. As far as Charles and my mom went, once I had a sister, my life was here, period."

"Do you talk to any of them now that you have all this business in L.A.?"

"Why are you so interested in California? Really, it's not significant and we don't need to talk about it. What did you think of Aubrey? She's great, isn't she? I think Adam will be a good husband for her too, steadying. She can be flighty for such a smart girl."

"She's only twenty-six, Alex. She's allowed to be flighty." Charlotte recognized Alex was diverting her attention from something, but he was clearly rattled, so she let him change the subject.

"Well, you're only 30 and I have never seen you be flighty."

"No," Charlotte agreed sadly. "I was born serious. I wouldn't mind being flighty now and then."

"Really? What would you do if you just let loose?" he asked, intrigued.

"I am not sure. I have never really thought about it."

"Well, think about it. Then, let me know. I would love to see you when you finally cut loose and go wild." After a few minutes of silence, Alex asked Charlotte, "So, why were you always serious? What was your childhood like?"

"The usual, you know," she demurred.

"No, I don't know. In fact, considering all the time I have spent with you, I actually know very little about you. I know you are from an esteemed and powerful Boston family, went to Harvard, got a job in a NY real estate management company that you left quickly to return to Harvard. I know you were looking for a change from your job at Independent Life when you met Regan through some big-donor Harvard fundraising event, but I don't know why. I know you have a brilliant financial mind. You're funny and sweet. That is all I know.

Oops, not true. I know you have a gorgeous body, which is all I am interested in at the moment."

"Alex!" Charlotte sounded affronted by the last statement, but secretly, she was very pleased. "You are such a pig."

"Are you kidding? You are so hot in that dress. And be honest. Where was I supposed to look when you ran with me in next to nothing? I am a normal, healthy guy, for god's sake. I have resisted you for ages and believe me, it was difficult."

Charlotte was grateful for the darkness hiding her smile. So, he'd noticed her efforts after all. After waiting a beat, Charlotte admitted, "it hasn't been easy for me either."

Alex looked away from the road just long enough to flash her his irresistible smile, his teeth blindingly white in the dark interior of the Mercedes. "Really?" he asked with a touch of insecurity interlaced with bravado.

"Mm hmm."

As they sat in the shadows, Alex took her hand in his, raised it to his mouth, and placed a long, hard kiss into her palm. He felt her shiver in response and nipped lightly with his teeth before letting go to return his hand to stroke along her arm.

"So, you were saying?" he probed. "I'm waiting."

"Saying? Are you that insecure? Yes, I find you very attractive."

"Good," he gloated, "but I meant you were telling me about your family."

"Actually, I wasn't saying," she corrected with a tiny laugh. "I have parents who are overprotective and two brothers, one older, one younger. The youngest is at the Culinary Institute in New York, studying to be a chef. I am so proud of him."

"I still can't get over your parents being okay with that. A chef in the high-brow Roche family. And your older brother and father?"

"Yeah. My brother, Jake, got his MBA from Harvard two years before I did. We are very boring compared to being a chef. We are just boring period. I would rather hear about you. How did you like Stanford? Did Aubrey go there too?"

"Aubrey went to my mother's alma mater, Vassar. As for Stanford, the education was great, of course, the weather was fantastic, and I loved living in Palo Alto."

"But you didn't stay there?" Charlotte was struggling, focusing hard to follow the thread of the conversation. Her body was tingling everywhere Alex ran his hand, heating under his touch, leaving her craving more.

"This is home for me."

Before either of them could learn more about the other, Alex was sliding the car smoothly into his reserved parking space. "Enough of that now, though." Charlotte waited for Alex to continue, but he sat in the compact car, shadowed and quiet, until finally he shifted in his seat to face her fully. "We have other things to discuss. Important things that we probably should have discussed sooner."

"Such as?"

"Plans, protection, the night ahead."

"Really?" Charlotte asked as a twinkle lit her eyes.

"Yep. I should probably warn you I am planning to make love to you until you can't stand up," Alex stated bluntly. "Any objections?"

"Well... I guess since I am having trouble standing already, I can approve that plan."

"Good point. Okay, next. There is no delicate way to say this, but I think you already know that I have slept with a lot of women. I get tested frequently, so I know that I have no STDs, etc., but just say the word and I will use protection."

"Wow, I guess we really are covering the nitty gritty here." Charlotte had gotten a pained look on her face in reaction to Alex's blunt statements, but chided herself with a mumbled reminder he was correct. It was nothing she didn't already know about him. Still, he could see it hurt her.

"Once I touch you, Charlotte Roche, I know I won't be able to stop, and this I will promise you: from that moment forward, there will be no one else but you," he reassured her. "Still, we better discuss all of this here and now."

"Very practical, Mr. Gaines. Okay, since I do not sleep with many people, not even close, I can tell you I too have no diseases to speak of. However, I have not really needed to think about birth control in a while."

"Then we have our answer. Protection it is." With that, Alex unceremoniously ended the conversation, jumped from the car, and went around to open Charlotte's door. Taking her hand, he dashed to the elevator as she did a little skip step to keep up with his long strides. He realized he was moving too fast, slowed down, and wrapped his arm around her waist to assist her.

"Sorry. I completely forgot about the boot. You really look stunning tonight."

At the elevator, Alex inserted his key, pressed the penthouse button, and waited beside her, facing forward, while the doors closed. As soon as they were enclosed in the quiet space, with almost seventy floors to travel undisturbed, he turned Charlotte into his embrace and bent to claim her mouth. His arms moved about her hips, drawing her tight against his body as his mouth locked to hers in a skillful, scorching kiss. Alex felt Charlotte melt into his embrace, returning his kiss with fervor. He increased his heated caresses on her back and butt, feeling the slide of silk and round woman underneath his fingers. With each move up her back, he took a small amount of the full skirt, lifting it higher until he felt the bare skin of her behind and a tiny scrap of panty.

Charlotte inhaled sharply at the glide of Alex's fingertips along her exposed skin, and he took that opportunity to plunge his tongue between her lips. He felt the moist heat of her mouth, felt her pillow soft lips give under his firmer ones as a small moan of pleasure escaped her. He was lost in the kiss, drowning in the feel of this woman under his mouth and hands when the elevator slid to a smooth stop and the doors opened into his penthouse with a 'ding'.

Alex scooped his arms under Charlotte's knees and lifted her off her feet, striding toward his bedroom quickly, carrying her effortlessly in his arms despite his muscles bulging under the fine material of his suit.

"Can't wait," he explained. Charlotte responded with a sexy smile, then laid her head on his shoulder, licking her tongue across the bare skin of his neck as she fussed to loosen his tie.

Placing Charlotte carefully in the center of his bed, Alex bent to yank the Velcro straps that held the heavy boot in place, then slid his hand gently up her bare calf to the knee. He stopped there, removed her small sandal, and did the same with her right leg, but this time, his hand didn't stop at the knee. Rather, he moved up slowly, tantalizing her with the soft feel of his hands lightly skimming along the inside of her thigh. He lifted her dress only enough to reach under and grasp the tiny bit of fabric at the apex of her thighs. Charlotte lifted her hips helpfully and Alex slid the lavender thong down her legs and tossed it to a chair in the corner. He removed his jacket, tie, and shirt and added them to the pile. He was enjoying the play of emotions he saw cross Charlotte's features as she drank in the sight of his broad shoulders and washboard abs. She had seen him in running clothes and going to and from the pool, but he could tell that this felt very different for her.

"You're magnificent," she muttered under her breath, eliciting a smug grin of pride from Alex.

"I am sure you are, too. Let's find out," he said as he lay beside her and rolled her to a side so he could reach for her zipper. His mouth captured hers as his hands moved unerringly to slip the zipper lower and undo her bra, all one handed.

"How do you do that?" she marveled.

"Practice." When she scowled at him, he added, "and a strong desire to see you naked." He rolled the colorful dress off her shoulders and low enough to expose her breasts, trapping her arms in the material as he first gazed at her, then lowered his mouth. She felt the moist heat of his breath just seconds before his mouth wrapped around one tight nipple. He sucked it deep into his mouth as Charlotte's hips reflexively rose from the bed in need. Without removing his mouth from the taut bud, Alex lifted his own hips to undo his pants and kick them off.

Alex circled Charlotte's tender nipple with his tongue before moving to her other breast and wrapping his mouth around it. The cool air on her moist skin brought goosebumps to the surface, that quickly disappeared as Alex brought his hand up to stroke and squeeze Charlotte's tender flesh. He tightened his fingers around her hard and highly sensitive peak until a small mew of surrender came from her mouth. Alex abandoned the tantalizing breast with a last tingling flick to her nipple and lifted himself to draw her bottom lip, then her tongue, into his mouth.

Pulling her dress from her body, Alex freed Charlotte's arms, which she immediately used to run her hands over his tight stomach muscles. "You are beautiful," he sighed at the light touch of her fingertips. Bending close to her ear, he repeated the words in a warm whisper as he lowered himself until his body crushed hers to the mattress. Only his black boxer briefs came between them.

As Charlotte writhed beneath him, he felt the soft heat of her skin trying to get closer to him. He was holding himself in check, his kisses demanding, his hands roaming over her rounded body, mesmerized by the feel of her. He was straining hard against the fabric of his briefs, longing to plunge deep into her luscious body but stalling, touching her, kissing her until she was begging him to enter her, to take her, to satisfy the growing need in them both.

After long minutes of mutual torture, of feeling her long fingers massaging the strong muscles of his shoulders and back, of being squeezed by the legs she had wrapped around his torso, trying to pull him into her, Alex knew he couldn't take another minute and suspected neither could she. He had pushed them both to their absolute limits with the prolonged foreplay.

Alex grabbed a condom from the drawer and removed his briefs in a single fluid movement, his blatant masculinity now on proud display. Charlotte took the condom packet, opened it with her teeth, and slid the prophylactic slowly and hypnotically over him. Charlotte's grip was tight and firm around him, stroking down, then slowly up again, then down lower. Alex feared he would explode from the exquisite play of her fingers.

"You ready?" he asked in a steamy breath, his lips nuzzling her ear.

"I'm desperate," Charlotte replied, placing her hands hard on his butt, wrapping her legs tighter around his hips and gasping as he inched the hot length of himself slowly into her. "Oh, God, not so slow!"

She was gloriously tight, and Alex savored every sensual movement as he sheathed himself inch by tantalizing inch into the slick heat of her body. Settling himself deep inside her, he felt her shudder and knew she was already close to orgasm. Charlotte was so responsive, her every feeling expressed in her eyes, the little sounds that escaped from her mouth, her restless hands moving again and again over his heated skin. Her touches burned him; her kisses sucked him into her mouth. His body desperately wanted to give in to her demands, but he willed himself to make it last as long as possible.

Moving slowly out of Charlotte's moist heat, he felt Charlotte grab his ass, trying to hold him still, and he inhaled sharply and sank back into her, taking her mouth with his, swallowing her exhaled breath and returning it to her. He swiveled his hips as he finally moved in and out of her, steady and deep, with increasing speed. Charlotte trembled under him, and he felt the pressure of release building in them both.

"More," Charlotte kept saying as she ground her hips hard against his. "Please."

"Come on, Charlotte," he rumbled low in his throat, urging her to let go. "Yes, that's right, yes."

Their sweat-slick bodies were pinned close from breast to groin, her legs wrapped like a vise about Alex's hips as the muscles of his ass tightened with his efforts. Her small hands roamed every inch of his hard body, her mouth glued to his as their tongues did a sensuous dance of desire. Alex increased the pressure of his thrusts slightly and felt Charlotte convulse under him in a glorious release. As she clung to him, the feel of her pulsing around him was all it took to catapult him over the edge. Shouting his pleasure, Alex came hard with a mind-blowing orgasm.

Alex felt incredible. His heart was soaring and hammering in his chest, his brain was mush. Alex was bursting with male pride and accomplishment. He felt like a lion, powerful, masculine, and dangerous. He felt protective of this woman. Looking down at Charlotte, eyes closed, Mona Lisa smile on her lips as her skin cooled and her body continued to flutter around his. He also felt an unfamiliar, unsettling, but not unwelcome tug near his heart.

CHAPTER ELEVEN

"Oh my god," Charlotte said when she could finally breathe. "That was incredible."

"No kidding," Alex said, claiming her mouth for small a kiss that gave way to playful nips at her mouth. "Charlotte, you were amazing. I think maybe we have figured out what you would do if you let yourself loose."

"Perhaps we have," she laughed.

They lay together for some minutes, stroking each other lightly, alternating between simple and breathtaking kisses, their passion spent. After a grunt from Charlotte indicating he was crushing her, Alex pulled from where he rested, still deep within her, and lifted himself from her body. She watched as he padded into the bathroom, his long legs built like a warrior, his butt tight, his back broad and muscled. She feasted her eyes until the door shut behind him.

Alex emerged a few minutes later wearing an elegant and obviously expensive robe. "Can I get you anything?" he asked her. "Water, a glass of wine?"

"Mm. Water would be great."

Laying in his bed, watching him disappear down the hallway silently, Charlotte revisited what had just occurred. She had limited experience with men, a few short dating stints during her college years, then her long, disastrous relationship with Gil. But she knew that tonight had been special. Sure, the sex had been skilled and heart stopping, but the connection had been complete as well. Charlotte was helpless to deny it; she was falling for Alex.

Why on earth did I ever suggest no strings? I am not a no-strings girl, and he was offering more. Or was he?

Charlotte scooted into the bathroom in his brief absence, washed up, found a brush to run through her short locks, and jumped back into bed before Alex returned with both water and wine. Her ankle throbbed slightly from the short effort, but she pushed the pain to a corner of her brain, hoping it would subside.

"So, Miss Charlotte Roche..."

"Yes, Mr. Alexander Gaines? When did we become so formal?"

"I guess I became formal when I realized I needed a bit of distance while I recovered my wits after a wild beauty stole them from me," he confessed.

"A wild beauty? I like that," she beamed.

Alex removed the burgundy robe in a confident gesture and slid back into bed with Charlotte. Lightly stroking her belly, then her breasts, he repeated a hypnotic pattern with his fingertips, soothing and arousing her simultaneously.

"You are a wild beauty, Charlotte. You are so responsive and exciting. I would never have predicted that. I knew I desired you—I have for quite a while, you know?" He didn't wait for her response. "But I don't think, until now, that I realized the depths of you."

"I think you were just in the depths of me," she responded coyly.

Alex laughed hard, shaking the entire bed, drowning out the sounds of Charlotte's gentle snicker. He pulled her in close, stopped laughing abruptly, and kissed her. She sensed his eagerness and surprised herself by her matching response. She felt her desire building again, felt proof of his against her thigh, and reveled in it.

Reaching behind Alex's head, she wove her fingers into his hair, holding him to her as she sought his mouth with her tongue. He met her demands in hot, drugging kisses until she used her shaking hands to push him flat onto the bed and straddled him, never breaking the kiss.

Bent low over him, kissing him like he was her very breath, Charlotte was only vaguely aware when he reached for a condom and slid it on. It was all the foreplay she needed before she sank her hips over his, seating him deep inside her. After savoring the sensation as long as she could, she began moving.

Charlotte looked at Alex. His face was tight with desire, focused on hers. His eyes widened as she took in the full length of him, and she watched a soul-deep satisfaction settle in them. With that reassurance, she increased her movement, rolling her hips over his, grinding their bodies together as she slid up and down the length of him.

He was filling her completely, and Charlotte felt the rasping heat of every inch of him. She felt complete with him inside her, empty when she slid up so that only the tip of him teased her. She loved watching the play of emotions on his face as she pulled back before gliding down to the intense pleasure of them both. Charlotte recognized the raw hunger, the spiraling desire that matched her own.

Alex wrapped his large hands around both of Charlotte's breasts, squeezing until she shuddered from the sensations. His hands wandered over her body until finally they grabbed her hips. She only resisted a moment before allowing him to control the speed and force of her movements. He leveraged her faster and Charlotte gave up sitting straight, bending forward to push against the mattress and help him and herself. It was only moments before she shuddered hard and felt her body release in a powerful orgasm that went on and on and on.

Seconds after her orgasm began, Alex took full control, flipping Charlotte to her back without uncoupling their bodies and pounding into her as the tension coiled in her again. Within seconds, Charlotte felt the blood course through her veins and the swelling inside her build to another shattering orgasm. Clinging to Alex through her shivers of release, her body drenched in sweat, Charlotte struggled to catch her breath. Alex's expression looked almost pained in the seconds before he came, straining for that last bit of pleasure, shuddering with his release before collapsing his weight on her, replete.

The two lay together, sweaty, and completely exhausted, until finally Alex rolled off Charlotte's smaller frame, a look of complete satisfaction on his smug face.

"What are you so pleased about?" Charlotte lost the battle with herself to say nothing.

"You, I am pleased about you. You make me feel incredible." He lay silent for several heartbeats before adding, "And if I am not mistaken, I just made you feel pretty incredible — twice."

"But who is counting?" she said with a laugh and a drowsy, satisfied grin, then, finally, a huge yawn she was unable to conceal behind her hand.

"Very cute. Sleepy?"

Charlotte nodded yes and Alex reached over, covering her bare shoulder.

"Go to sleep, Charlotte." Alex wrapped his long body around her back, holding her close but not too tight, and soon she was asleep.

CHAPTER TWELVE

A lex awoke incredibly rested, harder, and hornier than usual. When he got past the first huge yawn and his brain kicked in, he realized why. Wrapped against his back with her arms around his waist was Charlotte. She felt womanly with her breasts flattened to his back, soft and rounded. She smelled good, a faint hint of last night's perfume and their lingering sex. Her steady breathing told him she was still asleep.

Wake her or try to disentangle myself, but let her sleep?

Alex knew he wanted to wake her and slake his desire hard and fast in her warm body, but instead he disentangled gently and went to make coffee. His emotions were in turmoil, and he needed the caffeine to help him think straight.

Today was Charlotte's last full day at his place, and the weeks of confinement had certainly done the trick. They had moved from friends to lovers, as was his goal. Not just casual lovers either, despite Charlotte's flippant words. Sometime last night, while he was buried deep in her moist heat with their lips locked together, Alex realized this woman was different from the bimbos he had been with before and not simply because she was smart. This woman had wormed her way into his life, and likely into his heart.

That absolutely cannot happen. How can I protect my family—hell, protect myself with her close by? It is too dangerous.

It was a good thing she was leaving tomorrow. Another week like this one and he knew he would be irrevocably bound to her. He needed to focus; he needed to handle things in California, help his parents get Aubrey through this wedding. Then, just maybe, he could start something with Charlotte.

Absolutely not before. She will be all right with that, too. Remember, no strings.

Repeating the phrase, he poured two fragrant cups of coffee, and noting that it was already after 9:00, he went to wake Charlotte. He was quiet as a mouse moving about the condo, but the second the aroma of coffee entered the bedroom, her big brown eyes shot open.

"Do I smell coffee?"

"You do indeed," he confirmed, handing her a steaming mug. Charlotte took a sip, blew on it to cool it, then took another. She sighed with satisfaction at both the liquid and the sight in front of her.

"Well, Mr. Modesty," she smiled, checking out his naked form from head to toe, "thank you for the coffee... and for last night," she finished in a shy whisper, a blush coloring her cheeks. He placed his mug on the bedside table, climbed back under the covers, and gathered Charlotte into his arms.

"Believe me, last night was my pleasure."

"And mine," she added, dipping her head in further embarrassment.

Lifting her chin, he leaned his head down to hers. Alex was soon kissing Charlotte with increasing passion, running his hands over her silky skin, tracing the curves of her body first with his hands, then with his tongue. He ran a line of kisses from her mouth to her jawline and along her neck to her collarbone, listening to her sighs of pleasure as he moved lower, latching firmly to her breast, and staying there.

His hands continued roaming along her trim waist, across her flat stomach and finally his fingers twined into the small patch of hair between her legs to find the tiny hub of nerves there. He rubbed her gently, then harder, until she was squirming under his thumb and pulling at his shoulders.

"Want something?" he mumbled as he moved his mouth from one breast to the other, laving the tight nipple with his tongue before letting go.

"You, please."

"You have me, Charlotte," he responded with more emotion than he intended, his voice husky. He hid his confusion by wrapping his tongue around her nipple, circling the tightening morsel, and then sucking it hard into his mouth so that Charlotte inhaled sharply at the combination of pain and pleasure. Alex released the pink tip and gently took her entire breast in his mouth, increasing the pressure of his thumb between her legs and sliding a long finger inside of her.

Charlotte was ready, wet, hot, and literally panting for him. He lifted his head to her mouth and sucked her lower lip gently into his mouth before moving his body away to reach for a condom.

"We need to get you some birth control," he stated curtly before sliding on the condom, rising above her, and slipping into her fully and without hesitation.

"Oh, yes," she responded, releasing a long, slow breath. "Better."

Laughing, Alex supported himself on his strong arms and began to rock inside of her, plunging deep then sliding out until she moved to meet him, demanding his return. He set an unpredictable rhythm, leaving Charlotte desperate for more as he swelled larger, his arms trembling, his need growing. He held on, pressing against her as he rolled his hips to maximize the sensations for them both.

He watched her face and waited, feeling her kisses grow more needy, her breath hitch with his thrusts as he held them both in a sensuous grip. The coiled tension in his body was screaming for release as he slowed down, then sped up, gliding smoothly in and out as her hips lifted to meet his again and again.

Charlotte was making those little mewing sounds, clawing her fingers on the muscles of his back, almost climbing him in her need to be closer and then closer still. Her hands trailed up and down his muscles, soft fingers massaging and digging into him in raw hunger.

He ran his tongue over the outside of her mouth, then lowered his head and demanded from her kiss everything she had to give, feeling her flutter hard and repeatedly around him and catapulting him into a shivering release. He shouted his pleasure into her mouth as he swelled inside her and exploded into her heat until he had nothing left to give.

As he stilled, Alex could feel Charlotte's body squeezing around him, still trying to milk him, still shuddering in her own heart-shattering orgasm. When she lay still at last, breathing as if she had run a marathon, he lowered himself from his trembling arms to rest upon her, flattening her breasts with his broad chest and sinking them both deep into the pillow-topped mattress.

Coffee forgotten, Charlotte was breathing the deep, even breaths of sleep. Alex watched her with satisfaction, taking in her pixie face, unblemished skin and straight nose. Her lips in repose were bow shaped, not wide, and full as they were when she smiled. Right now, they were pink and bruised from his kisses. He enjoyed seeing her like this, bearing the signs of their lovemaking. He swelled with male pride.

Alex watched Charlotte sleep. She had a firm chin, the only sign of her determination until her eyes were open, wise, and full of challenge. She showed none of her fierce independence when she was like this, and he felt felt a strong desire to protect her.

From what? He wished he knew.

He loved Charlotte's brilliant mind and willingness to spar with him on almost any topic and thoroughly enjoyed her willingness to be playful and teasing in bed. She was the perfect woman for him.

He knew it was a cliché, but Alex had never felt like this before. This warmth and fullness around his heart gave him joy and concern. He felt conflicted. Alex was limited in what he could offer her right now, but undeniably, she was becoming vital to his happiness.

He drank tepid coffee and watched her chest rise and fall until he finally shook himself from his thoughts, rose and went to shower. He'd had all the exercise he needed for today. Running would just have to wait until tomorrow.

Tomorrow, when she has moved back into her own home, and I need to burn off my frustration.

Alex threw on a pair of shorts and a clean tee, tossed an old, faded Stanford sweatshirt over his shoulders and wandered down the long corridor to his office. After checking the headlines and email, he verified his flight to California and mentally prepared himself for the trip West, jotting notes on reports and papers on his desk. He was fully immersed in his work when Charlotte came up behind him and planted a kiss on his cheek. How had she gotten so close?

How had he let her?

Scrambling to put the papers in order and turn them over, he fumbled them a bit. Flustered, he abandoned them and pulled Charlotte into his lap, kissing her soundly.

"Hiding something?"

"It's nothing. Just work. Hungry?"

When she said yes and they rose to get breakfast, Alex realized why she had been able to sneak up on him. "Where is your boot?"

"Oh, Alex, I am so sick of the damn thing."

"I'll go get it," he said, rising from the chair and heading back to his room before he remembered he left her alone in his office.

"Let me get you to a chair," he offered, returning to the office instead of retrieving the boot. He didn't want her exploring anything. Once he had her settled across the room, Alex went in search of the dreaded boot. Surprised to see that Charlotte had made the bed as well as showered and dressed, Alex glanced at the clock. He had worked longer than he'd realized.

Returning to the office, he helped Charlotte put the heavy device on her foot, pulling the Velcro closure tight, then softening the blow by running his hands up her inner thighs almost to the edge of her panties.

"Tease," she accused when he rose to fix breakfast.

"Ready again?" he eyed her openly, eager to see her response.

"I guess I can wait until after breakfast." She flashed him a saucy grin. "Maybe."

"Well, if you can, I guess I can too," he tossed back, then he walked over, trapping her by gripping the arms of her chair and leaning in, giving her a long kiss thick with promise. "That'll have to hold you."

He wandered to the open kitchen and swaggered under her gaze as he scrambled egg whites, low fat cheese and turkey sausage into an impressive omelet. He had been enjoying learning to cook. Charlotte was a good and patient instructor, and he knew he would miss their lessons. For the moment, he basked in showing off his new skill.

Why did I wait so damn long?

Alex was mentally kicking himself as he moved about the kitchen. He had wasted so much time, squandered so many opportunities. Even now, he wanted her again, his hunger fueled further by the knowledge that she was leaving in less than 24 hours.

Two entire weeks wasted—or maybe not. If I feel this attached, think how much worse it would have been if we had been sleeping together the whole time. Right, get on the plane and forget this. Learn to be friends with benefits.

"This is delicious," Charlotte praised Alex as she dove into her omelet. "So, back to the real world tomorrow. What are your plans like this week?"

"Now that you are on the mend, I will finally take that trip to California."

"Oh, of course."

Did she sound disappointed that I will be away?

"Where will you be? What will you be doing?"

"Well, Miss Curiosity, I will be in tons of meetings in L.A. with boring business people. What will you be doing?"

"I am sure my place needs a thorough cleaning." At the mention of her apartment, Charlotte stared off into space. She seemed far away to him, preoccupied. Had she already mentally transitioned back to her home and away from him? He suddenly felt very lonely.

"Maybe I will go see my family," she chirped with excitement, as if she had just now thought of the idea. "They have been pressuring me."

"Boston? Are you sure you are up for traveling? Why not wait at least until that boot comes off?"

"Yeah, good idea. My parents will worry about me even more if they see me wearing this thing. Besides, I am sure I have tons of work to catch up on. What about you? Do you need to work today?" She sounded so forlorn at the possibility.

"No, Ms. Roche, my work can wait. This is our last day living under the same roof, and I plan to take advantage of it." He flashed her a wicked grin and she rewarded him with a pink blush warming her cheeks.

"Swimming perhaps? It is a beautiful day. There won't be many more of these warm weather days, you know," Charlotte teased with a twinkle in her eye.

"Oh, swimming, I actually had not thought of that..."

"No? I thought it was a perfect option. We can begin with you diving into me," she laughed, reaching for his hand, and rising from the table.

"Oh yes, diving is definitely in order." Alex took her face between his hands and kissed her breathless.

Pulling gently on her hand, Alex led her back to the bedroom, where they happily stayed for the rest of the day.

CHAPTER THIRTEEN

S unday, Charlotte awoke sore from the prior day's acrobatics and still full from the sumptuous dinner at Les Nomades. When Alex suggested they go out for their last night 'living together' she had laughed. But he was serious, going all out with dinner at the chic, romantic French restaurant. She should have expected no less from him even though a last-minute reservation on a Saturday night was a near impossibility at the Michelin-starred establishment.

Not only did Alex get them a table, but he also got them a quiet and romantic table. It surprised Charlotte until they entered the restaurant and she discovered everyone knew Alex. It appeared he was a regular here, just as his friends had promised. The host recognized him and called him by name. It didn't shock her when the manager came from the kitchen to shake his hand, but when all the servers stopped by the table to greet him, she finally understood just how much of a regular he was.

Charlotte felt lovely in the simple cream Akris Punto dress Joanne had chosen. The woman clearly had impeccable taste and, with an unlimited budget on Alex's credit card, she had gone all out. The basic sheath with the fishnet overlay was sexy and classy, exposing her chest and arms even while covering them up. Alex's reaction added to the overall pleasure of wearing the beautiful garment—his eyes almost popped out of his head when she emerged from her room.

"Men are so funny," she observed. "You saw me naked almost the entire day. You even showered with me. But now that I am dressed, you look at me like sex on legs."

"Charlotte, that is just what you are. Sex on legs," Alex said as he swooped in to kiss her. "With a brain, of course."

"Ooh, wait," she barked, holding a hand against his chest to stop him. "I just put on this lipstick, and I want it to last at least a few minutes, please."

"I'll buy you a new lipstick," Alex promised as he took Charlotte into his embrace and kissed her firmly on the mouth. Once she relaxed into it, he softened his lips upon hers, coaxing her response with his tongue, exploring the recesses of her mouth, reaching every sensitive nerve ending as his hands moved relentlessly up and down her back, pulling her tighter against his hard body with each pass.

When they pulled apart, Charlotte looked dazed for a moment, standing still as Alex ruffled through her tiny handbag until he found a tiny tube of color. Then he turned her silently from his arms and gave her a gentle push back to the bathroom to repair her lipstick, laughing under his breath as she wandered out of sight.

With no further mishaps to her appearance, the couple entered Les Nomades, looking elegant together and turning heads as they moved to their table. Charlotte tried not to stare at the décor, the people, or the elegantly plated dishes as she walked through the restaurant, but once they were seated, she dropped her sophisticated façade.

"Alex, do you have your phone? I forgot mine and I want to be sure to get pictures of the food presentation and the room to send my brother. He would love this place. It is just the elegance he wants to achieve as a chef."

"Of course," Alex handed her his phone, took it back to unlock it with his thumbprint, then handed it back again. "You know, you could just point him to their website."

Charlotte laughed and handed back the phone. "Of course I could," she said, laughing at herself.

"So, your brother prefers traditional French to more hip cuisines?"

"My brother is like something straight out of old Europe, all tradition and history," Charlotte admitted.

"Where do you think he gets that influence?" Alex asked as they handed him the extensive wine list. He allowed his eye to wander down the list for a few quiet moments before selecting both a bottle of white and red for them.

"That is a lot for just the two of us," Charlotte observed with surprise.

"Then we can share it," Alex responded cryptically. "So, you didn't answer me about your brother. Has he spent a lot of time in Europe?"

"Not really, although he spent a semester of school cooking in Paris."

"Well, that would explain it." Alex seemed content with the answer, and Charlotte relaxed back against the cushioned banquette, the menu hiding her relieved expression.

Everything I say is a potential minefield. Alex asks too many damn questions. Keep your head, Charlotte.

Safely turning the conversation to food, Alex offered to get the five-course prix-fixe dinner while Charlotte got four courses, but they agreed to choose all different dishes so that Charlotte could taste everything. Alex recommended some of his favorites- the Pates Maison appetizer, the lobster and shrimp salad and the duck—then warned her to save room for a soufflé dessert.

"It all looks heavenly," Charlotte breathed on a sigh. "How on earth am I supposed to choose?"

"You are such a contradiction to me," Alex confessed, leaning forward on his elbows to move closer to Charlotte across the table. "You come from a privileged background, yet you act as if a dinner like this is a rare and special event."

"Dinner like this is a rare and special event, Alex," Charlotte explained as a blush stained her cheeks. "For me, cooking at home was always the norm. Fancy dinners out were always unusual. My family gathered together around the dinner table, discussing their days, helping in the kitchen..."

"No cooks? No housekeepers?"

"We were the cooks. Why else would my brother choose to become a chef?"

"I guess I had not really thought about that. Upscale restaurants were the norm in my world. I never even asked your preference, though. Do you prefer to eat at home?"

"I enjoy doing both," Charlotte answered easily. "With you," she added under her breath before taking his hand across the tablecloth and squeezing it. "Besides, you are helping me to explore the best of Chicago cuisine. How on earth can I complain about that?"

They ordered from the attentive server, sipped a fabulous crisp white wine with their fish course, then the fruity red with the duck and venison. They laughed and talked together until, over the soufflé, raspberry for her, Grand Marnier for him, they finally discussed her return home. It was like a wet blanket being thrown over their effervescent evening.

Lightening the mood for a moment, Alex offered the rest of red wine to the table beside them, while Charlotte enjoyed the couple's surprise and delight. Then they offered the white wine to the server to share with the kitchen. They had made a dent in both bottles, but neither of them was the least bit tipsy.

"We have done well living together, Charlotte, and I really love having you in my place. You fit there. I don't see why you need to leave."

"Alex, are you suggesting I move in with you?" Charlotte's shock at the offer was apparent in her voice, along with her skepticism.

"You could keep your apartment if it made you more comfortable, but why not move the rest of your things in and take up with me?"

"How long have you been thinking about this?"

"Since today," he admitted.

"Alex, you've had no time to think this through. We haven't even discussed it or the details of how it might work. This is not a decision to be made lightly."

"We are discussing it now, Charlotte, and believe me, I am not being light about it. You and I are both very private people and I get that. But we are not children. I'm almost 37 years old. I want to get married, have a family. I think you do, too. It may be too soon to know if I am the one for you, but I think living together is a good next step."

"You want to marry me?" Charlotte asked, stunned. She couldn't believe that this famous playboy wanted to settle down at all, let alone settle down with her. She was too overwhelmed to be happy, yet. Was she happy? She had considered Alex as a husband, assuredly, but not on this timetable. Not to mention, this was certainly not the romantic proposal of marriage she had dreamed of all her life.

"I want you to move in with me," Alex corrected. Charlotte was disappointed and relieved, and confused. "Then we can see where things go. I think we show promise, together. That's all I'm saying."

"Show promise? That sounds very business-like, Alex." Where was the romance Charlotte always envisioned?

The more she acted surprised and concerned, the more Alex grew impatient. The conversation escalated noticeably in the quiet restaurant.

"Let's get out of here," Alex said, taking Charlotte's hand and helping her up from the table, holding on to it firmly until she was seated in the car.

"Is the idea so impossible to you?" he attacked in the dark silence. "Can you honestly say you never considered it?"

"I thought of it," she admitted quietly, "I thought about it a lot, if I am being completely honest, but you never even mentioned it, so I stopped thinking about it. This has completely blindsided me, Alex."

He was silent in the driver's seat, but his driving reflected his emotions, aggressive and impatient. Charlotte wanted to talk about this rationally, but she knew Alex's feelings were too hurt. Despite her best efforts, he was feeling rejected and defensive.

"Alex," she said cautiously after a full minute of total silence. "I love the idea of living with you. We just need to think it through. I need to consider timing, logistics. I need to be mentally ready to make that commitment and besides all of that, I have six more months on my lease."

Finally, Alex smiled, and the tension broke. "You're right, of course. I was too impetuous asking like this. We need to talk it through and plan."

"Yeah, you are usually the logical one. I've never seen you be impetuous before."

"Yeah. I am usually the most logical person I know, Charlotte. People seek me out for advice and counsel because they can count on me to be dispassionate in problem solving." Charlotte nodded agreement in the dark car. "This is all your fault," he accused.

"My fault? What did I do?"

"Isn't it obvious? You swept me off my feet and now I can't think straight."

Charlotte laughed, and Alex joined in.

"Laugh all you want, but it's true. You know me. I am like Mr. Spock, weighing options with no emotion. You, Charlotte Roche, have turned my brain to mush."

"I would apologize," Charlotte offered, "but you have made me worse." The confession seemed to clear the air, and Alex reached for her, twining his fingers with hers.

They held hands in the darkness, his long fingers stroking the palm of her hand, sending frissons of desire deep into her body just from the small movement.

"So, my place?" he asked when he had to choose a right or left turn ahead.

"I think we should keep it as planned for tonight. It's time for me to go home. At least for a day or two, so I can think straight," Charlotte said gently. She could feel Alex's disappointment radiate off his body, mirroring her own. But she held steadfast. "You are heading to L.A. this week anyway. Besides, I need to check on the place if nothing else."

Alex agreed reluctantly and soon he was parking illegally in front of her building, unloading the first wave of her belongings. He had arranged for someone to bring the rest over later in the week, thinking he would never actually need the services.

Alex carried a light bag in one hand and helped Charlotte up the steep front steps with the other while she fumbled in her small purse for keys. Holding them up proudly, she unlocked the door and pushed it open, stopped to pick up the last few days' worth of mail that Jo had not already delivered to her, then ambled up the inside stairs to her walk-up apartment.

Charlotte opened the double lock and pushed the door far enough to reach inside for the wall switch. When the lights illuminated the apartment, she gasped and fell back against Alex. Alex shoved Charlotte behind him, not sure what he would see until she no longer blocked his view.

The apartment was in shambles. There was glass shattered across the floor from a window that had obviously been the point of entry, papers strewn everywhere, overturned furniture. Cabinet doors sat gaping open; their contents spilled to the floor in front of them.

"Stay here," Alex ordered, moving into the apartment on silent feet. Charlotte begged him not to go in. "What if someone is still here?" she asked, clinging to his arm. Alex waited a minute, listening carefully, but there was silence.

"I mean it, Charlotte, don't move," he commanded as he stepped carefully over the broken glass and into the dining room. Charlotte lost sight of him, and her heart beat out of her chest until he emerged safely again. When he moved toward the bedrooms, she held her breath. Silence.

After what felt like a lifetime, Alex appeared, signaling for her to enter. "Don't touch anything," he ordered. "I called the police and they're on their way. You'll need to figure out what's missing."

"You called already? Really?" Charlotte asked, but she didn't actually sound surprised. "I won't know what good the police will be until I look around." She was unusually calm.

"Charlotte, what's going on? You don't seem surprised. Do you know who did this?" Alex helped her to a chair that was still upright and gently lowered her to the cushion. She looked like a warrior princess, dressed elegantly but with a fierce expression on her face that brooked no argument.

"Damn it," she muttered under her breath as they heard sirens growing closer. Charlotte needed more time.

When the police arrived, they questioned Alex, who explained that Charlotte had been away from home for weeks. He could not pinpoint when this might have occurred. When the police questioned Charlotte, they focused on what was missing. A quick look around the small space, followed by a cursory inspection, revealed that the expensive TV was unharmed, right where she had left it. Her desktop computer and the small amount of jewelry she owned were also safely in place. Everything was there.

"Is there anyone who might want to harm you, Ms. Roche?" the young officer asked politely. "Have you received any threats?"

"No, nothing." Charlotte looked toward Alex, who watched her like a hawk. "Perhaps it was all a mistake? Maybe someone had the wrong apartment?"

"We should check the answering machine, just in case," the officer suggested.

"It's broken."

Alex gave Charlotte a surprised look. She didn't dare make eye contact. Alex would know the answering machine was fine when she moved in with him. He had used it the night before she fell to schedule their morning run.

The police checked for fingerprints, increasing the chaos with their black dust, took lots of photographs and notes. They promised to canvas the neighbors for information. Charlotte thanked them, then sat still and silent right where Alex had placed her.

Alex thanked the two officers, shook hands with them and closed the door quietly before crossing the room and dropping to his haunches eye level with Charlotte.

"You'll come back to my place. Jo can arrange for a cleaning crew to get in here tomorrow, okay?"

"Okay," Charlotte whispered through barely moving lips. She made no move to get up.

"Do you need anything from here? What should we take back to my place?"

"Nothing. But could you get me a glass of water, please?"

"Of course. I'm sorry. I should have offered that before."

As soon as Alex was in the kitchen, Charlotte bolted from the chair and walked across the room to the answering machine. Hitting play, she listened, holding her breath.

"You have twenty-seven messages," the mechanical voice said, but as Charlotte played them, all she heard was hang up after hang up. She kept pressing forward, trying to get through them before Alex returned from the kitchen. She was unaware he was already standing in the doorway watching her when the message finally held a voice.

"I warned you, Querida. I warned you in the park and I am warning you now. It's time to stop pretending. It's time to come home. Don't make me hurt you."

CHAPTER FOURTEEN

Charlotte turned to see Alex standing in the doorway, white as a sheet, fury radiating from every pore. Clearly, he had heard the message. She was shaking and so pale that Alex feared she would faint. He wanted to help, moving to take her in his arms before stopping himself. He suddenly feared he was in over his head.

"Charlotte?" he approached warily, like she was a hurt animal or a threat.

"Thanks for the water," she said in a firm voice, taking it from his hand and gulping it down. "I needed that."

"Charlotte, tell me, what is going on?"

"My place has been trashed, and we are getting out of here. That's what," she responded crisply. She said nothing about the phone message and Alex battled with himself about how to broach the subject. He just assumed that Charlotte would offer the information, unburden herself to him, but she said nothing. He was wary of sounding too accusatory, but she owed him an explanation.

"I guess I have everything I need at your place," was all she offered, picking up the small bag, the mail she had just retrieved and moving to turn off lights. "Let's get out of here."

Alex took the bag from Charlotte and followed her back down the stairs and to his car. Just before he pulled away from her building, he looked her full in the face. "What's going on Charlotte? Who is trying to hurt you?"

"What are you talking about, Alex? I told you. I suspect someone realized they were in the wrong apartment, or it was a robbery that was interrupted. I am sure it was nothing personal."

"Nothing personal?" Alex was incredulous. Was she going to pretend that they had not both heard that threatening phone message? Had Charlotte also lied to the police? What the hell was going on? Alex was so certain he knew this woman. He had just asked her to move into his apartment. He believed he might be falling in love with her.

Falling for whom, though? That's the question. This woman is a complete stranger.

"Charlotte, you know if you are in any kind of trouble, you can talk to me. You can tell me anything – anything at all. I am there for you. I want to protect you and keep you safe." Alex had known she had a secret, but not one of this magnitude. Even as he told her he wanted to keep her safe, he wondered if he could.

But the quiet, frightened Charlotte, who sat down in her destroyed apartment, had disappeared and a phoenix had arisen from her ashes, with a ramrod straight back and an impenetrable expression on her face. He did not know this woman sitting beside him in the close interior of his small car.

"Seriously, Alex, you sound just like the hero in a novel, ready to slay dragons for me. Sorry, but I have no dragons. Perhaps I could find a ferocious dog so you can save me." Her words were biting and sarcastic, causing Alex to recoil. Alex felt as if she had slapped him in the face.

"Sorry, that was uncalled for," she acknowledged, immediately contrite. "I appreciate the offer of help, Alex. I really do. Seriously though, there is nothing I need besides a place to crash. I have no idea why someone would choose to break into my apartment. I find it all very strange and inexplicable. Especially since they didn't steal anything. Or at least anything obvious."

"And the incident in the park? And the threatening phone message?" he finally asked outright when she wouldn't offer any information.

"Oh, Alex," she said, leaning over to plant a kiss on his cheek. "You are so sweet when you worry like this. But I think you have been watching too many spy movies."

"Movies?" Alex's disbelief was obvious.

"Absolutely. I fell in the park. I have told you that repeatedly. Nothing sinister happened. I was just a klutz."

"And that awful phone message and all those hang-ups on your answering machine? Charlotte, how can you explain those?"

"I didn't realize you heard those," Charlotte responded, dragging out her words almost as if she was buying time. "Not sure about the hang-ups. Salespeople, I would imagine. They never leave messages."

"And the threat to hurt you if you don't go home? Charlotte, please just tell me what is going on."

"Of course, Alex. I have nothing to hide. That was a joke. I am sorry if it frightened you and I can see how you might misinterpret it."

"A joke? That is one screwed up joke. What did I 'misinterpret'?" Alex could already tell that Charlotte was fabricating some wild story, but he could not figure out why.

"Yes, misinterpret. It was my brother trying to be funny. He leaves me weird messages like that all the time. It was just a coincidence that it happened after the break-in. I can see how you would believe it was real."

"Your brother? That threat was from your brother? A brother who loves you? A brother you are so close with?" Alex recognized a threatening voice versus a teasing voice. He had heard enough threats of his own recently. This was definitely the real thing.

Why is Charlotte denying this? What is she hiding?

"So, it was just your brother who wants you to come home?"

"Well, I was supposed to be in Boston weeks ago. This is his silly way of giving me grief. I will take care of it when I am there. He will clearly be happy to see me."

"Clearly," Alex said without conviction. Charlotte had put an impenetrable wall between them, and Alex could nt find a way to knock it down. He just knew she was unable to trust him with the truth and that hurt.

"Have it your way, Charlotte, but I'll tell you this. I sure wish I could follow you East and find out what the hell is going on. Sadly, I have to go to California."

California. I should only tell you about the mess I have to go deal with. Shit. Who am I to pry into Charlotte's secrets when I am keeping so damn many of my own?

CHAPTER FIFTEEN

A lex was reluctant to leave. He had been hovering over Charlotte since Sunday, making it impossible to have any privacy just when she needed it most. She had avoided any more questions—barely—but she could see that the incident at her apartment, combined with the accident in the park, had stretched her credibility to its breaking point. He knew she was lying, but for a reason known only to himself, Alex stopped pressuring her for answers.

Charlotte concluded that the only thing saving her from further probes was Alex's reluctance to answer questions in return. He had become even more tight-lipped about his own activities, too. She cared for him. She wanted to live with him, to see where it would take them, but it didn't prepare her to bare all, and she was quite certain he couldn't either.

"What a pair we make," she whispered, shaking her head.

Alex would be out West again for another four days, his second trip in the four weeks that had passed since the break-in. Charlotte had not been back to her apartment since, avoiding the evidence while enjoying an opportunity to play house at Alex's. The house part was going fine, except the comfortable ease they had discovered before the robbery was no longer present. In its place was a strained truce and long silent moments.

Charlotte would catch herself staring at Alex, wondering what he was thinking, wanting to bare all. She wanted to find her way back to that place they had found together based on understanding and caring—that place that might bridge the mistrust and lies. She would shake herself, returning to reality by reminding herself of all that was at stake.

Instead, Charlotte was about to heap more untruths on the pile. She planned to take advantage of Alex's absence by slipping away herself, without letting him know. She made plans last minute, just yesterday in fact, hoping to fool Alex—among others—about her whereabouts. Charlotte was going to do her best to slip in and out of Boston undetected.

"Regan, I know I have only been back a few weeks, but I really need to get to Boston and reassure my family that I am alive. Can you do without me the rest of the week?" Charlotte had approached her boss with the request early yesterday morning. "I completed the deals for the new building. The acquisition papers are still with the lawyers, and we are waiting on a response for the property bid in St. Louis. I figure it is a good time to get away before things go crazy again."

"Charlotte, you can always go, you know. You don't need my permission," Regan had replied. "I know if something comes up, I can find you by email or cell, so just head out."

"True, but with all your recent trips back and forth to D.C., I thought one of us should be here."

"Good point. I really have been traveling a lot lately. But Ethan can handle an emergency if one comes up. He's learned so much and he's itching to show what he can do. Besides, I trust him to call if he is in over his head."

She was right. Her brother Ethan had come far in just the five months since Charlotte had joined the company. Initially Regan had let him learn the residential side of their complex holdings, but now he was doing more commercial and development work.

Charlotte enjoyed working with him. He was a quick learner, full of creative ideas and willing to roll up his sleeves to get the job done. Charlotte suspected he was eager to move up to working on development deals until he knew the entire business inside out. He made no secret of his desire to run LHRE some day, but he was still young, and a little immature. It was better for everyone to have either Regan or Charlotte on hand to provide a steadying influence.

Regan Howe had only been at the helm of LHRE a short time herself, since her brother, Wyatt, had started his own company and her father had retired after narrowly avoiding total ruin. The potential scandal had shaken her father so much that he relinquished the reins to Regan "even though she was a girl." If Ethan had been older and more experienced, everyone knew she would never have gotten the opportunity, no matter how deserving she was.

And she was incredibly deserving. Harvard educated; Regan had studied everything that she needed to run LHRE. An MBA plus summers and holidays following her father and big brother everywhere, absorbing the business into her pores, had left her more than capable when the opportunity arose. She had proven herself repeatedly since taking command and business was thriving.

Recently, Regan's success had caught the eye of politicians in Washington. They had asked her to testify before this Senate committee or that House hearing. The housing market had bounced back, but real estate was still under scrutiny, and people often sought Regan's expertise. She did well in the spotlight, better than anyone had expected, so the back and forth to Washington was increasing in frequency. Charlotte suspected that there was someone drawing Regan to the capitol as well. After all, she could only wait so long for Tyler.

"Ethan," Charlotte poked his head into the young man's doorway. "I just spoke with Regan, and I am going to head east for a few days to see my family. Can you handle everything here while I am gone? Anything you need before I leave?"

"You two fuss too much," came Ethan's calm reply. "I've got this covered, Charlotte."

"Great, call my cell if you need me. I'm here until late this afternoon."

Charlotte was comfortable now that she could leave, regardless of Regan's schedule. She and Ethan usually handled anything that came up. Ethan had the knowledge of how his family made decisions and Charlotte had a strong real estate and financial background. Whenever she thought about it, Charlotte recognized that the move to Chicago and LHRE had been a fortuitous one.

When she met Regan at the Harvard Alumni fundraising event in Boston, the two women clicked immediately. Similar in age and temperament, they were soon laughing over stories of their Harvard days and getting to know each other's activities since graduation. It had not taken long for Regan to find out that Charlotte had a wealth of experience handling real estate investing down the street at a major insurance company. Regan jumped to secure the skills she was seeking for LHRE.

Over entrees, Regan picked Charlotte's brain and found her smart, assured and a great fit for the Chicago company. She just had to lure her to the Midwest. By dessert, Regan had floated the idea of a move to a new job and discovered that Charlotte was ripe for a change. Over coffee, she found out that the woman was very close to her East Coast family and started pitching LHRE hard to overcome any potential reluctance. By the time they got up to leave the event, Charlotte was seriously considering an advantageous job change and relocation.

"My insurance job is really fine. It pays very well, and my colleagues respect me as a capable, hard worker," Charlotte had explained, unintentionally playing hard to get.

"I am sure they do," Regan had agreed. "But I can pay better, and you will be one of the top executives in the company. Why wait to get a series of well-deserved promotions when I am offering them to you in one leap?"

"I am due for promotion," Charlotte had considered, "and the work is always interesting. Plus, I really enjoy my coworkers. I just assumed I might stay there until I was ready to retire. It has the added advantage of being close to my home and family."

Why am I arguing? I need to leave Boston and I need to do it as quickly as possible. Regan was offering her the perfect chance. Stop fighting so hard and let her make an offer.

"Just how close are you to your family?" Regan had queried. "How often do you see them?"

"I am the only daughter," Charlotte had explained. "They are overly protective, but I love them. My brother is Harvard MBA too." She pointed to Jake in the far corner of the room and asked if Regan had met him. She said that she had not. "I do love being nearby, though, I admit. I can take the bus or a train home on Sundays to go to church with my parents or just to sit around the dining room table. Our conversations get very boisterous, and we laugh a lot. I leave totally weighed down with my mother's outstanding meals."

Charlotte had painted quite a picture and unbeknownst to her, Regan had upped the opening salary offer after that description of Sunday dinner. Charlotte never mentioned that her family was encouraging her to move. They all wanted her to be safe.

It was only after Regan made her that offer she could not refuse that Charlotte worried about all the misconceptions Regan had about her.

Before that, Charlotte believed it didn't matter. She never expected to see Regan again. Now she was being offered a job.

"I need to come clean," Charlotte had whispered to her brother over the phone later that week.

"I can't hear you," Jake complained.

"I can't talk any louder. I am at work," Charlotte had explained. "I need to come clean with Regan, Jake."

"Did you lie to her?"

"Not exactly," Charlotte conceded, "And I tried to have the conversation twice, but Regan took me off the topic and I never got back to it."

"Charlotte, seriously, this is personal anyway. You have never once lied to Regan about your work. You need the new job and the move out of town badly. Leave it alone at this point. Don't risk it."

"I guess you're right. It will not impact my work, after all. I have never lied about being qualified."

"And she checked your references, I am sure. And I am sure they were glowing."

Jake was correct. Her references had been glowing and plentiful, so she dropped the subject. How could she know that the assumptions Regan made regarding her personal life would continue to haunt her as the lies spread to more and more people? Now she was enmeshed in deceit and could not figure out how to set the record straight without risking the new job that mattered so much.

Standing in Regan's doorway yesterday, listening to her say that she trusted Charlotte, and that she was free to come and go, just added to Charlotte's guilt. Charlotte planned to set the record straight with Regan at some point, and with Alex, too.

But what if she told everyone the truth too soon? What if she lost her job because of it? Isn't omission the same thing as lying when applying for a job?

Charlotte never told Regan she came from a blue-blood family. She never said she was at the Harvard event because she was a major donor to the university, like the other attendees. She had actually volunteered no information about her background except that she had been a Harvard undergrad and MBA who ate Sunday dinners with her family after church. Regan just assumed a different Roche family sat down to those dinners, and Charlotte failed to correct her.

She hated keeping her family background a secret, as if she was ashamed of it. That was so far from the truth. She loved her close-knit family, her brothers, and parents. She was bursting with pride for all they had overcome, all they had achieved. But more details about her family never came up in conversation until Charlotte was safely ensconced in her new job and her new Chicago apartment. By then, Charlotte could find no easy way to broach the topic without embarrassing Regan and herself. She did not know Regan well enough to know if a bit of embarrassment might lead to her firing.

Instead, I am living a lie.

Until recently, all the lies and sacrifices had been worth it. Charlotte believed she was safe. She traveled back and forth to Boston many times to see her parents or her brothers, even a few friends that were sworn to silence. She believed she was flying under the radar. With airline security being what it was, a false name was no longer an option, but she took care of everything else. She was cautious, never reserving a hotel room in her name, always paying in cash. Charlotte moved around the area, never staying in the same place twice. She never saw her whole family at once, causing her to miss birthdays and anniversary parties that she dare not attend.

After only six months, it was already taking its toll on her. She could hide her identity, but when she had to keep secrets in Chicago too, she found herself more easily confused and likely to slip. She resented the need for secrecy and considered risking everything for the truth. Instead, she chose her only other option, keeping a bit more distance from co-workers and friends. Everything had been fine until Alex.

She liked him immediately. Despite his complaints to the contrary, she shared more about her background and personal life than she had with anyone else. Still, she hid a great deal. As they became running partners, she noticed he pried more and more from her with each mile they clocked. She wanted to be close to him, but he was smart—too smart. She feared slipping up, or even worse, endangering him too.

She had berated herself repeatedly since the incident in the park. Charlotte replayed the episode in her brain over and over. It could have been a disaster if she had taken Alex up on his offer of a ride. That could have put a target on his back without him ever being aware of the danger.

That was not an option. Charlotte cared for Alex as she had never cared about anyone before. She needed to keep her presence in his apartment a secret. That was the only way to keep him out of danger. She had to maintain a presence at her apartment. She had to be seen going in and out, to and from work. Alone.

Her sprained ankle had curtailed her marathon plans, at least. Now there was no risk of being accosted in the park again. Perhaps when Alex ran alone, it would look like a coincidence that they were together that day. She needed to distance herself from him in public in every way.

"Charlotte, are you listening to me? I don't think you heard a word I said," Regan said, raising her voice and waving her hand in front of

Charlotte's face. "Where were you?" she asked when Charlotte's eyes focused on her again. "You were a million miles away."

"I am so sorry, Regan. I was thinking about what to pack and going through the plans for the next few days. I am just excited about going home."

"I bet you are. Are you going for anything special? I know there is that big cancer fundraiser this weekend, because I met a congressional representative heading back from D.C. to attend. Will you be there? I could tell him to play escort if you like."

"No matchmaking, please!" Charlotte replied, sidestepping the question about the event entirely. "I have been spending some time with Alex Gaines and I think he is enough for me to handle without adding a long-distance relationship."

"I wasn't sure," Regan mused. "You two looked very cozy at the engagement party, but I couldn't tell if it was just because Alex was housing you while you recovered or if there was something going on."

"Actually, the night of the party might be when things changed from friendly to more," Charlotte confessed, her cheeks turning a becoming pink. "I like him, Regan. I really like him a lot."

"Well, he is a serious catch, Char, but I think I mentioned before that he is elusive as hell. He is notorious for dating models and actresses, so you may have your work cut out for you. But it would be really nice to see him settle down and he would be very lucky to win your heart."

"Well, it's too early to say where things are headed," Charlotte prevaricated. "Still, there have been some promising signs and I am not muddying the waters with a congressman."

"Of course not. Anyway, all I want to know is when will you be back? Do you want a company car to take you to the airport?"

"Oh, no. I already have a ride, and I will be back in the office on Monday. Just call my cell if you need me before then."

Charlotte thanked Regan and went back to work clearing work off her desk. A few hours later, she jumped into a taxi in front of the building. After the cab weaved through traffic for a few blocks, Charlotte told him to pull over, tipped him well for the short ride and jumped out.

Quickly diving into the nearby office building, Charlotte took an escalator to the basement, watching around her constantly, and waited for the blue line train to the airport. She found the easiest place to get lost was on public transportation. And right now, she needed to get lost. If she were to make it to Boston, she would have to be careful and be in stealth mode.

Alex would appreciate how much I've learned from those spy movies of his. The woman in a business suit, heels and sleek bob that got on the train would never be recognized as the ponytailed, baseball cap wearing tomboy in the hoodie and heavy boots that emerged from the train at O'Hare.

CHAPTER SIXTEEN

Alex resisted the urge to slam down the phone. Where the hell was she? At first, he had called only to say hi, to hear her voice, to idly chat about the day. Now, after listening to the phone ring incessantly all day, he needed to know she was okay.

The time difference had really messed him up. He had gone for a run, making it too late to catch her before she left for work, and Alex hated to bother her during the workday. Meetings last night had kept him out too late to call and it had been almost two full days since he had heard her voice.

Except on her damn machine.

She was slow returning his text messages, but at least she usually answered them. Not today. Today nothing but silence. She was not answering the phone at his place or at her office. He had called her cell and texted, but received no response. In desperation, he had even tried her apartment number, but thankfully, it was disconnected.

So much for believing that call was from her brother. If that was the case, why disconnect the phone?

A young man in a t-shirt and surfer shorts poked his head in the door of the large formal office, looking out of place. "We're ready to resume, Mr. Gaines," he told Alex in a respectful and business-like manner.

"Thanks, Tim. I will be right in," Alex responded with a nod. He put the phone back in its cradle slowly and rose with a scowl that sent Tim scurrying back to the boardroom.

Alex reentered the meeting he had chaired earlier. While he had been trying to call Charlotte, most of the meeting attendees had grabbed organic tea, fresh-pressed juice, fruit, or a granola bar. Looking around the crowded room, Alex knew that he was back in L.A.

California is just different.

Unlike meetings at the bank in Chicago, a much younger group of people currently surrounded Alex, all dressed in shorts and tees, Hawaiian shirts, sundresses and Croc's or flip-flops. Everyone sat with an innovative laptop or tablet in front of them. The team was different; the clothes were different, and the food was different. Even the looks on their faces were different. In that moment, Alex longed for a roomful of suits and a tray of Danish.

"Relax, everyone. Nothing has changed," Alex reassured everyone as he strode to the front of the room. He wore the trousers from his suit, a crisp white shirt, and a Bijan tie he had purchased on a whim on Rodeo Drive the day before. "My lawyers have assured me we can find a solution and avoid a hostile takeover. Right, Stu?" Alex pierced a young man at the foot of the table with a glare from his azure eyes.

"Right, Alex," the lawyer stammered. "They don't have a leg to stand on."

"Everyone feel better?" Alex asked. He looked down the table, watching everyone visibly relax shoulders and necks. "The company is fine. We have plenty of cash on hand but not too much. Sales are strong, up four percent year to year. We look great on paper, but not so great that a major conglomerate will back this deal. My family can go to hell if they think they are taking my legacy away from me."

A lot of heads bobbed in agreement up and down the polished table and Alex turned to look out the window at Southern California, traffic crawling on I-5 in the distance. How had he ever thought of living here? Alex loved coming out here as a kid, but he hated it now. He hated the casual clothes, the palm trees, and the god-awful traffic. He even hated the granola bars.

"Jeez," he mumbled. "I miss her worse than I thought."

"Okay." Alex cleared his throat, returning his gaze to his rapt audience. "This is the agenda for the rest of the day. Stu will take us through the case, explain the data and documents that we need to collect, and then Joanie will take us through the financials before we adjourn for the day. Does anyone have anything else that we need to cover?"

"Sir?" a young woman asked from a seat against the wall. "Would you mind giving us an update on your father? Are we allowed to visit or anything?"

"Same as last time, Sheila, no visitors. I am sorry."

There was a brief murmur around the table, but Alex offered no additional information, nodding instead to Stu to take the floor.

Alex, normally extremely attentive, allowed his mind to wander. Where the hell was Charlotte and how was he supposed to deal with his miserable family when he was growing frantic about her whereabouts?

Over the last four weeks, Alex had replayed that day in his mind and wondered how a budding love affair had soured so fast. He knew the phone message he heard was no joke between Charlotte and her brother, that the break-in was not a random thwarted robbery, and he was sure that Charlotte was attacked in the park. All of that was awful, but the rift it had caused between them was worse.

It was a time for them to come together and fight whatever and whomever this threat was. He wanted to assist. He felt increasingly protective of Charlotte. Still, he could get nothing from her. She was more tight-lipped than ever. The longer she stayed silent, the more withdrawn he became, and the further apart they grew.

This is the exact opposite of the direction I wanted us to be moving.

It seemed obvious to Alex that someone was stalking Charlotte, but he could not figure out who or why. Was someone trying to abduct her? He knew she came from a wealthy family, but he did not think that was it. He had talked to Regan since the break-in. Charlotte had never even mentioned it to Regan, which surprised and unsettled him. There were no hostilities at work, Regan had assured him, and she felt certain there was no abduction threat. There were no acquisitions, no mergers, no evictions, and no foreclosures that could explain someone wanting to attack Charlotte. He had no explanation, and she refused to discuss it.

Who or what is she protecting? I just know it is something from her past. Something to do with all those trips to Boston.

Even more troubling to Alex than the stalker was the fact that Charlotte didn't trust him enough to talk to him about it. He really believed that she cared about him. The break-in had forced her to live with him, although she wanted time to think about it. They were doing well together, better than well. They were doing fantastic. He was learning to cook beside her in the kitchen; she was learning to swim well enough to compete someday. He had turned the extra guest room into an office for her and they lived and worked side by side during the day, cuddled, made love, and slept side by side at night. They did everything but talk.

Alex watched her during the long silences, brooding and far away. He was a problem solver, but she would not let him solve this issue, or even tell him what it was. He thought of calling her family, but didn't know which of the famous Roche brothers was her father.

He was reluctant to bring his friends into any potential danger, so he kept the whole situation to himself, feeling cut off, lonely and hurt.

Why couldn't she trust him with this? After all they had shared, didn't she understand he would be there for her, no matter what? No matter what... Wait a minute, asshole, it's not like you are telling her the truth either.

Alex shied away from the realization that he too was keeping big secrets. How could he expect her to trust him if he refused to trust her? Maybe he needed to have a serious talk with his mother. It was long overdue. He would do it immediately following his sister's wedding. Alex and his parents needed this wedding to come off without a hitch. He had to be sure that not a whiff of scandal touched his sister before her dream wedding to her dream partner. She was blameless in everything, and Alex refused to allow her to pay the price for the mistakes of others.

But after the wedding, what did they have to lose? With the problems here in L.A., Alex recognized that he was rapidly losing control. Sure, there would be ugly fallout, but it was long past time that he got his life back. After the wedding, he would sit his mother down and they would have it out, once and for all.

Of course, if I don't contain this situation here and now, I won't have a choice about when and how this all comes out.

"Back up Stu, and go through it again," Alex demanded as the reality of his situation hit him. "I want absolutely no stone left unturned." Turning back to the discussion in the room, Alex gave it his full attention.

CHAPTER SEVENTEEN

The stress exhausted Charlotte although the trip was uneventful. She gratefully slipped off her dark glasses, pulled the too-tight ponytail loose from its band, pulled out the pins holding the shorter ends under her cap, unlaced, and kicked off her heavy boots. Sinking into the lumpy, pillow-top mattress of the Holiday Inn Express, she took her first calm breath of the day. She had taken two taxis and the train to get to the Foxborough location, paying cash for everything and backtracking more than once. She could only hope her brother took similar precautions. Foxborough was too close to home for comfort. Anyone might recognize her here.

"Be careful. Smithson," she texted. She waited, holding her breath, until she received the brief text in response to hers.

"You too. Gerard."

Picking up the phone in her room, she waited for the front desk to answer.

"Hi, this is Susan Smithson in 206. Please let me know when Mr. Gerard checks in. Yes, a message would be great. Let him know I am in room 206. Thank you very much."

Charlotte hated all the subterfuge, but years of experience had taught her to be cautious. She suspected she was not the only one being watched. They needed to be so careful not to go anywhere or see anyone. She had mentally prepared herself for a couple of days with nothing but four walls and a delivery pizza. It was worth it. She sat back to wait and finally responded to the increasingly desperate texts from Alex.

Alex. She wished she could tell him everything. The tension between them was growing despite the pretense that everything was fine. They shared the condo comfortably, shared a bed happily, but conversations were stilted and painful. Every question was fraught with danger to her since the break in. She could no longer keep her lies straight in her head. Who had she told what? What excuse had she used last time?

Poor Alex. He sounded frantic, even in texts. Charlotte began by apologizing for the delay in responding. She fabricated a story about traveling to a client meeting in St. Louis. Alex knew she was negotiating an important deal there and by now she was certain that he would have figured out that she was away from home. It would explain being unreachable because of flights and meetings.

It was only seconds before he responded. "I was worried," his text said.

"No need," she replied. "Home before you."

"Miss you," he replied.

"Ditto. Later," she said before turning away from the phone to unpack her few possessions and wait. She wished Alex were with her on this trip. She longed to bring him home to meet her family. They would all love him and he would forgive her for everything. She just knew it.

Someday. Maybe.

She flipped through email messages, channel surfed, read some contracts for work, bored and restless until a knock on the door almost sent her flying from her perch on the end of the bed.

"Ms. Smithson?" a deep voice inquired. "It's Mr. Gerard."

Charlotte flew to the door, yanked it open, and pulled the handsome man into the room. She covered his face with kisses.

"Stop, Char, stop," the deep voice said laughingly, but the big man allowed her to continue hugging and kissing him. "Stop and let me look at you."

Charlotte stepped back and twirled around before grabbing her brother's hands and dragging him into the room. "Oh, Jake, it is so great to see you. I missed you so much," Charlotte gushed, hugging her brother fiercely.

"Char," he hugged her back, "let go, Char, I can't breathe." Stepping out of her arms, Jake checked out Charlotte from head to toe. "What's with the bandage?" he asked harshly. "And no bullshit."

"I was running in the park, and I sprained my ankle," Charlotte explained, staying close to the truth. "End of story, and end of chances to run in the Chicago marathon. I was bummed."

"That's it? Just a sprain from running?" Jake seemed skeptical and Charlotte turned away from his piercing gaze to grab a sweater off the back of a nearby chair. She would never survive his scrutiny. He knew her much too well. Thank God he only saw the ace bandage she was wearing these days. She would never have been able to explain away the boot.

"Charlotte. What aren't you telling me?"

"I just feel guilty. This is the reason I cancelled my last trip here," she explained. "So, how are Mama and Papa? Any chance I can see them this time?"

"I don't think so, honey. I am so sorry. But Don said he would come down from school Friday night to be with us if he thinks it's safe."

"Damn it. I have to worry about Don now, too? This is so unfair."

"Relax, Char, Don is fine. We just want to be very careful since the break-in. You are our only sister. Forgive us if we worry."

"Okay. So, tell me about Mama, and Maria and work," Charlotte demanded. "I feel so out of touch lately. I want to know everything."

Jake pulled up a chair and Charlotte sank to the floor with her back against the bed, knees pulled to her chest. Her brother caught her up on all the news of home. Business was good, growing faster than they had planned and overwhelming all of them, especially her father.

"Too much growth? That is a good problem to have," Charlotte complimented.

"Not if it gets out of hand. Are you sure you won't reconsider and come work in the business?" Jake asked, although they both knew the answer. Charlotte couldn't come home.

"You aren't letting him work too hard, are you?" she asked with concern.

"I promise. Papa just oversees things and tastes. He tastes everything. We can never replace his discerning palate."

"I think you're right, so you better document everything while you can," Charlotte warned. "I thought you were crazy when you hatched this scheme, but the market was certainly ripe for artisan baked goods. You are so good at Internet marketing and social media, too. No wonder business is exploding. You and Papa make an unstoppable team. Of course, there is Maria. She was quite a bonus."

When Jake finished his MBA, he approached his father with a radical idea. Take their small Rhode Island bakery and become a specialty bakery with a worldwide reach. With the old-world recipes of her father and the marketing expertise of her brother, Old World Bakeries had taken off like lightning. They were shipping overseas now, even back to Portugal, in an ironic twist.

It had been almost forty years since the Rochas had left Porto to start a new life in America. With virtually no money, Charlotte's father had fallen back on his skills from home, going to work in a local bakery. The bakery served the strong Portuguese communities in Fall River and Providence. Those customers were soon asking for her father's recipes, which were so reminiscent of home. He became the critical resource, eventually taking over the bakery and then expanding. With three children to feed, Luzia joined her husband in the bakery, bringing her recipes with her. They created wedding cakes and pastries, sweetbread, and muffins. Luzia created takeout meals with spicy chorizo and fragrant stews. Soon they were getting a lot of press, reaching far beyond the Portuguese community.

The day that Charlotte met Regan, her brother was delivering a huge food donation to the fundraising event from Jake and Old-World Bakeries. Jake, also Harvard alum, teamed with the whole family to give back to Harvard the only way they could. Old World Bakeries had donated the desserts and baked goods for the event. Charlotte had been on a lunch break from work when she walked over to see her brother and ended up staying for the event.

It was only natural that Regan might make the mistake she had. Charlotte was in business clothes and seated at an event for some of Harvard's largest donors. She introduced herself as Charlotte Roche, her legal name, and was immediately mistaken for a member of the extremely wealthy family that owned one of the largest pharmaceutical companies, and much more. After all, the family lived in Boston and had made many large donations to the University.

Far from being born with a silver spoon, Charlotte had been fortunate when she received a full scholarship to Harvard, allowing her to attend the prestigious but very expensive school. Her brother received only a partial scholarship and had worked in the bakery to fund the rest. That had turned out to be providential.

He learned the business from the ground up and when he found himself using real-life experiences from the bakery in his marketing classes, Jake realized he had an opportunity in front of him. Upon graduation, he proposed a risky expansion into an online business. Charlotte was supposed to follow in his path by running the back office and her younger brother planned to bring his culinary training to the business in the future.

Although Charlotte hadn't followed through on the family dream, Don was developing new recipes to further expand their business. He would join the company when he graduated in December. Charlotte's plans were dashed when she fled Rhode Island and the East Coast.

Now Maria was stepping into the role she had hoped to fill. A local Providence girl they all knew from childhood, Maria assumed responsibility for all their financial operations and was soon Jake's fiancé as well. They made an impressive pair, both in the business and in life. They were planning a wedding for late the following summer.

"So, tell me about things in Chicago. I want to know everything, but first, run through the break in. Did he take anything? Do you know what he was after?" Jake asked in rapid fire. "I still think we should hire security and let you come home."

"Unnecessary, Jacobo. I told you I am staying with Alex."

"Does that answer the security question or the home question? What does 'staying with' mean exactly? What do we know about this Alex person? Is the fact that you are living in sin supposed to make me feel better about things?"

"Oh jeez, now you sound like Papa. Staying with Alex means I am in a secure building and don't need security. It also means that I am—maybe—in an interesting relationship that might have a future. Speaking of which, you haven't told Mama I am living with a man, have you?"

"Are you kidding?" Jake shot back. "Do you think I want to give her a heart attack? She will ship you off to Porto to live with cousin Adolfo in a heartbeat."

"God forbid," Charlotte rolled her eyes and clutched her chest, falling back in a fake heart attack that made them both laugh. "I may as well shoot myself or join a convent. Adolfo would keep me under lock and key, and my life would be over. Are you hungry? I'm starving. Do you think we can find a decent Chinese restaurant that delivers?"

Opening her computer, the pair perused the local restaurant choices before deciding that they could take their chances at a nearby Chinese restaurant.

"It looks like a dive," Jake observed.

"Exactly," Charlotte agreed. "Not likely we'll see anyone we know in a place like that. But just to be safe..." Charlotte picked up a Red Sox cap and her hoodie and shoved her hair under both. Soon they were crossing the parking lot toward the nondescript car her brother had rented.

"You didn't even drive your own car?"

"I didn't want to risk anything. Gil has been hanging around a bit too often and a few of his buddies have been, too."

"I don't want to talk about it or think about it again tonight. Deal?" Just thinking about her old boyfriend sent a frisson of fear skating up Charlotte's spine.

Over Szechuan chicken and spicy-hot shredded beef and celery, the siblings discussed Jake's wedding plans, the newest menu items for the bakery and Charlotte's work. After 90 minutes and replete with food, Jake finally brought up the topic they had been skirting.

"Char," he finally ventured, placing his hand gently over his sister's, "what about going to the police? I won't let anything happen to you, but I will not allow you to miss my wedding because you can't come home. I don't understand what's stopping you. It seems like the logical solution."

"I am not proud of what I did when I accepted this job, Jake, but how do I retract it all now without looking like an outright liar? I had to get out of Boston. You know that. Jake, I need to keep my job. I really love it and I cannot risk all this drama becoming public too soon. Eventually I will explain the misunderstanding to Regan—my boss," she clarified, "but I need more time. If I do a fantastic job for her and LHRE, Regan will be fine when I tell her about the deception."

"It wasn't your mistake, Carlotta, it was hers. Just tell her. Don't you hate living this lie, anyway? What does this Alex guy think? Does he believe you are some blue-blooded daughter of the American Revolution too?"

Looking at Charlotte's face, Jake instantly understood the problem. "So, it's not your job at all. You are too talented for them to fire you over your personal background. We both know they can't fire you over something personal, anyway. It's the guy, right? He thinks you're a rich bitch. He must be some snob. Maybe you are, too." Jake finished with a sneer.

"Oh, Jake, he's not. I swear, but he comes from an old, established family. The right side of the tracks, the right schools..."

"You went to Harvard, Char. How much more right can you get?"

"Yeah, on scholarships."

"So what? You should be damn proud of that, and you know it."

"Jake, his sister is marrying a U.S. Senator's son. The guy is an Illinois congressman. A baker's daughter just isn't in the same league. Besides, think about Papa's secrets. We need to keep those, too."

"I see," Jake said, a sadness coming into his deep brown eyes. "It really is you who is the snob. You're ashamed of your family. I would never have thought that of you, Carlotta Rocha."

Charlotte knew her brother was furious. He never called her by her birth name otherwise. She changed her name legally when all her problems started, but to her family, she would always be Carlotta Rocha, not Charlotte Roche.

"I just need a little time to explain everything, Jacobo," Charlotte said, stressing Jake's full name. "I am not ashamed. How could I be? I love you guys more than anything. It's just, you know how things go. It starts with a little omission at a party and pretty soon everyone thinks you have tons of money and influence. I feel like my life spun out of control overnight. First Gil, then this."

"This is minor, compared to Gil. You need to get that injunction reinforced and keep him away from you. Then you need to come clean at work."

"I know, Jake. I know."

"And then, Carlotta, you better bring this Alex fellow home to meet your parents before it gets too serious. They will never forgive you if you don't."

CHAPTER EIGHTEEN

C harlotte was sitting with her feet up on the oversized sofa in the media room, television blaring, computer in her lap, and the Sunday papers scattered all around her. Alex drank in the sight of her, stunned again by her beauty. No, she was not a model with perfect features. Instead, she looked lovely—wholesome, and healthy, like a woman who took care of her body but didn't obsess about it.

Best of all, she looked perfectly at home in his room. Their room. Charlotte hadn't gone back to her apartment in more than a month now, and neither of them had discussed the possibility of her doing so. The anxiety that had clouded her eyes and caused a tightness around her mouth was gone. She felt safe here, and that was of paramount importance to him.

Alex thought long and hard before asking Charlotte to move in with him, even though when he proffered the idea, it sounded spur of the moment. Alex never acted in the moment. Never. He considered the fact that he was turning his back on other women but he no longer wanted any woman but Charlotte. He considered the fact that he would be sharing his space with someone, day, and night, but if the someone was Charlotte, he found he loved the idea.

Most of all, he considered the fact that Charlotte was hiding something from him, something sinister and potentially dangerous. She was lying to him, too. Alex hated her reluctance to trust him with the truth. He hated not knowing Charlotte viscerally. He wanted to be intimately familiar with the minutiae of her life, from what toothpaste she used to every playground episode from her childhood.

But he was keeping secrets, too. What a hypocrite he would be to demand the truth from her when he was lying to her face. If he could not trust her with his secrets, how could he demand that she trust him with hers?

So, he had taken the plunge. He'd intended to take her back to her place and let her miss him a few days before asking, but over dinner Alex realized he didn't want to wait. Barely okay with letting her go home to sleep on it briefly, Alex would have pressed her again before even two weeks passed, but the burglary resolved the waiting issue. Charlotte returned with him that night and they never discussed it again. Alex wasn't sorry. He loved seeing her sitting there, loved coming home to find her in his home—their home.

"Hey there, Gorgeous," he said sneaking. up behind her and kissing her cheek. She was startled, then pleased, reaching to turn off the television and put her laptop aside.

"Hey there, yourself," Charlotted stood and stepped into his embrace. "I missed you."

"With all your travels, you still had time to miss me?"

"Are you saying, Mr. Gaines, that you didn't miss me?"

As an answer, Alex swooped down and pulled Charlotte tight against his body from neck to knee. He captured her lips in a hot, moist kiss that went on and on, allowing her to come up for air briefly before claiming her mouth again. His lips were firm against her soft ones, his tongue hot in her cool mouth, sending shivers of electricity through his veins.

"Does that answer your question?" Alex raised his head, breathless, without loosening his hold on Charlotte. "I missed you so much."

Charlotte's face split into a wide grin, her heart-shaped face completely lit up by the compliment. "You could have fooled me. You never called."

"Are you kidding me?" Alex pulled from her arms to feign being shot. "You wound me. I called and texted every single day and you know it. You were the one who was too busy to answer. I had to wait and wait for you to throw me a bone."

Alex tried to keep the annoyance from his tone. While he had faithfully texted Charlotte multiple times a day during his travels, she had clustered her responses, which he had to concede were many, in a single thirty-minute window each day. She had been funny, open, and sexy in her brief phone messages and longer texts, but still Alex was left wondering what she was doing for the other twenty-three plus hours. He wanted to give her the benefit of the doubt, but...

"So, tell me all about St. Louis. How did it go?" he probed with an innocent look on his handsome face.

"What's to tell? The business was good. The contract is progressing."

"Where did you stay? Did you see any sights? The arch? Eat any good food while you were there? I didn't even ask, were you alone or did Regan go too?"

"Well, aren't you just full of questions? I stayed at some downtown hotel that looks like every other downtown hotel, saw a lot of conference rooms, and ate room service. It was long days and frankly exhausting. How about L.A.?"

"Lots of meetings there too, but I got a little chance to do some shopping on Rodeo Drive. I might have a small present somewhere in my luggage and if you are a good girl..."

"Oh, Alex," Charlotte oozed, draping her body around his, putting her lips very close to his, and running her fingers through his thick hair. "I can be very, very good. Try me."

Alex needed no other encouragement before lifting Charlotte in his bulging arms and tossing her down on the sofa. He had her tee-shirt and yoga pants off in a flash and was yanking at his shirt when he felt her fingers stroking his stomach and her hands moving to undo his belt buckle. It seemed she was as anxious as he was. He fell on her the moment she had his pants down, hungry to feel her sheathed tight around him, desperate for that closeness he missed when he was away, grateful she had obtained birth control.

After a frenzy to satisfy their lust, Alex slowed the pace, taking time to savor the feel of Charlotte's whole body. He reveled in the tingle of her fingers lightly stroking his arms and chest, then her hands massaging the length of his back muscles until they slid down to his butt and sank into his flesh. Charlotte pulled him hard inside her. Alex picked up the pace again, sliding deep into Charlotte's waiting body, pulling back to enjoy the unbelievable sensation of sliding in again. She was so responsive, clinging to him, kissing him deeply, drawing his tongue to tangle with hers as she pulled him back into her body.

Little whimpers came from Charlotte each time Alex pulled back from her and she sighed with pleasure when he returned to sink farther inside her. Soon he had her panting and gasping for breath, begging for release. He barely kept himself in control, but he wanted this to last, to make up for five days without this woman.

He had been a starving man when he fell upon her lithe body and felt her muscular legs wrap around him. He knew now he would not be content with one meal.

Alex pulled Charlotte tighter under him and moved quickly, plumbing her depths over and over until he felt her spasm beneath him, her breath hitching, her hands wild on his skin. He loved watching her climax, knowing that he had brought her that pleasure.

Taking several deep breaths, Alex stilled in Charlotte's body, resisting the urge to let go as he felt the last of Charlotte's orgasm flutter around him. Then he kissed her deeply and slowly, thoroughly ravaging her mouth. Choosing the exact moment when she was just about to calm completely, he wrapped his hands around her breasts, kneading and stroking them and sending fire surging back through her veins. He watched her face, kissing her again before moving lower to replace his hand with his mouth, sucking hard around one taut nipple. Charlotte writhed beneath him, almost lifting them both off the sofa. Alex chose that moment to move inside Charlotte again, stoking her pleasure and his own with long, slow, rhythmic friction.

Alex felt Charlotte spiraling to her release, felt her body begging to let go as he dipped into her with painstaking slowness. His warm lips closed over her other breast, teething her nipple, and causing her to cry out. He gently tongued the tight bud as she tried to increase the speed of his thrusts, her hips lifting to his. Her ruthless hands were everywhere, pulling him tighter against her, trying to draw his body deeper into hers. Alex moved to her mouth, scoring her lips with his teeth before he took her mouth in a brutal kiss. Bucking wildly himself, he reached for their mutual release. Desire surged through his body as Charlotte repeatedly whispered "please".

Feeling swamped by the storm surging through his body, Alex made one last futile attempt to hold back. "Come with me, Char," he begged between gasped breaths.

Charlotte strained briefly for that last bit of pleasure before ripples of satisfaction ran through her body, squeezing and milking Alex until he thought he would scream from the intensity. He felt her body softening into his as they came down from their mutual high, catching their breath.

"Welcome home, Alexander," Charlotte said with a coy smile and a brief peck on Alex's lips.

"Good to be here, Charlotte," he responded with a soft nibble of her lips. "Very, very good to be here."

They lay together for several minutes as their breathing slowed, stroking each other's skin gently, making small talk before Alex finally got up from the couch and scooped up his clothes.

"Between traveling and you, my dear, I am in dire need of a shower. Join me?"

"Not sure my legs will hold me yet. You go ahead, I will be there in five."

Pulling his suitcase noisily behind him down the hall, Alex dropped his clothes on a chair and went to stand under in the hot shower, letting it revive him. He was already out of the shower and dressed, but there was still no sign of Charlotte, so he wandered back to the living room to find her sound asleep on the sofa.

Alex put a soft cashmere throw over her naked beauty before grabbing a juice from the fridge and heading to his office. His body was still on Pacific time, and he was wide awake.

May as well get a little work done for the bank.

Instead of working, Alex sat staring out at the night sky, allowing his mind to wander. When they were lying in each other's arms, he and

Charlotte were a formidable pair, close and connected. But he knew he was hiding himself from her, and he was pretty damn sure she was hiding herself from him.

Alex wanted to move their relationship forward. The more he was with her, the more he wanted to be with her. She was brilliant and funny, lovely, and sweet, softly feminine, and tough as nails. His family liked her. His friends adored her. He hated being away from her, even for a day. Everything was better shared with Charlotte.

But how would things be when he told her the truth? How could she ever learn to trust him again? Would she look at him differently, perhaps think he no longer deserved her? How could she bring a man with his history home to her family?

Staring out the window, eyes unfocused, he realized he had to come clean before she found out, anyway. Otherwise, she might never trust him again.

He wanted more with Charlotte, but at this moment, the hurdles in his way felt insurmountable. He had been keeping secrets almost his whole life, living logically and thoughtfully to assure that he never slipped up.

Now he had made the biggest slip up of all. He had fallen for Charlotte and invited her into his home and his life. How could he stay hidden with her right here, and how could he not? There was still too much at stake. He could not blow it now, not after all these years.

Soon, he would tell her soon, and let the chips fall where they may. It wasn't fair to ask him to keep this secret even if he could, which was questionable. Enough was enough. It was time to come clean.

But then what? After all, he only knew about his lies. What about the secrets and lies she had yet to reveal? Perhaps it was Charlotte who would blow them apart, not him. She had mentioned no hotel, no landmark, no restaurant. Alex suspected Charlotte had been nowhere near St. Louis.

So, where has she been and why can't she tell me the truth about it? After all, how long am I supposed to be a liar—or love one?

CHAPTER NINETEEN

The day was perfect for running, and the crowds were thick. Too much adrenaline was coursing through people's veins and Charlotte could barely hear herself think over folks talking too loudly with each other. Organizers had trouble getting out their messages despite the loudspeakers.

The entire gang had assembled to cheer on Alex. They were co-ordinating their positions throughout the course so that Alex would see a friendly face at least every four or five miles. Charlotte would see him off and then hang around to be there at the finish line since the course both started and ended at Grant Park. Wyatt and Keeli would be at the four-mile mark, Regan and Tyler at the eight. Aubrey and her Congressman, Adam, were taking the halfway point at mile marker thirteen and Alex's parents would be just down the road from her at marker eighteen. So it went until the finish line, where they all would converge.

She had offered to work her way through the crowds to egg him on after the halfway point, but he had refused. A marathon runner herself, she knew that frustration and burn would set in before the last third of the race. She knew too well how it felt to run sixteen or more miles, be exhausted, and still be facing ten more. Fatigue would set in, and he would have to rely on willpower, determination and training. A friendly face would go a long way at that point. She had wanted to do this for him, but he assured her that other friends and family paced along the route would suffice.

Charlotte had invited everyone back to their place after the race for what she hoped would be a late breakfast or brunch. Alex expected to finish in the middle of the pack, as he had the previous year, and with a 7:30 start time, everyone would be back at the house before noon. The biggest problem was traffic. To avoid it, almost everyone would be on foot. Those covering the northern edge, and Sloane and Randall, covering the southern corridor, would take the public transportation. Both groups assured Charlotte that they could get there on the "L" and then there was some good-natured teasing of Sloane. It turned out she had never ridden in any kind of public transportation.

Charlotte was bummed. she couldn't run, but at least the boot was off at last. She would never take a pair of light-weight shoes for granted again. Now, in sturdy running shoes, she made her way through the crowds to give Alex one last kiss and a proper sendoff.

"You'll do great. Just don't start out too fast. You always want to start fast," she told him now. "Remember that it is a fast course, and flat, so you have to pace yourself."

"Char, I've got this, ok?" he responded, humoring her with a hug to take the sting out of his words. "Do not make me nervous, please."

"I'm sorry. And even more sorry I am not running with you. Next year."

"I'm holding you to that."

"You do that. You ate enough?"

"Yes, Mom," Alex teased.

"You have clothes to discard as you heat up, right?"

"Yes, Mom. I am wearing the stuff you picked out, smarty-pants, and you know it. Just give me a kiss and let me get going."

"Okay, watch for everybody along the route and I will wait near the finish, as close as I can get."

"Gotcha. Now go." Alex took Charlotte into his arms, gave her a swift, hard kiss, and then pushed her away to join his fellow runners in the starting corral.

"Love you," she said reflexively to his retreating form.

WHAT! What has she just said?

Charlotte turned around to see Alex's response, but she'd already lost him in the crowd.

Perhaps he hadn't heard her? Where the hell did that come from? Things had certainly changed for her.

Charlotte reflected on her recent trip to Boston. It had been so great spending time with her brothers, after she took heat from both of them about calling the police. Once they finished scolding her, they had settled into a typical family visit with lots of stories of what had been happening, many "remember when's" and a lot of telling each other how to live their lives.

Jake and Don had a lot of questions for Charlotte about her new job, her new friends, but especially about Alex.

"I don't love the idea of you living with someone this quickly," Jake complained, "but I confess I am thrilled you live in a building with security people." Charlotte didn't offer information about Elizabeth, focusing on other door staff instead. While she was beautiful, Elizabeth was no match for Gil if he should he decide to force his way in. There was that key to the elevator requirement, so Charlotte volunteered that information to her brothers to reinforce her decision to stay with Alex.

"Now I feel even better," Jake responded, relief clear on his face.

Charlotte told them all about Regan and her job, bragging about how quickly she had increased responsibility, sharing information that was not confidential about acquisitions, development projects, and deals. They were both pretty impressed. Don missed many of the fine points of the negotiations, but Jake appreciated the sophisticated nature of Charlotte's work and the skill and nuance required to do it well.

Most of the time, the three discussed the online specialty food operation and their plans for it. "Papa may have been reluctant at first," he reminded them, "but even he is enthusiastic now that we are selling back to Portugal."

"I cannot believe that you turned Mama and Papa's recipes into a multi-million-dollar business," Charlotte fawned over her brother. "It's amazing to think that you grew one little corner bakery into a huge manufacturing plant shipping world-wide."

"What's amazing to me," Don had chimed in, "is that you can charge so damn much for a cake."

"That happened after all the publicity. Once celebrities started talking about our cakes on their talk shows and in 'People Magazine', we got to charge celebrity prices." Jake explained proudly. "People pay those prices happily. It is pretty wild."

They all laughed at the notion that a $10 cake in her dad's bakery now sold for $30 to $50 dollars or more. "We can't keep them in stock," Jake bragged.

"Amazing," Charlotte agreed. "And what about you, little brother? What are you going to contribute?"

"Well, obviously I will take over the baking when Papa is ready to retire, but I am working on variations of Mama's jams and soups, and I have some ideas of my own regarding traditional Portuguese dishes that will ship easily. Nothing that needs refrigeration. So far, that is my biggest challenge."

"I also suggested to Don that we open a restaurant in Providence to serve the Portuguese community, and the community at large, while testing recipes and promoting our business."

"It worked for all the famous chefs. Why not for you?" Charlotte agreed, ruffling her brother's hair like he was still five. He slapped her hand away and soon they were all teasing each other like children.

The time had flown by but soon Charlotte was donning a baseball cap and a new oversized Bruins sweatshirt, watching over her shoulder as she boarded a plane back to Chicago. The uneventful flight got in early enough for Charlotte to look like she had been sitting on the couch all day when Alex arrived home. In fact, she had only beat him home by two hours.

When Alex started asking questions, Charlotte thought he had found her out, but he had cut the interrogation short and taken her to bed where things were as good, if not better, than before they parted. They were close in bed, attuned to one another's needs and wants, attentive to each other's desires. The sex was hot, and the cuddling was close. Everything seemed better than ever.

Of course, Charlotte hated lying to Alex and wanted desperately to let down her guard and tell him everything, but she would have to let Regan know the truth before she could come clean with Alex. She was not yet ready to risk her job. But if she was falling in love...

Alex was smart and curious, though. He was asking more questions and settling less for her usual vague responses. Charlotte either needed to be cleverer about her fibs, she needed to come clean, or she needed to distance herself further from a man she cared for. While she did not want it to be the latter, Charlotte wasn't ready for the second. That left getting cleverer, but Charlotte feared Alex was too smart and Gil was too aggressive. She expected trouble, but couldn't figure out how to head it off.

Still, in the two weeks since Alex's return, there had been fewer questions and no issues. Alex was attentive but distracted by serious marathon training and work. Despite his long runs, Charlotte knew Alex was not sleeping as well as usual. Something big was happening in L.A. but she couldn't get him to say more than that he was fighting a hostile takeover. She loved he cared so deeply about his clients. He behaved as if the company was his own.

The noise brought Charlotte back to the present as the marathoners were off and running. Charlotte waved to Alex as he flew past her—his pace just a tad too fast, she was sure—but she couldn't tell if he saw her. She moved through the diminishing crowd to find a place to hang out until she watched for Alex at the finish line. She had a book to read, some work to do too, so she headed to get a cup of coffee and then find a shady tree under which to park herself.

There were two coffee places almost across the street from each other if she walked up to Michigan Avenue, but Charlotte headed for a pancake place instead and pushed her way to the front of the line of hipsters and yuppies waiting for a table.

"A cinnamon roll and coffee to go, please," she told the cashier, pacing from foot to foot, eager to get back out into the perfect autumn day. "Large, black."

Charlotte reached for her wallet, extracted a couple of singles, and went to hand them to the cashier.

"Here, let me get that," a familiar man's voice said, placing his hand over hers to prevent her from paying.

Charlotte didn't turn around, didn't acknowledge the generous offer. She froze like a statue, her blood running cold.

CHAPTER TWENTY

When Charlotte wasn't visible at the finish of the race, Alex was not concerned. The crowds were enormous, noisy, and undulating. She could be nearby, and he wouldn't know it. Then he remembered she had worn that hot-pink tee just so he could spot her in the crowd. She was nowhere to be seen. He would have checked his phone, but he had left the device with her while he ran.

What a stupid plan that had been.

Perhaps she wandered away a bit or miscalculated the time. He had finished faster than last year by a full twenty minutes. He couldn't wait to share his success with her.

There was that 'mile twenty-seven after party' down the street. Perhaps she had wandered over there. Alex was sweaty and exhausted, but he headed that way anyway, only to run into Sloane and Randall coming toward him in the crowd.

"Hey there. Very nice work, my friend," Randall bellowed, slapping Alex on the back in congratulations. "I think you finished even faster this year. Not bad for an old man."

"Watch it with the old man comments, Rand. After all, you are three full months older than me. When am I going to see your sorry ass out there on the course?"

"No running for this guy," Sloane offered. "You know that will never be his sport. He is just too big a guy to let his knees take such a pounding."

"Where's Charlotte?" Alex changed the subject abruptly. "She said she would be here at the finish."

"Oh, yeah, she texted all of us she would meet us back at your place. She wanted to get lunch organized and waiting for you. She figured you would be starving."

"Oh, okay. Thirsty, really, but soon I will be ready to eat a bear," Alex told them as he swiped a bottle of water from a nearby table filled with Gatorade and Vitamin Waters.

"Anyway, we said we would stand in and get you back home safe and sound," Randall explained. "Can you walk the few blocks, or do you need a rest first?"

"I can walk," Alex told Randall impatiently. "I am not an invalid."

"Of course you aren't," Sloane said, keeping the peace between the two blustering men.

When did Sloane become such a diplomat? Man, had she mellowed.

"But I have been on my feet for hours, so let's take it slow."

Ethan and Alex's parents were sitting in the living room chatting about Chicago politics and sipping mimosas when Alex entered the apartment. He could hear voices in the kitchen, so after accepting hearty congratulations, he moved in that direction.

Wyatt had his head in the refrigerator and his muffled voice could be heard asking something about fruit salad. Keeli and Aubrey were standing at the counter surrounded by platters of meats, cheeses and pastries that Charlotte had been preparing for days. But there was no sign of Charlotte.

Alex dragged his weary frame to the dining room. No Charlotte. He checked the pantry. No Charlotte. Finally, he went back to the dark bedroom and saw her laying on the bed, eyes closed, face white as a sheet.

Kneeling on the floor beside her, Alex took Charlotte's clammy icy hand in his and in just above a whisper called her name. "Char, honey, are you okay?"

After what felt like an interminable delay, Charlotte turned her head toward Alex and gave him a weak smile.

"I am so proud of you," she said, as if they were standing at the finish line. "You did so great today."

"Are you okay? Why are you back here, lying down?" Her stillness and chilled skin frightened Alex. "Are you sick?"

"I'm fine, Alex. Relax. I just got a bit too much sun or too much caffeine and came to lie down for ten minutes before our guests arrived."

Charlotte never got too much sun or too much caffeine, and they both knew it. Still, by tacit agreement, she told her lie, and he pretended to believe it.

"Well, they are here now, so do you think you can get up?"

"Of course I can, silly. Let's go throw a party and celebrate our champion," Charlotte said, bouncing from the bed with verve and excitement.

She is definitely not sick. So, she must be upset. What upset her and why won't she talk to him?

"You're sure you're okay?"

"I'm fine, worry wart, tell me all about the race."

The couple made their way back to the living room and Alex dropped exhausted to the sofa, not caring about his sweaty clothes. His friends and family gathered around, sipping cocktails or coffee, nibbling on canapes that Charlotte had handmade yesterday while he regaled them with stories of mishaps and accidents, triumphs and tribulations. He told his friends how he hit at a wall at mile marker twenty-one and how much having a cheering section waiting for him at thirteen helped. He thanked them all for their encouragement and support.

Charlotte emerged from the kitchen with a casserole in her hands and invited everyone to take a seat at the table. With family, friends and two neighbors from down the hall, they comprised a party of sixteen. It was relaxed and friendly, with lots of good food. Alex ate the equivalent of a bear it seemed and took a lot of ribbing for it before he finally announced he needed a shower and excused himself for a few minutes.

Conversation turned to the upcoming elections, Aubrey's wedding plans, and the rumblings of wedding plans for Randall and Sloane.

"My mother is planning an enormous event for late spring," Sloane told them. "She is in seventh-heaven." They all laughed, envisioning Marianne Huyler throwing the social event of the year. All who knew her understood she would pull out all the stops for her only child.

Alex stopped just outside the dining room when he returned, out of sight of everyone, listening to the conversation swirl around the table. Charlotte fit right into the group, tossing in her opinions without fear, accepted by all as if they had known her forever.

But of course, no one really knew her, did they?

Alex was listening to the wedding talk and wondering if he and Charlotte would ever get to where they could consider marriage. He was certainly falling in love with her. But she had not suggested introducing him to her family. In fact, she was surprisingly silent on the subject considering she called home, or they called her daily. She never took their calls without leaving the room for at least part of the conversation. The only exception was when she spoke with her brother,

Don, at school. They would discuss recipes and cooking techniques until Alex's eyes glazed over, but not speak of much else.

Alex was coming to understand that whatever Charlotte's secret was, it had to do with her family as well. She was in some kind of danger. He knew that her brother Jake called specifically to check on her safety. Every conversation began the same way between the two of them, at least what he could hear of it as she left the room.

"Hi Jake. I'm fine. Really. Things are quiet here."

What did that mean, 'things are quiet here'? It was code for something. Alex was tired of wondering. It was time to put a plan in motion. He was chomping at the bit to sort this out, but he needed to get through Aubrey's wedding, clear up things with his family, then his friends, and finally Charlotte. That could take months, and based on Charlotte's appearance and demeanor when he came in today, Alex feared he didn't have months.

Forcing a smile back on his face, he entered the room to a hero's hurrah, and the conversation turned back to the marathon. There was tons of bragging by Alex's family because he had shaved twenty minutes off his time—as if they had been the ones to train or run.

"That was all my doing," Charlotte interrupted. "I ran his ass off before this race. If he hadn't trained with me, he would have done much worse."

"Oh," Randall quipped, "so now they call that training."

Everyone laughed, and Charlotte blazed bright red. Alex loved her embarrassment. It made her feel more his, for some reason. Perhaps because all around the table acknowledged that every night, he took this special woman into his bed.

"Speaking of training," Wyatt interrupted, "can we talk about the Tahoe schedule?" The men all began talking at once and the afternoon proceeded around a discussion of skiing and travels.

The conversation came to a halt when Keeli announced that she could not possibly get away before her Christmas rush. "Not until mid-December for me."

"What about your family, Kee?" Wyatt asked, ending the silent brooding. "Aren't they expecting us for Christmas? Sorry guys, but I think we have to push things out until January."

"Speaking of Christmas," Alex began, getting a collective groan when they all realized someone else was messing with their ski plans, "are you planning to spend Christmas with your family?"

The question was addressed directly at Charlotte.

"Well," she began, and then she stalled. "Well," she started again, "I have no idea." It seemed an innocuous enough response, but Alex saw an opportunity to dig for more information. She couldn't hide with all these people watching.

"But Charlotte, you are so close with your family and your brother will be home from school. I would imagine this is a big deal for them, right?"

"Right," Charlotte choked out.

"So, they must have some traditions, some plans," Alex was relentless despite her discomfort.

"Of course you can have the time off, if that is what's worrying you," Regan announced from across the table. "I know you have only been able to take a couple of days here and there to see them until now."

"Really?" Alex dragged out the word. "I didn't realize you had been going to Boston lately."

"But she was just there," Regan responded, confused.

"Boston? Not St. Louis?" Alex asked, already knowing the answer.

Charlotte was sitting still in her chair, looking at her lap. Alex suspected she wished she were anywhere else, and that Regan would shut up.

No such luck, my dear. I am going in for the kill.

"Charlotte, would you care to explain?"

CHAPTER
TWENTY-ONE

S ensing the tension in the room, Aubrey jumped in to break it.

"I am sure it is just a misunderstanding, Alex. Besides, I thought we were all going to Aspen for Christmas this year."

"Yes," Laurel Gaines agreed quickly. "We made plans ages ago to be in Aspen for Christmas. You promised us the house, Alex. You wouldn't go back on your promise, dear."

"We are counting on it, Alex," Aubrey continued. "We have everything planned."

Alex was forced to pay attention to the women from his family before things got out of control. He had indeed promised that the family could use his ski lodge for two weeks over the Christmas holidays. Aubrey would just have returned from her November honeymoon in Europe before her husband had to be in Springfield for the January session. She had announced she wanted to get away for a couple weeks of "R&R" after her wedding, her honeymoon and her move into a new house. Their mother had been quick to invite the rest of the family along.

"Well, that settles it," Charlotte said, finding her voice again. "It's Aspen for Christmas and January in Tahoe. My goodness, you all live tough lives."

The table full of privileged people took a moment to appreciate their good fortune as calendars came out to lock down dates. The four friends agreed to meet at Randall's Tahoe home right after the new year, and the women agreed to join them for a week at the end of that two-week vacation.

Once that was resolved, the party began to breakup. Charlotte wanted people to stay, expecting a blow up with Alex when they left, but it had been a very early start that morning. People had errands and activities, and Charlotte soon found herself alone with Alex. And silence. Dead silence.

"I guess I should clean up," she offered to fill the quiet. "You must be exhausted. Why don't you go lie down?"

"Leave it and come sit with me. I will help clean up later," Alex offered, reaching for her hand and pulling her with him to the sofa where he dropped like a rag doll.

"I am totally wasted," he confessed, "but happy. It was perfect weather; I had a great run, and that was a superb lunch. You did a beautiful job."

"Thanks. I loved entertaining your family and friends."

"Our friends, Charlotte. You are definitely part of the group now. If Randall embarrasses you when he is sober, you are part of the crowd."

"That's all it takes?" Charlotte laughed, reaching to run her hands up Alex's calves stretched across her lap.

"That's all. Mm, that feels so good. Charlotte, we have to talk. You know that, right?"

"Mm, hm," she agreed quietly. "But not right now, okay?"

"When?" Alex pressed.

"Soon. I promise I will tell you everything soon."

"Just tell me if you are okay. Something happened today, didn't it?"

"Yes, I won't lie. For a brief second today, I thought I saw an old boyfriend. It was a nasty breakup, and the idea of running into him shook me. Fortunately, I was mistaken."

"That's all? Just an old boyfriend?"

Just! He should only know.

"It was a truly ugly breakup, and I hoped never to see him again. It was a false alarm, of course. He must be in Boston, not Chicago."

"Sure, of course. That makes perfect sense." Alex agreed, his eyes closing, his shoulders relaxing. "So, you're fine."

"Yes," Charlotte told his already sleeping form. "I am totally fine."

It had been a very close call, Charlotte knew. In all the excitement of the marathon, she had let her guard down. Of course, Gil would take advantage of the crowds and open spaces to insinuate himself closer to her. She was a fool not to be prepared for the possibility.

"I can pay for my coffee," she had told him briskly. "And I have a court order that says you have to stay 100 feet from me."

"Come on, Car, give me a break. Just talk to me. I promise not to lay a finger on you."

"That is what you always say. Go away, Gil. Leave me alone."

"Leave you with your fancy job, your pretty boy, and your rich friends? Now that you have a hoity-toity degree from Harvard, none of us are good enough for you?"

"That's not it and you know it. Go away." Charlotte pushed through the lines of waiting people for the door. "Don't follow me and stay out of my damn apartment!"

"What do you care if I'm in your apartment? You haven't been back there once. I simply want to see you, Carlotta. We could be good together, Querida, you know we could. It could be like before. I want to be with you."

"Gil, we're done. It is never, ever going to be like before," Charlotte heard her voice rising sharply, unable to reign herself in. "Leave me alone before I call the police. I mean it." Taking a calming breath, Charlotte pulled herself up to her full height and threw back her shoulders, trying to give extra force to her words.

"Go head, bitch, call the police. But if you avoid me, I promise, all your important friends are going to hear the truth. How long do you think you keep that posh job of yours once I talk to your boss? How fast do you think that fancy boy of yours will run in the opposite direction? Do you think your father will live through it, Carlotta, if I start talking? Think of the consequences, Querida, before you chase me away."

"You wouldn't dare!" Charlotte hissed.

"Just try me, Carlotta. Just try calling my bluff. I'm done being patient. I am through being understanding. You need to come home and you better do it soon. You cannot hide from me or the truth much longer. I intend to have my way."

Gil had taken hold of Charlotte's arm again, wrapping his heavy hand around the soft skin of her wrist and twisting. Charlotte felt frightened and unsure of what to do when a police officer rode by on a bicycle and Gil dropped her arm and disappeared into the crowd.

For a moment, she thought she had imagined the whole thing, but the pounding of her heart, the pain where he twisted her wrist and the cold seeping into her pores despite the sunny morning reminded her that the threat had been very real.

It still was.

She didn't see how she could add this mess to the problems she was already struggling with. How could she juggle Alex, Gil, her work, her family, and her damn lies? How much longer could she keep all these balls in the air? She felt ready to crack now.

"Charlotte?" Alex's sleepy voice brought Charlotte back to the present.

"Hmm?" she leaned over, kissing his lips lightly.

"You would tell me if you were in real trouble, right? You understand we are a team now. Your problems are my problems. I am here for you. Promise me you will tell me if you need my help."

"Yes, sleepyhead, I understand that. You rest and I will go clean up a bit, teammate," she said, sliding out from under him and heading for the kitchen.

Good thing he was tired. Otherwise, Alex would have realized Charlotte never actually promised. She needed to figure this out soon before dragging LHRE and Alex down with her. Carlotta Rocha, I think it's time to go home.

CHAPTER
TWENTY-TWO

"Regan to the rescue," Charlotte teased when the car pulled up to the curb Wednesday morning for a day of shopping.

"Actually, it's not me that's the hero today, it's Missy," Regan pointed to where her older sister sat in the backseat. "She swears Katie can outfit both of you perfectly and get it all done today. I have to wear that hideous bridesmaid's dress."

"It's not hideous and you know it," Missy corrected. "It may not be what you would have chosen, but it is a beautiful dress."

"It's green." Regan responded. She could not have sounded more miserable if she had said they made it of alligator skin and died it chartreuse.

"A beautiful pale green that looks great on you," her sister retorted. "So stop bitching about it."

"Yes, Melissa. Whatever you say, Melissa."

"Cut it out, you two," Charlotte ordered. "You promised me a fun day."

"Oh, it will be." "You'll love it," the two replied almost in unison, all sibling animosity quickly forgotten.

The three were spending the day with Missy's professional fashion stylist, Katie Schuppler, founder of KS Styling. Katie had been enlisted to help them find dresses for the wedding and style them to perfection. Charlotte had waited until the last minute to find a dress, assuming she would wear something that Jo had selected when she was first injured. Shopping was not her thing, so the shortcut had suited her.

Regan had been quick to point out the flaws in Charlotte's plan. One, she needed an evening gown, not a cocktail dress. Second, Jo had shopped months ago, buying clothes for late summer and early autumn, not early November. Third, her friends and coworkers had seen much of her wardrobe and, as the Howe sisters had explained, she could not be seen wearing something she had already worn. They all knew that Charlotte would show up in a business suit if they didn't intervene.

"Do they not have the same problem in Boston?" Missy had asked Charlotte. "You don't wear the same outfit to multiple benefits, right? Not after you have been photographed in it? Besides, don't the designers offer you dresses to wear to those things? Even I get offers from second-tier designers."

Thinking quickly, Charlotte had answered with what she believed was a plausible reply. "It's Boston, Missy. We have that Puritan work ethic thing going there. People take pride in saving money, giving to charity. Being too flashy is not seemly in Boston. Wearing a dress twice is totally acceptable."

"Oh, yeah. I had not thought of it that way."

"Well there are a few flashy types, but I was never one of them."

That had ended the conversation, but not the argument. The sisters insisted Charlotte let Katie find her a dress. Having never worked with a stylist, or even met one, Charlotte was nervous, but excited, too. It would be so much fun to shop with her friends and a professional stylist. Charlotte had never done anything remotely like it before and had no idea what to expect, but she agreed with a little persuasion to let Missy set things up.

She was unprepared for the very young, very petite Katie. Her first impression was that this woman could not be out of school yet, let alone be an experienced professional. Born and raised in nearby Wisconsin, Katie was a fresh-faced girl of thirty, slender, not much above 5' tall and with a smattering of freckles across her nose. Her dark hair hung to the middle of her back simply, but her outfit was fantastic and very chic. Charlotte immediately coveted the short boots Katie was wearing and the insouciant way she had accessorized.

As soon as she began talking, it became obvious that Katie was savvy and connected with Chicago stores of every style and price range. She handed Charlotte her card and Charlotte tucked it safely in her wallet, knowing that she would be back to Katie to help dress her for everything.

Katie suggested they start at Neiman Marcus, with a follow-on trip to Ikram or Saks if they needed it. Once they had a game plan, and a parking space, they moved quickly to the gowns and then Katie became a whirlwind of activity while the women were shown to seats and handed bottles of water. Soon, the petite stylist had gathered what appeared to be the entire stock of gorgeous gowns, all in the correct sizes.

"For you, Missy, I have selected deep greens and blues, predominantly. They will look great with your coloring and it's a big season for jewel tones. I am leaning toward Oscar de la Renta, but I have brought a variety that I think will work. Just let me get Charlotte set up, then I will come help you."

Grabbing Charlotte by the hand and leading her to the dressing room next to Missy, the tiny Katie took control like a soft-spoken drill sergeant, demanding Charlotte's attention. Charlotte looked like a kid in a candy store, thrilled but completely overwhelmed by more than a dozen gorgeous dresses hanging on the hooks.

"I know it is a lot to take in," Katie understated, "but just try on everything I brought you until one speaks to you. Trust me, the right dress is here, and we will make you gorgeous. I brought a lot of Roberto Cavalli for you, but I like these Tadashi Shoji dresses, and they are a fraction of the price."

"I would like to avoid spending a fortune," Charlotte whispered to Katie.

"I can dress you at any price range, Charlotte, so don't feel any pressure to buy here. I have clients I take to TJ Maxx. We can make this work."

"Okay, but that is just between us, okay?"

"Of course," Katie reassured her as she passed her the first gown to try. Speaking louder, she added, "I think these orchid and violet colors will be fabulous with your dark hair, and many of them are on sale, so you might snap up a bargain too." She winked at Charlotte and the two women were instant friends.

"How did Missy find you?" Regan asked minutes later as Katie helped zip her sister into a gorgeous flowing gown.

"Word of mouth, my usual way," Missy answered before Katie could even open her mouth. "The Junior League women were talking about this woman who cleaned out their closets and then took them shopping to fill in the gaps and I was hooked."

"What can be more fun than shopping with an expert?"

"What is your background, Katie?" Charlotte shouted over the flimsy wall separating the women.

"I have been doing this about five years, I guess. I have a degree in Fashion Merchandising Management and Business. Now I consult, I write for Chicago Women Magazine and work with lovely people like you guys. I have been a wardrobe consultant for TV personalities, but I do that less these days. This is more fun for me."

"She writes a great blog," Missy added. "She knows her stuff."

Charlotte had to agree that Katie knew what she was doing. Each dress was flattering, highlighting her trim figure, playing up the deep brown of her eyes, her skin tone. Many were dresses she would never pull from the rack, but Katie had a discerning eye. It would be very hard to choose.

"Where do you usually shop?" Katie asked Charlotte. Charlotte hesitated, trying to formulate a response. She certainly couldn't answer with the truth, Banana Republic, or Old Navy. Besides, Regan had pointed her toward some fun boutiques in town, like Sara Jane, and she was moving up in the world.

"She is a recent transplant to Chicago," Missy explained.

"She will certainly be introduced to a lot of Chicago society and politicos at this wedding," Regan added. "Just about anyone who is anyone will be there." Regan started listing names, many of whom were unfamiliar to Charlotte, but several had been on her radar since starting her job and she recognized that these were very important people.

"Do you have a lot of political connections back in Boston?" Missy asked when they were done oohing and aahing over the bigwigs that would attend the wedding. "The Roche family has so much clout, after all. And the big pharma lobbying organizations, you must be involved with those, too."

"Well, I was never attached to any of the Roche pharma activities, of course," Charlotte answered quickly, trying to stick as closely as possible to the truth. "I went straight from Harvard to real estate investing."

"You knew that didn't you, Missy?" Regan interjected. "That was why Charlotte was such a catch for LHRE. She had all that real estate investment expertise from her years with Independence. Her background was really impressive," Regan continued, as if Charlotte was not present.

"First were the back-to-back Harvard degrees. No slouch, this one," she said, thumbing in Charlotte's direction with a broad smile. "Then she started at the bottom of the REIT group at Independence and in three years managed to leapfrog everyone to be second in command. She was just starting the conference, lecture, spokeswoman circuit when I grabbed her up."

"I think I did know something about your background, Charlotte, but it sounds to me like the job you left would have more prestige than heading LHRE finance. Nothing personal, Ree," she added when her younger sister shot her a scathing look.

"Maybe, maybe not." Charlotte took a diplomatic approach. "I liked Regan. I liked the idea of being a bigger fish in a smaller pond, too. Besides, I hated the idea of being a spokesperson. I needed a lower profile."

Boy, did she ever!

"Needed, or wanted?" Missy caught the slip.

"Well, both, I guess," Charlotte struggled for a believable response. "I needed it because I hated being on the road. And I am shy."

"She is shy," Regan confirmed. "I am guessing you didn't want to travel so you could be close to home. But then you moved. I could never understand that one."

Oh, jeez. I am just getting in deeper.

"What can I say, Regan? You made me an offer I couldn't refuse." Charlotte's miserable imitation of Marlon Brando sent the four women into peals of laughter.

"Ladies, please. Can we return our attention to some serious shopping?" Katie took control and the conversation thankfully moved off of Charlotte for a while.

With help from the stylist, Charlotte had narrowed her selection down to two dresses. Missy had suggested she reconsider a third, but when she saw the price tag, Katie subtly suggested putting the third one back.

"Alright, ladies, come see Charlotte's final selection. I think you will agree it is a showstopper. Charlotte emerged from the fitting room outfitted in a gorgeous and unusual gown that was called African Violet, but was actually vivid blue over an underskirt of red. The embellished waist was reminiscent of ancient handcrafting, and the fitted bodice with a deep V-neck and back opening to a flowing skirt gave Charlotte a perfect hourglass figure. The dress was dramatic in its coloring but otherwise simple for a Saturday night, lacking beading or sequins that would have been too much.

"You look gorgeous," the sisters gushed, and the decision was made. At well under $1000, Charlotte was thrilled.

"What about you, Missy?"

"I need help."

"You need lots of help," Regan taunted. Missy shoved her lightly in response, and Regan pushed her in return.

"What are you, two-year-olds?" Katie asked, drawing a laugh but getting them back in line.

Missy provided a small fashion show, trying on three dresses and parading them in front of the women for their opinions. Eventually, they agreed on a Rubin Singer gown of a metallic navy in a strapless mermaid style that flattered Missy's figure. The small, pleated train really appealed to Missy and the $6000 price tag didn't even phase her.

"Now, shoes and bags," Katie announced. The woman was a bundle of energy.

"I'm starved," Missy whined. Checking her phone, Charlotte was astonished to see that over three hours had passed. It was way past lunchtime.

"Can we break for lunch?" she asked Katie.

"Of course. I am not your mother. I am your stylist," the small fashionista said. "I know a glorious spot around the corner."

"Missy, no pigging for you," her sister warned. "You still have to zip that dress in a month."

"Please, don't remind me. Why, oh why, can't I be thin like you two?"

"Are you kidding?" Charlotte responded sincerely. "I have gained about seven pounds since I stopped running. Spraining my ankle was painful and fattening."

"Yes, but you live with Alex now," Regan reminded her.

Breaking into a smile like the sun coming out from the clouds, Charlotte's face took on a dreamy look. "Yes, there is that."

"Oh my," Missy observed to Katie. "Looks like we will shop wedding dresses before you know it."

That brought Charlotte abruptly back to reality.

"So much has to happen before I can even think about marriage," she responded in a daze.

"Like what?"

A pack of lies stood between her and Alex. Charlotte knew, as these women did not, the hurdles they presented. It would take a lot of understanding and patience to move forward after she told the truth. Would Alex be interested in a woman with her background?

Definitely not. Not with his family pedigree. Not considering the circle in which he travelled. Would these women even speak to her once they knew?

"Like what?" Charlotte repeated, trying to conjure up a suitable answer.

"Well, he hasn't even met my family. And it hasn't been that long."

"Easily remedied," Regan pointed out. "And you've known each over six months."

"And he has to give up all those other women," Charlotte challenged.

"Oh, Char, are you really that dense?" Regan queried, not unkindly. "He only has eyes for you. Any other woman now is just designed to make you jealous."

Charlotte was surprised to discover that she wanted the picture her friends were painting. She wanted to walk down the aisle and see Alex's handsome face gazing on her, waiting for her to begin a life with him. How had things come to this so quickly? Charlotte had promised herself no complications.

Charlotte vowed that Alex would not know how she felt. She would keep things light and simple while she cleaned up more messes than Mr. Clean. Then she could consider a serious relationship with a man like Alex.

Until then, friends with benefits. I don't want to be his damn friend, though.

Charlotte promised herself that as soon as this wedding was over, she would head home and take care of everything, once and for all.

CHAPTER
TWENTY-THREE

I t was THE event in Chicago. The wedding of an Illinois State Congressman to a society princess was big news by itself, but add the bonus of all the Washington politicos on hand and the invitation became even more coveted. Six hundred people were invited to the Saturday night event, snarling traffic for a mile or more in every direction.

A lucky 180 were hotel guests able to avoid the logjam outside. The Four Seasons had closed three floors for the event besides the eighth-floor ballroom. There were suites for the wedding party, of course, and changing rooms for the eight bridesmaids and eight groomsmen, but Washington and Springfield insiders had flown in yesterday to make a weekend in Chicago. The governor was up from Springfield with his wife. nineteen US Senators would be in attendance besides Senator Jensen, 31 US congressmen and women and about the same number of representatives from Springfield, as well as aldermen from Chicago and suburban government people.

Security had been tight since they concluded a Thursday sweep, with numerous men and women trying to blend in despite their soldier like stances, constantly roving eyes, and plastic earpieces. They fooled no one, but guests of the hotel who were not there for the wedding felt safer than usual. Passes that barely fit in women's tiny handbags were required to enter the cordoned off floors and spectators loitered in the lobby hoping for a glimpse of someone famous.

Aubrey and Adam had moved into the hotel once it was secured, along with Laurel and Charles. They had to move in early to be readily available to Annie, their wedding coordinator. The women had been hounding Annie, nervously revisiting details that had all been finalized weeks ago. Finally, they were satisfied, and by Thursday night, the bridal couple could behave like tourists, going for a romantic dinner at Tru, then strolling to Navy Pier to complete their date on the new, 196-foot-tall Ferris wheel.

Her bridesmaids took over on Friday, keeping Aubrey busy all day with brunch and the spa before the rehearsal dinner and a final bachelorette fling. They had invited Charlotte to tag along, along with Missy Howe Wilder and several other friends. Regan was a bridesmaid and, although she denied it, the two women suspected she was the reason they were included.

Charlotte thoroughly enjoyed spending rehearsal day with the bride to be. Aubrey and Adam were well-suited and very much in love. They were wistful leaving one another after dinner, when the bridesmaids separated the couple to take Aubrey barhopping in the rented stretch limo. Adam would not see her again until Aubrey appeared gowned in white at the end of that long aisle.

Charlotte reflected on the wedding to come. She was excited about the wedding, all the important people she would see and about looking beautiful for Alex. Things at home had been comfortable, but she felt the undercurrent of unspoken words like a living, breathing creature comfortably settled in a corner easy chair. Her secrets had made themselves at home and they weren't leaving anytime soon.

The tension came and went between the couple. Communication was more strained, conversations purposely vague or avoided altogether. She knew Alex was stressing over the deal in California, but he rarely spoke of it, except to mention that he had a meeting or travel plans. He would head west again in just a few days. Charlotte said nothing at all about her family, about the break-in, about the mysterious bad breakup, but she did give Alex a heads up that she would be gone for several days while he was out of town. She didn't pretend it was for work this time, admitting freely that she was going home to see her parents. She offered no additional information, and he didn't pry.

But this weekend they were forgetting all of that. This weekend they hoped to strengthen their tense relationship. Alex had checked them into the Four Seasons last night and they had a romantic dinner at Spiaggia, a long stroll to window shop the Michigan Avenue boutiques and back to their room for long, slow, sizzling hot sex. It was perfect, and Charlotte drifted to sleep exhausted and well satisfied.

The wedding day began with coffee together, but Alex was busy with the groomsmen, his family and with organizing logistics for the many and demanding out-of-town guests. The hotel, used to people who demanded only the best, had most of the details handled. However, arranging limos to and from the airport, last-minute tailoring emergencies and assuring that a brash republican did not share the elevator with a democratic diva fell to Alex.

"I don't envy you your job today," Charlotte told him as they parted ways that morning. "But, if anyone can keep their cool around all that chaos, it's definitely you."

"Why thank you, Charlotte. So sweet of you to tell me I am the reigning king of chaos," he bowed before taking her in his arms to smother her laugh with kisses. "I will think of you being pampered in calm luxury."

"Luxury, undoubtedly, but calm will remain to be seen. Think of all the women invading the salon today - insanity." Charlotte knew of at least nine other women with appointments at her salon today for professional hair, makeup, and manicure services. She suspected there would be far more wedding guests there as well.

"Well, call me if you need help," Alex offered.

"Not a chance. I will see you when you are tuxedoed and glorious. I will be one of the many women fawning over you."

Alex laughed again. "You will be the only woman I have eyes for," he responded in a husky voice full of emotion. With a quick "have fun" and tight hug, they separated until the wedding.

Charlotte hated to admit it, but she missed him all day long. His smoldering eyes when he had told her he would have eyes only for her had made her heart skip a beat. She wished they could skip the wedding and spend the entire day in bed.

Several hours later, Charlotte was pleased she had stuck to her plans. The women had enjoyed a thoroughly hedonistic day. Four of them had met for a sumptuous brunch complete with champagne, then headed to the salon for manicures, pedicures, makeup application, and hair services. Alex had offered to pay for Charlotte when Regan invited her, and Charlotte had accepted the gift with alacrity. The moment she started her sugar and honey foot scrub, she was grateful to both Regan and Alex for the indulgent experience.

Now, dressed in the violet gown that Katie had helped her select, Charlotte felt gorgeous. She hated having to enter such a sizable crowd alone, but knowing she looked elegant certainly helped overcome her fears.

Wobbling unsteadily after months on low shoes, Charlotte exited the elevator on the eighth floor into a fairyland of flowers, candlelight and beautiful people. Servers moved on silent feet through the enormous and noisy crowds, passing cocktails and canapes. Elegant men and women talked politics or rehashed their day in the windy city trying to outdo or out argue each other. Charlotte looked for a safe group to attach herself to and was relieved when a hand steadied her on the plush carpets.

"You look ravishing tonight," Randall Parker offered sincerely, not a hint of flirtation in his voice. "My fiancé has sent me to fetch you and bring you safely through the assemblage to our little nonpolitical enclave."

"Thank you, kind sir. That would be welcome indeed," Charlotte said before giving him a peck on the cheek, wiping off the lipstick she left there and then taking his arm.

Randall navigated the outskirts of the room and delivered Charlotte to a small seating area where Sloane was waiting, ravishing in a Zuhair Murad gold beaded gown. She was chatting with Missy, who was a perfect foil in her silvery blue dress. Hovering over his wife was Missy's husband, Stephen, conversing with Tyler, Wyatt and Keeli, who wore a necklace that took Charlotte's breath away. The heavy gold piece was incorporated into the chain creating a single large shape encrusted with diamonds and sapphires. Charlotte knew it would be the envy of every woman in the room.

When Charlotte gushed over the piece, Keeli fingered the necklace gently, smiling in gratitude. "Tell Alex you like it, Charlotte. I am sure he will buy it for you."

"Oh, I wish I could," Charlotte gushed, looking at the piece with longing. "I have never seen anything like it."

"Well then, seriously, if you won't tell him, I will get Wyatt to do it. Christmas is right around the corner."

"Don't you dare," Charlotte told Keeli, scandalized at the thought. Charlotte realized things were different for this crowd. The idea that the gowns, the jewelry, the vacations were easily afford-able was second nature to these people. Before entering this world, Charlotte would have considered a new pair of running shoes an extravagant Christmas gift. Economizing was something they had never experienced and could never understand.

"I would never take advantage of Alex that way. But I might have to discuss buying it for myself. I will call you next week," Charlotte promised, realizing she had the financial wherewithal now to buy herself such a gift. She didn't need a man to drape her in gold and diamonds. She could do it herself.

Oh, Carlotta Rocha, if only these people knew how far you have come.

"Okay. Have it your way, but jewelry is always so nice as a gift. And the guys are always at a loss about what to get us. A gentle hint...."

"I mean it, Keeli. Not one word."

After hugs and compliments on appearance, the group moved in unison toward the ballroom to find seats where they could see the processional. Alex came forward quickly to usher them to the bride's side.

"Charlotte, you take my breath away," he murmured in her ear as he placed a soft kiss on her bare neck. "Don't tell Aubrey, but I think every eye will be on you."

"Tease," Charlotte accused, but she blushed with the compliment, kissed Alex lightly, and moved out of the way and into a seat. Getting this many people seated and quiet would be a challenge. She knew they were counting on the change in the music to do the trick, which it did.

A hush descended on the room quieted as soon as the string quarter played the soft sounds of Jeremiah Clarke's Trumpet Voluntary.

The processional began when the groom's parents, bursting with pride, took their measured steps down the flower-draped aisle. They were followed by the bridesmaids on the arms of the groomsmen, all looking elegant. One, who briefly caught a stray heel in the white fabric draping the walkway, even stumbled without looking awkward.

There were a large number of attendants, so it felt like forever, but finally Aubrey was standing at the end of the aisle on her father's arm, looking lovely and innocent. Her Marchese gown of tulle, lace, beading, and pearls showed off her figure without overwhelming her small frame, and the simple bouquet of calla lilies was perfect. She was a storybook bride. Adam, at the top of the aisle, was gazing upon her with so much love that Charlotte, who didn't believe she was sentimental, felt a tear well in the corner of her eye. She dabbed at it quickly and noted several women around her, as well as a man or two, doing the same. Gazing at Alex, she saw him looking with soft eyes as his sister was joined with the man of her dreams.

The service was lovely, performed by a woman pastor from Aubrey's Lake Forest church with a wonderful combination of humor and gravitas and with warm personal references. It was obvious that Aubrey had grown up in the church and was well known and well liked. Soon Adam was kissing his blushing bride, and the ceremony was over. The huge crowd followed the recessional from the room, politely exiting row by row, as if they were disembarking a plane.

Alex skipped the reception line to find Charlotte, sneaking up behind her with two glasses of champagne and a large, public kiss. He looked so handsome in his classic tuxedo. His shoulders looked broad, and his legs looked especially long with the satin stripe creating the illusion of additional height. Alex had his thick hair combed from his rugged face, and the cleft in his chin appeared more prominent than usual, his eyes bluer.

"I must be the luckiest girl in the room," Charlotte told him. "You look breathtakingly handsome." Holding her hands, Alex planted small kisses her lips in response.

The ceremony had touched them both, leaving them more loving and attuned, in their own bubble, until well-wishers and friends or businesspeople asking Alex for advice or support repeatedly interrupted them.

"Okay if I call you next week?" they would ask before walking away. There were directors of organizations wanting to chat briefly about donations. Alex politely deflected them all.

"This is my sister's wedding day. Please call my office next week." Turning to Charlotte, he added in a low voice, "Thankfully, the election just ended, or I would be inundated with requests for support from that corner as well."

Watching the interaction, Charlotte realized what a powerful man Alex was in the community. Everyone wanted to assure they said hello, did some small talk that he would find memorable, pay him some compliment. They knew he had the financial capability to make or break them, either personally through his philanthropy or through business bank loans and deals.

When it was just the two of them, or when they rejoined the group of his childhood friends, it was easy to forget his wealth and influence. Then he was just Alex. She could see him physically change, dropping his guard and relaxing again.

No wonder he kept his friendships from childhood. He had known these men since they were boys, since the days when they could offer each other only a buddy to share a walk to school, defense in a game of football, a setup with that cheerleader they were eyeing or perhaps a stray answer to a test question. Alex was assured that they loved him for himself, not what he could offer them monetarily.

Besides, all of his friends had become successful in their own rights. Tyler and Wyatt were setting the world on fire, running Lyons Technical Solutions. The small startup was a powerhouse in real estate sales applications after only a few years. Tyler also kept his connections from his time as a partner in a prestigious law firm that handled Chicago's biggest clients. Randall had transitioned into running his family's private investment firm, scooping up all the new wealthy sports and entertainment figures to add to the firm's traditional old-money wealth. None of these men needed to get a handout from the others, but they always covered each other's backs, working as a team to solve problems.

How Charlotte wished she could team up with them to solve her problems now. In less than a week, she would be home, brainstorming with her family about how to get out of the mess with Gil and the problems she had created with her lies. She desperately wanted to clear the air with Regan and Alex and move forward in her new Midwestern life. The combined brainpower in this group of friends would have easily helped her out of her predicament, if only she could have asked.

"Charlotte," Alex interrupted her thoughts, "I want to introduce you to one of the newly elected Massachusetts representatives. I thought you might already know Ellen, since she represents the 7th congressional district, but she says you have never met. Charlotte Roche, may I present the honorable Ellen Barron. Ellen, this is Charlotte Roche, of the famous Boston Roche family."

"So pleased to make your acquaintance," Congresswoman Barron said, formally giving Charlotte a firm handshake. "I know your family well. They have been among my best supporters. I am very surprised we have never met."

"Well," Charlotte stammered, "I have been living here in Chicago during this election."

"But before that?"

"Yes, Charlotte," Alex added fuel to the fire, "I know how politically active you are. I can't believe your paths never crossed."

"Well, last election, I was still a student. Very heads down. But it is so nice to meet you now. Congratulations on your recent win. Massachusetts is lucky to have your cool head on the hill."

"Thank you so much. I am looking forward to getting some good work done."

"Actually, Ellen, Charlotte is planning to head home next week for some family time. Perhaps you can all get together while she is visiting." Charlotte threw Alex a pleading look, but he ignored it, forging ahead. "Don't you think that would be a great idea, Charlotte? I am sure Ellen would love a chance to say thank you in person before the session begins. Maybe you could set something up?"

"Oh, I would love to," Charlotte began, scrambling for an intelligent excuse to get out of this latest discussion without digging an even bigger ditch to crawl out of later. "But actually, my family is planning to spend the week in Rhode Island. We have a house on the shore."

"Oh, how unusual for November. But lovely. Newport this time of year is rather chilly, but at least it is less crowded." Ellen observed with polite surprise. "I assume you are heading to Newport?"

"Yes, Newport. There is always lots to do, even in November, and we just want quiet time together," Charlotte replied, promising to take a drive down to the beach while she was home.

That way, this conversation will have at least a kernel of truth.

"Really? I had no idea." Alex gave Charlotte a seeking look. "You never mentioned it."

"Well, with all the wedding plans, it didn't seem important." Alex looked at her askance, but at least he dropped the topic.

The three talked politics for a few minutes before the Congresswoman excused herself to say hello to other influential people. Alex left as well to get them each another glass of champagne.

Charlotte took a coconut encrusted shrimp off the tray of a passing waiter without even thinking, focused as she was on the mess she had almost stepped into.

How would I have wriggled out of a 'family' meeting if the Congresswoman had insisted?

What was Alex about, anyway? He had brought the newly elected official over to meet her intentionally, trying to stir up trouble. Charlotte had seen that mischievous gleam in his eye.

He's trying to trip me up. Damn him. I should have known he hadn't dropped this when he stopped pressing me for answers.

Charlotte wanted to be furious, but she had a hard time being angry at Alex for wanting to know the truth. They both understood that trust was the foundation of a solid relationship, yet both could not trust the other.

What a friggin' disaster.

"Ready to go in?" Alex asked, taking Charlotte's hand. "I am absolutely starving." Alex escorted Charlotte into the ballroom, transformed during the hour of cocktails and small talk into a gorgeous dining room set up to feed an army. The lights reflected off the silver and mirror place settings, the flowers filled the room with white and pale greens and a fresh outdoorsy fragrance. Despite the enormous crowd, there was a dance floor, a large band playing on a dais and on display off to one corner, a magnificent wedding cake wrapped with the same delicate flowers and greenery.

Alex and Charlotte took the last two seats at the head table beside the newly elected senator and his wife. In addition, Laurel and Charles, Aubrey and Adam, Adam's brother and best man, Stuart, and his date, Ashley, and the maid of honor, Jenna, and her date, Ron, sat at the table. Talk was interrupted often by well-wishers stopping by, speeches and toasts, and of course, the ping of glasses demanding the bride and groom kiss.

Charlotte and Alex moved past the earlier tension caused by the conversation with Congresswoman Barron and joined in the festivities. Dancing began even as the food was served, with the requisite introduction of the newlyweds, followed by their first dance, dances with father, mother and in-laws.

The food and wine were plentiful and delicious. A winter greens salad with candied walnuts and fried goat cheese was followed by passion fruit sorbet to cleanse the palate before they served a perfectly seared filet mignon beside a succulent lobster and crab cake. Charlotte had intended not to overeat, but she had mindlessly eaten too many appetizers to quell her nerves in the large crowd, and the dinner was too good to resist.

"Dance with me a lot," she begged Alex. "I ate so much; I will have to dance off the calories."

"Nothing would please me more than to provide your aerobic exercise this evening," Alex laughed, offering his arm in a chivalrous move and leading her to the dance floor. "I promise to dance your feet off if you promise to be careful of that ankle."

"It's been months, Alex. My ankle is fine now."

"And we want to keep it that way, please."

The musicians struck up a medley of slow, romantic Beatles songs, and soon Alex was spinning Charlotte in his arms. He was a polished dancer, light on his feet, holding her lightly. Their heights were well matched for her to rest her head on his shoulder and nuzzle his neck.

"Have we danced together before?"

"Just that once at the fundraiser, the one at Navy Pier."

"Why don't we dance more, Char? I love holding you in my arms like this," Alex admitted as he spun Charlotte in a fast turn that left her lightheaded.

"I love being in your arms, Alex, on the dance floor and off. But if you spin me like that again, after all the champagne and food, I don't promise to remain upright."

Laughing, Alex slowed his steps for the rest of the dance before he took his sister in his arms while Charlotte watched from the sidelines. Looking at them together, it was obvious to Charlotte that they were not fully related. Their size and bone structure, and their coloring were all too different. It was equally clear that they loved each other. Alex was bursting with joy over his sister's happiness, combined with brotherly pride.

The night flew by. Charlotte ate the luscious dessert of mini-Crème Brule's, then found she couldn't resist the cake, a chocolate and white cake combination oozing with buttercream. As she polished off the last forkful, she was grateful to Katie for being wise enough to keep her out of a skintight dress.

Charlotte danced until her feet hurt, kicked off her shoes, then she danced some more. She met politicians, business magnates, and the mayor of Chicago. She danced with the senator and both of his sons. These men were easy to follow through the complex steps. So were Ethan Howe and all of Alex's childhood friends, so light on their feet. Finally, Ethan explained that in Lake Forest, ballroom dance was still alive and well in junior high classrooms.

"Oh, I wish I could have seen you guys at that age, learning to waltz," Charlotte laughed, pointing to Alex standing just off the dance floor with Wyatt and Tyler. "Having to ask a girl to dance? That must have been hilarious."

"I wasn't there when Alex and those guys learned, but it was pretty embarrassing when it was my turn."

Charlotte couldn't remember having a better time at a wedding in her entire life. She admitted as much to Alex as they headed back to their room long after 1:00 in the morning. She held her shoes dangling from her fingers, her toes peeking out from under her dress. In the elevator, she leaned hard against Alex's side, her head resting on his chest, exhausted and giggling. Charlotte never giggled.

"Are you drunk?" he asked her when she refused to stand on her own two feet.

"No, just tipsy. I am completely done in. I can't remember ever dancing so much."

"Ok, sleepyhead," he told her as he flashed his security pass to a stalwart guard, guided her down the hallway and dug in his pocket for the keycard. "Let's get you to bed."

Giggling some more, Charlotte batted her eyes at Alex. "I thought you'd never ask."

Alex deflected her remark, but once the door was closed behind them, he leaned her gently against it. He pressed his body fully against her, kissed her thoroughly, running his hands up her arms until he reached her neck, then her face, which he captured in his hands as he deepened their connection.

"Bed?" he suggested when they came up for air. Charlotte's lips were cherry red from the kisses, plump and inviting. Alex dipped his head again, closed his mouth over hers, and pushed her harder against the door, unleashing a storm of sensation in her blood.

Charlotte responded immediately, pushing against Alex, turning in place, and presenting her back to him. He slowly lowered the zipper of the Shoji dress, trailing moist kisses along her spine until she shrugged slightly, and the confection fell to the floor. Stepping over it like it was rubbish, she glided to the king-sized bed, moved the chocolate from her pillow to the side table and flipped off the light above it.

Laying back in a tantalizing, barely-there cream-colored bra and thong, Charlotte gave Alex a come-hither look and patted the bed beside her. He was yanking off his bowtie, jacket and ripping at the shirt-studs as he made his way to her. When his frustration grew, she assisted with the cufflinks that were suddenly more than he could manage. Then she reached for his zipper and slid it down, trailing her hand behind it to feel the hot, hard length of him.

Inhaling sharply, Alex kicked off his shoes and pants and fell on Charlotte like a starving man. They ripped at the remainder of each other's clothing clumsily, his breath warm and moist against her ear as he told her what he wanted. His lips closed down upon hers. Then he was sheathing himself in Charlotte's moist heat with a deep sigh of satisfaction. Charlotte felt molten heat in her veins and a flood of emotions. Wrapping her arms and legs around Alex's hard body, she clung to him. Moving slowly, inch by inch, Alex controlled the pace, keeping Charlotte painstakingly edgy and wanting, making things last for them both until they were clawing at each other in need.

Bearing down on her body, Alex drove into Charlotte, withdrawing slowly. She rose to meet his thrust, the slow rub and heat, the friction of her wrapped tight around him. His powerful hands skillfully explored every inch of her skin, leaving her begging with her body. Scoring her lips with his teeth, tongue delving deeply into her champagne flavored mouth, Alex pulled every response from Charlotte, who shivered with desire and insinuated her hands deep in his hair, holding his mouth to hers and drinking from it as if it gave her life. Charlotte was on fire for this man, clawing at his muscles, digging into his buttocks with her heels to pull him deeper inside her. Finally, rigid and demanding, Alex moved hard and fast into her waiting warmth, taking them both over the edge into oblivion, overpowering her with a flood of emotion.

She hugged Alex fiercely to her chest as they soothed each other in the aftermath of their lovemaking. Their mingled breaths were labored, slowing eventually as they continued to kiss and stroke each other. Charlotte's fingers wandered over his sweaty skin, gently kneading his muscles, then sliding across his skin. She still felt impossibly filled, Alex already growing hard again. The exquisite pressure was building inside of her, causing her to crave him yet again.

Alex caught her eye in the shadowed room, his eyes questioning her. Her inviting smile provided the answer, and he began to move slowly inside of her again. This time, he was slow and tender. Her body softened into his hard one and she met him kiss for kiss, thrust for thrust, until he picked up the pace. His movements grew more urgent, as did her desire, and he quickly surged forward, demanding that her body relent. He teethed her nipples that already ached from the friction of his movements, but the sensation just toppled her over the edge as she clung to him. Alex came into her, spilling his seed as her limbs folded around him.

Charlotte longed to stay like this forever, safe from the reality of the world, locked in his arms, feeling his warmth under her fingertips and his breath fanning through her hair. His body was heavy on her, but when he attempted to move away, she held him fast against her, trying to hold onto the feeling as well as the man. She loved feeling small beneath his weight, sheltered from the world, hidden under the solid feel of Alex. At times like this, Charlotte believed Alex capable of whisking her away from the spiraling web of lies, away from Gil and his mounting threats.

Charlotte loosened her grip reluctantly and allowed Alex to roll to his side of the bed before following behind him to wrap herself around his back. Laying there, feeling his heartbeat under her hand, listening to his breathing slow and even into a pattern of sleep, Charlotte realized she wanted this man forever.

She loved him. She was certain of it. She wanted to care for him, be there for him and have him be there for her, always. Lying there, allowing herself to feel the love, to bask in the realization of her emotions, Charlotte knew Alex was worth fighting for. This relationship was worth fighting for.

It was time to tell Alex the truth.

CHAPTER TWENTY-FOUR

Alex tossed the keys to Joe, the valet at Gibson's, and ran inside to meet the guys. He was late for their regular Friday night out, rare for him and not because of the usual hideous traffic. He was unable to extricate himself from yet another horrible phone call to the West Coast and he was more than ready to shake off the resulting frustration.

"Sorry," he mumbled, sliding onto a stool, and signaling for a drink from the server. "Widow Jane, light ice," he ordered, quickly grabbing the attention of his old friends.

"Bourbon?" Alex queried. "What's going on AJ?"

"Why does anything have to be going on?"

"Bourbon," Randall replied, knowing the one word was self-explanatory.

"You never start with bourbon unless something bad happened," Tyler added unnecessarily. "We all know it."

"Just a bad business situation, a call that I had trouble ending. It's why I am late. Just catch me up while I unwind from it."

The others had only been there about twenty minutes before Alex joined them, so they quickly brought Alex up to speed on what he had missed. They rehashed the week: work, a few missteps that had cost them a win in last week's hockey game, wives and girlfriends. They were just getting into vacation details when Alex arrived. Alex was happy to leave business behind and talk about vacation instead. Just thinking about the ski trip helped relieve the tension between his shoulder blades.

"My dad will be at the Tahoe house as early as next week," Randall told them. "The snow is already good, so he will head there earlier than usual. He will be champing at the bit for some friendly competition by the time we arrive."

"Do we want to skip Aspen then and go straight there?" Alex queried.

"You trying to get out of playing host?" Tyler ribbed Alex good-naturedly.

Aspen. Shit, will the trip still be on after I tell them everything? Will I still have a place there after this lawsuit? Maybe this is my last vacation in the house. I hadn't thought of that. Don't tell the guys that.

"Not at all, but I was thinking maybe we should reverse the order. The women might like a week in Aspen. The shopping alone should appeal to them, even if the slopes don't. Not all of them are skiers after all." Alex dropped his mask in place, hiding his thoughts from his closest friends. "I'm happy to host you, as always."

"Sloane will not be happy if she doesn't get some time at my place in Tahoe," Randall rightly observed. He knew his fiancé was wild about the house she had visited last year. It had been the fact that he owned the house that had sealed his marriage proposal and he still teased her she was only marrying him for the house. Good thing his ego wasn't fragile.

"Take her to see your dad," Wyatt suggested. "I am sure Keeli would have no problem with Sloane working from there."

"Even with the Christmas rush?" Randall asked, intrigued by the idea. "Couldn't hurt to ask her."

"Great idea. What do you guys think? Alex? Earth to Alex."

"What? Oh sorry, my mind was wandering."

"This must be some problem at work, man. C'mon, shake it off," Tyler encouraged as he signaled for another round of drinks.

"You're so right. I need to let it go. We could go to Randall's right after the New Year, then use Wyatt's plane," Alex looked over to get a nod of approval from Wyatt, "to hop over to Aspen with the girls."

"I love the idea," Randall agreed. "And maybe Sloane and I can spend the holidays with my dad instead of here. Now that her mom has a boyfriend, it might be easer to get away. I hate the idea of my dad being alone over Christmas."

"Not that he cares," Tyler tossed unsympathetically. "Your dad is used to being alone."

"That is harsh, Ty," Wyatt chided. "He has gotten used to being a widower, but that doesn't mean he likes it."

"Sorry, Randall, no offense meant."

"None taken."

"Does this mean Sloane's mom is getting a divorce? I wouldn't blame her," Tyler asked.

"I know officially they are separated. I think all those affairs and jail have worn her down. Not that I blame her either." Randall's disdain for his future father-in-law was clear in his voice.

"You're right about my dad, he may not care," Randall continued, "but since my mom died, I am not sure how he really feels. He might be lonely and just not saying anything." The men nodded their understanding and went silent for a moment, remembering the lingering illness that had claimed Randall's mother years earlier. His father had been chasing the best ski conditions ever since then, avoiding dealing with his grief.

"This is getting morbid," Alex told his friends. "Back to happier topics. You're supposed to be distracting me, remember?"

The conversation turned to the logistics of their travel, reminiscences of prior vacations and soon they were ordering another round of drinks. The Friday boys-night-out had started as a weekly ritual when they were in graduate school and although they met less frequently these days, the four men always made time to get together, have a drink or two and hash over their lives and their problems at least once a month.

"How was the honeymoon?" Tyler asked Alex about Aubrey and Adam. "They are back from Europe, right?"

"Yeah, I think so."

"You think so? Haven't you talked to them yet?"

"This business in California has me swamped."

"You know, AJ," Wyatt began gently, "maybe if you would tell us what the hell is going on out there, we might help."

"It's a long story. And it's complicated," Alex mumbled under his breath.

"We have all night," Randall offered.

"None of us are stupid," Wyatt added. "Just spill."

Alex hesitated. He wanted to unburden himself and he planned to do so in the near future, anyway. The men sat silently, watching the conflicting emotions cross his face but exuding no additional pressure.

"Oh, what the hell," Alex took a deep drink, finished his bourbon, and put the glass down with a thud.

"Promise to forgive me for everything—and I mean absolutely everythin—when I am finished telling you all of this. And swear not to tell anyone—and I mean anyone — until I tell you otherwise. That means Keeli, Wyatt. Or Sloane. Or Regan."

"Why would I tell Regan?" Tyler asked defensively. "There is nothing going on between me and Regan."

"Of course there isn't," the men all chorused sarcastically. "Let's save that problem for our last round," Randall suggested. "Okay, Alex. You're on."

"First, this is not really my secret to tell. I have not discussed it with my family and without their permission, I really shouldn't be saying anything. But now that the wedding is over, I am beyond ready to let this one go."

"Whoa," Randall interjected, leaning forward to rest his elbows on the table, "now you have me intrigued."

"Okay," Alex lowered his voice conspiratorially, and the rest of the men leaned in over the table. "I am having problems with my father's company. My real father, not Charles. You guys know Charles is not my father, right?"

"Sure, we all know your father died when you were a baby," Tyler answered for the men. "But we never knew he left you share of a company." The men all nodded in agreement.

"Well, that's not completely accurate," Alex offered, shamefaced. "Not shares, and not dead. I have a father I have been keeping secret for thirty-plus years. I made a promise to my mother that I would never tell anyone, but now things are blowing up. I want to tell Charlotte everything and I am sick of keeping secrets from you guys and the rest of the world. Besides, I am pretty sure it will be public knowledge soon, whether or not I want it to be."

"You have a father still living in California and you never told us?" Wyatt spoke for all of them, astonishment obvious in his tone. "You kept a secret this big from us—your best friends?"

"I promised my mother, Wyatt. She was embarrassed. Once she remarried and Aubrey was born, it became critical to her to keep up the appearance that we were a typical Lake Forest family. She wanted us to have all the advantages that Charles's money and pedigree could give us. She was afraid of a scandal, and sadly, after all this time, she may be about to get one."

When the men interrupted with questions, Alex begged them to lower their voices and to wait until he finished with the complete story. "I have been wanting to tell you all of this for ages, so just let me get through it and then I will answer whatever questions I can."

Alex took a deep breath and exhaled it loudly. "My mother grew up in California, and back in her teenage years, she would sneak out of the house to hang out on the beach in Laguna. The summer between high school and college, she met a surfer dude there, Zack, a Stanford drop out who was late in embracing the sixties. The guy was a complete stoner, but he was handsome and smooth talking, and my mother was head over heels in love with the guy by the end of the summer." Alex's friends sat riveted and silent. Alex could see that Wyatt was already piecing things together.

"Fall came. Her parents shipped her off to college, and Zack followed the waves to Australia. By Christmas, my mom was pregnant, and her family mortified. They threw her out, and she had no one to turn to. My dad was still halfway around the world. He didn't find out anything until the following summer when the baby, me I mean, was already born." Alex stopped to sip the drink the server delivered, waiting until they were alone again to continue.

"He wanted to marry my mom. I think he really loved her, and I think he was happy to raise a child with her. But my mom had been scrounging for six months by then, with no help from her parents. She went home with Zack to say she was getting married, expecting them to forgive everything."

"I gather that didn't happen?" Tyler prompted.

"You guessed it. My mom's family values were deep-seated. It was easy for them to make her see things differently. Zack had been a tolerable summer romance, but they saw he was lousy material for a marriage. After a few lectures from my grandparents, my mother loathed the idea of raising a baby with a man who lived chasing waves, getting high and surfing. All the things she had loved about him, she hated now—his life, his friends, his lack of ambition. She was no longer interested in marrying Zack, but she still had this baby on her hands.

"Well, you can figure out what comes next. Her family offered their help, after all, making up a story about a dead husband, and shipping her off to Chicago to live with her Aunt Connie. Within a few weeks of my mom's arrival, she met Charles, and not long after, she married him. She made a deal with Zack. She would send me West for the holidays when I was old enough to go on my own and in exchange, Zack let her take me away and have Charles adopt me. Those days, my dad didn't seem to care much. I think my mother had hurt him badly, and he gave me up without much of a fight."

Alex stopped, feeling the loneliness and rejection afresh after all these years. "I had way too much anger. Zack didn't stand a chance with me. We tried staying in touch with emails but cut off all visits when my mother worried that someone might find out the truth. I was more than happy to end the relationship. I just found it all confusing."

"But it's the 21st century, AJ. No one cares about shit like that anymore," Randall spoke for them all. "We care about secrets, asshole. You may not keep secrets from us. Although, this is a doozy. So, what if your father was a stoner who gave you up? I kind of like that you're a bastard. Gives us something to lord over you at long last." He gave Alex a gentle punch on his arm to let him know he was teasing, but the underlying hurt and distrust was there, and Alex sensed it.

"I reconnected with my dad late in high school. He influenced me a lot senior year and is a big reason I chose Stanford when you guys went East."

"I always wondered," Tyler admitted.

"I just assumed they gave you the biggest scholarship or something," Randall countered.

"Once Aubrey met Adam, keeping our past in the past was more important to my mother than ever. She was afraid that anything but a squeaky-clean background might be an excuse for a U.S. Senator to prevent a wedding. I never understood why it needed to be a secret, but I love her, guys, and I love Aubrey, So I kept her secrets all these years. And believe me, it wasn't easy. Other than immediate family, you are the only ones who know. Charlotte knows I am hiding something, but she doesn't know what."

"Hey, we get it wasn't your secret to share, man," Tyler spoke for them all. "But we appreciate you coming clean now. I hate the idea of us keeping stuff from each other."

"I can't believe we never figured anything out." Randall shook his head in disbelief. Wyatt remained silent, and Alex could see that he was just waiting for the other shoe to drop.

After rushing through the story of his childhood, the confusion of trips to stay with a stranger for vacation, Alex moved forward with his tale. "There were advantages, then and now. I learned to love the water. I was a beach bum when I was out there and a pretty good surfer. Once I was in college, I reconnected with my dad. He's a great guy and has a brilliant mind. My choosing his school was a bond, and we got along great during those four years. He became active in my life, and we have been solid together ever since."

"Now we know where you get your brains," Wyatt observed. "Okay, so what's going on now? When are you going to tell these guys who your father is?" Alex spun to look Wyatt full in the face and the knowing grin that met him was all the answer he needed. Wyatt knew who Zack was.

"Well, Wyatt, since you asked..." Alex began with a smile, "my family is fighting over controlling interest in the multi-billion-dollar company my father and his sister started. That would be the company I have been managing the last several years."

"What?" two voices asked in unison, while Wyatt just smiled more. "Your dad started the bank?"

"Not the bank, you idiots," Wyatt couldn't resist.

"Yeah, I thought that might catch your attention. No, not a bank. This bank I run," Alex offered, trying to drag out the suspense a bit, "has exactly one client, Maverix." He sat back, picked up his drink, clinked glasses with Wyatt, and the two waited while the information sank in.

"Maverix, the chain of stores?" Tyler asked.

"I thought they owned some sports channels. Aren't they that big media company?" Randall asked.

"I thought they were a clothing line," Tyler reiterated, confused.

"Yes, the stores, clothing company, media people. That Maverix. It started as a surfboard company back in the '80s. They are ubiquitous in California, Hawaii, Australia. They are also a $115 billion world-wide conglomerate and I am about to become their CEO. That is, if my father has his way."

Alex looked smug as he sat sipping his bourbon and watching the shocked and wondrous expressions move across the faces of his friends. "My father is stepping down from the company he founded and handing the reins to me. He has been grooming me for years."

"That's fantastic, Alex." "That's amazing." "Congratulations," his friends offered in unison.

"Oh my god," Tyler added, the light finally coming on for him, "your father really was a stoner. He was famous for it. You are talking about Zack Fairchild."

"Yep," Alex acknowledged, unashamed.

"Zack Fairchild. It was obvious. I cannot believe you two didn't figure it out," Wyatt taunted. "Geez, they have written enough books about him. Wild life, unbelievable surfer, rags to riches story."

"No rags. There was always some family money, but he ignored it when he was young. When he became a father, he decided he needed to take things more seriously. The family was in the HVAC business, not interesting to him, so Zack made some money off his passion. I think he thought he would win my mom back, but he was too slow getting there. But he did start the business with his sister, Joan."

"I fail to see a problem here," Randall cut to the chase. "You are running the largest company of its kind, raking in the dough and close with your father again. Where is the downside of all of this?"

"Yeah," Tyler added, "and you get a great dad in Charles, too."

"Well, it seems that I have a cousin, my Aunt Joanie's kid. Greedy little S.O.B. who wants to stop me from gaining a controlling interest in the company. I guess we kept the secret too well, because this little shit thought he would inherit alone. We kept him in the dark for too long. The good news is that we also kept the business world—and my mother's friends — from hearing that a hostile takeover was brewing."

"Do they have a legitimate claim?" Wyatt asked, jumping into the business, ready to problem solve immediately.

"I have 55 percent, he has 45. He wants to flip that. If that happens, I might get to stay president but cannot move to CEO. He is a VP now and wants to be CEO himself. I think if he got the job, he would work to oust me."

"I can't see any legal issue here," Tyler observed, putting on his legal hat.

"My father is losing his memory. Early signs of dementia," Alex explained. "Or he fried too many brain cells in his younger days. So, my cousin is threatening to sue for power of attorney to gain control of my father's affairs and, of course, his shares. The bank, i.e., me, has that power now. It's a disaster, really. It is tearing apart the family, making a lot of lawyers rich—no offense, Tyler—and driving down the company value."

"None taken," Tyler responded. "But AJ, if you have POA, I don't see how your cousin can take it away."

"He is claiming my father was not of sound mind when he signed it over to me. It's completely ridiculous. He did the paperwork ten years ago and immediately started grooming me in the business. Under his direction, I have been progressively taking on more and more responsibility. The paperwork has been in place for ages since we set up the bank a decade ago."

"Yeah, why the bank?" Randall asked.

"As a front to protect my mother and sister. It takes some digging to put the bank and Maverix together and then it is still a leap to connect the family dots. This protected everyone's secrets."

"Well, they can have no embarrassment that you run a huge and successful company, can they?" Wyatt asked.

"Unless someone asks how he came to run it," Tyler answered for Alex.

"Exactly."

"So, the wedding is over. Just come clean and take the bastards to court before they take you."

"Great plan, Randall. Of course, technically, I am the bastard." They all laughed at the weak joke, breaking some of the tension that had built around the table. "In truth, that is what I would like to do. But it would break my mother's heart, might mess up the business, and then there is Charlotte."

"Charlotte? What does she have to do with any of this?"

"Well, how do you think your father would feel, Wyatt, if Regan brought home her prospective bridegroom—a bastard child who was running a company started by a famous stoner? Yeah, there is wealth, but is that the bloodline he wants for his grandchildren? Charlotte comes from a Mayflower family. They are wealthy, influential, old New England stock. I can only imagine how they would feel. They would never look at me as acceptable husband material for their only daughter."

"Husband?" Wyatt gasped. "When did I miss all this? Did you ask Charlotte to marry you already?" Three sets of eyes were boring into Alex in surprise.

"No. Not yet, but I would like to think things are moving in that direction. We have a lot of issues to work through still, including this one, and it's major. I promise I will not keep a proposal secret if it comes to that."

"Absolutely no more secrets," Randall ordered, looking each man in the eye for agreement. They all nodded heads.

"I really like her," Tyler admitted. "I do not think she is the snobby type, AJ, despite her blue-blooded ancestors. In fact, she is more down to earth than any of us. She doesn't act like a blueblood at all, if you ask me. Have you seen her? She cooks and cleans, she told Sloane she always takes the bus. She's cautious with her money. I think she is the least snobby rich girl I have ever seen. Besides, if she loves you, she won't care."

"Well, I think I am about to find out if you are right. After that call today, I don't see how we can keep this fight out of the courts or the press. It will be the lawsuit of the decade," Alex told them, dejected.

"Especially with 24-hour news and Twitter," Wyatt agreed sadly. "I just know it will be all over Twitter. This is that business story that crosses over to news, like messy divorce stories. Sorry AJ, but I don't see how you avoid the sleaze factor."

"You know, I think Charlotte has secrets of her own," Alex continued, ignoring Wyatt's gloomy prediction. "I have been surrounded by family members keeping secrets from each other—me obviously—but my mother has kept this from Aubrey all these years and my grandparents were willing accomplices, pretending my father was dead. I am not sure how much Charles knows, either."

"I am so sick of secrets and lies," Alex stated vehemently. "I am not sure if I will ever completely forgive my mother for insisting I be her co-conspirator in all of this. It's exhausting, unethical and frankly, it puts up a wall between people that only honest, open communication can tear down. I wonder if Charlotte is even capable of open communication, and I wonder if I can get past it if she isn't. You know what I mean?"

"Sure," Wyatt sympathized. "Of course, we know what you mean. After having secrecy your entire life, you must crave honesty in ways we can only imagine."

"You know," Randall added, "I knew exactly what I was getting with Sloane." The men groaned, remembering Sloane's manipulative ways, teasing Randall about how she tried to get the upper hand repeatedly, first with Wyatt, then with Randall.

"I still don't understand how you worked things out," Wyatt admitted.

"But back to Alex," Tyler reminded them. "Either you get to a place where you can trust Charlotte or you have to move on, man. Trust is critical."

"Especially for me," Alex added. "But enough. That is my saga, the good, the bad and the ugly."

"You will have celebrity status, AJ," Randall told him, gleefully adding, "like when Anna Nicole Smith died, and they fought over her daughter." The guys groaned at the tawdry reference, sending Randall into guffaws at his own joke.

"I am sure you have a slew of fancy lawyers, bro, but I would love to help where I can," Tyler offered, getting back on track despite Randall's continued laughter.

"And I will spare him for the task," Wyatt added.

"Oh yeah," Tyler looked sheepish, "I guess I should have asked first, boss."

"Thanks, Ty. That means a lot to me. I will let you know if I need you. So, you guys aren't mad about the secret?"

"Of course we are," Randall answered, all signs of laughter stopping abruptly. "But we'll forgive you as soon as you pay for the next round."

Alex laughed and did just that.

CHAPTER
TWENTY-FIVE

Charlotte disembarked in the overcast November afternoon, looking around the Providence airport for signs of friend or foe. Thankfully, there was no sign of Gil, but her parents were present, waving like mad from the other side of the security checkpoint. Charlotte broke into a run as she grew close.

"Mi Palomita," her father said, hugging her tight against his broad chest and smothering her in his thick coat.

"Papa, I can't breathe," she told him gently after a moment, stepping back as he reluctantly loosened his grip. She immediately wrapped her arms about her mother and held on fiercely. It had been almost six months since Charlotte had last seen her, the longest they had ever been apart.

Her mother, her hair grayer but otherwise unchanged, held her at arm's length and looked her over carefully. "You look tired, Carlotta. Tired and fat."

"Gee, thanks, Mama," Charlotte said, laughing and hugging her mother again before taking the handle of her roller bag and moving them toward the exit.

"She's not fat, Mama. Don't be unkind. But Carlotta," her father conceded, "you look a little chubbier."

Taking no offense from the honest statements, Charlotte explained to them. "I stopped running, but I haven't stopped eating. I will take the weight back off by the spring." She had gained seven pounds, and on her lean frame it showed. Fuller cheeks surrounded her delicate features and her middle was softer, not that they could see that hidden beneath her winter layers.

"Is this any way to welcome your prodigal child?" Charlotte continued, teasing them as they walked toward the parking lot. "I thought you would be happy to see me, but if I am an embarrassment..."

"Not at all, Little Dove, not at all," her father assured her, wrapping his arm around her.

"Are you kidding?" her mother asked in her accented English. "I am never letting you go back to that terrible city. You stay away too long."

"How do you know it's terrible if you never visit?"

"Who has invited us?" her father asked pointedly. Charlotte had the good grace to blush furiously and stammer something about being busy settling in.

"You must be busy. You never call anymore either," her mother commented. "So, what's his name?"

"I don't know what you are talking about," Charlotte lied.

"Of course, you do, Pequena. You call every day for months. Then suddenly you call once or twice a week if we are lucky, and you can't talk long. You never say where you go, who you spend time with. I am your mother, Carlotta, and I am not stupid. It must be a man."

"We weren't born yesterday," her father added in Portuguese under his breath.

"I know you weren't, Papa. Okay," Charlotte conceded, throwing her hands in the air. "I have been seeing someone, but it's still very new.

It might be nothing, and besides, I thought I would just wait and tell you all about him when we were together."

"Is he Catholic?"

Count on Mama to cut to the chase.

"Mama, could we at least get in the car before you grill me?"

"Ach, he is not Catholic," Charlotte's mother whined to her father, as if Charlotte were not there.

"So, where are the boys?" Charlotte asked, hoping for a reprieve. "I thought they would come to the airport. It feels so good not to be sneaking around." Charlotte had contacted both the courts and the local Providence police about being in town, wanting to assure that Gil could not violate her restraining order. She could only hope now that it would be enough.

"Go ahead. Change the subject for now. We can discuss this later," her mother promised.

"Your brother Jacabo is at the factory today and Donato won't be home until tomorrow. We are all going up there for his graduation, Carlotta. It better be on your calendar."

"It is, Papa. I promise. I wouldn't miss his big day for anything."

"Will you bring your fancy new boyfriend?" her mother asked pointedly. "Or maybe you could bring him for Thanksgiving?"

"Mama, would you just lay off? He's not my boyfriend, and he's not fancy. And I am not sure I can come for Thanksgiving."

If Charlotte could have, she would have dropped to her knees on the spot and clasped her hands together in prayer. Instead, she mumbled under her breath. *"Please, God, forgive me for lying straight to my mother's face. Oh yeah, and for the thousand other lies I have told lately."*

"You stayed away to avoid Gil, but he obviously knows where to find you, Carlotta, so I think with or without your man, you better be home for Thanksgiving." Her mother was certainly an expert at laying on the guilt.

They spent the congested I95 drive from the airport to their Fox Point neighborhood home discussing both Charlotte's new job and current activities at the Old-World Foods plant. Business was booming, and the online business had doubled again this year. The biggest issue concerning her father was that they were growing too fast. It was a realistic concern. If they could not handle orders in a timely manner and continue to manage quality, their reputation would be on the line.

"Jake understands all of this, Papa. I am sure he has it under control."

"Don't you think he would do better if you helped, Palomita? You have those impressive Harvard degrees, after all. What about your man? Is he well educated?" her mother tossed in.

"So does Jake, Mama. He can handle it," Charlotte responded a bit too sharply. Her mother's interrogation was getting under her skin. She should have seen this conversation coming from a mile away, but she was caught off guard and allowed a bit too much irritation to creep into her voice. "Sorry, Mama. You are right, it would have been nice if I could help, but I had to get away and we all know it."

"I just miss my little Principessa," her mother admitted, wiping a tear as it slipped down her cheek. "You are my only daughter."

"Don't, Mama, please. I am here now, aren't I?"

Oh no. The dreaded tears, complete with childhood nicknames and heavy guilt. Mama is a master at this, damn her. Charlotted conceded. She really needed to come home more often, if only to avoid this guilt trip.

"I miss you too, Mama. And you too, Papa. But I love my new job and Chicago is such a fun city. Let me tell you more about it," she offered, trying to buy some time.

"I would rather hear about the man." Her mother was relentless.

Fortunately for Charlotte, they turned onto her street, and she used the last few minutes of the ride to ask about the neighbors. Then the sight in the driveway stopped the conversation completely.

"What is he doing here? Did you know about this?" Charlotte directed her sharp tone at her mother. "Did you? I have a restraining order. Did you forget?"

"No, Carlotta," her mother's exasperated reply came quickly. "I did not forget. But we are here to keep him in line, and he promised he would behave. He just wants to talk."

"And you believed him?" Charlotte was furious, and more than a little frightened. "Call Jake and tell him to come home, or I am calling the police instead. Now!"

"That won't be necessary, Carlotta. Gilberto promised us."

"Papa. You cannot believe his promises." Charlotte reached for her cellphone and dialed quickly, dispensing with niceties when her brother answered. Charlotte wrapped her voice in steel. "Gil is here, Jake. Come home now."

"I am not calling the police, not this soon," Charlotte whined into the phone. "Can't you just come, please?"

Her brother said something while they all waited in silence and then Charlotte responded, "okay, but not one minute longer." She hung up. "He will be here in 20 minutes," she told her parents. "I am not setting foot indoors until he gets here, and you are not leaving me alone with that man. Do you understand?"

"Carlotta, we will freeze out here," her mother pointed out.

"Too bad," Charlotte replied stubbornly. "Outside or not at all." She stepped from the car and repeated the words loudly to Gil, who raised his hands in innocence and agreed to her terms. "We will talk about this later, Mama. This is not the way to get me to move home."

She pulled her coat tight around her, moving further from the car, barking, "What the hell do you want?"

"I just want to talk, Namorada. I swear."

"Stop calling me that. I am not your girlfriend. Gil. I am not your anything."

"But you could be. You should be."

Gil looked handsome standing there looking innocent. Listening to his softly lilting accent, looking at his trim fit body, Charlotte felt the pull that had attracted her to him back in high school. He stood tall, dark, and exotic. His chocolate eyes were nearly black and mesmerizing. His smile was broad and white against his olive skin, lighting his features as if he were an angel.

He was certainly no angel. Anything but.

Charlotte was reminded of the day she looked at Gil with maturing eyes, no longer seeing the little boy she had grown up with but a young man, handsome, confident, and full of promise. Charlotte felt emotions that were new, exciting. Attracted to him, she flirted uncharacteristically, neglecting her studies when he was around, opting to go for rides in his parents' car, parking on dark street corners and making out until she was restless with wanting.

That was old history. Charlotte knew better now and refused to let him worm his way back into her life. "Remember who Gil really is. Remember Alex," she repeated as a mantra while Gil tried to sweet talk her.

Alex. He was everything that Gil would never be. He was her future, if she was lucky. This man in front of her was her past—over and done with. And an ugly past, ultimately.

"You need to come home, Carlotta," he interrupted her thoughts. "Your parents need you at the plant. Your brother needs your help in the front office. They miss you. I miss you. It's time to shed this false persona and get back to being you. You belong in the neighborhood, in this family, and with me."

"Over my dead body, which, if I stayed with you, would be my future."Gil stepped back, shocked by the harsh words, but Charlotte gained strength from his affront and continued in a more powerful tone.

"It was you who chased me away, Gil. You should have thought about that before. We were children when we got together. Children. Things changed for us both. We have gone our separate ways. I have moved on and you should, too. You need to let go."

Charlotte had started the conversation by leaning against the door of her parents' car with Gil at the curb, a good thirty feet away. She had not been paying close enough attention as he stepped on quiet cat feet, closer and closer to where she was standing. He was menacingly close now and, with the car at her back, she had no escape route.

"Not such children, Carlotta. Your mother was eighteen when she got married."

"In Portugal. In a small town and so that she could come to America with my father. They would have waited otherwise. Don't come any closer, Gil."

"But look at them. They are happy. They have built a wonderful life, children, a successful business, friends. We should have that, Car. We deserve that." Gil pointed at her parents, huddled together for warmth in front of the open door to their house.

"Maybe we do, Gil, but not together," Charlotte insisted, trying to remain calm. They had been over this time and time again. "Don't come closer," she barked as he took several steps toward her, closing the gap. "I mean it."

Standing still again, Gil reached his arms toward Charlotte, palms up as if to show her he meant her no harm. He could have reached out and touched her had he chosen to, and her skin crawled with the realization.

"I love you, mi Amada. I always have. I want to marry you and take care of you. Not like that pig you live in sin with back in Chicago. What does he offer you? Nothing. He shames you. He shames your family. I offer you marriage and a future here in your community, where you belong."

"You leave him out of this," Charlotte spit. "This is about you and me, Gil, no one else. You do not love me. You love a childhood dream. You do not want to take care of me. You want me to take care of you, to find you a place at New World, a place near the top where you can push people around."

"That's not true."

"It is true," Charlotte insisted, her voice rising sharply as her patience wore thin. "You could have gone to college, Gil. You had the grades and the financial wherewithal. Your parents begged you to go. I helped you with applications. You could have made something of yourself."

Charlotte was gesturing rapidly, passionate in her speech. The man had thrown everything away. "Instead, you stayed in the old neighborhood, hanging out with the old crowd, and going nowhere, getting in trouble, bullying, and hurting people. Why would I want a loser like you, Gil? Give me one good reason."

"One reason, Querida? Alright, Carlotta Rocha, let me give you one reason," Gil stood taller, his demeanor more like the threatening Gil she had learned to fear and avoid. "I know you, Car. and I know you lied your way into your new job. You let those people in Chicago think you come from the Boston Roche fortune. I know all about you, Car, and I am not keeping your secrets if there is nothing in it for me."

Gil stepped closer as he spit the alarming words, grabbing Charlotte's shoulders and squeezing tight. She would have bruises there within the hour.

"I told them all the truth a long time ago, Gil. No one cares. Let go of me." Gil knew her well, but she kept a blank face and prayed he would not see through her bravado.

"You're lying, Carlotta. You always were a terrible liar. But I am not lying. First, I will expose you and cost you your big shot job and your millionaire with his swanky life." He squeezed harder, lowering his face to within inches of hers so that her father, across the yard, would hear nothing. "Then I will ruin your family, Carlotta. I am not bluffing. You know I can. I can destroy the business they are building, maybe cost someone their entire future. Are you willing to risk that?"

Charlotte stood still and cold, tears streaming down her face at the reality of Gil's threat. He knew too much.

"Then you will come crawling back to me with nothing but your fancy degrees. No friends, no family, no job. A lesser man would walk away, but I love you, Car, and I will take you back. And I won't hurt you again, Carlotta. Just come home and marry me. I will never raise a hand to you again. I told you I was sorry. Hitting you was a big mistake, but a mistake I won't repeat. I swear, Car. Just come home to me. Come home to help your family."

Gil released his hold on her arms, as if only then realizing he was gripping her painfully. Then he lowered his mouth to hers and kissed her gently, but thoroughly. "I will keep your secrets, Querida, but you must give up Chicago and come back here. Come home to me, Carlotta. Make this right."

Tires squealed behind Charlotte, breaking her trance and causing Gil to jump back from her. Charlotte wiped the back of her hand across her lips to remove any trace of the snake that had slithered into her life again. Jake leaped from his car the moment it stopped and ran to stand between Gil and his prey.

"Get out, Gil. Go now, before I call the police."

"I'm going," Gil told Jake, hands up in surrender. "Remember what I said, Carlotta. I mean every word. Come home before year end or else."

"Saia!" Jake hollered as he wrapped his arm around his pale and shaking sister protectively. "Get out now!"

Gil walked past the house to his parked car and climbed in without another word as Jake turned to walk Charlotte into the house. "I am only doing this because I love you," he called to Charlotte from his open window as he drove away, the sound of the souped-up engine loud in the stillness.

She recalled the triumph in his voice long after he was miles away.

CHAPTER TWENTY-SIX

A lex took Tyler up on his offer of help, even though he wasn't sure what he could do. It was just nice to have a friendly face around when the shit hit the fan, and even nicer to introduce a friend to his father. He had wanted to bring the boys to meet him for years. Now he wanted Zack to meet Charlotte, too. He knew he was running out of time.

Charlotte. He wondered how she was doing with her family and reached to call before he remembered the time difference. It would have to wait until tomorrow. He could not believe how much he missed her. She had become critical to his happiness and the sooner he resolved everything with the business and his family, the sooner he could stop these incessant trips West and tell her the truth. He just hoped that she would forgive him for lying, and that her family would accept him as he was.

"Earth to Alex," Tyler teased him now. "Oh man, you've got it bad, my friend." Tyler had simply asked what Charlotte was up to while they were in L.A. In response, Alex's face had softened, and his eyes had glazed.

"Yep. Guilty as charged," Alex admitted.

"Why didn't you invite her out here with you? You have talked or texted with her enough."

"I would talk to her more, but she's in Boston with her family. Well, in Newport actually. They own a house on the beach, of course."

"At this time of year?" Tyler's surprise matched the shocked face Alex had made when he had heard the news.

"I know, weird huh?" Alex agreed. "Those New Englanders. They do things differently, I guess. I thought we appreciated cold winters, but I hear they are hearty souls."

"I guess," Tyler agreed as they headed back to the hotel after a long day of meetings. "Let's stop in the bar. I could really use a drink."

"Sounds good to me."

"Nothing personal, Alex, but your family is pretty awful. Not your dad. He's very cool," Tyler corrected, "but that greedy cousin Jeffrey is revolting."

"You noticed," Alex responded drily as they found a quiet table and ordered drinks. "He has worked hard, don't get me wrong, but not like I have. Nor has he worked as closely with my dad. He hasn't bothered to understand Zack's vision for Maverix. Now, he wants controlling interest. That can only be to stop me from moving forward in the direction my father laid out. He wants to prevent him from fulfilling his dream for the business."

"Not his. Yours," Tyler corrected.

"You're right, of course. It's my dream he wants to destroy. And all because of some stupid, petty jealousy."

When Tyler had volunteered to come to L.A. with Alex as both legal counsel and friend, Alex didn't realize how much it would help. First, Tyler was a sharp legal mind, able to assist the Maverix lawyers think innovatively. Second, he could translate all that lawyer-speak so that Alex understood the nuances of the lawyers' actions in ways he had not previously. Third, and best of all, he was supportive, an unconditional friend on his side when he really needed one.

The two men sat huddled over drinks, discussing the case for about an hour, nursing their drinks, nibbling on a bowl of nuts that the server replenished twice before leaving menus and suggesting they might want food. It was late for dinner, but the two men ordered sandwiches and, with a legal pad in front of Tyler, they strategized yet again. Tyler believed Jeffrey had no case, but admitted his lawyers were trying to create a stranglehold of legal mumbo-jumbo until Alex caved in and bought him off.

The crux of the threat was simple, according to Tyler. It seems anything but simple to Alex.

"Just listen, Alex, and try to put your emotion aside for a sec," Tyler said. "Your Aunt Joan when she died recently... By the way, I am very sorry for your loss. Were you close?"

"No, but I know she and my dad were. Joan was the whole reason he could start Maverix. She put up money, and he put up sweat equity. She never interfered, though. He made all the decisions."

"Well, now Jeffrey has Joan's forty-five percent of Maverix and is your partner in the business. Quite simply, he wants controlling interest, or maybe all of it. That is not clear yet. I can't tell if the scumbag actually wants to run the show or if this is just a knee-jerk reaction to all those years of mounting jealousy and anger."

"Jeffrey has never moved past the fact of my existence," Alex acknowledged. "It didn't help that he was the golden boy. Someone should have told him about the lay of the land a lot sooner. I will concede we were unfair to him. After growing up never seeing me, not even aware that he had a first cousin, it must have been a shock to Jeffrey to find out at age fifteen that he had a cousin and that he had to share everything with him."

"You were what, seventeen? Not much older? And look at everything you had already been through with this damn family."

"Jeffrey was already laying out the life that he would lead as the head of Maverix, Inc. when he was just a teen. He could taste all that money and power. Suddenly, he's forced to share ownership of the highly successful company and the power and money that went along with it. Until that moment, he had always believed that one day it would all be his. His uncle Zack had no children to the best of his knowledge. It had seemed obvious to him he would inherit it all and run it all."

"Well, he's predictable about some things," Tyler observed. "The Maserati and the models were a bit of a giveaway, although you did the model dating thing, too. And you have that fancy Mercedes. Hmmm, maybe you and Jeffrey have a lot in common besides genetics."

"Bite me," Alex retorted with a laugh. "I am nothing like that money-grubber."

"No, but you are so easy to bait," Tyler laughed. Alex was sensitive now, so the simplest effort to tease went a long way. "You need to find your balance again, AJ."

"Yeah, you're right. I am just so furious that my dad did all this hard work, and it may be for nothing."

"Not nothing. Jeffrey has a good grasp of the business and I don't see him running it into the ground, after all. He prepared to inherit, and even you said he earned that VP position."

"You're right, Ty, as usual. But he doesn't want to share, he wants it all. Can't you feel it? He did great in marketing and even better running things on assignment in Australia, but he cannot see past his greed long enough to understand that there is plenty to go around."

"True. It would be great if he could embrace you as his older cousin instead of challenging you every step of the way."

"That's Jeffrey though. He doesn't want to share the attention or the company. Not after wanting the top spot for years and all the dreams he envisioned to go with it. He intends to get it all or ruin us both trying.

"I am determined that Jeffrey will not bring this lawsuit forward. Not if I can stop it. First, it's obvious that Zack intended his shares to go to me, and Zack had made it clear he wanted me in control now that he no longer feels as confident of himself. Zack completed all the necessary and legal documents to assure this occurred."

"Right." Tyler was nodding his head in agreement as Alex continued, devouring his sandwich.

"Second, no one wanted Jeffrey with complete control of anything, not with the selfish greed he displayed. They feared he might be too busy taking cash upfront to consider the long-term health of the company. Third, when Zack died, his will would return the voting rights of those shares to me anyway, opening the door for yet another fight with Jeffrey. No one wants to see that happen. Another fight would be toxic."

"I agree with everything you just said, Alex, but it doesn't get us closer to a solution."

"Finally," Alex continued as if Tyler had not spoken, "if the press gets wind of this, it will be terrible for business, which helps solidify the support of the entire Maverix board of directors behind me. Their unified front is supposed to keep the suit from ever coming forward, keeping the press from ever knowing of a potential fight for control."

"Of course, you need to avoid the press for personal reasons as well," Tyler reminded his friend. "A team of corporate lawyers has been pouring over documents both in L.A. and at the bank in Chicago trying to prevent Jeffrey from gaining power of attorney or bringing forward his suit. It's unlikely he would win, but keeping the suit from even being litigated is the primary goal. It's obvious that Zack is CEO in name only at this point."

Tyler shot Alex a sympathetic look and gestured to the sandwich sitting untouched before him. "Eat something. Not sure why, but it will help. Anyway, the bank, and by extension you, have the power to vote his shares and make his business decisions. You have Zack's personal power of attorney as well, right?"

"Yep," Alex agreed between bites. "All that would have stopped someone less determined than Jeffrey."

"Why would someone do all this if they know they are going to lose?" Tyler mused under his breath. "That is what I don't understand. He can't really want to ruin the company. It's the source of his income and, frankly, his prestige. So, what is he after?" Tyler let the thought trail off, staring at his empty plate, his mind far away.

Shaking his head, Tyler looked straight into Alex's face. "That is the key to all of this. Jeffrey has a very weak case. Any lawyer worth his fees is telling him to drop this suit, AJ. Or they should be. He will lose in court."

"But I really need it to stay out of court, and the press," Alex reminded his friend. "Jeffrey understands that there are secrets here. I believe his is counting on my aversion to this going public, that he is betting I will settle to keep the family issues private."

"An intrepid reporter might find and publicize the lawsuit if we filed it," Tyler conceded, "but it would likely be a business reporter less interested in the family back story."

"This is the age of 24-hour news. Everything is about digging up the dirt now. Privacy, decency, and personal consideration are things of the past. It would only be a matter of hours before it moved from the business press to TMZ and every talk show from there. I just want to keep my family background and my role in the company quiet, for my mother's sake."

The scenario Alex laid out was all too possible and would undoubtedly be damaging to his mother and Charles, and to Aubrey as well. Tyler understood, listening now that Jeffrey was using the threat of this exact scenario to manipulate Alex. Nursing his drink, Tyler was suddenly as sullen as Alex. He had no solution.

So far, they had all avoided getting Laurel involved. Many on Alex's side believed she might be able to help to calm Jeffrey. By taking the fall for keeping Alex's existence a secret, she might diffuse his anger at Zack and Alex. If she could do that, perhaps Jeffrey could abandon his need for revenge. But prior to the wedding, she was reluctant to step up, and Alex remained adamant about keeping her out of it, fearing a scandal that might jeopardize Aubrey's future.

"What about your mom, AJ? Maybe we should involve her after all?"

"Don't you recall my argument with her about this very topic? I told you that when Jeffrey first threatened me, I confronted my mom. 'What about my future?'" I asked her. I reminded her that I am just as much her kid as Aubrey is. I pointed out that I have worked years beside Zack to make this business the success it is."

"Yeah, I remember."

"I told her she reaped financial benefits from all that work, and so did Aubrey. All that time I was unable to acknowledge my real father, my real heritage, even my real job." Alex was getting angry just remembering the conversation. "Haven't I done enough? Don't you think I deserve this?"

"What did she say?"

You will be rich either way.' What kind of answer is that?" Alex didn't wait for Tyler to respond.

"My father's will assures that there will be plenty of money even if my cousin wins the case, and that seemed to be all my mother cared about. She reminded me that Charles has provided for me, too. To my mother, it is about money. To me, it is about my father's legacy, but she doesn't get that." Alex took a deep breath, trying to calm himself.

"I exploded at her, telling her it is not about the money. After all these years tamping down my emotions, feeling like a football passed between families, and avoiding the conversation, she boiled it down to money." Tyler was watching the frustrations of a child and a teen move across the face of an adult who felt he was losing his father all over again.

"I reminded her that the controlling interest is at stake. I was so exasperated with her, trying to remind her that Jeffrey is a greedy bastard."

"Does she really want you to just hand everything over to that bastard?"

"That bastard, as you so indelicately put it, is my family. Doesn't he deserve a share of the prize? My mother thinks he does."

"He has his mother's share. He has almost half." Tyler reminded Alex. "She can't expect you to give all this up without even a whimper?"

"She begged me to consider what I might be doing to Aubrey. She knew that would get to me."

"You are just claiming what is rightfully yours, AJ. Nothing more."

"My mother is concerned that I am claiming it publicly. 'You understand the scandal that will bring upon us? Upon your stepfather, on your sister, who is an innocent in all of this? Is that fair to her?' I hate when she uses Aubrey against me."

Alex could not fight his mother when she brought Aubrey into the equation, and she knew it. She had played that card repeatedly though out his life, every time Alex had asked about calling his father, or visiting him. He cared about Aubrey too much. It always worked. Alex would stop arguing with his mother after that, just as he did this time. But the hurt and the secrets remained.

"AJ?" Tyler brought Alex's focus back to the present. "I think the answer still lies in getting Jeffrey to think he has already won. That he has enough. You would think half of a company this size would be enough."

"You would think so, Tyler, but you would be wrong. He wants to be in charge."

"So let him be," Tyler answered after a full minute of silence. "We are so stupid. We are all so stupid. Let him be in charge."

Alex looked at Tyler like he was insane. "What are you talking about? The whole point of this is not to let that jealous, sniveling fox into my father's henhouse."

"Just hear me out," Tyler said, leaning forward and lowering his voice as he proposed his idea. Alex leaned in, nodding his head, a slow grin lifting the anxiety and exhaustion from his features.

"You, my friend, are a genius. I think you have something, Tyler. I think you have something that just might work."

CHAPTER TWENTY-SEVEN

The next morning, Alex took his father out to breakfast and told him Tyler's idea. Zack was all for it and suggested they have the board, and not Alex, suggest it to Jeffrey.

"That would remove any personal animosity," Zack explained. He was sharp today, firing on all cylinders, and Alex could see the brilliant mind that had propelled his father to such success. "If all goes well, we could neutralize Jeffrey as a threat of Jeffrey as early as this week."

"That would be fantastic, Zack."

"Anything to protect your mother, Alex. I did her a great disservice all those years ago, and she did the only thing she could that would allow her to keep her reputation and her family's dignity intact. She has certainly landed on her feet, and I believe she and Charles have been happy together. Still, I owe her this much. We need to allow her to keep her secrets."

Alex had heard this argument from his father many times over the years, but now, with Zack's memory fading, Alex pressed for more answers. "Do you still love her after all these years? You never married, after all."

"Now? I am not sure I would call it love anymore, or at least not the traditional definition of love. But I hold your mother in my affections.

She gave me my only son, for one thing," Zack smiled and reached over to stroke Alex's cheek, "and my memories of our short time together are very special. I will hate losing those most of all."

"Have you considered a video journal, Zack?"

"A video journal? After all the books written about me, all the newspaper articles, what's left for me to tell?"

"Well, your side of things, perhaps?"

"I granted a lot of interviews, Alex. I told my side of things."

"Not the personal things, Zack. Not the stuff I would want to know. No pressure, but you could think about it."

"I will, Son, and I promise not to take too long to decide. Time is no friend anymore. Speaking of which, when will you bring your girlfriend to meet me? I am sorry, I can't remember her name. I promise not to scare her away."

"Charlotte. I will bring her soon, Zack. As soon as I can."

Will there still be a lovely Charlotte in my life once she knows about Zack? How will I manage if she leaves me? I simply cannot allow that to happen. I just have to handle things perfectly. If only I knew how to do that.

Alex enjoyed spending time with Zack. Today he was alone, but he had brought Tyler by several times to meet his father. Tyler had commented on the simple beach house Zack owned and shared now with around the clock caregivers.

"You can turn me into a corporate giant," Zack had explained, with a laugh, "but the beach bum is never very far away."

In his lucid moments, Zack made Tyler tell him his versions of Alex's childhood stories, pointing out to Alex everywhere he had exaggerated with a wag of his finger. "So, you weren't the big shot of the game, huh?" he would challenge with a smile until Alex would confess, he might have built himself up a bit more than was true. He would apologize for the fibs and hyperbole, but Zack would just shake his head. "I would love you if you came in last, you know. I would love you no matter what."

Alex relished his time with his father. "If I had known twenty years ago that his memory would go like this, I never would have stayed away. Then it had been all about resentment and teen angst, but now, I want more time, Tyler. I want to do more work as colleagues. Now we're friends, but I never got to be a kid with him. I will always regret that."

"I know, AJ, but you still knew him well, and you still have a lot of years ahead, God willing. His mind may be going, but a lot of the time he is obviously all there.

"True, and by getting to know him as an adult, I have been able to respect Zack for what he has built and for his anti-establishment lifestyle. I might have had a hard time balancing one or the other years ago," Alex admitted. "Of course, it sure helps that I know he loves me, that he wanted me."

"True, but Charles loves and wants you, too. You were always wanted, my friend. Even we want you," Tyler joked, breaking the serious tone.

Taking advantage of this time earlier in the day, when he knew his father was more likely to be lucid, Alex ignored the legal threats, the problems, and spent hours sitting with him, speaking about life in general. Zack told him how much he enjoyed meeting Tyler. Alex told Zack about Aubrey's wedding, then he told him about Charlotte and his suspicions that she was hiding a big and dangerous secret.

"You cannot build a relationship on dishonesty, Alex. Just look at Jeffrey. Just look at the two of you. Look at the two of us."

"I know, Zack. I used to try pressuring Charlotte to spill her story, but now I just let her live her life, show her how I feel and hope that she will open up to me. What else can I do? Here's the thing, though. If she is frightened, I want to protect her and keep her safe, or help her keep herself safe. How do I do that when I have no idea what she is fighting?"

"I have faith in you, Son. You have never failed at anything you put your mind to. I can see that Charlotte means a great deal to you. I must admit, that pleases me. She sounds like a wonderful woman, and I look forward to meeting her. Don't wait too long to bring her out here."

"I promise, Zack," Alex offered yet again, wondering if his father remembered that they had discussed this earlier. It saddened him to realize they were running out of meaningful time together, despite Zack's good physical health.

"Can you try to get the emotion out of the way and let logic prevail? You might see things with Charlotte more clearly then, be better able to interpret the little signs and slipups. I imagine even Charlotte is not that good a liar. It would take KGB skills to fool you, Alex, if you were paying attention."

Alex pondered his father's words and realized that he was right. His reputation in business and with his friends was as the logical one, the puzzle solver and clear thinker. With Charlotte, he f clearly from the very beginning.

"I love you, Dad," Alex said with emotion.

"Dad. You haven't called me that in years," Zack observed.

"It feels disloyal to Charles somehow," Alex admitted.

"I don't want that, for either of you. But sometimes, when you slip, it feels good."

"To me too, Dad, to me too."

"Now," Zack continued, dropping all sentimentality, "give me a pencil and paper, and let's deal with Jeffrey so we can move on to Charlotte and solve this mystery once and for all."

CHAPTER
TWENTY-EIGHT

C harlotte knew Alex was disappointed when she failed to extend him an invitation to spend Thanksgiving with her family, but she could not take him home until she told him everything. How could she fly him into Providence and introduce him to the Rochas from Fox Point when he expected to fly into Boston and meet the Roches of posh and wealthy Beacon Hill? She wanted to stop lying, but Regan deserved the first explanation and Charlotte still believed it was too early in her job to have that conversation.

"I will be back before you know it," she told him as she waited in the chill November weather for the limousine he had called to take her to the airport. They had argued all week about this trip. They had argued about everything since Alex had returned from California. A weekend apart would do them both some good. They had been apart just two weeks ago, though, when she was supposedly in Newport.

More apart time was not helping.

"The blue line would be so much more efficient. It's Thanksgiving at the world's busiest airport. It's crazy to drive there."

"We aren't driving there," he had responded in exasperation. "I am hiring someone to drive you there. Think of it as creating jobs over the holidays."

"That just semantics," she had argued, but she had smiled at his logic and here she was waiting for the limo. Eventually, she had given in because of his logic and because they were struggling with so many bigger problems.

Alex had hinted broadly that he wanted an invitation to her home, but she was still hiding her background. There was no way he would have been comfortable with Chorizo stuffing, a lot of swearing in Portuguese, and too many bodies crowding around a family table. She could just imagine his surprise when she brought him to the federal-style two-flat where her parents lived on the bottom floor, and Jake on the top. It would be a far cry from the elegant Beacon Hill row house she had allowed him to think she was heading to, where servants would serve a sumptuous dinner to a historic and powerful family in a high-ceilinged, elegant dining room.

"I hate being away from you again so soon," she told him, resting her forehead against his suit coat. He was not even wearing a jacket as he stood waiting with her in the chill air.

"Then don't go," he responded. "Call your parents and tell them you saw them two weeks ago and you are staying here."

"I can't Alex. Not my first Thanksgiving away."

"You and your Mayflower ancestors. Thanksgiving must be a pretty big deal for you guys, I guess."

"We have a lot to be thankful for this year. Me especially. I found you."

"Go ahead. Sweet-talk me." He laughed before kissing her gently. "I am just going to miss you, that's all."

"Me too."

She was saved from giving in to the tears gathering behind her eyes by the arrival of the limo and the jostling of luggage. She was waving goodbye before she knew it, and in the quiet interior of the car, she had time to let her mind wander and to review the last few days. Charlotte was grateful someone else was left dealing with the heavy, stop and go traffic.

Alex had returned from L.A. in a fantastic mood, although he refused to tell her why. "The business went really well," was all he offered, despite a myriad of questions from her. It rankled her that he shared so little since he asked for details about her work all the time. When she pointed this out to him, they argued. Then they fought repeatedly about her trip to Boston. The worse battle had come when they tried discussing Charlotte breaking the lease on her apartment.

It had been almost three months since Charlotte had moved in with Alex after the incident in the park. The only things left at her apartment were some dishes and her out-of-season clothes. She had moved her few pieces of furniture and found places for the beat-up antiques within the modern décor of Alex's place. The closets held her clothes, the drawers held her underwear. They now shared the bathroom equally. Her books filled his shelves, and her pots filled his kitchen. He had converted the back bedroom into an office for her, assuring that the Wi-Fi connection was strong there and installing a dedicated land line for the phone.

Alex kept repeating that they were living together, and she should just pay the penalty to be released early from her lease. She said she was just staying there for a while, insisting that she wanted the ability to go back home again. She knew she was denying the truth. He had converted a room to an office, for heaven's sake. She had moved all her belongings. She was just fooling herself. When he pointed these out to her, a huge argument had ensued, their biggest to date.

"Just admit that you live here," he had demanded, after several dead-end discussions on the subject.

"But I don't live here," she had countered. "We never discussed my moving in or anything. I am just here because of circumstances."

"Do you really believe that?" She could see that Alex was hurt by her statement. "Why do you need to keep one foot in that other world? Why can't you commit to this? To us? I have."

She understood his logic. She loved the relationship and his willingness to commit to her, but she also knew that she had to tell him who she really was, where she really came from. Until she did that, she could not be sure he would really want to live with her. She would no longer be the rich, important Charlotte. She needed to know that Alex could love the poor, working-class Charlotte, and the lying Charlotte. But she couldn't tell him that yet. Instead, she gave him excuses even she could see were feeble; then they clashed.

That recurring argument spilled over, tainting everything. Soon they were fighting about what to have for dinner, what to watch on TV. Everything. Alex's post-California high was gone, replaced by a tense and frustrated mood. She knew she was hurting him, confusing, and disappointing him, but Charlotte needed a little more time. She had committed to telling Regan the truth before the New Year. After that, she risked that Regan would hear it from Gil instead.

Charlotte was glad to be getting out of town. She needed to do something about Gil so she could tell the truth. She was losing sleep, filled with trepidation whenever she went out. It was hurting her work and damaging her relationship. Charlotte made herself a promise to move up her timetable and reveal everything before Christmas.

"Just until Christmas, Alex. After all," she teased, trying to lighten the mood a bit the last time they had argued over the lease, "I'll need a good place to hide presents."

"Like this place isn't big enough," he had responded sarcastically. But he dropped the subject, at least for a while. Back in the present,

Charlotte tried to lay out a plan for her big reveal while the limo inched forward in traffic. Each idea had a flaw that stopped her, and when she alighted from the limo a full hour later, she was no closer to an answer.

Gil was disregarding the court order to stay away, calling more frequently and showing up outside her office. She wondered where he was getting the money to fly back and forth so often, but she would not engage with him to ask. She tried to ignore him, hanging up or walking away, but he was getting more persistent and, she feared, more desperate. Charlotte knew that a desperate Gil would be more aggressive, more dangerous.

At least all his actions had allowed her to stop sneaking around. It was obvious he knew how to find her, so she decided to take advantage of it where she could. She was thrilled to be flying home for the holiday. A few days with her burly brothers would give her some security. They would help her work out a plan, once and for all.

That encouraging thought allowed Charlotte to relax, and she fell asleep on the plane. It felt like only an instant passed before the hard bounce of the wheels hitting the tarmac jarred her awake.

Home. I am home.

Charlotte was wearing an enormous grin when she passed the security guard and looked amongst the waiting crowd for a familiar face. Although she had just seen them, she was thrilled to find both her brothers waiting for her. Holding her in tight bear hugs and covering her face with kisses, Don grabbed her luggage, and they moved through the Thanksgiving crowds toward a full parking lot.

Charlotte was so happy to see them that she didn't even complain when they were parked in the far corner of the big lot, or when they got off 195 and took back roads to avoid the traffic. She was happy to look at the familiar scenery and catch up with the siblings she adored.

"We are going to eat like pigs tomorrow," Don promised. "I have been planning this menu for weeks." The conversation turned to stuffing recipes for the rest of the journey and soon she was inhaling the smell of sweet bread that permeated the house. The kitchen counter was buried under tantalizing desserts that Charlotte craved right now. She could almost taste everything as she crossed the well-worn carpet of the living room straight into her mother's full-bosomed embrace.

"Carlotta, Carlotta," Luzia sighed as if she had not seen her in years, "I love having my baby girl home with me."

"Mama, it smells so good in here," Charlotte ignored the guilt-trip and hugged her mother in return. "What have you been baking today?"

"Everything, of course, but now you are here, you can help."

Energized by her family and home, Charlotte happily took her spot in the crowded kitchen, measuring and kneading amongst the family banter. Tonight, they would eat a delivery pizza. The kitchen was not fit for anything else. But tomorrow would be a feast.

Her family would host aunts and uncles who had followed her parents, immigrating from the small towns around Porto, looking for a better life. Most, like her parents, were hard working and middle class, but thanks to her father's success, they were all moving up economically. Two of her relatives were managers at the factory and her cousin, a recent Johnson and Wales graduate, would be joining her brother in the kitchens after the new year. Cousins were working in the offices, or the factories, and she even had young cousins hurrying to get driver's licenses so that they could drive the delivery trucks. It was a family business in the truest sense of the word, although in the last year they had swelled to over 300 employees.

It had only been six years since her brother had come up with his brilliant idea to take her father's bakery items, famous throughout the neighborhood, build up some capital and then expand to internet sales. Rocha Bakery had ballooned into Rocha Specialty foods quickly and then a parent company, Old World Foods, was formed. Now they were shipping her father's famous sweet bread and pastries to twenty-two countries, along with other delicacies.

Don's role would be to continue her father's legacy with old-world inspired recipes of his own. He had been experimenting with his mother's soups this past week and they bragged to Charlotte that they had figured out how to flash freeze them for shipping. The celebrating was premature, but Charlotte knew her brother would succeed. Jake was a business wizard, but Don was an even greater chef.

Charlotte settled into her childhood room, with its faded quilt and even more faded wallpaper, and caught her breath before dinner. She was overwhelmed by the noise and bustle of her family. The quarters were close. They lived on top of each other in the three-bedroom, one bathroom house. Her father had paid to add a second bath since she had moved out, a master bath that had pleased her mother beyond its worth. Her brother had moved out, but only to the top-floor apartment. She was used to it being more quiet these days, living in that big space with Alex, but once her nerves adjusted, she loved hearing the voices and chaos of her family home.

Not exactly a Beacon Hill Thanksgiving. Wouldn't Alex laugh now?

Charlotte mumbled under her breath as she hung up the jeans and t-shirts she had packed. Alex had stood over Charlotte while she had packed a bag of dresses, wool trousers, and cashmere sweaters but the moment he had left the room she had tossed all of that in the back of the closet where he wouldn't find it and packed her ankle boots, running shoes, jeans, and pullover sweaters. Her family would have laughed her out of Rhode Island if she had worn a dress around them.

"Wanna go for a run before dinner?" Don asked after knocking lightly on the doorframe and sticking his nose into the room. "I need to work off Mom's lunch; you missed a great meal by the way."

"Count me in," Charlotte accepted with her broad smile. "Just give me five minutes to change. But remember, I am a newbie on this ankle."

"Excuses, excuses," her brother tossed over his back.

Fifteen minutes later, Charlotte was wheezing lightly, trying to keep up with Don's moderate pace.

"Jeez, Char, you really are out of shape," he said, not unkindly. "When's the last time you ran?"

"It's been a while, but it's the hills. Chicago is flat as a pancake. Even these little hills are killing me. I am not used to them anymore."

Don slowed down and waited, jogging in place, as his sister caught up, then he dropped to a slightly slower pace. Charlotte fell in with him easily and soon they were running and talking comfortably. When they had exhausted the history of her brother's last semester at school and Charlotte's job, Don cut to the chase.

"Okay, Char. First, who is the guy and second, what the hell are you going to do about Gil? You need to get rid of him once and for all."

"I thought I had," Charlotte replied, "but he keeps turning back up."

"We'll get to him," Don commanded. "You can't avoid this anymore. Give me the scoop on the guy first."

"Who said there is a guy?" Charlotte stalled.

"I did, Carlotta. I have known you for too long. You have only had that moon-eyed, far away look once before."

"And we know how that turned out."

"It was a long time ago, Char, and obviously, you are finally over it. Do you trust this guy? Are you safe with him?"

"How sad is it that the first thing you have to ask is if Alex keeps me safe? He does, Don. Very safe."

"Alex. Okay, he has a name."

"He does indeed. Alexander J. Gaines. Banker. Mid-thirties. Successful. Generous. Handsome. Funny. Runner. Swimmer. Smart. Sexy. Very sexy." Charlotte said between breaths. "You'd like him. He can't boil water."

"From Chicago?" her brother asked, laughing easily as Charlotte again labored for breaths. She vowed to get back in shape, and soon.

"Yes. He has a sister there. I just went to her wedding, remember?"

"Some political blowout, yeah, I remember. You love him?"

"Well, let's not get there slowly."

"Why waste time?"

"I think I might," Charlotte admitted.

"Catholic?"

"That's enough, Mama."

"Well, is he?"

"We have never discussed it, actually, but I don't think it would be a problem. He is Episcopalian."

"Okay, we'll leave that alone for now. Does he love you?"

"He might, Don. Oh god, I hope he does. I am falling hard." Charlotte stopped running to give her brother a desperate look.

"How could he not love you, Carlotta? You are brilliant, beautiful, and you have a kind heart."

"Spoken like a perfect loving brother," Charlotte leaned in, kissing her brother on the cheek. "Let's turn back, please, before I drop like a stone right here in the street."

The pair slowed to a walk as they turned and headed back toward home. The neighborhood felt unchanged to Charlotte, as if she was walking home from Girl Scouts or the numerous after-school activities that had helped her win a scholarship to Harvard. Her life was so different now, but she had loved this life too.

"So, if you want to be with this Alex guy, you have got to get rid of Gilberto."

"I know, believe me, I know. I have told him for years that we are finished. Most guys would have taken the hint long before now. I have asked him to stay away, and after last year, well, you know. But he doesn't leave me alone. I am sick of hiding. Besides, he is like a bloodhound. He finds me anyway."

"We could ask Papa's family..."

"Don't even joke about that, Don. Not even a little."

"No one heard me, Char. I promise."

"You shouldn't even know about any of that."

"Give me a break, Char. I am not a two-year-old."

"You are still my baby brother, though, and safer not knowing any of that."

"Did you tell Alex?" Don asked, ignoring his sister's admonishment. "Did you tell Alex anything yet?"

"Nothing. How can I?"

"Charlotte, if you love this man, how can you not?"

Stepping into the over-warm house, Charlotte kicked off her shoes, yanked off her sweaty socks and wandered down the hall to the kitchen and the sound of voices and merriment.

"Good run?" Jake queried.

"Very good," Charlotte answered. "But now I am starved."

"No problem. We ordered pizza as soon as you left. It should be here any minute. You two barely have time for a shower."

"I go first," Don announced, disappearing down the corridor.

"Leave me some hot water," Charlotte shouted to his retreating back.

"Who wants wine?" her father held the bottle high above his head, shaking it lightly to catch his family's attention. Everyone said yes and soon they were pouring and passing glasses and toasting to the family, to a sweet life and to each other. Her father moved about the room, bestowing wet and noisy kisses on the cheeks of his wife and children.

Charlotte's brother, Jake, did the same, moving carefully through the crowded space. Don returned, hair dripping, and Charlotte ran to change before the pizza arrived. She was just emerging from the steamy bathroom, clad only in a towel, when the doorbell rang.

"Pizza" they cried out in joy as Jake went to answer the door. Charlotte ducked back into the bathroom until the delivery person was gone, then threw on clean clothes and ran for the dining room.

"Is there anything left?" she joked, grabbing a slice as she moved into her usual seat.

"We waited to say grace with you, Carlotta," her mother scolded. Charlotte dropped the pizza to her plate as if it scorched her fingers and bowed her head.

The family devoured the pepperoni and vegetable pizzas oozing with cheese and cut into squares. Something they have in common, Providence and Chicago. Pizza in square slices.

The meal was gone in what felt like moments, but the family sat around the table sipping wine and then coffee, sharing stories and enjoying their time together for another two hours.

No one was paying attention when Don bent close to refill Charlotte's cup and leaned over to kiss her cheek. "You need to fix this, Carlotta. And you need to tell Alex. Tell him soon."

CHAPTER
TWENTY-NINE

The sedate Thanksgiving dinner at the Gaines' home was as different from the boisterous event in Rhode Island as two dinners could be. The conversation swirled around stories from the honeymoon and planning for their upcoming ski trips. There were no raised voices, no controversies, and, by prior agreement, no politics. It was polite and controlled...

... and boring.

Alex sat in the understated luxury of his parents' dining room, listening to the quiet clink of sterling silver on fine porcelain and longed for Charlotte. Even a fight with her right now would be preferable to this staid and proper dinner. He missed her. The excitement went out of a room without her in it. Even this experience could have been fun if he could have looked across at her and rolled his eyes. It would have been fun rehashing everything with her later too, but not long distance. Their conversations were stilted and confined. He needed her home.

Surprisingly, he missed the casual comfort of his father's beach house, too. Alex, who had never known anything but luxury, had found the simple cottage near the water easier. The sound of the water had soothed him and despite the situations with the business and his father's health, it had been a calm place for him. His father had changed him by letting him get close. Without him realizing it, Charlotte had changed him, too.

They stayed in more, cooked more. Although he still had a housekeeper, he did his own laundry now and washed dishes without complaint. He was less of a snob, which he realized he had been despite his philanthropic efforts. Now he rolled up his sleeves and painted schools instead of just writing checks to them. He was more engaged in the world, and he was happier.

The first time Charlotte had suggested they work at the soup kitchen as well as write them a check, Alex had been mortified. Now, he was on the Board of Directors there, helping strategize long-term methods of funding, and helping to build a larger shelter. Painting the school building had led to adding a playground. He would never have known they needed it if he hadn't actually made the effort to see what his money was funding.

Oh yes, she had changed him,

Sitting here, he realized that Charlotte was unlike any woman he had ever met. She was hands on, boisterous and engaged. Alex liked that he found his family and their isolated luxury boring. He loved them, just as much as always, but his father's genes were coming to the surface and he was learning that he wanted a simpler, more engaged way of life.

With Charlotte.

Charlotte. How had she pulled him in this new direction? Even with a Puritan background, there was no way she had ever been exposed to it in her family. With her upbringing, she should fit right in with his family. He was probably experiencing a less opulent version of the dinner she was having right now.

Maybe she would invite him to join her in Boston, where he could see how descendants of the Mayflower celebrated this day of thanks. Of course, she would know the truth by then, he realized with a start. Perhaps they would not be together a year from now.

Thinking about it gave Alex a physical pain, and he decided then and there to do something about it.

"We need to talk," he blurted out, disrupting the conversation. "Mother, I want to share everything, and I want to do it now. It is important to me, to my future." Laurel needed no explanation to understand what Alex wanted to share.

"This is neither the time nor the place, Alexander," Laurel said, a strained look tightening her face. "It's Thanksgiving, dear. Let's save serious talk for another day."

"There is no other day, Mother. There never is. Aubrey is a married woman now. What the hell are we doing hiding things from her?"

Laurel grew agitated at the foot of the table, trying to stop her son from going down the path where she knew he was headed. "I don't want to discuss it, and I don't want to think about it, Alex. You know that. We are having a lovely holiday. Let's leave it that way."

"Laurel," her quiet husband said from the head of the table, "it's beyond time we brought our skeletons out of the closet."

"You mean my skeletons," she responded bitterly.

"After 35 years of marriage, dear, I think your scandals are mine. Don't you?"

"Scandals? What scandals, Mother?" Aubrey chirped in excitement. "We have scandals? Do tell."

Trust Aubrey to find the fun in all this.

"This is serious, Aubrey," her mother upbraided her. Aubrey fell back in her chair, shoulders drooping.

"It was serious, but the truth is no one cares anymore, Mother. Right, Charles?"

"Or if they do, Laurel, they are petty and unworthy of our friendship."

"Would someone please tell me what is going on?" Aubrey demanded as her husband sat embarrassed, clearly wishing he were elsewhere. He tried to excuse himself, but Alex barked at him to stay put before apologizing for treating him like a dog.

"It's simple, really. Adam, Aubrey, I'm a bastard," he announced boldly.

"No, Alex. You are always so sweet," Aubrey countered quickly.

"I love you too, pumpkin, but not that kind of bastard."

"Please don't use that word," Laurel begged. "I loathe that word."

"Your brother was born out of wedlock, Aubrey," Charles clarified. "His father was out of the country when you mother became pregnant and did not find out about Alex until after he was born."

"And my father is not dead, Aubrey. Mother is just embarrassed by him."

"That is not true," Laurel insisted. "I may have been once, but I got over that."

"It is, Mother. But here's the thing. You are embarrassed by a 25-year-old stoner dropout that you knew one summer. You say you got over it, but you were never completely okay, even after Zack accomplished so much. Not me. I am proud of the world-famous surfer turned media mogul who started with a beach shack business and grew it to a multinational company. I am proud that he followed his dreams, that he never forgot what was important to him, including me. And I am damn proud that he never lost sight of who he is."

"You should be proud, Son," Charles agreed. "Zack has accomplished a great deal, and he has been a great father and friend to you these last fifteen years or so."

"Zack Fairchild?" Adam asked, finally entering the conversation. "Your father is Zack Fairchild?"

"Close your mouth, Aubrey dear. That is not lady-like. You look like a fish," Laurel remarked, getting everyone laughing and causing the tension to break. Soon, the whole story was spilling out with everyone talking over each other.

"Now what, Alex? You obviously brought this up for a reason," Laurel finally asked.

"I want to tell Charlotte and my friends. I am about to become CEO of Maverix and I want to be able to do it openly."

"What about that slimy Jeffrey?" Charles asked with a look of distaste on his face. "Have you figured out how to resolve that problem?"

"Well, for one thing, if the world knows about this, his threats of exposure are moot. Second, Tyler came up with a great solution. We spun off the entire Australian operation and gave it to Jeffrey. Now he can feel in charge. He loved living in Australia when he was on assignment there. His mother is dead. What is holding him in L.A. anymore? It's a perfect fit for him. We transferred some of Zack's shares in Maverix Australia to Jeffrey so that he has the controlling interest in it, while I retain controlling interest of the holding company and corporation. Jeffrey gets to be CEO of something big and I get him off my back."

"But the entire Australian operation?" Adam asked. "That must be huge."

"Worth it. He will move to Sidney, and I won't have to look at his ugly mug anymore. And in truth, Jeffrey will be happier Down Under.

We might even find a way back to being true cousins. I would like that."

"That is wonderful for you and for Maverix. I am happy for you, really, and I hate to be petty, but what about my standing in the community?" Laurel asked in a tearful voice.

"Since Jeffrey is not pursuing this lawsuit, I imagine it all goes away. There will be no press, and it will simply be announced that Alex has taken a new—and exciting position as CEO of Maverix. He is well known in the business community. They will all believe he applied for and earned the position. Closed case. We volunteer nothing and I imagine no one hears anything. If they do," Charles told his wife calmly, "we deal with it. It is old news, Laurel. No one will care."

"How can you be sure?"

"Well, I am sure I don't care," he told his wife, coming around to give her a tender hug. "It's time for Alex to claim his birthright."

"Wow," Aubrey finally piped up. "I had no idea, Alex. It is so cool to have skeletons in the family closet. I always felt so average, but this is so 'reality TV'."

"God forbid," Laurel swooned. "Bite your tongue, young lady."

"Can you even surf?" Aubrey challenged.

"Try me little sister, just try me."

CHAPTER THIRTY

He was acting differently. Not bad, just different. Something was up, but he was offering no explanations. Something had definitely happened over the holiday weekend. Charlotte had asked repeatedly if everything was okay and, in a perfect imitation of an irritated woman, Alex kept replying, "fine."

But everything was not fine. It was awful. True, they weren't fighting as they had been before Charlotte traveled to Rhode Island, but they were miles apart. Sure, they were speaking. Alex had described his Thanksgiving meal, football with the guys over the weekend, some Black Friday shopping and filled in details here and there, but he was miles away, thinking about something he was keeping from her. She had seen him mull over problems before, and knew that he was secretive, but never had she seen him so preoccupied.

Charlotte was very careful to describe a Thanksgiving unlike anything she experienced. She went into detail about the elegant meal shared with prominent Boston families she had researched in detail. She talked about shopping for Christmas gifts and even brought home presents in boxes from stores unique to the Boston area. She was exhausted from the effort.

So, what was wrong? Charlotte had been home for two days now. He kissed her good morning and good night, seemed genuinely happy to be with her, but there was no conversation, no laughter, no cuddling, no sex.

Something was wrong.

"Alex," she asked again now, "did I do something or say something?"

"No, of course not, Char. I would tell you if you did. Why do you keep asking me that? Everything is fine."

"Fine. There is that word again," she bit.

"What word do you want me to use, Charlotte?" Now Alex sounded exasperated. Every time she started this conversation, he got exasperated, and she backed off. But she knew that something bad was brewing and when it exploded, she feared she would be the casualty.

Charlotte needed to do something and if she couldn't make headway with Alex, she would make headway elsewhere. Deciding that she could not maintain her lies and keep her distance when she was struggling with Alex, Charlotte made good on her promise to get the truth out in the open before Christmas. Well, as much of it as was her secret to tell.

With that in mind, she asked Regan for an hour of uninterrupted time at the end of the day Tuesday, then suggested they head to a quiet spot and talk over drinks. Regan accepted happily and suggested the hotel bar around the corner from their offices. By the time they arrived there, well after seven, she reasoned that it would be quiet enough for them to remain undisturbed.

Walking through the first snow of winter closer to 7:30, the two women rehashed their day. Deals were closing quickly now. No one wanted unsettled business as the holidays approached, so their clients were sewing up loose ends and everyone in the office was slammed.

Sliding into a booth, Regan kicked off her shoes under the table and sighed with pleasure as she wiggled her toes.

"Your ankle is fully healed?" she asked as the server approached. They ordered wine and a small cheese platter.

"Fully, I even did some running with my brother at home. It will take me a while to get back in shape. Why, oh why, is it so easy to get out of shape and so hard to get in shape?"

"Charlotte, if you ever figure that out, write a book and do the talk show circuit. You will be in high demand. Try to cut yourself some slack. Those Boston hills can be murder up around your house. You didn't try to run around Beacon Hill, right?"

"Actually, that is what I wanted to speak with you about," Charlotte began. The server returned with their drinks and food, then disappeared quickly.

"You were saying," Regan prodded.

"Regan, I have not been completely honest with you about a few things. A few crucial things."

Regan leaned forward. "Go on. You have my interest now."

"Remember when we met at that event for top Harvard donors?"

"Of course, I remember, Charlotte."

"You and I got to talking about Harvard women's programs, real estate, and pretty quickly, we were talking about a job for me here with LHRE."

"Right, we clicked instantly. I was so happy to find you. Of course, I remember."

"You offered me the job right after that, well, after you checked my references, but fast. And I am thrilled to be here, believe me."

"We are lucky to have you, Charlotte. You are doing a fantastic job for us. I knew you would be the right woman for the job, and you are."

"Thank you, Regan. It means a great deal to me for you to say that."

"But..." Regan prodded.

"No but. It's just that when I was finalizing the plans to move here and we were talking, I realized that you had made some assumptions about me that first day that were not accurate. I should have corrected you then, Regan. I know that. I have no real excuse, except that I wanted the job badly. I just thought at that point that it would be easier not to correct you. Then I didn't want to disappoint you and I didn't really think it would hurt anyone. I never intended it to go this far, but now I am heaping lie upon lie and everything is a mess," Charlotte took a deep, calming breath. "Oh God, I am rambling."

"I checked your references, Charlotte, so I know you didn't lie about your education or experience. You were obviously qualified for the job."

"Oh Regan, I would never have allowed you to hire me if I didn't think I could do a good job. Never," Charlotte stressed. "This seems so stupid now. I am not proud of what I did, but I am not even sure how to explain it."

"Just talk to me."

"Okay." Charlotte took a deep drink of her wine and a deep breath. "You thought I was there that day, at the luncheon, because I was a big donor. But I wasn't, Regan. I was just keeping my brother company. He was working there. I am not from the big pharma Roche family. I am from a little Rhode Island family. My father owns a bakery. My family's name isn't even Roche. It's Rocha. I changed mine to hide from an annoying boyfriend—a stalker, actually. I should have told you. I should have told you right away."

"So, you have been living a dual existence. That must have been exhausting," Regan said calmly.

"I just got caught up and couldn't find a way out."

"Why tell me now? You could have kept up the charade indefinitely. It would not have affected your work. There was no reason for me to find out."

"I hate having any lies between us, Regan, even ones that only hurt me. I have wanted to clear the air for ages."

"Well," Regan said solemnly, "I am very sorry you didn't tell me this at the beginning. Very, very sorry."

"No, I am sorry, Regan." Charlotte felt her perfect job slipping through her fingertips and she gripped the table edge as if to keep herself upright. Her knuckles turned white from the pressure.

I have blown everything. How did I let this happen?

"Oh, Charlotte. Relax. You didn't hurt anyone but yourself with all of this. I have known since the day after I met you that you were from Rhode Island, who your family is. Hell, I did so many background checks. I probably know what you ate for Christmas dinner when you were ten."

"Chorizo. Something with chorizo," Charlotte replied automatically as the words sank in. "I can't believe you have known all this time. Why didn't you say something?" She was laughing with relief and drinking her wine too fast. She started choking on it, her face turning beet red from the coughing.

"You okay?" Regan asked in concern. Charlotte caught her breath and nodded yes as her coughs subsided. "Slow down there, Charlotte. Sip. You sip wine, not chug it." The women laughed together, and Charlotte felt free for the first time in months.

"Two reasons," Regan continued. "First, I wanted you to tell me the truth, to trust me with the truth on your own, when you were ready. Second, I figured you had some reason for not admitting things. If you needed to keep your history a secret, Charlotte, I was prepared to help you."

"Regan, I don't deserve this, but I will take it. I cannot tell you what a weight this is off my chest. Now I really wish I had said something sooner. I was a fool."

"Does Alex know?"

"No, I felt that I had to tell you first. I owed you that much. I am terrified to tell him, though. How will he ever learn to trust me again after I tell him I have told him lie upon lie? How will he feel when I tell him I am not who he thinks I am?"

"Carlotta Rocha, you listen to me..."

"You really do know everything, don't you?" Charlotte interrupted, surprised to hear her old name on Regan's lips.

"Almost everything. You will have to tell me about your stalker. Seriously, I mean this with all my heart. You are exactly the woman you say you are. So, your name is a little different. You come from Rhode Island and not Beacon Hill. You are still smart and talented, funny, and kind. You are a hard worker and a good friend. None of that is a lie."

"Regan, you are a better friend than I deserve. A way better boss, too. I am sincerely sorry for the deception."

"There was really no deception, Charlotte. I made an assumption—a wrong assumption."

"But I should have corrected you, then and there."

"Maybe. But it is behind us now. Let's just move forward. We have lots of work to do and you have a man to go home to. Go tell him the truth, Charlotte. Do it tonight. I imagine you will sleep a lot better after you do."

"You're right. I am exhausted from keeping this from him. It has caused so many damn arguments, too. But Regan, what if I tell him and it goes badly?"

"You can always call me if you need a place to sleep."

Please, God, don't let it come to that.

CHAPTER THIRTY-ONE

I t was almost 10:00 at night when Charlotte walked in the door. She should have been exhausted, but she looked calm and beautiful. Her winter white suit was still pristine despite the long day. Her hair was perfect.

Hell, she was perfect. How could he tell her the truth? It could cost him everything.

"Alex," she said before she even had her coat off, "we need to talk." Feeling his stomach drop to his feet, Alex could only nod yes while he tried to find his voice.

Is she breaking up with me? Moving out? This looks bad and I haven't said a word yet.

"Where have you been?" he finally asked, sounding more accusatory than he intended.

"Having a drink with Regan," she responded. "I sent you a text hours ago telling you I would be late."

Oh great. Now she is feeling defensive.

"I know. I was just wondering if you needed dinner or if you had been at dinner." It was a lame answer, but it was the best he could think of with his heart beating in his chest this loudly.

"Actually, we had a few nibbles, but I wouldn't mind some ice cream if we have any."

"Ice cream? You never eat ice cream."

Oh god. Is she pregnant?

"I'm a little stressed, so I want sugar."

Oh god, she is pregnant.

"What are you stressed about, Char? Come sit down and tell me." She came to the couch two minutes later, shoes and suit gone, dressed in sweatpants and a long-sleeved, bright red Henley, and carrying a huge bowl of mint chocolate chip ice cream.

"Sorry, did you want some?" she asked as an afterthought.

"Just give me a spoonful and I will be fine."

Having shared far more than one spoonful, Charlotte ate in silence until the bowl was empty. Placing it on the table beside her, she turned back to Alex, looked him straight in the eye and announced without preamble, "Alex. I am a liar."

"Excuse me?"

"I am a liar and I have been lying to you since the day we met. I know you knew I was hiding information from you, but actually I have been making up stories right and left."

"Good stories?" he joked.

"This is serious. I got my job under false pretenses, and in order to keep it, I told small lies, big lies, and boldfaced lies. I couldn't find a way to keep my secrets at work unless I kept my secrets from you."

"So, all of this," Alex swept his hand to indicate the two of them, "is a lie?"

"Oh no, Alex. What we have is about the only real thing in my life. But my past, my family, they are not what you think. I am not a daughter of the American Revolution. My ancestors did not come over on the Mayflower. They came over with the clothes on their backs in the cheapest steerage passage they could book. They came from Portugal. My father owned a bakery until a couple years ago. My brother is turning it into a hot online specialty foods business now, but we grew up down the block from the bakery in Providence, Rhode Island. And we grew up poor."

Alex sat there, letting everything soak in. Finally, Charlotte was telling him what she had been hiding. It was nothing like what he expected, although he had imagined almost everything.

"But why pretend to be from Boston?"

"I told all this to Regan tonight. She was the reason I started this. It seemed innocent at first, but I just felt I could not tell you the truth until I told her. At first, I just wanted to keep my job. Then it just became easier to keep up the lie than to admit it. I didn't want to disappoint Regan. But then I didn't want to hurt you and it became a bigger issue. I knew it was wrong, but I was all tangled up in it and couldn't find my way back."

"I understand," Alex responded woodenly. "What else have you lied about, Charlotte?"

Charlotte seemed surprised by his suddenly bitter tone and took his hands in hers. "I m still me, Alex. I never did any of this to hurt you." Charlotte explained Regan had mistaken her for a wealthy Harvard donor and a member of an aristocratic family, and she had allowed the mistake to continue.

"That's all, Alex. That is all I did. But to keep it up, I told you I was in Boston when I was in Rhode Island, things like that."

"And the break-in? What about the break-in Charlotte? Or the 'accident' in the park that we both know was no accident?" Alex asked in a clipped voice. "If you are going to stop lying, then stop lying already. Tell me everything."

"That is nothing, Alex. Just an old boyfriend who wanted me back and was angry that I have moved on. He is nothing."

"He's not nothing, Charlotte. He tried to hurt you and he trashed your apartment."

"He lives in Rhode Island, Alex. I live here. With you."

"Well, he seems to be in Chicago an awful lot," Alex spit at her. For years, he told lie after lie, but inexplicably, he could not get past his anger with Charlotte.

"You made a fool of me, Charlotte. A total fool. You have not been completely truthful with me one day that we have been together. Not one. You had a million opportunities to tell me the truth. I would have kept it from Regan if you had asked me to, but noooo," he raised his voice, "you didn't trust me."

"I wanted to, Alex. I really wanted to. It has been killing me not to tell you. You need to believe me."

"Believe you? How can I believe anything you say to me now? I have never seen a deception that permeated every aspect of a life like yours has. Even now, I had to ask for the complete truth. Even now, you tried to hold back some of the story. That is the same as a lie, Charlotte. Shit, I don't even know you."

Alex strode from the room, his anger a tangible thing that was choking his throat and cutting off the air to his brain. He threw open the patio door, indifferent to the cold, paced the patio several times and then came back in, passed Charlotte without a glance, and went down the hall. Charlotte heard the door to his office slam with a thud.

Only after she was numb with crying did Charlotte pick herself up from the sofa. She walked past the silence behind the closed office door, hesitated there, then continued to the bedroom. She threw clothes for work and exercise in a bag along with toiletries and hastily scribbled a note to Alex. Sobbing uncontrollably; Charlotte grabbed the keys to her old apartment and her coat and quietly closed the door behind her.

It was a full hour later when Alex emerged from the office, calm at last. What was the big deal about her story? She had not hurt him. She had just protected her job. He had completely over-reacted.

What had caused this awful outburst from him? Perhaps his own guilt? Alex had been completely unfair with her, overreacting and behaving like a brute. He owed her an apology.

And more. I owe her the truth in return.

Even after she told him everything, he had failed to tell Charlotte about his background. After four days of worrying about nothing else, of acting like a zombie for fear that she would leave him, he had stayed mute about his birth.

He couldn't wait to tell her now. How she would laugh when he told her he was afraid her blueblood family would not accept him. It would be so great to have that weight off his shoulders.

He wandered to the living room, the media room, the kitchen. No Charlotte. He realized it was almost midnight and went to find her in bed. Instead, he found a post-it note on the bathroom mirror.

"I hope someday you will forgive me. I'll send someone to get my stuff."

CHAPTER
THIRTY-TWO

He was there again. It was a fourth day in a row that the guy was hovering outside the building. Alex was pretty sure he had seen him when he went running. The man was no runner, and it was mighty cold to take a stroll in the park. Had Charlotte hired a detective? Had his cousin? Alex assumed they'd resolved their issues, but maybe not.

This person didn't really look like a private investigator, although Alex admitted, his image of a PI came from watching too many movies. From the glimpses he had taken, someone was following him young and pretty good looking; too good looking to just blend in with the background or get lost in a crowd. Actually, the guy didn't even look like he was trying to blend in.

He just stood there, as if he was issuing a challenge. "Notice me," his posture said. His clothes were nondescript enough, blue jeans and a leather bomber jacket that couldn't be keeping out the brisk December wind, but his expression and features commanded attention.

He wore sneakers. Was that so he could make a quick getaway? Was he a thief? No, he was definitely trying to get in Alex's face, even from a distance. His face and stance were a come-on to Alex to get involved. It was an invitation to something sordid or dangerous.

Alex was relieved that Charlotte was not around, if only so this guy couldn't harm her.

He had been trying to reach Charlotte, but in the two weeks since she had walked out, she had not answered his calls, his texts, or his emails. He had not received a thank you or even an acknowledgement for the huge bouquet of flowers he had sent with the 'I am so sorry. Please forgive me' note. Nothing.

Two days ago, he had come home to find her belongings gone and his keys returned. Not a trace of her remained in the apartment, and yet she was everywhere. His memories of her filled every corner of the place. He could picture her chasing him around the house threatening with a twisted dishtowel, in the kitchen cooking, at the table chatting over a meal, snuggled into the corner of the sofa, cuddled with him. The bed was now a torture chamber of loneliness. He hated to be there. It felt so damn empty.

He had run out of ideas to win her back. Wyatt had suggested he buy her an expensive piece of Keeli's jewelry. Wyatt told him she had admired a piece at Aubrey's wedding. He thought that was a great idea, but when he called Keeli, she told him she'd sold the piece.

"It was a one-of-a-kind, Alex," she had explained. "I am so sorry."

Randall suggested going through her parents to get her back. It had worked for him when he had burned his bridges with Sloane. Her mother had helped get him in front of the furious Sloane over dinner one night so that he could apologize in person.

"Her parents are in Rhode Island, idiot," an exasperated Alex told Randall. "I don't even know how to find them. Charlotte Roche may not even be her real name."

Tyler had been cool and logical, very lawyer-like. "Charlotte is the guilty party here, Alex. She lied to you, not vice versa. She owes you the apology. You stand your ground and wait for her to recognize your value. She will come around."

"How's that working for you and Regan, Ty? You know you love her, asshole. Maybe you should get off your high horse and tell her. Waiting around is definitely not the answer here."

"Well," Tyler had responded in a huff, "remind me never to give you advice again."

The four men had laughed together over that reaction and there were no hard feelings, but Alex was no closer to a solution. "I am running out of ideas," Alex had complained for the tenth time that night.

"What about Regan?" Randall had suggested innocently. "She sees Charlotte every day, man. Maybe she can help."

Alex kicked himself. Why hadn't he thought of that sooner? He called Regan at the office the very next morning.

"Meet me after work," he pleaded. "I need your help."

"I wondered how long it would take you to call me," Regan had laughed. "Can you come to my office instead?"

"Do you think that is wise, Ree?"

"Don't worry. I am confident you won't run into Charlotte. Just come by after six."

Alex was tired at the end of another long day, but he was alert enough to notice that same strange man across the street from Regan's office building. In a city the size of Chicago, it was a wild coincidence that Alex would keep seeing him everywhere. Alex, always logical, did not believe in coincidence. The man was following him, plain and simple.

Changing direction sharply, Alex was across the street and confronting the dark-haired man before he registered he'd been spotted.

"Are you following me?" he demanded.

"Maybe yes. Maybe no," the man answered in a mildly accented voice.

"What are you? A two-year-old? Give me a damn answer," Alex barked.

"Yes. Happy now? Yes, I am following you."

"No, I am decidedly not happy. Why? Why are you following me?" Alex felt an awful suspicion building somewhere in the back of his brain. The man had an accent. Not a strong one, but it was distinctly there.

The New England 'a' mixed with a hint of Portugal, perhaps? Was this Charlotte's brother?

"Why are you following me?" he shouted close in his face.

"Leave Carlotta alone, Alexander. Leave her alone or I will hurt her, and I will hurt her family. I can do it. I can damage them forever."

Not the brother, the boyfriend. The stalker.

Alex was still digesting the words spit in his face, so he didn't see the fist that followed. He was down on the ground with a bloody nose before he realized it. And the man was gone.

Passersby stopped to ask if he was alright. Someone offered to call 911, but Alex insisted it was just a friendly spat, and grabbing a handkerchief from his pocket and holding it to his nose, he went to meet with Regan.

Her alarmed face when she saw him told Alex he looked worse than he felt.

"What the hell happened to you?" she asked. "Let me get some ice and then you can tell me."

Five minutes later, Alex was stretched flat on the deep blue leather sofa in Regan's office with a dishtowel of ice on his face. He was still trying to assimilate what had happened. This man had threatened Carlotta's—holy shit, he didn't even know her real name—life.

"Is she really in that much danger? If so, she needs to be back where I can protect her."

"Alex, right now it looks like you can't even protect yourself," Regan chided kindly. "Are you sure you don't want me to call a doctor or the police?"

"I'll be fine, Ree. But Charlotte needs help. She needs to be back in my apartment, in a secure building. That apartment of hers is a joke. That animal already trashed it once."

"Gil."

"Gil?"

"That animal has a name. It's Gil. She has a restraining order to prevent him from coming near her, Alex. All he can do it threaten."

"Are you sure? He implied to me he could hurt her. 'Damage her,' is what he said. And her family."

"She isn't even here, Alex." I sent her out of town on business. She has been gone all week."

"Okay, I feel better knowing that. The guy has been following me everywhere."

"I think he was after you this time, not Charlotte," Regan reassured him. "And despite the current evidence to the contrary, I think you can take care of yourself."

Alex smiled at the remark, then grimaced. "Ow, that hurts," he whined.

"Keep the ice on it, and tell me what you are doing here." Regan was all business now.

"How do I get her back?"

"Do you want her back, Alex? You told her you couldn't forgive her, from what I heard."

"It hurt, Ree. She told me a lot of lies."

"She told them to me too, Alex, but I understood. I forgave. I empathized. You attacked."

"I know. I was wrong, but she was gone before I could tell her. Now she won't talk to me. I want her back, Regan. I need her in my life."

"Very nice, Alex. You almost have me convinced."

"That's not fair, Ree."

"Sorry. I just needed to make you suffer for a second. She won't take you back, Alex. She thinks you are too good for her, that she is beneath you now. I would have sworn that people were over all that class nonsense, but I guess I would be wrong. The woman is Harvard educated, brilliant. Look at all she has accomplished before age thirty. She thinks your parents won't approve."

"That's ridiculous. They love her."

"Of course they do, and your father would, too, I am sure."

"Wyatt told you?"

"Wyatt never could keep a secret from me. Didn't you know that? Missy too. We can always tell when he's hiding something. Don't worry, Alex, your secret is safe with us. No one cares anyway, except that your father is a legend."

"Yeah. I hope Charlotte thinks so too."

"She would if you had her back. You must really be in love. Want to know how I know?"

"How?"

"You reacted to Charlotte's news with your heart, not your head. Logical Alex wasn't logical about something. She touches something in you, Alex."

"I can't be logical around her, Ree. All my logic goes right out the window. I take one look at her and I can't think straight."

"Poor Alex. You've got it bad."

"So, will you help me, Regan? Help me get her back."

"I want to, Alex, but I am not really sure what I can do. It might be too late. I can tell her we talked, but I am prevented as her boss from giving you her home address."

"I have her home address. I need her to pick up the phone or answer the door, though."

"While I can't promise anything, I can ask her to pick up when you callcan't promise anything. She won't answer the door at the address you have for her. Charlotte is gone. She quit last week. She went on her last business trip for me this week and then headed straight back to Rhode Island.

"She went to Rhode Island?"

"She went home to marry the animal."

CHAPTER
THIRTY-THREE

C harlotte wondered again, for the thousandth time, what she could have done differently. How did she end up here, the one place she had been running from for the last ten years?

"Char, do you have those figures for me yet?"

"Sorry, Estelle, I am getting them now," she called back through the office doorway. At least she was helping her family. Working in the family business beside her brothers was the only silver lining in these clouds. Even her mother did not seem completely happy. And if her mother wasn't happy planning a wedding for her only daughter, things were dire indeed.

Thinking back, Charlotte decided she had made the right decision. She had been running these scenarios through her memory day and night, trying to replay a version that had a different ending. After two weeks of wracking her brain, she still landed right where she was.

Two weeks. That meant it had been almost a month since the last time she saw Alex. He had been so hard, so judgmental, and unforgiving. It hurt, but she had long ago forgiven him for it. The messages, the flowers, the apologies had been so sincere that she realized the reaction she witnessed was hurt, not anger; it was his hurt and defensiveness.

Once Alex let his defenses down, he wanted to work things out, understand, try again.

Of course, by then it was too late.

By then, Gil had done his damage, and done it well. The man was a complete snake, a wolf in sheep's clothing. He had looked at her with those melting amber eyes, flashed her those pearly white teeth and threatened the safety and happiness of everyone she loved.

Really, what options did she have at this point but to cave in to his demands? It seemed ridiculous to her, archaic even. Why would a man even want to marry a woman that he knew was only agreeing to the marriage under duress? She asked him this very question and his answer was the same as it had been since high school.

"You are the only girl for me," he told her when he invited her to senior prom. "Carlotta, we were meant for each other." He believed it then, and he believed it now. "I will do whatever it takes to win your heart."

Back when they were eighteen, that had meant splurging for an orchid corsage and a decent tuxedo. Now the stakes were much higher, but it was Charlotte who was doing whatever it took to make things work.

First, she had walked away from a job she loved, from the opportunity to succeed at LHRE and by extension to make a difference in real estate investing and the future landscape of the Midwest. The conversation with Regan had been stilted. She felt foolish lying to her again, just after she finally cleared the air and started being truthful.

"Regan, I have received bad news from home," she began, crossing her fingers behind her back in case the old wives' tales were true, then praying to God to forgive her and not make her lies come true. "My family's new business has been growing by leaps and bounds, faster than they can manage. That has been good news for all of us. But now the cash management is a mess, and my brother is too busy in the front office to manage the back office. He has begged me to come home and help. How can I say no? It's my family."

Her brother, Jake, could run circles around her business-wise. He had attended URI for undergraduate school, unable to afford more, but he had worked in his father's business the entire four years, then two more before taking the time off to complete an MBA from Harvard. He had planted the seed in Charlotte to pursue a business degree, to aspire to Harvard. His smarts and work ethic were legion. She dreamed of someday being as good as he was. The notion that he might need her help was ridiculous, but Regan didn't know that.

"Of course, Charlotte. You must go help your family if they are need you. Trust me, I run a family business too. I completely understand. How long do you think you will be gone?" Regan queried. She was being so supportive. It broke Charlotte's heart to lose her as a boss and a friend. Charlotte hoped that someday she could tell her the truth and resume a relationship.

Stop kidding yourself. It will never happen. You're shutting that door forever.

"I don't mean temporarily, Regan. I need to resign. I am giving you my two weeks' notice. In fact, if there is any way I can leave sooner, I really need to get home."

Charlotte could not look Regan in the eye, but she delivered the words. Taking a deep sigh, she turned to leave before she lost it in front of such a kind, strong woman.

"Oh." She had caught Regan off guard. "I didn't realize that was what you were saying. I hate the idea of losing you, Charlotte. You have been a valuable member of the team here, a real asset."

"Thank you, Regan," Charlotte mumbled, near tears. "That means a great deal to me. I will miss you and everyone at LHRE."

"Well," the soft moment over, Regan was all tough business. "I will need you to go close out things in St. Louis before you leave. They will not want to deal with anyone else after all this time."

"Of course, I'll go Monday." Charlotte was standing in the door, still trying to skulk away, but Regan kept talking.

"And from there, I guess you can head home. What about your apartment?"

"The movers are coming later next week. I will arrange for my landlord to let them in. I already paid him to break the lease," Charlotte explained.

"So, you have known about this for a while?" Regan sounded hurt and surprised. "Only about a week," Charlotte could to tell her honestly. "I was planning to make my move in with Alex more permanent."

"The more I think about this, the more I think you should take a six-month leave of absence. Ethan can try to hold down the fort with some help from me and the rest of the finance team. I will do my best to hold your job for that long, just in case."

"Regan, that is more than I can ask. You need to get a director of finance in here."

"I have a director of finance, Charlotte. I am looking at her."

"Well, if you are sure. But I cannot make any promises."

Hopefully, it will be easier when I am not face to face with her to tell her it has to be a permanent break.

"Understood," Regan confirmed. As Charlotte turned to leave, Regan came from around her impressive desk. Giving Charlotte a brisk hug, she whispered in her ear, "What about Alex?"

"You know we are through."

"Yeah, sure," Regan responded sarcastically. "I never saw two people more perfect for each other."

Tears welling in Charlotte's eyes, she quickly changed the subject and moved through the door. "I am so sorry, Regan. Believe me, I wish things could be different."

Remembering that moment now, Charlotte worried. Had she said too much? Given away too much? She was the radiant bride. This was her choice. She had to be sure everyone, even her family, believed that. Closing up the apartment in Chicago had been easy. She didn't even unpack her belongings when they moved over from Alex's. Why bother when she already knew that everything was shipping back to Providence? God knew where she would put her things in the overcrowded house. She had suggested getting an apartment of her own, but Gil had nixed that immediately.

"I will know where you are and who you are with at all times," he had outlined. "I will take your cellphone—don't worry, I will get you a new one. You will be with family, at work, or with me. Understood?"

Charlotte had responded with a dejected nod, afraid to speak for fear that she would start screaming. She had worked so hard to build an independent life. It had been heartbreaking for her parents to let their only daughter move away to college. She had fought like hell just to end up back here.

"I will be an hour away, Mama," she had reassured her mother repeatedly. "And it's Harvard," she added, like the prestigious words would erase her mother's fears. "And I am eighteen years old, Mama."

"Let her go, Luiza," her father had said. "Carlotta worked hard for this scholarship, achieving all the dreams we had coming to America. She will be someone important someday, with important friends. Our daughter will make a difference in the world, just like you taught her."

"I know," her mother had conceded, wiping her eyes. "But I hate to let her out of my sight."

"Don't worry, Querida," her father had promised his wife, "she will call home every day."

And she had. Every single day of college, of graduate school, and once she moved to Chicago, she spoke with her family daily. Until she moved in with Alex, she touched base with her parents every night, even if only for a minute. "I'm safe, I'm fine and I love you," was often the entire conversation.

They had let go over time, less worried, prouder of what she was accomplishing. But not Gil. He never let go. He would arrive unannounced in Cambridge, asking to stay the weekend or call relentlessly, begging her to come home.

He was an above-average student, from a proud Portuguese family, and they wanted to send him to college, wanting more for him than they had themselves. His older brother was studying to be a research biologist and Gil had filled out an application to attend URI to study business, but the idea of accounting classes bored him and Gil never attended. He would have received scholarships, earned when Charlotte was helping him study. Instead, he stayed around the house until soon he was hanging out on neighborhood streets, tinkering with cars at the local garage, filling in at the textile factory's second shift, making ends meet. When Charlotte pointed out that he could get so much further if he just applied himself, he brushed her off.

"Not everyone has to go to Harvard, Carlotta. When did you begin looking down your nose at people who did an honest day's work?"

He grew to resent Charlotte's success, disparaging her 'snooty' friends and her clean fingernails. "Come home, Querida. You can work at the bakery. I can work there with you. They are expanding, you know. You would see it for yourself if you ever came home," he complained. "Your brother is doing amazing things. Come home and see. Come work by my side."

Gil may have thought that the constant pressure and whining would win her over, but it just pushed her further away, until things came to a head her junior year.

One frosty November night, Charlotte returned late to her dorm walking with a young man, a fellow student. They had been studying together, and he had offered to walk her home to assure her safety. There was no more between them than friendship.

She never had time to explain that to a drunk and waiting Gil before he threw the first punch. Gil had arrived at 7:00 and between the three-hour wait and the chill in the air, he had consumed a bottle of Jack Daniels and laid in wait for Charlotte. When she arrived with a man, she could not reason with a drunk and angry Gil.

"It was nothing, Gil. We were just studying," Charlotte tried again to reason with him. "I wasn't with him. But we broke up, remember? We agreed to see other people." That had been a mistake, fueling his animosity. Punching and kicking the fellow, he broke his nose and three ribs. He was down on the ground, trying to fend off the worst, when Gil heard the sirens in the distance.

"You bitch," Gil spat at Charlotte. "You called the police on me? You cheat on me and then you call the police?"

When Charlotte nodded the affirmative, Gil had grabbed her and shaken her hard. She heard the sirens and prayed they would get there fast enough. She had never seen Gil this out of control, and she was scared. He had never threatened her safety before. Until that night, she would have argued he was incapable of harming a hair on her head.

Slapping her hard across the face until she saw stars, Gil had called her every vile name he could think of, screaming in her face until spit foamed at his lips. Then he punched her once, hard, in the stomach and pushed her away with force.

She had awakened at Mass General, in the emergency room. The nurses and doctors explained she had hit her head on the concrete and passed out. She was concussed, bruised, but after asking questions and having her walk and move for them, she had been pronounced fit to go home. Her study partner would remain overnight.

She had not intended to press charges, but when the tough policewoman who interrogated her suggested a restraining order, she had leaped at the opportunity to follow through. Her study partner did press charges, though, and Gil went to jail for sixteen months for assault.

If Gil's prospects had been lousy before that, they only got worse. While Charlotte graduated from Harvard and received her MBA, she heard tales of Gil's spiral down. He was in prison briefly, serving only six months of his sentence. Once released from prison, his family wrote him off. He needed a place to live, and that meant he needed money. While Charlotte had not heard from him except for the collect calls from prison that she refused to accept, she heard from him once he was out.

Gil tracked her down in Boston and begged her to help him find work, come home. Be with him again. He barraged her with phone calls, letters, and visits.

"We were good together, mi amada. You know we were," he would plead. "I can be someone again with you by my side." Instead of assisting, Charlotte reminded Gil of the restraining order and the calls mercifully stopped. Charlotte was able to obtain her degree, change her name, and move into an apartment with an unlisted number. Until the insurance company started making her a 'face' for them, she had lived in quiet, undetected, and unmolested.

But once Independent sent her to do CNBC and Bloomberg talk shows, news of Charlotte Roche got around and Gil easily tracked her down. He began showing up at her door again, leaving small, unwanted gifts of candy and flowers. He would not take no for an answer, although he always maintained a physical distance, honoring the restraining order.

Until late one Saturday night. Charlotte had been sleeping in her first-floor apartment when she heard the glass in the front room smash. Reaching for the phone to dial 911, her intruder was on her before she completed the call.

Terrified, Charlotte had scratched and kicked, fighting for her life.

"Stop, Carlotta. It's me." Recognizing Gil's voice, she calmed a bit, but her brain continued to work furiously. She had to get him out. His breath stank of alcohol, and he had broken into her apartment.

"You need to get out, Gil," she had hollered, pushing him away from her.

"I am done waiting, Querida," he had slurred. "I came to take you home."

"Don't be insane, Gil. I am not going home with you."

"Carlotta, I cannot get a job. No one wants me. I need you, Querida. I need you to get me a job at Old World, a good job. I deserve it. You owe me."

"You are acting crazy, Gil. I don't owe you. You need to get out." She was shouting and trying to get around his broad shoulders to reach for the phone. He would not budge, cornering her like a mouse in the center of the bed. Charlotte needed a way out of the vulnerable position.

Leaping away from him toward the other side of the bed, away from the door, she realized she would have to traverse the entire room, but it would put some distance between them. Gil caught the movement early though, grabbing her arm and almost yanking it from its socket. He pulled her back onto the bed before lying across her nightgown-clad body.

Charlotte was defenseless now, her arms pinned beneath Gil's body. His foul breath in her face, he began kissing her while she bucked beneath him and turned her face away.

"Don't you dare turn from me, bitch," he barked at her, slapping her face hard. "I was good enough for you before, and I am good enough now."

Charlotte felt Gil's hands on her naked legs and started screaming at the top of her lungs. In a haze, she realized he was undoing his jeans. He had every intention of raping her.

"Shut up before I make you," he hollered above her noise, slugging her with one fist while he pulled his jeans lower. "You will love this, Querida. It will be great."

Charlotte felt the weight lift from her and the air flow into her lungs with a whoosh. Gil was being yanked from the room by two burley Boston policemen. His feet never touched the floor until they had him on his knees in the next room. He was handcuffed and taken away while a young EMT soothed her and suggested in the kindest of tones that they get her to the hospital.

"I'm okay," Charlotte kept repeating. "He didn't do anything."

"You mean he didn't rape you? But you are beat up pretty bad."

Charlotte refused to go with them, gave a brief statement saying that her old boyfriend had gotten angry. She should have pressed charges. She was an idiot. That was where she had made her big mistake.

Instead of making Gil go away, she was forced to run and hide again. At her wit's end, her meeting with Regan and an opportunity to move to Chicago were godsends.

Charlotte disappeared again and stayed happily hidden until August, when a shadow in the park turned into her worst nightmare. Except this time, Alex had been there to rescue her, to protect her.

I should have known it couldn't last.

There was no escaping Gil, Charlotte finally acknowledged. This was her reality, and she gave in to it. Gil was growing more desperate for money; his family was pressuring him to leave his rough crowd behind and become the man he had shown as a teen he could be. He said he wanted that, too.

Sort of.

He wanted it the easy way, or the trappings of it. Getting it honestly, through his own hard work and effort? Not a chance. Instead, he would blackmail his way into a job, into a marriage, into the right society with the right opportunities.

He knew all of Charlotte's secrets and he would divulge every one of them, no matter who he hurt or endangered.

"You will come home. You will tell everyone you want to marry me. Tell them you are eager to start a family, that you are sick of working so hard. I don't care what you tell them. But make them believe you, Charlotte. You better be the best little actress ever born."

"Why would you want me knowing I hate you?" she had thrown in his face.

"Hate is very close to love, Charlotte. Isn't that what they say? You loved me once. You will learn to love me again."

"After everything you have done, I could never love you. And back then, we were kids, Gil. That wasn't love."

"It was for me," he told her, running a hand through his dark locks, and flashing his deep brown eyes at her. He looked handsome in that moment, and very, very dangerous. "You'll make them believe you, Carlotta, or people will get hurt. Your precious Alex—I can get to him.

Your father, do you want me to go public about him? It would destroy your family. You decide, Querida. It is up to you."

"I will convince the world, Gil. You just name the day."

Gil reached forward to kiss her, and she pulled away as if he was a viper.

Gil was furious. "You love me, Car, remember?" he said with a sneer. "You want to marry me. Now, come give your Gilberto a loving kiss. Make them believe."

So she did. She lived the lie everyday day for two weeks, letting him kiss and hug her in front of their families and friends while her skin crawled. Her would-be rapist was now her fiancé.

There is no other scenario, she determined, returning to the present. She could never, ever let anyone believe otherwise. Make them believe or people will die.

CHAPTER
THIRTY-FOUR

"**S**omething's not right about this," Sloane told Randall as she snuggled with him in front of the fireplace and looked out the window at the dark night. All she could see was her own stunning reflection, and the gorgeous open and rugged space that was their Lake Tahoe home. She loved being here, in this house where Randall had proposed marriage. They had been here with only his father since New Year's Day for two blissful weeks, but tomorrow their friends would arrive for a week of relaxation and skiing.

Sloane knew how much Keeli needed the break. Business had been insane for the last ten weeks of the year, filling and delivering on a record-breaking number of orders to major distributors and overseeing the production of custom pieces.

Business had never been better or harder. Thank God for Keeli's creativity and calm demeanor. Left to her own devices, Sloane thought she would tear off a few heads, but running things with Keeli was fun, even when it was exhausting. It never failed to amaze Sloane that she and Keeli had gone from competing for the same man, to colleagues, to true friends. Especially since Sloane was a sore loser.

Randall had gone through all the year-end paperwork associated with the world of high finance, so that he would have no trouble getting away. He ran a smooth ship and delegated where he needed to. Tyler, too, had come into the year-end with no major issues, although he warned the group that Wyatt would be exhausted from growing the tech company he started for another consecutive year.

Regan was in the worst shape, desperately needing a getaway. She was more emotional than usual and horribly overworked since the departure of Charlotte. For the last three weeks, Regan had been doing both jobs and trying to get through Christmas.

The group was unhappy with Alex, who had bailed on them and taken off for Aspen alone, brashly telling his friends they were un-invited for the skiing holiday that had already been planned. No one dared challenge him. He was an ogre since Charlotte moved out. She had left Chicago a month ago, but the hole she left in their lives remained hollow.

"You need to stay out of this," Randall warned Sloane. "Charlotte is a grown woman. She knows her own mind." The commotion at the door saved Randall from a spat with his fiancé, who loved to have her own way and had just opened her mouth to argue. "They're here!"

"It is about damn time," Sloane noted. "They should have been here hours ago. They will help you see that I am right."

"Let it go, Sloane," Randall pleaded. "Think how tired they all are if it is this late here. Do not get into it. Promise me."

Sloane agreed reluctantly, and five minutes later she was the most gracious of hostesses.

"You must be exhausted," she told the women as they preceded the men and luggage into the house.

"And starved," Regan added. "I cannot believe we are two hours behind schedule. Can you ever forgive us?"

"Of course we can, Regan. We all know how tough it is to get away for a week. We all have so much on our plates."

"Do not let her off the hook," Tyler jeered. "She held us all up so she could do an extra hour of meetings." His words were rough, but the look he gave Regan, and the soothing arm he placed around her shoulders, belied his words.

"It's just a good thing we had Wyatt's plane."

"You wouldn't have kept us waiting if we were on a commercial flight," Keeli observed. "Maybe we should have thought of that."

"Okay." Regan threw her hands up in a sign of surrender. "Guilty, guilty, guilty. Now, can I get some food?"

Sloane reached into the fridge and took out platters of meats and cheeses, salads and rolls and started reheating a large pot of soup on the stove, then opened a bottle of wine to breathe. Meanwhile, Randall showed the couples to their rooms and laughed when Tyler and Regan took separate rooms.

"When are you going to make a move?" he challenged his friend.

"Never, asshole, so just drop it."

"Idiot," Randall muttered under his breath, but he indicated a room far from Regan's and they said no more despite the longing look Tyler gave Regan's retreating form.

Sloane i Randall's father, Mark, to join them, but he declined, and the group of friends fixed heaping plates of food, then gathered around the large table.

Conversation was a rehash of the travel that day, the Christmas holidays, and excited plans for the week. Still, it didn't take Sloane much effort to turn the discussion to Alex and their efforts to get him to join them.

"I have called twice," Sloane announced, "and Randall sent a slew of emails."

"He didn't even respond to me," Randall revealed. "That is why Sloane finally called him. The guy's a mess. We need to drag his ass up here for a few days."

"It's Charlotte," Sloane announced. Randall shot her an 'I told you to stay out of it' look, but Sloane ignored him and forged ahead. "Don't you agree Regan? Something fishy is going on."

"I told you, Ree, leave it alone." Tyler said from beside her, earning a high-five from Randall. "It's Charlotte's choice."

"Is it? I keep thinking about the way she gave notice. There was something going on."

"Yeah, her family was in trouble," Tyler pronounced. "Of course, something was going on."

"No," Regan contradicted. "Something else. Something weird."

"What do you mean, Ree? Weird how?" Keeli asked.

"Oh no, Keeli, please just stay out of this. We are in big trouble if you all put your heads together," Wyatt pleaded.

"Watch it, Bro," Regan warned before turning back to Keeli. "She said she wished things could be different."

"Yeah," Tyler interpreted, "she wished her family situation could be different."

"Exactly," Randall agreed.

"Then why such a hasty wedding?" Sloane asked. All eyes shifted to her except Regan's.

"You guys didn't know? Didn't you tell them, Regan?"

"I might have failed to mention it," Regan said now in a small, innocent voice. "I got an invitation this week to Charlotte's wedding."

Chaos erupted around the table, with everyone firing off questions at the same time. "What wedding?" "When?" "To whom?" and finally, "Does Alex know?"

"I have the invitation in my bag, so I can show you. In Rhode Island, March 1st, to a childhood sweetheart and I think Alex might know. I think that is why he's not here," Regan stated.

"How can she be marrying someone else when she loves Alex?" Keeli asked the room at large.

"Exactly," Sloane agreed. "That is my point exactly." She fired a look at Randall who was pointedly looking elsewhere.

"Charlotte is a smart and strong woman. You are such a drama queen. If she didn't want to marry this guy, she wouldn't be marrying him."

"Oh Wyatt, do you have to be so logical?" his wife asked him. "What if he is forcing her?"

"Or her family is forcing her?" Regan added.

"Or she is being blackmailed by them all?" Sloane suggested.

"You ladies read too many novels," Tyler announced. "Things like that don't happen anymore. Not in America at least."

"But how do you explain the guy that beat up Alex that night outside my office?"

"Alex got beat up?"

"He never told you?" Regan looked from one friend to the next, astonished. "I wonder why he never shared that."

"Maybe 'cause he lost the fight," Randall mocked.

"Oh shut up, Randall," Wyatt tossed across at his friend good-naturedly. "What happened, Regan?"

"Right when Charlotte gave her notice, Alex came to see me. He wanted me to help get her to return his calls. But of course, she was gone. Anyway," she continued, back on point, "he had blood all over his shirt and his nose looked broken to me. I guess it wasn't, but it was bad. Anyway, he told me a man had jumped him right across from the office and punched him."

"That could have been anyone. It's Chicago," Sloane interjected. "Yeah, but the guy threatened Charlotte, her family, and Alex."

"Shit, why didn't he tell me?" Randall said, angry. "I would have beat the crap out of the guy."

"Well, my friends," Regan announced, waiting for their undivided attention, "the guy who punched Alex is now Charlotte's fiancé."

After the shocked "What?" and "Are you serious?" questions had filled the air, Sloane asked what she wanted to know all along.

"So, team," she queried, like she was speaking to her high school cheerleading squad, "what are we going to do about this?"

CHAPTER
THIRTY-FIVE

T he women wanted to problem solve that night, but the men's objections of exhaustion and needing time to think prevailed and soon everyone went to their own rooms to consider the problem, unpack, or sleep.

Over coffee the following morning, the conversation picked up right where it had left off. There was disagreement on how to help, but the group all agreed on two things—something was not right, and Alex needed to get involved. All three men fired off emails effectively saying the same thing—get out of Aspen and over to Tahoe or they would come get him. Then, while they waited, the skiers hit the slopes with Randall's father, a ski bum if ever there was one.

By mid-afternoon, everyone reconvened in the enormous living room before a roaring fire and picked up the morning's conversation. No one had heard from Alex, so Wyatt took it upon himself to fly to Aspen and bring him back to Tahoe to join the planning. He promised to deliver the reluctant man to their care by nightfall and was quickly gone.

In his absence, Regan shared with her friends the formal wedding invitation she had received just days ago. The heavy velum contained the traditional words for a wedding invitation, her parents cordially invited Regan to attend "the marriage of Carlotta Maria to Gilberto Arelo, son of... "

"Carlotta Rocha? What the hell is going on here?"

"A Catholic wedding in Providence, Rhode Island? I am completely confused."

Regan field their questions, explaining that Charlotte had a hidden past. When her friends tried to accuse Charlotte of attempting to fool them, to pass herself off as more important than she was, Regan was quick to defend her.

"The mistake was actually mine. I just assumed she was a Roche from 'the' Roche family. They are donors at Harvard, and a large number live in Boston, and so I leapt to a few conclusions. Charlotte tried to tell me right away, then she saw her opportunity to get out of Boston and she took it."

"I knew as soon as I did a background check, and eventually Charlotte admitted everything." Regan chose not to tell the group how long it had taken for her employee to fess up. It didn't matter, they had moved to the subject of her lying to Alex instead.

"She told him everything right after Thanksgiving," Regan told them. "He didn't take it well."

"The hypocrite!" Tyler announced before he could check himself. "How dare he get mad at her for hiding her past when—"

"Tyler," Randall cut him off.

"Are you keeping secrets?" Sloane asked.

"Not our secret to tell, Sloane. I have to respect the request of a friend."

The three women tried to get a kernel of gossip from the men, but all were tight-lipped. Later, in the hot tub, Sloane and Keeli made a game out of guessing what it might be before giving up in frustration.

"We will have to corner Alex about this," Keeli suggested.

"Maybe we should fix this Charlotte mess first? I may have accused her of trying to 'pass herself off' earlier, but the truth is, I really like her. We need to get her back with Alex. It needs to be our top priority, ok?"

"I see your point. Charlotte and Alex first, but then we get to the bottom of this secret. Promise?"

The hours passed quickly, and, true to his word, Wyatt dragged Alex in shortly after midnight. He looked like hell, and he certainly did not look happy to see his friends.

"What is this? Some damn intervention?" he snapped in lieu of hello.

"It's the vacation we all agreed to take together," Sloane retorted.

"I was fine vacationing on my own. Thank you very much."

"You weren't fine, Alex. The Aspen house was a shambles. You look like you haven't eaten, slept, or shaved in weeks," Wyatt observed. "I got you out of there just before the laundry reached the ceiling."

"So what? That's my business."

"Maybe," Regan agreed. "But this isn't. This requires us to put our heads together and solve a problem." She handed Alex the wedding invitation. "The wedding is just around the corner, on the first of March. We need to do something now."

"She's marrying him?" Alex asked in shock. "March first?" Alex looked like someone had just run over his dog, stolen his favorite toy, and flunked him in a class he thought he was acing, all at the same time. "Well, I guess this is what she wants."

"Do you really believe that?" Sloane snarled in his face.

"Back down, my love," Randall said, taking his fiancé by the hand and physically pulling her back into her chair.

"You don't believe that she loves this man, Alex. You know she doesn't. She told you enough to know that she was afraid of him, didn't she?" Sloane was like a dog with a bone between its teeth.

Mimicking Charlotte, Alex explained. "He lives in Rhode Island, and I live here." With scorn in his voice he continued, "that's what she told me. That's all she would tell me. I knew there was more. That was why I got so angry. She denied he was an issue. I even asked her outright, and she still denied it."

"Oh Alex. There was a lot more. You saw him. He was stalking her. She had a restraining order."

Alex was up and pacing now. "I had no idea it was that bad. How could I when she kept telling me there was nothing to worry about? I met the animal. Did Regan tell you? He pummeled my face one night," Alex confided to them now.

The whole story came out in bits and pieces. Alex talked about his suspicion that Charlotte was accosted in the park. Regan told them she suspected Charlotte so desperately wanted the Chicago job to get away from Gil.

When they had answered each other's questions as well as those of the rest of the group, Alex looked at each of them. "Does this sound like a man Charlotte would want to marry?"

"Not a chance," Randall told the group. "Sloane, honey, you were completely right."

"I know." She beamed with pleasure at the statement.

"What have you done to Randall?" Tyler asked in alarm. The group laughed, enjoying a moment of levity before tackling the serious problem.

"She has to be afraid of something. Gil has something on her. It's the only explanation," Wyatt proposed to the group.

"Or on her family. Or on you, Alex. She would do anything to protect the people she loves," Regan offered.

"You think she loves me?" Alex asked in awe.

"Jeez, you are a complete idiot," Randall said on behalf of the whole group.

"Okay," Tyler said in his best lawyer voice, "we need a plan."

"Let's recap what we know and come up with some possibilities," the ever logical Alex suggested.

"Ah hell, boys. Let's call this trip over and head to Rhode Island," Randall suggested instead.

Seven heads nodded agreement.

"I'm so damn sick of flying," Wyatt admitted, sheepishly. "Can we wait until tomorrow?

CHAPTER
THIRTY-SIX

R egan handed the invitation to Alex on the plane, thereby providing him with Charlotte's address without ever divulging anything from her employment records. The group would check into the Biltmore Hotel downtown and then Alex would go see Charlotte alone. There had been a long discussion about taking 'backup,' but the group agreed that they should assume the best, not the worst.

Both Alex and Regan had tried calling Charlotte repeatedly once they arrived. The number Alex had for her was disconnected. The updated number Regan had got no answer. She sent a text saying she just wanted to find out some details about the wedding and got a call immediately. It wasn't Charlotte.

"Hello Regan, this is Gil, Charlotte's fiancé. She is at work right now and unable to take calls, but I would be happy to answer your questions."

Regan was nonplussed by this turn of events, but quickly recovered. "Nice to speak with you, Gil. I am so sorry to bother you about something so trivial. I wanted to know where you two were registered and discuss gift ideas with Charlotte. Perhaps I would be able to join with some of her friends here, I mean in Providence, to throw her a shower. Girl stuff. You understand. Please, just have Charlotte call me to discuss it further. Or her mother, if she isn't too busy."

After disconnecting, Regan turned to Alex, white as a sheet. Alex jumped down Regan's throat. "Her mother? Why would you agree to talk to her mother? We need to be able to talk to Charlotte." He was fuming from the delays and crazy with worry. The animal was answering her phone. He had her completely cut off.

"I didn't want to seem too anxious. This might throw him off the scent a bit."

"Good thinking," Tyler praised. "That's my girl." Blushing red at the slip of the tongue, Tyler left Alex's hotel room where they had all congregated and moved back to his own room for a while. "That boy has it bad, Regan. Why don't you just step up and save him?"

"Oh Alex, I would if he would just give me one clear signal, but he is all over the place. I can't really tell what he wants."

"Trust me, Ree. He wants you."

"Let's solve this problem first, guys," Wyatt suggested. "Please."

"Yes, sir," Regan told her brother. "You're completely right."

"So now we wait?" Keeli asked.

"Not a chance." Sloane stepped forward. "I didn't come all this way to do nothing. We go to her office. Oh, not you, Alex. He will be watching for you. We girls go. That should be less suspicious."

"That is a great idea, Sloane. You always did have a devious mind," Regan offered before adding, "I mean that as a compliment, of course."

"And I took it as one," Sloane told her friends.

Using GPS, they mapped out a route to the Fox Point location for the specialty foods business. The three women said their goodbyes and made their way there, sightseeing Providence a bit along the way, and planning their next few days.

"Assuming this goes well," Keeli reminded them.

Soon they were parked in front of the nondescript building for Old World Foods. There was a storefront for carryout and, although none of them believed they would find Charlotte that way, they agreed it was their best way into the building.

"Oh my god, this smells good," Keeli gushed as soon as they were in the door.

"That's either the chorizo or the sweet bread," a young man stepped forward to explain. "They are both homemade here. Do you smell sweet or spicy?"

"Spicy," Keeli gushed.

"But I smell sweet," Sloane said, stepping forward flirtatiously. She knew she had what it took to get into the back, and she intended to use it.

"We are visiting from out of town, and we met a couple that told us we just had to take home some of your cooking," she oozed, resting a hand on the young man's arm.

"They were right," he told her, flattered. "We make the best authentic dishes in Providence. Real Portuguese cooking. I would know," he bragged, "I'm the chef."

"The chef?" Regan stepped forward. "So young? That is so impressive." The women were laying it on thick, but it was working.

"Well, I am one of them. I finished The Culinary Academy of America last month," the young man told them, puffing himself up a bit.

"I am getting married in a few months. I hear your wedding cakes are divine," Sloane continued before she realized she had given up her flirtatious edge. The man, his nametag said Don, deflated visibly. "Perhaps you have samples, or pictures?"

"In the back. Let me get someone to show you," Don said, no longer interested in the unavailable woman.

"I understand it is a family business," Regan stepped forward to ask. "Are you family?"

"Yes, my father, brother, sister and I run the place, using my mother's recipes."

"Wow, so your sister will show us the cakes?" Sloane asked.

"My brother," he announced. Disappearing briefly, he returned with an older version of Charlotte. "This is my brother, Jacabo Rocha, but call him Jake."

"Jake," Sloane turned on the charm, "we have heard such fabulous things about the food here. Would it be possible to see the wedding cake collection?"

"They are from out of town," Don explained when Jake looked about to say something about an appointment.

"Oh, then come in the back with me and we can take a look." Jake showed them to a small windowed office with a worn Formica table and pulled forward two large albums of photographs. Keeli and Sloane sat at the table, but Regan leaned on the door before shutting it quietly.

"Jake," she interrupted, "where's Charlotte?"

While the ladies explained who they were, Jake carefully began turning the pages of the first album, looking out the glass behind the women regularly. "Gil has a job here now. He watches Charlotte all day. She is never alone. He doesn't let her answer her own phone."

"We know."

"She doesn't drive to or from work alone. He brings her straight to our house after work."

"That's where we will get her, from your house," Regan announced. "As soon as he drops her off."

"He calls to speak with her hourly. If she were not there to answer the phone, I don't know what would happen. He is a violent man, ladies. I would hate to see any of you come to any harm. My brother and I have been discussing this nightly, trying to find a way to spirit her away. But I should warn you, she doesn't want to go. She will fight leaving and he will come after her. She is afraid of something. Something very bad."

"Can we talk to her at least?"

"Not here. But if you give me a number, I will have her call the moment she gets home. You will probably have 30 minutes before he checks on her."

They exchanged numbers while Jake calmly sifted through the photos and Keeli and Sloane appeared completely absorbed. Shaking hands in the doorway, the women moved to leave.

"I will help however I can. We all want to see Charlotte far away from him."

Almost exactly three hours later, Regan's phone rang. A shaky Charlotte was on the line, excited to speak with her friend after weeks apart. "I have missed you so much," she gushed.

"Me too," Regan told her before handing the phone to Alex.

"Me too, Charlotte," he admitted in a strong voice. "I wish you had told me everything. Now, tell us what he is threatening you with and we will fix it, and then we are getting you out of there."

"You can't fix it," Charlotte started to cry. "No one can. We have wracked our brains to come up with an answer, but he will destroy my family, Alex. Completely destroy us."

"Sweetheart, it cannot be that bad. Please just tell me so I can help. I cannot lose you now that I found you again."

"I have to go before he calls. I will call again." With a click, she was gone. Alex stood holding the cell phone in his hand, looking bereft.

"She'll call, Alex," Sloane reassured him. "She'll call."

But it was an accented male voice that called less than fifteen minutes later. "Take the phone off speaker, please," he said calmly. "I only wish to speak with Alex."

Alex spoke very little, but the man on the other end of the line spoke at length while Alex said, "I understand," repeatedly and nothing more. Finally, Alex said, "Yes, sir, I do. With all my heart." The man said something more and Alex handed Regan back her phone.

"Guys," Alex told the group gathered in the room, "this is going to be much harder than I expected."

CHAPTER THIRTY-SEVEN

T yler had been a wizard, working closely with international legal specialist and all-around savior, Jonathan Chen. Jonathan had already helped Wyatt and Sloane solve their legal problems when it looked like things were beyond hope, but he was honest and skeptical when Alex called.

"Alex, your friends were dealing with China. I understand China. We have people in the office who are EU specialists, but no one has a good handle on Portugal. We just don't get many requests. That could make things a little tougher. But we did find a paralegal with family still in Portugal. She called them and they called someone, and I am waiting for them to get back to me. I want to vet them for you, of course, and make sure we don't need to look even further. You need to sit tight."

"Jonathan, I will sit tight, as you put it, for forty-eight hours and not a moment longer. The clock is ticking toward a Catholic wedding that needs to be avoided at all costs. You need to understand that if it goes through, there will be no undoing it. Divorce is not an option and annulment may be equally impossible. I need you to pull a rabbit out of a hat for me."

"Money is no object," Tyler called into the speakerphone from the background.

"That was a given," Jonathan laughed. "I love when you send me a client, Ty. I just love it."

The three men discussed a few details. Jonathan made sure he had the correct spelling on everything. Alex asked probing questions and took careful notes, and the wheels went into motion. Now all Alex could do was wait. He had run off as much nervous energy as he could and seen much of the famous East Side in the process. The hills had set his lungs burning, but the Brown University campus had been beautiful, and he had enjoyed seeing the truly first Baptist church in America.

January in Rhode Island was no picnic, and tomorrow would be February first. It was cold and blustery, and the days were short. Alex was watching the calendar and the clock with mounting frustration. He paced like a caged animal when he was in the hotel, but he refused to leave in case Jonathan called.

"He is calling your cell, AJ," Randall pointed out. "He can reach you anywhere."

"True," Alex agreed, "but I need to focus." Eventually, the group gave up their attempts to lure him sightseeing and left him behind. He was sorry to see them go, bundled in their ski clothes and off to explore Newport for a day.

Jonathan called while they were out.

"I have good news," he began. "We have cleared all charges on the Portugal end without no problems at all. How come no one thought about doing this years ago? I will overnight the papers to the hotel in a few hours, but you are set to go. I believe we have covered all our bases, but be cautious on your end just in case, and call me if you need anything else."

Alex was effusive in his thanks before he began jumping around the hotel room in excitement. It was only noon, and he had plenty of time to make something happen today. He dialed Jake at the office.

"We are a go," he told Jake, feeling like a character in a crime movie.

I *only wish this was a movie. This is too real for my peace of mind.*

"Okay, give me about 15 minutes and I will have her out of here. You know how she can be."

"Tell her your mother wants her," Alex suggested. "She always drops everything for Luiza."

"Good plan," Jake conceded before hanging up.

Alex was thrilled to hear from Jake only minutes after they hung up.

"You would have loved it. I had Charlotte out of here in seconds. Mama was the perfect excuse. But check this out. When she got home, I was on the phone with her, so I just handed it to Gil so she could prove she had arrived. He is such an ass about all this. He doesn't let her take a breath without checking in with him. And we know his buddies are still watching her."

"Good thing she isn't marrying the guy. Would he have had her followed after they were married?" Alex wondered out loud.

"Thank God, we will never know. Anyway, Mama grabbed the phone from Charlotte and shooed him away like a fly. 'I have Charlotte safe at home, but you need to know that we are going out. No, not now. We women have plans that do not include you. You may speak to her later tonight.'"

Jake struggled to keep a straight face, wishing Alex could have heard it all go down. "He didn't dare argue with Mama. She is a force when she wants to be."

"I'll keep that in mind."

"She told him it was a day for the ladies, not the men, and warned him to stay away or 'I will spank you like a child.' I swear that is what she said, and I could hear Charlotte laugh. Anyway, Mama explained they were wedding dress shopping and that it had to be done in Boston, on Newbury Street. 'We are not poor anymore, Gilberto,' Mama told him. 'We are getting the best.'" Jake laughed, recalling his mother's fierce speech.

"Honestly, Alex, my mother can be more frightening than ten rounds in the ring with Mike Tyson, so Gil gave up and they are on their way out now. I suspect one of his low-life friends is following them, so keep an eye open."

Alex thanked Jake profusely for sharing the story, grabbed his coat, and ran downstairs and around the corner to the front of an obscure menswear store. He had to wait less than three minutes before a car stopped sharply and the door flew open.

"Get in," Luiza shouted. "Hurry, someone is tailing us." Luiza was clearly enjoying the melodrama while Alex scrunched his lanky frame between the front and back seats, hunkering down on the floor uncomfortably.

A stupefied Charlotte tried to ask what was going on, but her mother was too busy weaving in and out of traffic like a Le Mans driver.

"This is so exciting," Luiza told them, confirming Alex's assumption. "Like a detective movie."

"Except we are living this one, Mama, so please slow down."

"I think we are safe now anyway," Luiza checked the mirror once more, nodding her head.

"I cannot believe this is all happening. We need to be so careful," Charlotte whispered. "If anything goes wrong, people will be seriously hurt."

Alex reassured Charlotte again that everything was covered. "No one can hear you, Charlotte. You are safe now. Gil won't discover your absence until after six or seven this evening, and by then we will be long gone."

"He'll follow us, Alex. You know he will," she was still fretting.

"Relax, Char. Even if Gil does, he will look in Chicago and we will be safe in Aspen."

Luiza pointed out that Gil might rail and threaten, but what could he do once she was out of his grasp? Alex offered to hire bodyguards again, as he had since they had hatched this escape plan. Charlotte was still considering the offer, weighing the peace of mind against her privacy.

They screeched to a halt at the front of the building. "I think you enjoy this cloak and dagger stuff," Alex told Luiza, kissing her cheek and promising yet again to look after Charlotte. He unfolded himself from the car and began pulling the small cases from the trunk. He pretended not to hear Charlotte's tearful goodbye.

"I love you, Mama, and I will miss you so much. I must admit I am relieved to be getting away from here. I am just sorry that I won't be here to see Gil's face when he realizes he's been duped by my mother. You were the last person he expected to be a problem."

"Oh Carlotta, he has been tailing your brothers and your father for weeks. Is the man such an idiot that he doesn't realize a mother protects her young most fiercely of all?"

"He'll know it now, won't he?"

"He will indeed, my child. I promise to tell you everything that you miss. And you, my man," she fixed Alex with a stern glare, "you have made me a promise that I expect you to keep."

"Yes, Mama," Alex said contritely, causing Charlotte to laugh freely for the first time in days.

"You take the best care of my daughter. Keep her safe. You make sure she calls home every day to talk to her mama and papa who love and miss her."

"Yes, ma'am. I promise." Alex bent to give the tiny woman a swift hug.

"Mama, I am sorry to leave you with all the wedding plans to cancel. I wish I could help you more."

"Carlotta, are you daft? We never made any plans except for show. We sent the invitations, but we never booked the church or reception hall. Your papa would have died before he would have let you marry that pig."

"That was my biggest fear, Mama. I knew Papa would understand that I was doing it for him. I was always worried he would do something noble."

"He should never have put you in harm's way in the first place, Carlotta. That was his fault. And mine."

"He didn't do it by choice, Mama."

"Well, Alex took care of everything, and we all owe him a debt for that. He was smarter than the rest of us." Luiza looked around nervously. They parked in front of the small private plane terminal in plain sight, but there were no other cars around, so she relaxed. "We are all so grateful, Alex. How will we ever repay you?"

"I just did my homework, Mrs. Rocha. When Jake told me that Gil was threatening your husband over something that happened more than thirty years ago, it sounded odd to me. I mean, we have statutes of limitations. Why wouldn't Portugal?"

"Not on murder, Alex."

"But it wasn't murder, Charlotte. There were witnesses. The bakery was on a busy street and had large plate-glass windows. Did your father really believe no one saw anything?"

"We left too quickly to know that."

"Now Jonathan has their statements, and they've dropped the case against your father. He never murdered anyone, only defended himself against an armed robber in his bakery. He had a young pregnant wife. He grabbed a knife. It made sense to everyone, including the judge we worked with last week. There is no case, no threat. Let Gil talk. There is no one he can harm now."

"Do not think you are in the clear, Alex. When Jake fires him and he realizes I am gone, he will be furious. He will hunt me. He will hunt you now, too."

"Let him. You will be with me, and I am not letting you out of my sight. I will keep you safe always."

"Hm, hm," Luiza cleared her throat to get the attention of her daughter.

"Yes Mama?"

"No living in sin. Do not make me ashamed of you, Carlotta."

"Mama, stop that. I am a grown woman."

"I know, Carlotta. That i what worries me."

CHAPTER THIRTY-EIGHT

Although she knew she was supposed to be impressed by the wide expanse of mountain view—and it was magnificent, no doubt about it—Charlotte could not take her eyes off the light filled space that was Alex's Aspen home. Arriving at night, it was a beacon against the night sky, huge plate-glass windows brightly lit and displaying the unparalleled elegance of the contemporary home on Aspen's exclusive Willoughby Way.

The sweeping panoramic views from Mt. Sopris to Independence Pass were visible from throughout the open floor plan, rising above the tree dotted landscape and gorgeous wood and rock architecture. The size and beauty of Alex's mountain getaway overwhelmed Charlotte. She thought she was prepared for opulence, having stayed in his Chicago penthouse, but the impressive home in Aspen still wowed her.

According to Marnie, the charming and unbelievably efficient caretaker, the house was almost 10,000 square feet of space. Charlotte discovered six big bedrooms each with private bath, a media room, an exercise room, multiple living spaces including the formal and informal living rooms, an office—nicer and larger than her's at LHRE and certainly with a better view—and a steam room/sauna area. Alex gave her the tour, where he also pointed out the wine cellar.

"We store over 2000 bottles," he bragged. Then he showed her the ski storage room and the enormous garage, bigger than her old apartment. Hell, her parents could have fit their entire Rhode Island house in the garage alone.

Charlotte had never experienced such excess and luxury. She was not sure she could have even imagined it existed. Alex obviously appreciated it and was proud showing and sharing it with her.

"I have owned it for over five years, so to me it just feels like home. It's different looking at it the first time. I have been here for a while now and so I have just become comfortable. You will too."

"I don't know about that, Alex. This is not my usual hangout, you know."

"My father wanted to buy it and he wanted to do a joint purchase with me. We are both skiers and we enjoy getting away together," he told her before awkwardly dropping the subject and moving forward to show her more of the amazing house. "It was in the right spot. We liked it. I guess we didn't really consider that it might be a bit much."

"A bit?" Charlotte teased. "Okay, it's a bit much."

Outdoors, Charlotte admired the decks, the small endless pool where Alex could swim against a current to stay in shape, and then he took her hand and led her a short distance into the trees to a magical hidden hot tub. The size of a small swimming pool, the tub was a small refuge. Charlotte immediately imagined relaxing in the moist heat, enjoying the view and Alex.

The house perched at the top of the road so that it had unfettered views of Aspen. Constructed of warm Spanish stone and rich wooden accents, it was an architectural gem. But the best feature for Charlotte—besides Alex, of course—were the windows. The soaring apertures created disappearing glass walls. Although she stood indoors, reflected against Alex with the cozy fireplace in the background, it felt as if she stood outside.

After she had seen most of the house, Charlotte stopped again to look out the dramatic windows. Alex waited behind Charlotte, wrapping his arms about her, and pulling him tight against his body as if he would never let go.

"I prayed for this moment," Alex bent his head closer and whispered in a husky, emotional voice. "I was so afraid I had lost you. I never want to be apart from you like that again. Promise me."

"I promise." Charlotte stood, safe at last in Alex's arms, savoring the feel of his breath, warm and moist against her neck, his arms holding her close against the feel of his muscled chest. They stood like that, silently, for several moments, until Alex spun her in his arms and kissed her soundly.

Despite her exhaustion, Charlotte came alive in his embrace, returning kiss for kiss, tongue teasing and probing for more. It was all Alex needed to trap her against the cool glass, placing hands on either side of her as he leaned into her body. Capturing her with his seeking mouth, he released her only long enough to divest them of their warm sweaters. As he reached to unfasten her bra, he pushed up against her body, his broad chest smashing her breasts as his hips ground into hers.

Charlotte let out a small squeal when her body came in full contact with the glass, but before Alex could back off, she had her arms tight around his neck, pulling him tighter against her.

"Let's go to bed," Alex offered.

"No, take me here, like this. Make love to me here against the glass."

"With pleasure, my dear," Alex responded. They shimmied out of their clothes and Alex fondled Charlotte, getting her wet and ready before he bent his knees, wrapped her legs around his waist, and surged forward. They both sighed with the pleasure of the moment before Alex began moving. Charlotte slid up and against the cool glazing behind her and the increasing heat of Alex in front. It was only minutes before they both found their release and slid to the floor in a tangle of arms and legs.

"I have missed you," Charlotte offered.

"Me too. Let's make up for lost time," Alex responded with a wicked grin. "Bed or floor?"

"If you take the bottom, floor," Charlotte laughed.

The days flew by as the two rediscovered each other. Charlotte was carefree and relaxed in a way Alex had never seen before. Free of Gil, away from work, in the mountains and the house she loved, Charlotte was like a young girl. She lounged with him in the hot tub, went for walks, took ski lessons, and leisurely naps. She sat in the corner of his office while he worked, pulling books from the library shelves, reading everything from Homer to business journals. When he completed his work, they wrapped in a blanket in front of the fire, her head resting on Alex's chest as they shared the couch. They made love long into the night, whispering of their future together.

Alex wanted to take Charlotte to some of Aspen's fine restaurants, but once she saw the gourmet kitchen, he could not get her out of it. Alex was enjoying the best of the Rocha family recipes and every night he left the table patting his flat abs as if he had a belly and praising Luiza. "No wonder your family has made such a success of Old World. I could eat like this every night, and I imagine your customers could too.

"Yes, my love, but you don't have to," Charlotte teased. "You have me to cook for you and these recipes are in my blood. Of course, you could wash a dish now and then." Alex, who cleaned every time

Charlotte cooked, took offense, and swatted her with a dishtowel. She threw ice at him in return, missing by a mile, and they were quickly enmeshed in chasing each other around the house until they were falling into each other's arms laughing, exhausted from the effort.

Charlotte returned to running, but the steep climbs and lighter air at these altitudes took their toll, forcing her to slow down and shorten her distances. Instead, she put her energy into her ski lessons. The kids skiing around her made it look so easy, but Charlotte struggled with the unwieldy skis and her fear of falling and re-injuring her ankle. The air and the views were exhilarating. Her instructor was a handsome and patient Argentine, but she still found the entire effort frustrating and exhausting.

Having taken her third lesson today, Charlotte was drained. She downed two Advil for the muscle aches and spent the late afternoon with her head tucked under Alex's arm, dozing.

"Are you asleep?"

"No, just quiet," she told him.

"I know we have talked about this before, but if Regan is giving you back your old job, and Gil has gone back to Portugal, I don't see what the problem is."

"I wonder what made Gil up and leave. That was quite a surprise, wasn't it?" Charlotte asked, ignoring Alex's point.

"I was shocked. I mean, I knew he had no job anymore, no help from the influential Rocha family, but I never expected him to just pick up and leave. I really expected him to haunt us for a couple of years."

"Me too. I wonder what changed his mind. No one seems to have a clue."

"Are you sure he really went? I mean, that is what his mother told yours, right? Why would she lie?"

"She wouldn't. She is a lovely woman, despite her son."

"So, if he is gone, what is the problem? Why are you resisting? Is it me, Charlotte?"

"Oh, no, Alex. Of course not. I am so thrilled to have my two lives converging at long last. No secrets, no lies. Regan is being so generous to let me resume at LHRE, and she even had some great ideas for recommending Rocha plant expansions as a potential investment for some of our big clients. She has been fantastic. You all have. I have a new and very protective family in Chicago. I am blessed. It is more than I could ever deserve."

"It is all wonderful and well deserved, Charlotte, but it still avoids the question of you moving in with me permanently. You already gave up your apartment when you went back East, so just blurt it out. Tell me what is going on in that complicated mind of yours."

"Oh, Alex. You try to make everything so simple, but it isn't. It isn't my mind that's complicated. It is life."

"It isn't complicated, Carlotta Maria Rocha. It's this simple. I love you. I love you with all my heart and with all my being. I want to come home to you every night, laugh with you, and make love with you for the rest of my days. How is that complicated?"

"You know I legally changed my name when I started college. Only my family still calls me that."

"Stop avoiding my question, Charlotte."

"Look at my family, Alex. Look at yours. Compare how I was raised and how you were. My family is working class, blue collar. Yours is as white-collar as they come. My father was accused of knifing a man to death, for God's sake. How can you expect your family to accept me into their world?"

"First, they already accept you. They love you. Why wouldn't they? You are funny and smart, well educated, and charming. You are a strong woman, Charlotte, and a catch. They think I am lucky as hell."

"They think I am from the powerhouse Roche Pharma family too. You have not yet disabused them of that idea, have you?"

"Well... no, not exactly. But not because I am ashamed," Alex rushed to explain.

"Then what? Why not tell them everything?" Charlotte prodded.

"I am not exactly speaking to them at the moment. That's why," Alex stated, with a hint of a blush on his wind-burned cheeks. Charlotte could not remember ever seeing Alex blush before. Something was up.

"And why are you not speaking to them?" Getting coquettish with Alex, she tilted her head and smirked, battling her eyelashes. "Would I be the reason why?"

"Actually, not at all," Alex stated baldly, instantly returning the mood to a serious one. "It's because I want to take their lies and make them public. Their lies and mine."

Alex had Charlotte's full attention. "What lies?"

"I have been wanting to tell you this for ages, Charlotte, but technically, it wasn't my tale to tell. I had to wait until after Aubrey's marriage and then I told my mother I was going public, but you had left me already. She is not happy with me. That is why we are not speaking."

"What? What story?"

"Charlotte, I am not technically Alex Gaines. I mean, I am. Charles adopted me when I was still a toddler."

"Right, I know that. When your father died, your mother married Charles, and he adopted you. That is not a secret, Alex."

"Except my father didn't die. He is very much alive, living in California. He is the skeleton in my mother's closet. I could tell no one my father was alive without showing her to be a complete liar for saying he was dead. So, you see the problem?"

"Yes, but why tell the world now and upset your mother? Is something going on? Are you in touch with your father again?"

"I have been in touch with my father all along, Char. I run his business, which will someday be mine."

"He owns the bank?"

"No, not the back. Of course not. The bank holds power of attorney for his business. I own the bank. He owns Maverix."

"The surfing Maverix?"

"Yep."

"Your father is Zack Fairchild?" When Alex nodded the affirmative, Charlotte started bouncing on the sofa like it was a trampoline. "I love Zack Fairchild. I saw him when he spoke at Harvard. I have followed his career in the "Harvard Business Review" and his personal life in... well, in every publication imaginable. When he took over the sports channels... My god, Alex. Your father is a friggin' legend," she finished, short of breath.

"Yep. That's my dad."

"But then, why would your mother want to say he was dead? Or make you pretend he was dead? Frankly, why on earth would she let another man adopt you? This makes no sense."

"Okay, you are right. Life is a little complicated." Alex explained about Laurel's days on the beaches at Laguna, of meeting the surfer Zack and spending a summer with him. Of her falling in love and of him chasing the waves. Of her family's efforts to break them apart.

"So, when my mother found herself pregnant while Zack was on the other side of the world chasing 'the big one,' they put the wheels in motion to send her off to Chicago to an aunt. They tried to keep the fact of my birth from Zack entirely, but when that failed, they simply convinced her he was a loser. So off she went to Aunt Connie, telling the world that her husband was dead. Next thing you know, my mother married Charles. How to keep him from adopting if there was no impediment? That was a challenge, of course, since there was an impediment.

"The made deals and I was adopted. Of course, then Zack reached out. As I got older, he wanted me back. Not happy about the arrangement, to say the least, he insisted on being part of my life and Laurel agreed. But everything has been hush hushed. I just told the guys about a month ago."

"You didn't even tell your best friends? That must have been so hard for you," Charlotte said. "Wow, Zack Fairchild. That explains so much about your looks, oh, and why your father would want to buy this house with you. You meant Zack, not Charles. Of course, he skis. He was into all those sports."

"You know how a secret can snowball, Charlotte, and this one did, too. I got sick of the lies. I wanted to tell you the truth. So, you see, my family has its own skeletons, Char, just like yours."

"You should have told me this when I told you the truth. I should be furious with you after the way you treated me. Why wait? You certainly could have told me as soon as we got here."

"I should have, but I wanted a little time with no drama. Forgive me?"

"But Alex, this is worse still. Now you have the blue-bloods and Zack Fairchild in your genetic makeup."

"Charlotte, I am a bastard, for heaven's sake. I don't think I am in a position to lord anything over you, do you?"

"Don't call yourself that, Alex," she admonished, giving him a stern look. "You were adopted, for starters. If you have to say anything, say you are illegitimate. Alex, how the hell could you get so furious that I lied to you when you were lying to me the whole damn time?"

"I couldn't tell you, Charlotte, not without talking to my mother first. That would not have been fair. Like you felt you had to tell Regan before you spilled your story to me."

"I understand, but that was not my point. I think I am entitled to storm from the room, slam a few doors and give you the silent treatment, not give you what you want."

"Look where that got us, Charlotte. Look at the mess I set into motion. I have apologized and admitted I overreacted. I felt a lot of hurt and distrust. You hit a nerve." Alex threw his hands in the air in surrender. "Not that I am making excuses, mind you. I was awful to you. My behavior was dreadful. But now, don't you think coming home is a better answer?"

"You were awful, but I get you had your reasons. To be fair, I think that mess you think you started was already in motion."

"You may be right about that, Char. Please, just agree to move back in."

"Are you sure you are done with all the models? Are you sure we have no more secrets? Are you absolutely, positively sure?"

Alex wiggled out from under Charlotte's head and reached into the space between the sofa cushion and arm. He produced a Keeli Larsen Design jewelry box and opened it. Laying against the chocolate brown satin was the most beautiful ring Charlotte had ever seen, a large emerald-cut diamond, easily four carats, with two large emerald-cut diamonds on either side. The stones were dazzling, almost overshadowing the unusual setting that raised the stones slightly above a filigree of platinum.

"I am totally sure that I want to share my life with no one but you, Charlotte Roche," Alex said solemnly, dropping to one knee in front of an astonished Charlotte. "I want to wake beside you and sleep beside you. I want to run with you and rest with you. I want to argue with you and make up with you. I want you to teach me to cook and I will teach you to surf."

"Really, Alex? Can you surf?"

"Don't interrupt, please."

"So sorry," Charlotte laughed. She tried to school her features back to a serious expression, but her wide smile persisted.

"I believe in you, Charlotte. I believe in us. You are brilliant and funny, kind, and loving. I have been searching for you without knowing it. Please walk beside me through life. Marry me, Charlotte Roche. Will you please make me the happiest of men and do me the honor of marrying me?"

Alex watched as tears slowly filled and dropped from Charlotte's eyes in spite of the dazzling smile. She could not stop the tears, wiping them sloppily with the back of her hand. Unable to find her voice, Charlotte sat there frozen until finally she nodded her head yes.

"Yes? Yes?" Alex confirmed.

"Yes, of course," she finally answered.

Alex lifted Charlotte into his arms and kissed her hard, twirling her about the room until her legs knocked a stack of books off the coffee table.

"Ouch. Alex, you need to put me down," she told him before resuming the all-consuming kiss.

"Never," he countered, adjusting her in his grip so that he could carry her to the bedroom.

"Never," he repeated in a whisper as he began removing her winter wear and pushing her back on to the overstuffed quilt.

Charlotte peppered his face with kisses as Alex pulled his turtleneck over his head, getting stuck when she refused to move out of the way.

"Stop kissing me," he ordered, causing her to pull back abruptly. "Only long enough for me to get this thing off, though." Charlotte helped him pull off the shirt, then made quick work of the rest of his apparel too.

"Anxious, are we?" Alex laughed as he dropped back onto her body, skin against warm skin. His scent teased her nose, and her hair tickled his face as he nuzzled into her neck, kissing his way down her body. Her strong, gentle hands pulled at the muscles in his shoulders, holding him close against her, small mewls of pleasure interspersed with her breathing.

"Make love to me, Alex."

His mouth closed over her breast, warmth and sensation unleashing an immediate response from Charlotte, who squirmed beneath him. She stroked him with long, lingering touches, as his ruthless hands sought her core and closed over it. Dipping into the well of her womanhood, he found her wet and ready for him and, wasting no time, he slid his hands around her hips and moved into her with slow, painstaking deliberation.

Alex scored her lips lightly with his teeth before sliding his probing tongue into the moist recesses of her mouth. The erotic stimulation of him in her mouth and in her fiery core sent sparks of electricity through her body. Alex gave her everything he could, helping her achieve her pleasure. He was totally exposed and vulnerable when he was with her, even as he controlled their lovemaking. She felt him strain to make it last, to give all he could even as he took. He was patient, caressing her with his strong hands, loving every inch of her with his lips, and she responded, writhing and moaning under his expert touch.

Charlotte slid her legs against his backside, pulling his torso deeper into her, stroking with her hands and feet, brash in her need. She pushed to overpower Alex, flooding him with desire. She reveled in her power as his body spiraled quickly toward a climax.

"Char, honey, slow down," he begged even as he pumped into her, straining for his release. "Please, before I lose control."

"I want you to lose control," her honeyed voice whispered, warm against his ear.

"Then come with me," he begged. "Come with me, Char."

He dropped his head to her breast, mouthing it, licking it, sucking the distended nipple, pampering her body. He moved to the other, gently kneading it with his fingers as he lightly scraped his teeth across it.

Charlotte's breathing increased, and he felt her bucking beneath him, her need rising. Her demands on his body increased in tandem with the friction of their bodies. The exquisite pressure and slide of him hard inside her was eliciting the response he had pulled from her, and she had tried to delay. She held her body tight, on the edge of release as Alex returned to her mouth, bruising her with his kisses and bearing down on her softness.

"Oh Alex," Charlotte let go with a shout as she felt her body spasm, her orgasm shaking her with its power. Alex pounded into her body once, twice, and fell upon her as he was wracked by the intensity of his own release. It just got better and better with Alex, she realized as she basked in the aftermath of their intense joining. A heavy drowsiness overcame her almost immediately, but she fought it off, allowing the sensations slowing but still racing through her blood to linger.

Dropping like a stone on her body, Alex attempted to roll away, but she held him tight as he softened inside her.

"Not yet. Don't go yet," she requested in a quiet voice. "I love the feel of you."

So Alex remained, wrapped against her as she held on like a monkey, arms and legs holding him lightly, her fingers soothing as she trailed them against his skin. She kissed him slowly, longingly, ending with a whisper of kiss, as she released his body.

Rolling beside her, he reached to fiddle with the ends of her hair clinging to her damp neck. He couldn't stop touching her as they came down and relaxed into sleep. In that moment, and all others, she loved this man fiercely.

"Alex." Charlotte said in a small voice just before she was dozing off to sleep. "You do know I am Catholic, right?"

"We'll deal with it, Charlotte. If we can deal with a potential murder, a dangerous stalker, my being a bastard, your almost marriage and everything else we have survived, we can deal with a little religious difference."

"Well," she conceded, "when you put it that way..."

"Sleep, my love. We can tackle that tomorrow."

CHAPTER
THIRTY-NINE

M alibu was more beautiful than Charlotte could have imagined, better than the movies she had seen over the years. Yes, there were crowds, but the beach and the ocean compensated for too many people. It even had its own special smell. Charlotte quickly discovered that she loved California. She wanted to stay here forever. Of course, she said the same thing about Aspen when she was there.

That was before she saw Malibu.

Alex had brought her here over a week ago to meet his father and to see his West Coast offices. She let him drag her everywhere he went, running errands, to the office, to the beach. The surfing lessons had been an education. Not that she was successful on a board but watching Alex and Zack together had been eye opening. She wondered if Alex was aware of how much he emulated his father. He copied his surfing style, had a similar inflection in his voice and swagger in his step. Alex showed a comfort and confidence with his father that exceeded anything she had seen previously.

It was love, . Alex felt unconditional love from Zack, allowing him a freedom he didn't feel in Chicago. He took more chances, thought outside the box more frequently. Alex took charge at work, but in a more democratic manner. She loved watching him with the young "granola gang" as she dubbed them. He encouraged their participation in strategizing, planning and executing plans, and they rose to the occasion. The meetings appeared to be a free-for-all, with people shouting over each other and throwing darts at a board to make choices, but Alex assured her they were accomplishing a lot and, at day's end, that seemed to be true. Although their styles were totally different, Charlotte found Alex to be a highly effective manager.

"You are having fun, aren't you?" she asked him as they drove home from his office one evening, the sun setting over the ocean in shades of pink and red that had her awestruck. "You are always so serious at home, but here you are—what is the right word? I know," she said, turning in her seat to face him. "You're silly. You are actually childlike and silly."

"Silly? Me? No one has ever used that word to describe me."

"I mean it though, Alex. You are completely different here. Are you happier here?"

"Char, I am happy wherever you are. You are my happiness. Are you happier here?"

The question stopped Charlotte in her tracks. She considered the time she had spent in California. It seemed unfair to ask if she was happier here, having been in Malibu only ten days and in 'vacation mode' the entire time. She had no work hanging over her. She was still on a leave from LHRE and had not set a date to return.

Her life had been ten days of decadence. She shopped on Rodeo Drive, eyes popping at the stores, the people, and the price tags. While she had been unwilling to splurge for herself, she bought Bijan ties for her father, brothers, and Alex. She skipped Zack only because he had said he'd never worn a tie and never planned to. Charlotte had never seen ties that were numbered like fine art, or that were sold in boxes covered in the same silk as the tie. She found it lavish, but Alex was happy with her choice and her family was over the moon.

"I saw so many celebrities too, Alex. They just walk around Rodeo Drive like normal people," she told him, her voice rising almost to a squeal.

"Hon, I hate to break this news to you. They are normal people."

"Are you laughing at me?"

"I would never," he assured her with a quick kiss.

Another day she wandered to Venice Beach, watching the skaters, swimmers, and surfers, wowed by the level of activity. Over the weekend, she and Alex flew to San Francisco, sailing on the bay, driving across the Golden Gate Bridge to dine on the Sausalito waterfront and pigging out on hot fudge sundaes at Ghirardelli's. When she asked if he would take her to Disneyland, he hesitated.

"Do we have to?" Alex asked. She offered to let him off the hook, but she was openly disappointed. He capitulated. Clearly, he could deny her nothing. They had ridden roller coasters and wandered past cartoon characters before Alex kissed her repeatedly under the fireworks exploding overhead. Her heart was so full it threatened to explode in her chest.

She spent ten days as the consummate tourist, but now she wondered, was she happier here? If it were not a vacation, if this were where she spent her daily life, would she be more content?

One month ago, Charlotte was living a nightmare, planning the wedding from hell to her nemesis. Now she was completely free of Gil. Although he would take no credit for it, and kept insisting that he couldn't understand what happened, Charlotte was sure that Alex had been involved in shipping Gil back to Porto. She suspected he had paid him to leave, but she couldn't confirm it.

Instead of living in misery, barely able to lift her head from the pillow, unable to imagine another happy day, she was living a dream beyond any she could have imagined. Charlotte was smart, she worked hard, and she had been fully prepared to take care of herself for the rest of her life. Now she would do that with a shoulder to lean on when she needed it—a strong, virile, and very handsome shoulder.

Alex loved her. He wanted to marry her. She still couldn't fathom that reality. No matter how many times he told her, no matter how many times she stopped in the middle of whatever she was doing to admire the gorgeous ring on her finger, she questioned her good fortune.

"I can't believe I am this lucky," Charlotte admitted on the plane coming west, taking his hand in hers and kissing him softly on the lips. "I feel as if you rescued me from the mouth of the dragon and now I have landed in Oz or something."

"You are mixing your fairy tales, but I understand. My colleague, Ann, told me years ago that in a truly great relationship, both people think they are the lucky one. I never forgot that."

"Well, I certainly know I am the lucky one here," Charlotte responded.

"As am I. The luckiest man alive."

Alex couldn't persuade Charlotte away from believing she had the better result. His family had embraced her as one of their own and Aubrey was already conspiring with Luiza on the wedding plans— happy plans this time. Charlotte feared she would get no say in things once the two of them took over, but she was content to let them plot and scheme. They could have the wedding. She just wanted the marriage.

She was definitely the lucky one.

Alex's dad was exactly as she had hoped, although his memory came and went. He recognized Alex without difficulty, but struggled to remember Charlotte from day to day. Still, his long-term memory remained intact, and he regaled her with stories of 'chasing the big one' around the globe, of sleeping under the stars in Hawaii, and of the girls he met in Australia. He made her laugh until she cried, describing how hard he hid his success when it came, feeling like he sold out his vagabond ways.

Charlotte was completely star-struck, shameless in her efforts to pick his brain about business, where his genius still shined through. He gave her some business advice, then he offered surfing tips, and they seemed to help, although she reconciled herself to being a minnow in a sea of sharks. His wit and wisdom were invaluable and with his permission, Charlotte began taping their chats to share "with future grandchildren."

"Nothing would please me more than that," Zack told Charlotte. "Grandchildren. Imagine. There was a time when I feared I would not even have access to my son and now I will have a daughter and someday grandchildren. I hope they have my brains, and your beauty," he told her.

"You flirt," Charlotte chided.

"If you've got it, flaunt it." He still had it.

California was a magical getaway for Charlotte. A time to see a different, more relaxed Alex. Although he ran an enormous company and was making consequential decisions daily, he was less stressed in California, as if being closer to the operation made it easier to lead.

"Would you prefer to live out here?" Charlotte asked finally, coming back to the present. She was afraid of his answer. She loved it, but Malibu was so far from Rhode Island.

"Would you do that for me?" he asked in awe. He maneuvered the car into the carport, and they walked arm and arm into the beach house they were renting.

"If it improved your life," she told him. After giving her a resounding kiss and telling her how much he loved her for offering, Alex declined. Charlotte hid her relief. "Whatever you want, Alex."

"I would like to come back and forth a lot while my father still knows me, but I want to live in Chicago with you. It has always been my home. I love Chicago, our friends are there, and it turns out to be halfway between all the other places we want to be. We can come here for a week, go to Rhode Island for a week, then spend a week at home."

"Oh my god, we would live out of a suitcase, Alex. That would be insane."

"I see your point. We will have to figure this out with a little trial and error. Charlotte, I just want to be where you are. I want to build a life together that includes my father, my mother and sister, Charles, your family, and their families. I want it all, but as long as I have you, I will be happy anywhere." Pulling her into his arms and looking deep into her tawny eyes, he asked, "How soon can we get married?"

"First Sloane and Randall have to have a wedding, Alex. I refuse to even try to compete with that. Then we can set a date. This summer, maybe?" She kissed the tip of his nose to soften her words a bit before continuing.

"Somewhere in Newport? What about one of those famous mansions on the Cliff Walk? Would that work for you?" Alex queried.

Charlotte was getting excited by the idea, visualizing the event in her head. "It would be a blast, Alex. A destination wedding for the Chicago brigade, but someplace where it is affordable for my family to attend."

"And we still get a one-of-a-kind Rocha wedding cake," he teased. "Make any plans you like. This wedding will be whatever you want, Carlotta Maria. Just do not make me wait too long."

"Waiting? Who said anything about waiting?"

With that, Charlotte took Alex by the hand, a seductive smile lighting her face. Tugging on him gently, she wandered down the hall, wrapping her arm about his waist as they moved and reaching up to kiss his cheek. Alex turned to lift her into his arms, taking her mouth with his as he moved into the bedroom. Charlotte returned his kisses with increasing fervor. Wrapping her arm tightly around his neck, she kicked the door closed behind her.

EPILOGUE

"**C**an you believe this? After everything we did, look where the guy ends up!"

Tyler shook his head in disbelief and took a sip of the 15-year-old scotch in front of him. He savored the fiery liquid moving across his taste buds before responding.

"The contract you wrote is iron-clad. He can't come back for more from you, even if he has nothing left."

"I never understood how you knew so much about buying someone off, but I was so glad to have you there when I needed you."

"I just knew, okay? I'm a lawyer, Alex. I am supposed to know."

"I think there is a lot more to it, but if that is all you're saying, so be it. Anyway, here is what I found out." Alex leaned close across the table of the crowded bar, even though no one was paying attention to the two friends conversing. "He bragged to his no-good friends one time too many." Alex couldn't stop the gratified smirk that broadcast his feelings.

"What did you expect, AJ? You gave the guy a million bucks! I told you to give him less. With less, he might have been better able to keep it under wraps. But you had to pay all that money. I warned you. It was too much temptation for him."

"I wanted to be sure he would never bother Charlotte again. Money was no object."

"So, you said before, a dozen times. So, wipe that grin off your face and tell me what happened?"

"He bragged to his buddies, and the low-life assholes robbed him." Alex paused like a seasoned storyteller, enjoying a look of astonishment spread across his friend's face. "Idiot converted it to cash, stashed it at home and told the world. What did he expect?"

"So, they took it all?" Tyler fell against the back of the stool, laughing.

"Most of it, I guess. Of course, Gil knew who did it and went after him with a gun. Dumb shit. Now he has no cash, and he's going to end up in a Portuguese jail. They charged him with attempted murder. Tons of witnesses. They will find him guilty for sure."

The two men sat drinking in silence, enjoying the moment, their drinks, and the apparent fairness in the world.

"I guess he only got what he deserved," Tyler stated. "No matter what, he can't come after you or Charlotte."

"You think a contract would stop him?" Alex couldn't hide his concern. "Or a jail?"

"Well, the jail will stop him for sure. At least for a while."

"At least fifteen years."

"Then I would marry Charlotte on schedule and live your life. Fifteen years in jail may be just what Gil needs to straighten out at last. Jail has a way of doing that."

"What do you know about jail? Do not tell me you're a lawyer either. You have never been a criminal lawyer and we both know it."

"That's true. The man is gone, and fifteen years is a very long time," Tyler responded, distracted. "You have a wonderful woman who loves you. Go enjoy your life."

"Do I detect a trace of loneliness, Ty? What about Regan? You two have been circling each other for ages. Go after her, Bro. You know you want to."

"Maybe you're right, AJ," Tyler mused. Staring off into space, Tyler was almost thinking out loud as he repeated cryptically, "Maybe you're right. Maybe enough time has gone by for me, too. I think it's time to find out."

Find Out How it Ends...

I t began with four bachelors, privileged, smart, successful—single.

Through it all Tyler has been pining for his high school sweetheart, Regan. Regan is the youngest sister of his best friend, but that never stopped Tyler in the past. He vowed to marry Regan, promising her forever.

But forever was short-lived, and twenty years later, Regan is offering him a job instead of her hand. Her own job, to be precise. Regan clawed her way to her CEO position. Is she ready to marry a rising political star and give it all up? Does she even love him?

Timing is running out for Tyler and Regan. But something sinister is holding Tyler back.

Is it time to face his demons and win the girl?

Find out in *Besotted,* the conclusion to the Beguiling Bachelor series, available from your favorite bookseller.

Introducing the All's Crazy in Love Series

Eight women—seven **single by chance or by choice. One dare—marry in twelve months or less. The stakes are high. Losing is not an option.**

When eight friends from childhood reunite at their twentieth high school reunion, they realize they only see each other at weddings and funerals. This is unacceptable to friends as close as this. The answer—obviously—more weddings. To get the ball rolling, the lone married woman, Gabriella, dares her friends to marry or else. When they laugh off her idea, she doubles down on her challenge and raises the stakes.

Gabriella doesn't care if Avery is so shy she's hardly even spoken to a man, or that Rachel can't choose between the multitude of guys she sleeps with each month. Gabby ignores every argument, instead exacting the worst price for each of them to pay if they lose.

The Dare is on. The women open their hearts to every opportunity that crosses their paths, no matter how unlikely or elusive the man might be. Gabby adds another six months to assure a winner. They'll help each other—as long as it doesn't cost them the win.

Within weeks, Avery finds a fellow cat rescuer, Sofia's heart flutters with new possibilities at work, and Willow spars and sparks with her horrible neighbor. Leah finds a long-distance love. Melinda has to be coached, but not Harper. After twenty years, she's finally flirting with her high school sweetheart.

The *All's Crazy in Love* series offers one dozen steamy romances—from first love to second-chance romance, from unexpected babies to unexpected attraction. Get to know a dozen wonderful women who find each other, themselves, and a chance to snatch the biggest prize of all—love. Read the eight stories of the Crazies and meet their friends and relatives in the *All's Fair in Love* series.

Travel with lifelong friends as they discover love, test friendships, and race to cross the finish line.

Let the games begin at www.madisonmichael.net/books.

Crazy to Wed - An All's Crazy in Love Prequel

Prologue: Six Months in the Future - Gabriella

"What do you mean, the wedding's off?" I'm sure the guests heard my mother's shriek. Nearly one hundred of them had gathered for our rehearsal dinner. "You better be joking."

Tears streaked my professionally applied makeup. I know it upset Mom. Hell, I was beside myself, but she didn't make this easier for me. I couldn't keep the annoyance from my voice. "Do I look as if I'm laughing?"

"What the hell." Hell was blasphemy for my mother, but I reduced her to swearing as the truth registered. She became blissfully speechless for once. Sadly, her silence was short-lived.

"What did you do, Gabriella?" she asked, pointing an accusing finger at me. Her teeth clenched, and her chin wobbled as tears formed in her eyes.

So typical of my mother, always jumping to the conclusion that made me look my worst.

"Why do you assume it's my fault?" How many times had I said those words to her? At least anger had replaced my misery for a minute.

I flopped into an oversized upholstered chair in the ornate powder room, wondering how long I could hide out and how I face the remaining rehearsal dinner guests. Thank god it was late,and half departed earlier.

Do I say the wedding w cancelled or do I let everyone show up tomorrow and find out for themselves?

Less than an hour ago, I looked forward to the happiest day of my life, laughing as Rob and Rachel, the best man and maid-of-honor, toasted our marriage. Now we had no future, and I sat crying my eyes out in a public bathroom, my world in tatters. I watched dispassionately as tears stained the raw silk bodice of my gorgeous Rachel Lowell original dress.

"Was it your fault?" Mom asked, lowering her voice and handing me a box of cheap tissues. My nose chafed. But who cared?

"No, Mother, this time it wasn't. All I did was give him his gift."

Crazy to Wed – Chapter One

Gabriella – The Four Seasons Rule

"**I**s six weeks too soon to plan a wedding?"

Strolling the streets of Georgetown with my seven best friends, I should have been sightseeing, window shopping, or choosing where to get lunch. I wasn't doing any of those. Nor was I appreciating this rare time together with the Crazy Eights. No. Not me. I was thinking about Brad. I thought of him morning, noon, and night. Now, I needed to shake him off so that I could stop grinning like a hyena and enjoy my besties. So far, nothing worked.

Images of Brad flashed into my consciousness, moments when he made me laugh so hard, I snorted, or brought me flowers, or sang to me. He wouldn't make it as a front-man for a band, but he was pretty good. And he got to me with this head-tilting, eye-locking thing he did, pouring his soul into love songs until I melted.

I couldn't ignore Brad's talented hands, either, whether he was strumming the guitar, tinkering under the hood of a car, pounding the keyboard of a computer, or especially caressing my body. Very skilled. I jiggled my head to clear the visions before Rachel caught my dreamy expression and harassed me. Like a sister, we were mind-melded, except she had a dirtier mind.

"Not if you're a professional wedding planner, which you are not. But if you met a guy six weeks ago and think it's time to drag him to the altar, then it's definitely too soon. Besides, Gabriella, has he proposed?" Rachel snapped me back into the moment with her pointed question. "Aren't you getting ahead of yourself here, not to mention breaking your famous four seasons rule?"

Rachel had a point. I was looking at wedding dresses, but I didn't have a groom—at least not yet. Brad and I hardly knew each other.

I scowled at the redhead, wanting this conversation to go differently. I was off-the-rails in love and needed my sister-from-another-mother to be on board with me. Instead, she offered a hard dose of reality.

"When I introduced you two, I said you were perfect for each other, and I meant it." Rachel looked away from me, stopping in front of the display window for an upscale boutique to study the merchandise. I watched her scan each mannequin from head to toe, her fingers itching by her sides. Meanwhile, I held my breath, desperate to continue on my favorite subject—Brad.

"I didn't imagine you would start shopping for wedding dresses after six weeks, Gabriella. This may be difficult for you, but you need to relax and let this run its course for a while. Shit, it's not a relationship yet. Before you hire the caterer and florist, someone needs to propose."

Rachel walked away from the window and me without waiting to gauge the impact of her statement. Typical. Not that she didn't care, it was simply that she always assumed she was right. Most of the time, she was.

I expected ridicule for bringing it up, and–not one to mince words–my girl, Rachel, had gone straight for the jugular. Drawing even with her when she stopped at another window, I vibrated with annoyance when she pulled out a tiny sketch pad. My future happiness was hanging in the balance, and she was sketching a chartreuse romper no woman would be caught dead in.

"Rachel." I stepped between her and the display, demanding her attention. She put away the notebook and focused on me with a sigh. Even after twenty years of friendship, her remarkable green eyes distracted me. You couldn't help noticing them, huge in her face, the color of new leaves after a heavy rain.

At that moment, they were staring at me above a mouth twisted with annoyance. "Is it the sex? Because you don't marry a stranger to get laid."

"You should know, I grumbled the words, hopefully quietly enough. Not that Rachel would balk. She knew who she was.

"Of course, you're right," I said. "But it isn't just the sex. I'm obsessed. I understand it's too early to be in love, but Rachel, it feels like the real thing, different from any relationship I've been in before." How could I make her see how Brad tilted my earth to a better axis and how I was a worthier human being with him? He introduced me to fresh ideas, and I was more optimistic. Especially about love. My cynical friend Rachel would laugh me out of D.C.

Melanie waved for us to catch up to the rest of the Crazy Eights. These were my friends since third grade when I had created our clique and named it for a card game. The moniker had stuck for twenty years as had the friendships, even if we touched a raw nerve sometimes. We had scattered for college, moved to different cities, married, had children, explored other careers, still the gang held together.

We emailed and talked often, but what helped keep us a unit was our annual long weekend, four days away from home, husbands, obligations. Trips like this one to D.C. assured us we could reconnect on neutral ground—a way to remember why we loved each other. Here we were on a rare vacation, but I remained preoccupied with Brad instead of engaging with my friends. I was there in body, not spirit. And believe me, my body wanted to be somewhere else, too. The man was like a drug. I was blissfully addicted.

As we rushed to close the gap, I hurried my words, trying to end the discussion before anybody overheard. "I have been looking at wedding dresses and buying those thick *bridal* magazines. I need you to find out Brad's position. See if he feels the same." I yanked on my friend's elbow a little too hard in my enthusiasm. She stopped and looked me in the eye, rubbing her arm. "Sorry," I apologized for the potential bruise, "but you have to help. You know him better than anyone."

Sometimes, I exaggerate a bit. Okay, I might have a habit of hyperbole, if I'm being honest. But in this case, I was right. Rachel and Brad had been thick as thieves for years. She'd dropped his name casually in conversations long before she suggested fixing us up. My curiosity had been worse than any cat's. I was dying to meet him, but Rachel would say the timing was lousy, or he was seeing someone. This had gone on for years until I was ready to rip her red hair out by the roots.

In fact, I hadn't quite forgiven her for taking so long. Had she introduced us six months sooner, I might already have that ostentatious diamond on my hand. Not that I was greedy, or wanted to bankrupt my future fiancé, but it needed to be eye-popping enough to equal Sofia and Melanie's jaw-dropping rings.

When Rachel at-long-last suggested I meet Brad, she confessed why she'd made the match. "You are complete people on your own. I don't see that very often. Neither of you needs a partner, but you would enrich each other's lives."

"What the hell does that mean, anyway?" I was a bundle of nerves and had trouble following everything she said.

"It means he is worth the wait." So worth it, if only she knew. Nah, better if she didn't.

The night in that dark bar when Rachel warned me her friend was going to call, I tried to pick her brain about Brad. But the man-eater was scanning the perimeter of the room. If someone caught her eye, she would be out the door with them in twenty minutes. I needed to work fast if I wanted info before this date. Luckily, that evening the pickings were too young and unappealing, so she returned her focus to our discussion.

"You aren't one of those women desperate for a man," she explained. "You never have been. It's just one of the many reasons I love you. Look at your life—you have great friends," she gestured to herself, "a close family, challenging work at which you excel. You travel to cool, exotic locations and even volunteer. You are a complete person, interesting and fun, without some guy on your arm." I rolled my eyes. "It's a compliment," Rachel insisted. "Brad is the same. Lots of sports, tight with his buddies and his siblings, involved in local politics, not looking for a wife."

The pep talk was great, but left me suspicious. "Why is such a paragon interested in meeting me? Is he a dog?"

"No, my dear friend, he's a looker."

Gotta love Rachel. Here I was six weeks later, goo-goo eyed. She'd been right about everything, except being worth the wait. She should have introduced us ages ago.

The moment I saw him, Brad's dark good looks and deep dimples appealed to me—and then some—setting the nerves in my belly fluttering. Finally, they settled, replaced by the welcome hum of sexual tension. He was laid-back, comfortable and when we were together, time flew. Our first drink became dinner, then more drinks, until the wait staff eyed us with longing—longing to see our backs as we left the restaurant. They bounded to lock the doors after us when Brad escorted me to my car.

I remember everything: the velvety purple of the sky, the moon hovering over the trees, and the wind lifting the hem of my dress. And that goodnight kiss—I felt the softness of his lips, the restrained power behind it, a zing to my toes and a shock of electricity everywhere in between.

Brad felt it too, I'm sure, because we sucked face and groped each other like two teenagers until we were on the verge of making love pressed against the trunk of my car. Rachel had nailed it. We were perfect for each other. Reluctantly pulling apart, we scheduled a second date before we left the parking lot.

As for enriching my life, if being a stellar kisser and a stud in bed was what she'd implied, Rachel was spot on. If she'd meant that Brad would make me laugh and cherish me, then she got that right, too. Surprising, really, since Rachel ran through men like a hot knife through butter. One-night stands were her specialty, yet Brad and I were the fourth couple she'd introduced who were talking marriage or already married.

Initially, I was curious. Why hadn't Rachel dated him herself? In fact, I'd been wary. Only natural when you mention Rachel and a man in the same sentence. Settling for her leftovers didn't sit well. Both Brad and Rachel insisted they were just friends. Then I wondered why she wasn't interested. Was something wrong with the man? Eventually, I got past all my suspicions and embraced the relationship.

Once I'd resolved that issue, nothing stood in my way. I clicked with Brad, and knowing he reciprocated, I saw no reason to keep my emotions in check. I was almost thirty. So was Brad. Briefly engaged before, "when he was young and foolish," showed me Brad could commit. We discussed vacations and his office Christmas party. He might not be proposing, but he was long-term planning. Wasn't that the same thing?

"Don't tell," I begged Rachel, as we caught up to the rest of the women. The Crazies had halted outside an Ethiopian restaurant. I was out of breath but wheezed out my opinion. "I'll eat anything but Ethiopian."

"That's what you said about Indian," Harper said, crossing her arms and jutting out one hip in defiance. "This town is famous for ethnic food, and you're rejecting everything. You rejected the Thai place, too."

"And that Southwestern restaurant," Avery added.

"You could tell us what it is you want and save us this incessant debate." Harper's scowling face flushed. Her exasperation was palpable. Did I say we got together to remember how we adored each other? Not so much when hungry.

The Crazies were like family. We loved each other, but we didn't always like each other. At that moment, Harper wanted to bitch-slap me. It had been over twenty minutes since she proclaimed herself starving, and I had nixed four potential lunch spots. I wasn't trying to be contrary, in fact I was famous for trying alternative places, but today I needed less fuss.

"We are eating at the next place." Harper gestured her arm to include everyone but me. "Majority rules," she stated with authority. She turned until she was facing me directly. "You can do what you want."

Subject closed as far as she was concerned, Harper spun on her heels and marched down the sidewalk with that enviable athletic stride. I would kill for those long legs, I thought, without resentment. I couldn't be angry with her. After all, the woman was 'hangry.'

I felt a little remorse. Harper was one of my favorite people, and I had brought out the worst in her. These were my peeps, the girls I turned to for advice, for a shoulder, for a laugh. They were the women I most admired and respected.

I'd often wished I could compose one ideal female from the best of each of us. She'd include Avery's logic and compassion, Harper's athleticism and inexhaustible energy, Melanie's faith and sweetness, Willow's sense of adventure. If I could sprinkle in Sofia's poise and unconscious beauty, Sydney's flair for the dramatic, and Rachel's fearlessness, I would be perfect. With Harper's legs, of course. But they would make me taller than Brad. I wasn't sure I would like that.

I halted before a crepe restaurant as sharply as if someone had yanked me by the collar. I vowed to think about food, not my sexy boyfriend, and spoke up. "How about this place?"

Harper scanned the menu posted in the window, calling over her shoulder when something caught her eye. "Ooh, the desserts look amazing. Oh, Willow, they have loads of vegetarian options. Okay, there are tons of choices," she conceded. "This looks great."

"So, we've decided?" Avery asked in her quiet voice.

Before anyone could argue, Harper was through the door, demanding a table. Once seated, Harper reverted to her usual sweet self, commenting on our good fortune. Getting a spot at a Georgetown restaurant between eleven and two was a miracle.

We emptied the breadbasket in less than sixty seconds. With food in her stomach, Harper's face relaxed and her tone softened. "So, Gabs, you've been quiet about your latest conquest." Harper lifted an eyebrow, offering me a sly glance. "Rachel says you've been inseparable."

I threw a look of trepidation in Rachel's direction, but her bland expression assured me she wouldn't share my secrets. Great. I could decide what to share.

"I like him," I admitted in the ultimate understatement. I waited a beat, rearranging my neatly arranged cutlery. "A lot.

"Yeah, we figured." Sydney tossed her head at the dry remark, then pushed a gorgeous mane of curls that fell into her face, securing them with an accessory that resembled a claw. If I envied Harper her legs, it was nothing compared to my longing for Sydney's hair. Total strangers stopped to complement it. "You've been too quiet about him, so Melanie and I guessed you have something to hide."

A pregnant Melanie blushed as she blew a kiss toward Rachel, whose matches stick. She could make a living at it. The pretty blonde would know. Years ago, Rachel introduced her to a serious, somewhat nerdy, speech writer. We attended their perfectly planned wedding last year.

I was selfishly concerned that Melanie would be too busy with the new baby to 'do' my party when the time came. She was a high-powered attorney, but her genuine passion was everything on HGTV and Food Network. Her creativity was endless, and I dreamed of an event as
beautiful as hers. "We can sit as long as you want," I said, too little too late.

"You've made it through winter," Avery acknowledged to me. I swear I say one hundred sentences for each of Avery's, but I love her—shy, lovely, smart as a whip. She doesn't say much, but when she does, everyone listens. Sadly, I have to keep her at arm's length, or I will sneeze my brains out. A pet-rescuer, Avery is never wholly free of cat dander.

"What does winter have to do with anything?" Willow asked, ordering buckwheat crepes filled with spinach and other disgusting things. How did I end up with such a healthy friend? She was our back to nature girl, no bra, no makeup. She was also a hell of a baker. Someday she would run a very successful bakery, and I would grow fat from patronizing it.

"Remember," Sofia answered, "when Gabriella created that rule. No serious commitments until you've been with a man through four seasons. She's made it through winter, so she has three to go."

Sofia was married to Nico, a handsome devil she'd known her entire life. They were a stunning couple, dark, tall, and fit. Once they got pregnant, and she was trying her best to do so, they would have gorgeous children.

One thing I loved about Sofia? She underestimated her staggering beauty. In fact, she always overdressed to compensate for her insecurities. Sitting beside Willow, she was wearing false eyelashes and make-up more appropriate for a Saturday night. She was an exotic peacock to Willow's brown wren.

Speaking of peacocks, I caught Rachel glaring at me from her seat at the end of the table, but she said nothing. We were so different. I was "the vault." Rachel couldn't keep her mouth shut, but I loved her. Her imagination was endless while I was logical, her behavior wild to my straightlaced. She was even pale skinned to my Mediterranean coloring. Rachel had flamboyant red hair and those eyes. She embraced her freedom and single state while I wanted a husband and a family. The budding designer was the closest thing to a sister I would ever have. She was the first girl to commit to the Crazies and had been in my life ever since.

Rachel couldn't stay silent any longer. "Yeah, Gabriella, what about four seasons?"

"Maybe I wasn't clear." There were seven sets of eyes glaring at me. I had no one to blame but myself for their derision. I was breaking my own rules. "To wed you should be together a full year, but you can get engaged as soon as you want."

"You're engaged?"

Avery's words acted like a bucket of ice water thrown over the Crazies. Harper stopped chewing bread, Rachel halted doodling on her napkin, Willow nearly choked on the organic juice she had swallowed. Melanie's beautiful blue eyes grew wide as saucers; as did Sofia's gorgeous brown orbs. The clatter of the fork Sydney dropped to the floor brought everyone back to life.

"No, ladies, I'm not engaged."

"But she wants to be," Rachel blurted. I knew I shouldn't have said anything to her. She never could keep a secret, especially not from the Crazies.

The food arrived, offering me a temporary reprieve while the server distributed our orders and took our requests for drink refills and more bread. Everyone settled too soon, and Rachel picked up where she'd left off. "Gabriella is in love, you guys. She wants to marry Brad."

"Waiting four seasons was Gabriella's rule." Melanie used her courtroom voice, getting everyone's attention, including two older women at a nearby table. "She made it, so she gets to break it. Also, you will recall Prom, when Rachel didn't have money for a dress, and we all pitched in to buy fabric?" Heads nodded. "Gabriella stipulated that when one of us wants something, we combine forces to make sure she receives it."

"I said that, didn't I?" my pride was clear in the lift of my chin. If we operated as a team to win Brad, the poor man wouldn't stand a chance.

A cunning smile curved up the corners of my mouth. "Okay, ladies, what's our plan of attack?"

Crazy to Wed is now available from your favorite booksellers. Grab a copy and join these women on their crazy journey.

Books by Madison Michael

Standalone Stories

Broken Time–A Time Travel Romance
Studmuffin

About Madison Michael

Meet Maddy. She loves romance: reading it, writing it, watching it. So, she made a career of it. Why not reside in an unpredictable, exciting, enticing world where rich, sexy men and smart, sassy women fall in love? Returning to her roots in Chicago after traversing the U.S., Madison embraced old friendships, family, Chicago pizza and hot dogs and began writing,   her trusted feline, Gracie, at her feet.

Maddy creates complex characters who navigate intrigue, suspense, humor and plenty of steamy sex before achieving their happy ending. Setting her stories against the most luxurious and elite Chicago offers, her billionaire heroes—or heroines—quickly learn the value of life-long friendships, and that money can't buy love.

Maddy loves exploring, reading a ton and writing more. She lives on Diet Dr. Pepper and coffee—not imbibed together—and the company of loved ones who provide her inspiration.

Author of more than a dozen romance novels, including the billionaire series, *The Beguiling Bachelors*, and the humorous *All's Crazy in Love* series, you can sign-up to receive exclusive content at her website, www.madisonmichael.net